The Gordian Knot

(Schooled in Magic XIII)

Christopher G. Nuttall

Twilight Times Books
Kingsport Tennessee

The Gordian Knot

Paladin Timeless Books, an imprint of
Twilight Times Books
P O Box 3340
Kingsport TN 37664
http://twilighttimesbooks.com/

First Print Edition, August 2019

ISBN: 978-1-60619-328-0

Library of Congress Control Number: 2019945206

Cover art by Brad Fraunfelter

Printed in the United States of America.

Prologue

"AND FINALLY, I'M GLAD TO ANNOUNCE THAT BOTH OF OUR PICKS FOR REPLACEMENT Charms and Healing tutors have accepted their offers," Grandmaster Gordian said. He allowed himself a thin smile at the whisper of relief that ran around the table. It had been a long meeting, even though they'd had a break for lunch. No one wanted to prolong it further. "They'll arrive tomorrow and take the oaths in the Great Hall."

He leaned back in his chair, silently enjoying the moment. Too many of the senior tutors were not bound to him, either through loyalty to Gordian's predecessor or through ambitions of their own. He could count on them not to do anything that would actively harm Whitehall itself—their oaths would see to that—but he knew better than to expect them to follow him unquestioningly. And it was difficult, even for an experienced political warrior like himself, to edge them out of their positions. They couldn't be dismissed for anything other than gross misconduct.

"You'll be invited to watch and bear witness, of course," he added. "Now, before we break up for the evening, is there any more business?"

Professor Lombardi cleared his throat. "The election of a Head Pupil. I believe we are running short of time to nominate one."

Gordian nodded, keeping his face expressionless. The senior tutors had the right to elect the Head Pupil for the year, if they wished to use it. He'd refrained from raising the issue, half-hoping they'd choose to leave the matter in his hands. There were pupils—several pupils—he would prefer not to see elected.

"Very well," he said. "Nominations?"

"Emily," Sergeant Miles said, immediately. "I believe her record speaks for itself."

"She had to retake four of her exams," Gordian said. It was hard to keep the annoyance out of his voice. His feelings about his most troublesome student were decidedly mixed. "That does not suggest a sterling academic record."

"She failed the exams because she was summoned to war," Sergeant Miles countered, his voice unyielding. "And because she was... *involved*... in that mess in Beneficence."

Gordian tried not to groan. No two accounts of what had happened in Beneficence seemed to agree on everything, save for one detail. *Emily* had saved the city, somehow. If the more extreme reports were to be believed, she'd battled a *god*. Gordian wouldn't have believed it himself, if he hadn't read the reports that hadn't been made public. He hoped the full story—or at least the version he'd heard—never leaked out to the rest of the world. Too many sorcerers—and religious sects—would see it as a challenge.

"There are others," Professor Gaunt said. "Melissa has very definite potential."

"But she's politically unacceptable," Gordian said. "She was disowned by her family."

"She does have the talent," Gaunt insisted. "And she is... more aware of social situations than Emily."

"Cabiria has talent," Professor Thande said.

"She was suspended for a year," Gordian pointed out. "What about Caleb or Cirroc?"

Sergeant Miles snorted. "And how many students have actually *saved the school?*"

Gordian met his eyes. The hell of it was that Sergeant Miles was correct. Emily was the *only* student who had saved the school once let alone twice. By any reasonable standard—certainly in terms of achievement—she stood head and shoulders above the rest of the students in her year. There had never been any sign that Emily *wanted*, let alone *expected*, to be Head Girl, but everyone else probably expected her to walk into the post. And she deserved it.

And yet, she was a menace too. He'd wanted to expel her last year, when he'd become Grandmaster. Putting her on probation—and forcing her to work with Professor Locke—had been done in the hopes of keeping her out of trouble—or convincing her to quit. It wasn't as if she would have had problems finding a place at another school, somewhere well away from Whitehall. Gordian certainly wouldn't have stood in her way.

She's not evil, he admitted, privately. Technically, she was a probationary student too, although he'd decided to ignore that as much as possible. *But she is disruptive.*

He kept his face impassive as he contemplated his options. Nothing had happened openly—not yet—but he knew that more and more important figures were growing... *concerned* about Emily. Child of Destiny, Necromancer's Bane... she was a knife that could cut both ways, something that could reshape the world or damage it beyond repair. A sorceress who'd bested two—no, *three*—necromancers would be alarming enough, but her... *innovations* had started a chain reaction she might not be able to control. And she didn't seem able or willing even to *try.*

And she owns the school, Gordian reminded himself.

Gordian wouldn't have believed that, either, if Emily hadn't shown an astonishing prowess at manipulating and *duplicating* Whitehall's wards. Even now, a year after she'd told him the full story, he still found it hard to come to terms with it. The Founders of Whitehall had been lost in the mists of time, known only by a handful of contradictory stories. And *Emily* had gone back in time, taught Lord Whitehall and his fellows the secret to controlling a nexus point, then returned to the present. It was unbelievable.

It was also intolerable. He was Grandmaster, not *her.* He'd worked hard to secure a position of boundless power and influence, only to see it turn to ashes. He couldn't have a student in a position to overrule him, perhaps even remove him from the school. He'd already started a very quiet program to do something about the whole situation, but he doubted he'd have time to complete it. Too many people wanted something done, now. And they were pressuring him to force her to divulge her secrets.

He cleared his throat. "Emily has earned her reputation. I do not dispute that. But would she be a *good* Head Girl? She is not the most... sociable of students."

"She has a gift for making friends in high and low places," Sergeant Miles reminded him, dryly. "And that has saved her life, more than once."

"She'd be required to do more than make friends," Gordian countered. "The Head Pupil has to do everything from organizing the mentorship program to carrying out a project of their own. She would be distracted from her work."

"The same could be said of almost anyone else," Madame Rosalinda said. The Housemother smiled at him. "And while she is not *that* friendly with anyone outside her circle, she doesn't have many enemies either."

Not in the school, perhaps, Gordian thought.

Madame Rosalinda tapped the table, meaningfully. "Melissa has been disowned from her family. Cabiria is seen as... as something of a freak. Pandora's marks are too low to justify promoting her into the Head Girl role. Jacqui and Cerise are... are too power-hungry to take on the role without causing problems. And The Gorgon is..."

"The Gorgon," Gordian finished. What, in the name of all the gods, had Hasdrubal been *thinking*? Allowing a Gorgon to study at Whitehall? "Are there no promising prospects amongst the boys?"

"None who match Emily," Sergeant Miles said. "Cirroc and Johan are both working on Martial Magic, while Caleb... has shown evidence of moral weakness. And those three are the best of the bunch."

Gordian pressed his fingers together, hiding his irritation. Jacqui had been *his* choice for Head Pupil, although Cirroc would have been a close second. The Head Pupil would find a multitude of doors opening for her, when she left Whitehall. It would give Emily the skills she needed—and probably keep her out of trouble—but it would also paint an even larger target on her back. Her enemies didn't *need* more reasons to step up their plans.

She might decline the nomination, he thought. *Does she understand that that would be held against her?*

"Let us vote," he said, instead. In hindsight, maybe he should have raised the issue with a handful of tutors privately. If nothing else, he might have been able to get Jacqui or Cirroc nominated before he held the final meeting. "All those in favor of Lady Emily, raise your hands."

He counted, slowly. "Ten in favor," he said. Five tutors hadn't voted, although that didn't prove anything. Professor Thande wasn't known for caring *that* much about the position—or anything beyond his alchemical experiments. Gordian was surprised he'd even bestirred himself to put Cabiria's name forward. "The motion passes."

"As it should," Sergeant Miles said.

Gordian shot him a sharp look. If he were forced to be honest, one of the reasons he'd allowed Sergeant Miles to take Emily to the war was an unexpressed hope she wouldn't come back. The war could have lasted months, if not years. She might have been killed or moved straight to a more regular apprenticeship. Instead, she'd bested her third necromancer and returned to Whitehall.

"She's due to re-sit her exams tomorrow," Gordian said, calmly. There was one last card to play. "They'll be marked immediately afterwards. If she passes—if she can enter Sixth Year—I will inform her of her nomination."

There were no objections. He hadn't expected any.

"I'll see you all at the Last Feast," he added. "Until then... dismissed."

He kept his face impassive as his senior tutors filed out of the room, some clearly intending to head down to Dragon's Den for a drink before the students started arriving to re-sit their exams. When they were gone, he sealed the wards and sat back in his chair, forcing himself to think. He was caught in a knot of conflicting obligations, of promises he'd made and rules he could not break...

And others are already moving against her, he thought. He'd heard rumors. Some of them had been nightmarish. *What will happen when their plans come to term?*

Chapter One

E MILY PLACED THE BRACELET ON THE TABLE, CLOSED HER EYES AND UNDID THE SPELL. There was a surge of *feeling* as Aurelius came to life, a wave of strange animalistic emotions that ran down the familiar link and through her mind. The Death Viper wasn't hungry—she'd fed him weeks ago, before changing him back to the bracelet— but he *was* a little confused. Emily steadied her mind, forcing herself to peer through the snake's eyes. Her head ached as Aurelius looked around, tongue flickering in and out of his mouth. It was hard to reconcile *her* vision of the room with his. To her, the room was tiny; to him, it was vast and cold.

She shivered, despite the warm air. The Death Viper wanted something warmer. His head moved from side to side, hunting for a warmer part of the room. Emily smiled, wanly, as the Death Viper looked at her, then she reached out and picked up the snake. Aurelius curled into her hands, enjoying the warmth. She looked *warm* to her familiar's eyes.

He sees into the infrared, she reminded herself. *And he wants to be warm.*

She felt an odd flicker of affection as she cradled the snake in her arms. It wasn't something she could do very often. The familiar bond kept the viper's poisonous skin—the rotting touch—from harming *her*, but the poison would be terrifyingly dangerous to anyone else. She'd have to make *very* sure she cleaned herself—and the room—before she left. Even a drop could do someone a serious injury. The handful of people who *knew* about Aurelius had been horrified, knowing—all too well—that accidents could happen. She simply didn't dare take the snake out to play too often.

The snake brushed against her fingertips, another wave of warm sensations washing down the bond. Emily opened her eyes and peered at the snake, admiring the blue-gold scales running along its back. Death Vipers hadn't evolved to remain unnoticed amongst the greenery. There was certainly no way they could hide from hawks, eagles and other predators. But they were so dangerous, so *poisonous*, that almost every other living creature gave them a wide berth. A hawk foolish enough to snatch a Death Viper off the ground would be dead before it could claw its way back into the sky.

Emily shook her head, slowly, as Aurelius started to climb into her sleeve and up her arm. It was a shame, really, that she *couldn't* keep the snake with her—other magicians had far stronger bonds with their familiars—but the danger was just too great. And besides, Aurelius *was* a secret weapon. The fewer people who knew about him, the better. She caught the snake as he poked his head out of her collar, then put him back on the table. Aurelius shot her a wave of betrayed emotions, silently pleading for her to pick him back up again. The familiar bond drove him to remain close to her at all times.

"Sorry," Emily muttered.

She worked the spell quickly, before she could talk herself into spending an hour playing with the snake. Aurelius shimmered, then became a silver bracelet. Emily felt her head spin, just for a second, as the familiar vanished from her mind. She picked it up and played with it for a long moment, then placed it back on the table and closed her eyes for a second, centering herself. It had been a long day.

And it isn't over yet, she thought, as she turned to the bathroom. *Lady Barb said she'd return in an hour.*

Her reflection looked back at her as she walked into the bathroom and closed the door. She looked pale, her face almost drained of color. The summer should have been a time to rest and relax, but she'd spent the last two months desperately cramming before retaking her exams. Lady Barb and Sergeant Miles had been merciless tutors, drilling her in everything from advanced charms to fiendishly complex potion brewing. And then she'd returned to the school to retake the exams.

She ran her hands through her brown hair, feeling drained. The exams had been harder than she'd expected, even though Lady Barb had told her—time and time again—that retaking the exams was always harder. She'd been expected to display a breadth of knowledge and comprehension that had been lacking from the original exams, something that irritated her even though she understood the logic behind it. A person who failed the exams *might* have failed because they hadn't been paying attention, rather than going to war. She'd lost weeks of study during the fighting— and another week in Beneficence—and it had cost her. She hadn't managed to catch up in time to pass the exams.

I suppose I should be relieved I didn't fail them all, she thought, as she removed her dress and stepped into the shower. *It was a very near thing.*

The warm water was almost hypnotic, cascading over her body and washing away the dirt and grime. She wanted to stay in the shower for hours—or perhaps years— but she knew she didn't have the time. Lady Barb *had* promised her she'd have her exam results today, even if that meant having the papers marked in a hurry. Emily wasn't sure she wanted to know, not after spending the summer desperately reviewing everything she'd learnt over the past year. If she failed—again—she'd have to retake Fifth Year from the start.

Which is a serious problem, she told herself. She climbed out of the shower, using a spell to dry her body. *I'd have to find a way to tackle the joint project without Caleb.*

The thought cost her a pang. Breaking up with Caleb had hurt, but she hadn't been able to cut him out of her life completely. They'd needed to finish their project—or at least show they'd moved forward over the past year—or they would *both* have been threatened with being forced to retake the year. The hell of it was that she didn't *want* to cut him out of her life, despite everything. And yet... Her emotions were a jumbled mess. There were times, when she'd been lying alone in bed, when she'd wanted to call him... and times when she'd wanted to make sure she never saw him again.

She walked back into the room, dug through her bag to find a new dress and pulled it over her head. It wasn't anything fancy—a blue gown designed more for comfort and practicality than anything else—but she felt it suited her. Alassa's mother had sent her a whole collection of dresses over the summer, each one expensive enough to feed an entire village for the year, yet Emily hadn't been able to wear them. They'd just been too bright and colorful for her tastes.

And I didn't have time to go out anyway, she thought. *I had to study.*

Emily couldn't help feeling another pang at the thought. She was still—technically—banned from Zangaria, but there was nothing stopping her from meeting Alassa and Imaiqah somewhere along the border. Or she could just cross the border and dare Alassa's father to do something about it. Or... she shook her head, grimly. She knew she hadn't had *time* to visit anyone, even her two oldest friends. There had been a time when she'd shared everything with Alassa and Imaiqah. And yet, she couldn't help feeling as though they were drawing apart.

And Alassa's last letters spoke of trouble in Zangaria, Emily thought. *And of her failure to conceive a child.*

There was a knock on the door. Emily glanced down at herself, making sure she looked reasonably presentable, then opened the door. Lady Barb stepped into the chamber, carrying a parchment scroll in one hand. She held it out to Emily without speaking. The charm on the seal glowed for a moment, reading Emily's magical signature, then faded away into nothingness. She could open the parchment at will.

Emily hesitated as she closed the door. She *really* wasn't sure she wanted to know. She *thought* she'd done well, but she'd thought that before. And *that* had ended badly. If she'd failed... she wasn't sure *what* she'd do. Accept Void's offer of an apprenticeship? Or swallow her pride and retake Fifth Year? She'd hardly be the *first* student to retake an entire year.

Lady Barb snorted. "It won't go away."

"I know," Emily said. Her fingers refused to open the scroll. "I don't want to know."

"I could read it for you," Lady Barb offered. "But you *will* have to find out eventually."

Emily looked up at her. Lady Barb had been up for hours, longer than Emily herself, but there was no trace of it on her face. Her blonde hair framed a patrician face that made her look striking—and timeless. Emily felt a sudden rush of affection for the older woman, mingled with a faint dismay that *she* would never have a presence rivaling her mentor. Lady Barb was formidable and everyone knew it.

"Yeah," Emily said, finally. "If I faint..."

"I'll catch you before you hit the ground," Lady Barb promised.

The wax seal broke under her fingers. She unfurled the scroll, feeling her heart starting to pound in her chest. If she'd failed... she forced her doubts aside as she searched for the summary. The tutors would provide a great deal of feedback—she'd been promised entire *books* of feedback—but that didn't matter, not now. All that mattered...

"I passed," she said.

She felt her face twisting into a smile. "I *passed!*"

"Very good," Lady Barb said. "Can I...?"

Emily wrapped her arms around the older woman, hugging her tightly. "I *passed!*"

Lady Barb took the scroll. "Four exams... good marks on all four, plus the joint project... I dare say you did very well."

"Thank you." Emily let go of Lady Barb. "I..."

"You won't get the *highest* of marks," Lady Barb added. "Retaking the exams will cost you, no matter how well you do. But you did well enough to pass into Sixth Year. Unless you've changed your mind..."

Emily shook her head, hastily. She didn't really want to leave Whitehall, but she didn't want to repeat a year either. It would have meant going over spells and rituals she'd already mastered, time and time again. And everyone she knew would graduate a year ahead of her, leaving her alone.

Frieda wouldn't, she reminded herself. *But she'd still be a year below me.*

She took back the scroll and skimmed through the detailed feedback. Professor Lombardi and Master Tor had attached a series of comments; Professor Thande had written a short note, asking her to pay him a visit after term restarted. She promised herself that she'd sit down, when she returned to her house, and go through the comments carefully. There was still a week to go before term formally restarted.

"Thank you." Emily felt her vision go blurry and hastily blinked away the tears. "I wouldn't have passed if you hadn't helped me."

"Don't forget, Miles helped too." Lady Barb winked, mischievously. "You owe him a thank you too."

"I will," Emily promised. Lady Barb and Sergeant Miles had driven her mercilessly. She sometimes thought she'd learnt more practical magic over the last couple of months than she'd mastered in the last five years. It made her wonder just how far she would have progressed if she'd hired private tutors during the summer holidays. "Do I get to rest now?"

"Not quite," Lady Barb said. "As you're staying for Sixth Year, the Grandmaster wishes a word with you."

Emily frowned. "Now?"

"Soon," Lady Barb said. "I advise you to go now, then... then you can decide if you want to go back to Dragon's Den or stay here."

"Oh," Emily said. She'd always had the impression that Grandmaster Gordian didn't like her. He'd certainly tried to make it clear he hadn't wanted her to return to Whitehall after Grandmaster Hasdrubal's death. Their relationship was frostily polite. "Did he say what he wants to talk about?"

"No," Lady Barb said. "It might be nothing more than a formal acceptance to Sixth Year."

She glanced at the clock. "If you go now, I'll be in the Armory until dinnertime. I'll see you there."

Emily turned and walked back to the table, picking up the bracelet and slipping it over her wrist. Gordian wanted to see her... why? To ask her to—finally—take the oaths? She couldn't still be on probation, could she? Or to... *suggest*... that she left the school and went elsewhere? Or... she sighed, inwardly. Unannounced meetings—in her experience—were always bad news.

"I'll meet you afterwards." Emily brushed her hair back as she headed for the door. "And have fun with Sergeant Miles."

Lady Barb snorted. "Mind your mouth," she said, warningly. "I can *still* beat you for cheek."

Emily concealed her amusement as she walked into the corridor and headed towards the stairs. Whitehall *hummed* around her, the wards welcoming her home. She could *feel* the complex network of spellwork that made up the wards growing stronger and stronger as charm masters and wardcrafters struggled to prepare the school for the next intake of students. There was so much spellwork running through the system that even *she* had trouble working out what had evolved over the years and what was new. It was the most complex set of wards in the Allied Lands.

Heart's Eye will grow to match it, one day, she thought. She had plans for Heart's Eye. A university, for starters. Caleb and she had talked about a *lot* of possibilities, back when they'd been lovers. She intended to go ahead anyway, with or without him. *And who knows what will happen then?*

She passed a handful of younger students chatting at the bottom of the stairs— they'd retaken their own exams over the last few days—and walked up, nodding politely to Master Kay as he walked down. He nodded back, clearly distracted with a greater thought. Emily smiled to herself as she reached the top of the stairs and walked along to the Grandmaster's office. A middle-aged couple was just coming out, looking annoyed. Emily stood to one side to allow them to pass, then stepped into the antechamber. Madame Griselda, Gordian's secretary, was sitting behind her desk, writing something on a newfangled typewriter. Emily couldn't help wondering if it had come out of Cockatrice or Beneficence.

"Emily," Madame Griselda said, flatly. She was a stern-faced older woman with a gimlet stare. Emily had heard she'd once turned an imprudent student into a toad and eaten him, although she was fairly sure that was just another unfounded rumor. "Wait here. The Grandmaster will see you shortly."

Emily nodded and sat down, resting her hands on her lap. Madame Griselda's office was bare, save for a bookshelf, a heavily-warded wooden cupboard and a large painting of Whitehall that someone had hung on the far wall. A handful of faces at the bottom were marked as Lord Whitehall and company, but none of them looked anything like the people Emily recalled meeting. Lord Whitehall had never been so handsome in his life.

He might have been, in his youth, Emily thought. *But they grew old quickly, back then.*

The inner door opened. "Emily." Grandmaster Gordian stood in the doorway, giving her a searching look. "Come in, if you please?"

Emily rose and followed Gordian into his office. It hadn't changed. The room was bare, save for a large wooden desk and a pair of chairs. A handful of scrolls rested on the desk, but otherwise it was empty. The bookshelves and paintings had been removed, leaving the walls completely barren of anything that might catch the eye. There was nothing to draw her attention away from him, nothing to distract her...

"Take a seat," Gordian said.

Emily sat, studying Gordian as he looked at her. He hadn't changed either, as far as she could tell. He was a tall, powerfully-built man, with long dark hair drawn back in a ponytail. His face seemed somehow ageless, yet lined enough to make it clear he was no longer young; his dark eyes peered at her, as if they could see into her very soul. She could sense the magic humming around him, a grim reminder of his power. Whatever else he was, Gordian was a formidable magician.

His voice was very calm. "Congratulations on passing your exams."

"Thank you, sir," Emily said, carefully. She didn't think Gordian actually *wanted* to congratulate her. There was... *something*... in his voice. "I look forward to going into Sixth Year."

Gordian's lips twitched. "You worked hard." He didn't sound pleased about that either. "I have been told that you deserved to pass."

Emily frowned. Who'd told him that? And why?

"You'll join the rest of your classmates in a week, when term restarts for you," Gordian said, curtly. "However, there is something that has to be addressed immediately."

The oaths, Emily thought, grimly. She'd anticipated a demand that she swear the oaths months ago. In some ways, it had almost slipped her mind. *Do you want me to swear them here and now?*

"There was a staff meeting yesterday," Gordian said, sounding vaguely displeased. "My staff saw fit to nominate you for Head Girl."

Emily blinked. "What?"

"You were elected Head Girl," Gordian said, patiently. "Do you wish to accept the nomination?"

Chapter Two

E MILY STARED AT GORDIAN IN SHOCK.
"They nominated *me* for Head Girl?"

"You were the prime candidate by a considerable margin," Gordian informed her. He seemed to be enjoying her surprise. "Congratulations."

"Thank you," Emily managed. She tried to force herself to think. She'd known there would be a new Head Pupil, of course, but she'd never imagined *she* would be in the running. She doubted *Gordian* had put her name forward. Technically, she was *still* on probation. Who had voted for her? And why? "Who... who nominated me?"

"The deliberations are private, I'm afraid," Gordian said. "Suffice it to say that ten out of fifteen Senior Tutors cast their votes for you."

"Oh," Emily said. Ten out of fifteen? She knew enough about the post to realize that it would be hard to decline the nomination, particularly when she'd been elected by such a considerable margin. It had just never crossed her mind that she *would* be nominated. She'd certainly never expressed interest in the role. "I..."

She looked down at her hands, trying to think of a proper response. She didn't *want* the post, not when she had so little free time. Her studies—and her private research projects—came first. And she doubted she'd be the most *capable* candidate. Being Head Girl required skills she knew she didn't possess. Aloha had made it look easy, but Aloha had been sociable as well as smart.

And yet, with so many tutors having voted for her, she couldn't decline the nomination.

Twenty-five possible candidates, she thought. She didn't think any of her peers were disqualified, certainly if *she* wasn't disqualified. *And I received ten out of fifteen votes.*

"I'm sure you will bring credit to the school." Gordian picked a scroll off his desk and held it out to her. "I look forward to working with you."

Emily took the scroll automatically. She felt as though she was still in shock. Head Girl wasn't a meaningless position, not in Whitehall. She'd be expected to do everything from supervising detentions to policing the corridors after dark and mentoring the younger students. She wasn't sure she had time to do everything, even with assistance from the other older students. God knew she had to work hard to pass the *next* set of exams.

She kept her face as impassive as possible as she unfurled the scroll. If she declined the nomination... she sighed, inwardly. It wasn't possible, not without offending everyone who'd voted for her. Lady Barb had once told her, years ago, that anyone who declined such an honor was unlikely to receive another one, even if they had *good* reasons to refuse it. And it *was* an honor. There was only one Head Pupil per year. She'd be in good company.

Assuming I don't mess it up, she thought, wryly. She'd read horror stories about Head Boys and Girls who'd accidentally created all sorts of problems. *They'll forgot I ever held the post if I make a real mess of it.*

"I look forward to working with you too," she lied, finally. She was fairly sure that Gordian wasn't looking forward to working with her. He'd done his level best to ignore her since she'd returned from Beneficence. "When do I have to accept the nomination?"

Gordian lifted a single eyebrow. "You *were* elected to the post. It is generally assumed that the person elected will serve."

And no one bothered to ask me if I wanted the post, Emily thought, sourly. Who had nominated her? And why? She knew she couldn't ask. *I wouldn't have put my hat in the ring if I'd been asked.*

"I see," she said.

She considered—briefly—declining the nomination anyway. There *were* good reasons to want to decline it. They couldn't *force* her to serve, could they? But it would cost her later on, she was sure. The Senior Tutors wouldn't be too pleased with her... she wondered, grimly, if Gordian had deliberately created the whole situation. Either she accepted the post and ran the risk of messing up or she declined, offending the other tutors. Or maybe she was just being paranoid. Gordian didn't like her. That didn't mean he was out to *get* her.

He knows I can control the wards, she reminded herself. *That can't sit well with him.*

"You'll be familiar with most of the Head Girl's duties," Gordian said. He nodded to the scroll in her hand. "However, there are two issues that I need to discuss with you."

Emily nodded, slowly. "Yes, sir."

"First, we will be continuing the mentorship program from last year," Gordian said. "You will be responsible for assigning the Fifth Year students to mentor First Year students, then supervising their progress over the first three months. I expect you to ensure that the newcomers get the sort of mentoring they need."

Without making life too easy for them, Emily thought. It was a fine balancing act and she suspected she'd fallen off, last year. She'd wound up helping her mentees more than she thought she should. But then, the entire school had nearly collapsed in on itself. The new students had endured a baptism of fire. *It won't be easy to supervise the older students without being far too intrusive.*

She pushed the thought aside and forced herself to think. Aloha had just assigned people at random, as far as she knew. She'd have to check the records to be sure. *That* wouldn't take too long. There were roughly two hundred new pupils every year. She could simply parcel them out to the Fifth Years, then watch progress from a distance. Aloha hadn't watched *her* that closely, had she? She'd have to check that too.

"I'll do my best," she said. The mentoring program was important. She knew *she* would have avoided a number of missteps if *she'd* had a mentor, back when she'd first entered Whitehall. "Did Aloha leave behind any records?"

"They'll be made available to you." Gordian held up a hand. "I shouldn't have to remind you that they're confidential. You are *not* to discuss them with anyone outside the staff without permission from myself."

Emily nodded. "Yes, sir."

She looked down at the stone floor, thinking hard. She'd have to read through the records carefully, then decide how to proceed. It wasn't going to be easy. Perhaps Aloha *had* put more thought into the whole process than Emily assumed. Pairing up the wrong students and mentors would be disastrous. It was something to discuss with Lady Barb, then perhaps Aloha herself. But the former Head Girl would be busy with her mastery...

And she'd expect me to stand on my own two feet, Emily reminded herself. *She won't come back long enough to hold my hand.*

"The *second* matter is considerably more important," Gordian added.

Emily straightened up and looked at him.

"You are aware, of course, that the Head Pupil is supposed to undertake a special project?"

"Yes," Emily said. "The mentoring program..."

Gordian smiled. "The mentoring program was *Aloha's* idea," he said. "You will need something different."

Emily's confusion must have shown on her face, for Gordian started to explain.

"The Head Pupil is required to design and implement a special project of their own," Gordian said. "The project can—and will—be maintained *after* the Head Pupil has left, provided it proves itself beneficial. I believe the mentoring program was beneficial, correct?"

"Yes, sir."

"You are required to come up with something of your own, along the same lines," Gordian said. "Something that actually benefits the school."

Emily looked down at the floor. She couldn't think of anything—offhand—that might actually benefit the school. The mentoring program *was* a good thing, but... what could *she* do? More importantly, what could she organize that wouldn't cut too much into her limited time? Everything she knew *she'd* needed, over the last five years, would be too difficult to implement for the entire school. And she doubted Gordian would *let* her implement some of her more radical ideas.

More experience outside the castle would be a good thing, she thought. She'd found herself hampered by a lack of proper experience. The Nameless World was nothing like Earth. And while she was the only student from another world, the upper-class students had little comprehension of the lives led by the lower-classes. *But students already go out on work experience over the summer months.*

"I understand that you might not have the time to find something suitable," Gordian said, after a moment. "Fortunately, there *is* a project that you could implement without much additional work."

Emily's eyes narrowed. Gordian was unlikely to be doing her any favors out of the goodness of his heart. He might be pushing her to implement something *he* wanted, rather than something she'd devised for herself. Or he might be trying to ensure that she'd fail—or at least do something harmless. Or maybe he was just trying to keep her busy. He'd certainly tried to keep her busy *last* year.

"Whitehall has *not* competed in any of the dueling contests over the past two decades," Gordian added. "Our failure to send contestants has... *weakened*... our position amongst the other schools. Many questions have been asked about our reluctance to take part in the noble sport. I believe that establishing a dueling club and running an in-house dueling contest would lay the foundations for a return to the dueling league. Ideally, we'd be sending an official dueling team next year and—perhaps—hosting a contest the year after."

"I was under the impression that dueling had little in common with real warfare," Emily said, carefully. She *had* dueled at Mountaintop—and fought both Master Grey and Casper—but both contests had been formalized. There were no rules in actual *war*. "I believe that was why Grandmaster Hasdrubal banned dueling circles."

"There is some truth in that," Gordian conceded. "But do we not play *Ken* even though it has nothing in common with actual *life?*"

He smiled, rather thinly. "No one *would* mistake a dueling circle for an actual *war*. But dueling is a game, not training for war."

Emily nodded. Dueling—at least, the dueling she'd been taught at Mountaintop—was one-on-one. There were no teams, not in a formal duel. Each contestant won or lost by his own abilities. There were rules, strict limits on what spells could be used... rules that had no place in war. Necromancers certainly didn't bother to restrict themselves when they invaded new countries, not when there was nothing to be gained by holding back. She couldn't help thinking that Grandmaster Hasdrubal had a point. Dueling taught bad habits for magicians who actually had to go to war.

Sergeant Miles is not going to be pleased, she thought, grimly. *He'll spend months teaching his students to forget everything they learnt in dueling club.*

"You'll be responsible for setting up the club and supervising the first set of contests," Gordian told her. "You may request assistance from the staff, of course, but it may be held against you if it is something you should be capable of doing yourself. I suggest you model the club on what you saw at Mountaintop..."

"If I can't think of anything else," Emily interrupted.

Gordian looked displeased. "If you can't think of anything else."

Emily shook her head, ruefully. She *couldn't* think of anything else. And she had to admit that a dueling club—and contest—might be fun, at least for the younger students. *She'd* never cared for team sports, but that made her fairly unusual in Whitehall. They'd have a lot of fun drawing up dueling rosters and preparing for the interschool championships. But it was going to be a great deal of work for very little reward...

Unless I can put it on my resume, she thought. *It might work in my favor.*

Her thoughts raced from point to point. She *wanted* to be a teacher, although she knew she needed to complete her mastery and gain more experience before anyone would consider her for a teaching position. This *was* a chance to gain experience, even if it was dueling rather than a more serious subject. Hell, it would be easier to teach dueling than charms or alchemy. *She* wouldn't have to worry about screwing up the basics, ensuring her students couldn't progress to the upper levels. Failing to master the fundamentals of charms, she knew from bitter experience, made it impossible to pass on to the more interesting levels.

"I'll try and think of something," she said, slowly. "How long do I have to decide?"

"You have a week to give me a proposal." Gordian cocked his head. "If I accept it, you may proceed; if not, you'll have less time to come up with something new."

Or just accept the dueling club, Emily thought. It wouldn't be *that* hard, she admitted privately. She could just copy the setup at Mountaintop for the club, then model the contest on the standard league rules. *It might just work in my favor.*

"I'll let you know," she said. She wished, suddenly, that someone had *told* her she might be elected Head Girl. A few weeks to think about it might have let her come up with something more interesting. "Do I still have to come up with a proposal for the dueling club?"

"You have to sketch out an outline," Gordian told her. "But you don't have to come up with a formal proposal."

Good, Emily thought.

A thought struck her. *Would it be cheating if I hired someone from the outside world to handle the club?*

She shook her head, mentally. It probably *would* be.

Gordian cleared his throat. "There are a handful of other matters that we will discuss over the next few weeks." He picked up another scroll and held it out to her. "Right now, your father has... *requested*... that we include you in Soul Magic classes. I have reluctantly granted this, as I believe you already have some basic training in Soul Magic."

"Very basic," Emily said. Aurelius—the *original* Aurelius—had shown her the basics, but he hadn't taught her anything more. She'd assumed it was something she was going to have to study later, after she graduated. "I thought that only Healers studied Soul Magic."

"Your father was very insistent," Gordian informed her. "He appears to believe it would be useful."

Emily frowned. Void—her father, as far as anyone outside a select group knew—wouldn't have found it *easy* to convince Gordian to let her study Soul Magic. Soul Magic was extremely dangerous, even in the hands of a trained Healer. It was normally hedged around with all sorts of warnings and oaths, just to prevent accidents. She wasn't even sure she could keep up with the other students in the class. Prospective Healers would have been studying it *last* year.

He thinks it might be useful, she thought. *Why?* She'd have to write to him, soon.

"Understood," she said, finally. She was going to be *very* busy. Perhaps she could work her way through her schedule, then put some of her classes off until she had a grip on everything else. Or perhaps that was a little optimistic. "Is that the only major addition to my schedule?"

"For the moment." Gordian shrugged. "You'll have quite a bit of free time on your schedule, but... you're *expected* to actually use it for study. Running down to Dragon's Den every day will cost you."

"I know," Emily said. She hadn't had much free time over the past year, not since she'd returned to Whitehall. It had been easy to decline the handful of invitations to visit Dragon's Den or go walking up the hillside. She supposed it would have been harder if she'd still been dating Caleb. "I'll be spending most of my free time in the library."

"And running the dueling contest." Gordian's lips twitched. "And doing everything else a Head Girl is supposed to do."

Emily groaned. "Is *sleep* included on the list?"

"I believe it's an optional extra," Gordian said, deadpan. "Pencil a nap in for some time next week."

Emily had to smile. "Is there no spell that allows someone to go without sleep for a full year?"

"Only if you don't mind seeing things after the first few days," Gordian said. "I believe the hallucinations can be quite unpleasant."

"I know," Emily said. They'd been warned, time and time again, not to abuse wakefulness potions. One or two doses might be tolerable, but after that the side-effects turned nasty. It was better to sleep than risk stumbling around in a daze. Cabiria had taken five doses last year and wound up sleeping for a week when they'd caught up with her. "I won't risk it."

"Very good." Gordian glanced at his watch. "We'll discuss the other matters later, when we have time. Make sure you bring your proposal to me before term starts."

"Yes, sir," Emily said.

"And one other thing," Gordian added. His voice was suddenly very hard. "Do you recall what you were told, last year, about punishments for younger students?"

Emily had to force herself to recall. "We were told that if we issued unjust punishments to our mentees, we would share them."

"Correct." He pointed a finger at her. "That is *also* true—perhaps *more* true—of being Head Pupil. You have significant authority over your fellow pupils, even the ones your age. Abusing it will not be tolerated."

Emily nodded. "I understand."

"Very good," Gordian said. "You may go now."

Chapter Three

A S SOON AS SHE WAS OUTSIDE GORDIAN'S OFFICE—AND ANTECHAMBER—EMILY LEANED against the stone wall and closed her eyes. It was hard, so hard, to think clearly. Head Girl? She had never expected to be Head Girl. No one had even suggested she might be in the running for the nomination! Hell, if anyone had suggested it, she would have assumed that failing four of her eight exams would have disqualified her. God knew she wasn't going to get *full* marks for the exams she'd retaken...

She took a deep breath, centering herself as she clutched the two scrolls to her breast. Head Girl... she could cope. She'd *have* to cope. It wasn't something she'd wanted—she'd always assumed that her feelings would be taken into account—but there didn't seem to be any way to get out of it. The election wouldn't even have been a close-run thing, not if ten out of fifteen senior tutors had supported her. *That* was enough of a majority to ensure that Gordian couldn't simply veto her election.

And that would be great, if I wanted the post, she thought. There were too many things she had to do to welcome more work. *This is going to keep me very busy.*

She opened her eyes and looked down at the first scroll. It was a list of duties, ranging from the simple to the complex. She would have to do all of them, while somehow keeping pace with the rest of her classmates. She'd assumed she'd have plenty of time to catch up and move ahead, now that she was single again. Instead, she was going to be wasting valuable time trying to handle the Head Girl's responsibilities as well as her schoolwork. Patrolling the corridors, supervising trips to Dragon's Den... offering advice to younger students... she had no idea how she was going to cope. She wasn't even sure what she'd be asked. *She'd* never bombarded the Head Pupil with questions.

The second scroll was an updated timetable. Emily glanced at it, wondering just why nearly all of her classes were in the morning. It *looked* as though sleeping in was going to be impossible, even though—as a Sixth Year—she wouldn't have the bed tipping her onto the floor if she didn't get up before classes began. She wondered, absently, why the tutors were punishing themselves too. *They* could sleep in too...

She put both of the scrolls in her pocket and walked back to the stairs, heading down towards the lower levels. The school was surprisingly quiet. She didn't see anyone as she reached the bottom of the stairs, not even a handful of cleaning staff. No doubt the students she'd seen earlier had headed back to their bedrooms, if they'd finished their exams. The library wouldn't be open until classes resumed, unfortunately. Emily *had* considered trying to sneak in herself, but she knew that would be far too revealing. Besides, she had no idea what protections Lady Aliya and her staff might have added over the last few months. *They* wouldn't be connected to Whitehall's wards.

They were trying to upgrade the whole system, after the entire school nearly collapsed, she reminded herself. The library had been a ghastly mess. Hundreds of students had worked hard just to put the books back on the shelves. *They didn't want to rely on the school's wards again.*

She frowned as she heard the sound of raised voices, dead ahead of her. Lady Barb was arguing with Sergeant Miles, their voices echoing down the corridor. Emily froze, unsure what to do. She couldn't quite make out the words, but they sounded angry... she shivered, remembering the one time she'd seen Sergeant Miles mad. He was so calm—normally—that his anger had been frightening.

The sound cut off, abruptly. A moment later, Lady Barb strode out of the office.

"Emily." She looked like an angry cat. Her voice was so tightly controlled that Emily *knew* she was furious. "Come with me."

She swept past Emily and headed down the corridor. Emily hesitated, then followed her into a small workroom. It was clean and tidy, the tools placed on the workbench or hanging from the walls. She wasn't surprised. Anyone who was allowed to use the workroom would *know* that it had to be kept clean, that they had to tidy up after themselves. Sergeant Miles would *not* be pleased with anyone who didn't take care of the school's tools. They'd spend *weeks* on punishment duties.

"Have a seat," Lady Barb said. Her voice softened, just slightly. "Just let me put up a privacy ward and I'll be right with you."

Emily eyed her, worriedly. Lady Barb didn't seem to be angry at *her*, but it was clear the older woman was *pissed*. She strode up and down, her fingers curling into fists as she cast a trio of privacy wards into the air. Emily watched her, sensing the wards falling into place one by one. Lady Barb wasn't just trying to keep their conversation private, Emily realized grimly. She was using the spellcasting to calm herself.

"That should do it," Lady Barb said, finally.

Emily braced herself. "Are you all right?"

"No," Lady Barb said, curtly. She shot Emily a look that warned her not to ask any more questions. "What did the Grandmaster want?"

"I'm Head Girl." Emily looked up at her mentor. "Is there any way of getting out of it?"

Lady Barb rolled her eyes. "Only *you* would try to get *out* of it," she said, her voice sour, as if she was still distracted. "Everyone *else* schemes to get *in*."

"I didn't want it," Emily said.

"I suppose it wouldn't look *quite* so good on your particular resume," Lady Barb said, with a grimace. "Necromancer's Bane, Baroness of Cockatrice, Savior of Farrakhan, Savior of Beneficence... Head Girl."

Emily had to smile. "It does look a *little* small," she said. "But... is there any way to get out of it?"

"Not without paying a price," Lady Barb told her. "If nothing else, they'd have to meet and elect a *new* Head Pupil."

"Ouch." Emily met Lady Barb's eyes. "He also wants me to set up a dueling club and run a contest."

Lady Barb looked irked. "As your special project?"

Emily nodded. "I can't think of anything better..."

"It's never easy to come up with something that hasn't already been done," Lady Barb admitted. "Finding something that will *succeed* is even harder."

She sighed. "There *has* been a push to reopen a dueling club for several years," she added, tiredly. "But it was never a possibility until a new Grandmaster took up his office."

"I was told it isn't good training for war," Emily said. "That's true, isn't it?"

"Yes." Lady Barb shrugged. "To be fair, it does teach *some* of the skills combat sorcerers need. Thinking on one's feet, snapping off curses and hexes at speed... they're skills that are desperately required in combat. But duelists are also taught to hold back, something that can be disastrous in a *real* fight."

Emily made a face. She knew hundreds of spells that *couldn't* be used in a duel without—at best—forfeiting the match. The risk of maiming—or killing—her opponent would be far too high. And yet, in a real fight, she'd use those spells without a second thought. Training herself *not* to use them would hamper her in later life.

"It will be fun, for everyone who wants to take part," Lady Barb added. "But not everyone *will* want to take part."

"They'll want to keep their skills a mystery," Emily said. She'd been cautioned not to show *everything* she could do. "What happens when younger students want to go up against older students?"

"The younger ones will get their butts kicked," Lady Barb said, dryly. "Or you'll have the perfect excuse to humiliate the older pupils."

Emily sighed. "I don't want to do this. But I just can't think of anything *else.*"

She looked up. "What about reorganizing the library?"

"That wouldn't be quite so spectacular," Lady Barb said. "You'd get more credit for something that lasted."

"Like the mentorship program," Emily mused. "But how much work did Aloha actually *do* after it got started?"

"Probably quite a bit," Lady Barb said.

She held up a hand. "You shouldn't have any trouble setting up a basic roster, perhaps selecting a few older students to serve as additional supervisors. That won't take *much* work. Then you can run the club one day each week. I don't think you'll have to do *that* much work, once you get started. It'll probably wind up running itself."

"I hope you're right," Emily said. She'd never liked dueling, even before she'd killed Master Grey. But then, she'd never liked team sports either. Just because *she* didn't like something didn't mean everyone else detested it too. "If I do as little work as possible..."

"Do enough to give the club a reasonable chance of success," Lady Barb advised. "It does have a great deal of potential. If nothing else, it *will* give dozens of other students—the ones who haven't been able to get onto sports teams—the chance to compete. It will certainly be more *fun* than Martial Magic."

Emily nodded, ruefully. Martial Magic wasn't *fun.* She had to admit she'd put on a great deal of muscle over the last five years—as well as learning countless spells and techniques—but it hadn't been *fun.* She'd ached every day until her body had grown used to heavy exercise, then crawled through mud and sneaked through woods...

she'd never *liked* it. She wasn't surprised that only a handful of pupils took the course every year.

"And do the same for the rest of your duties as Head Girl," Lady Barb added. "You have to show willingness to reap the full reward."

Emily rubbed her forehead. "Why didn't they ask me first?"

"Probably because most people would leap at the chance to prove themselves," Lady Barb answered. "Being Head Girl *here*, Emily, is something that will add breadth to your resume. It will definitely count in your favor when you start looking for an apprenticeship."

I already have an offer from Void, Emily thought. *And that comes without conditions.*

She frowned. Void had already made her the offer. He wouldn't care if she was Head Girl or not. Or would he? Aloha had had masters clamoring to take her as an apprentice... had *they* been impressed by her conduct as Head Girl? No one could deny that Aloha had been brave as well as clever, risking everything on a mentoring program that could easily have gone bad. Failure would have tarnished her future.

"I'll see if I can think of anything else," she said. "But if not..."

"Good thinking," Lady Barb said. "Gordian *wants* this to succeed. I daresay he'll be more inclined to help you if you're doing something *he* chose."

"And it saves me the job of coming up with something else," Emily said.

She looked down at her hands. "Which way did *you* vote?"

"I wasn't there," Lady Barb reminded her.

Emily scowled. It had been easy to forget, over the past three months, that Lady Barb was no longer a tutor. She'd hoped Lady Barb *would* return to Whitehall, even though Lady Barb herself hadn't been keen on the idea. If nothing else, she'd be near Sergeant Miles. But they had just been arguing...

"I don't know which way I *would* have voted," Lady Barb added. "You're not the only student with a heavy workload. And I would have wondered about your ability to handle the more... social... aspects of the job. And yet... you *did* save the school more than once. You deserve some kind of reward for your services."

I would have preferred permanent access to the library, Emily thought. *Or a place at the school for the rest of my life.*

She pushed the thought out of her head. She wanted to stay at Whitehall, but she knew that wouldn't be possible. There was too much else she had to do. Besides, Gordian wouldn't hire her as a tutor until she had her mastery and a great deal more experience. Merely having a certificate wasn't enough, not at Whitehall. A tutor who didn't know what he was talking about wouldn't last long at a school of magic.

"I'll do my best," she promised. "I..."

"I'll be leaving tonight," Lady Barb said, cutting her off. "I have to head back to the border. There might be more trouble to the south, near the Inner Sea."

Emily felt a stab of dismay. "So soon?"

"Work doesn't stop, not for us." Lady Barb reached out and squeezed Emily's shoulder. "I'll keep the chat parchment with me. You can write whenever you like."

"I wish you could stay longer." Emily swallowed, hard. "Why were you fighting with Sergeant Miles?"

"None of your business," Lady Barb said, her voice suddenly very cold. "Suffice it to say that we had a small disagreement."

Emily winced. "I..."

"Don't worry about it," Lady Barb said. Her lips twisted. "He managed to blindside me and... things went downhill from there. I'll speak to him before I go."

"Oh," Emily said. "I... was it my fault?"

"Not *everything* is your fault, Emily," Lady Barb said. She smiled, suddenly. "Although, if you want to accept the blame, I'm sure Miles will be happy to give you a truly appalling detention."

"I don't have time for detention," Emily said, quickly. "Will you be staying for dinner?"

"I think so," Lady Barb said.

She rose. "I believe Madame Rosalinda wishes to see you in the dorms," she added. "Go there. I'll see you at dinner."

Emily nodded, wondering just what had actually happened between Lady Barb and Sergeant Miles. They'd been lovers for the past two—perhaps three—years. She'd never heard them argue before, certainly not like *that*. They'd been so angry they'd forgotten to put up a privacy ward before starting to shout at each other. It didn't bode well for their future.

She hurried out of the door and up the stairs. The Sixth Year dorms were in the upper levels, isolated from the lower dorms by a layer of study rooms and spellchambers. Gordian had put a small army of wardcrafters to work updating the protections over the summer, according to Lady Barb. In hindsight, Emily suspected he'd been planning the dueling club for the last year or two. The duelists would need dozens of spellchambers to practice their arts before entering the dueling circle.

And I still can't think of anything else, Emily thought, as she stepped through the door and into the corridor. The wards shimmered around her, checking her identity before they allowed her to proceed. *There's nothing that will appeal to most of the school.*

"Emily," Madame Rosalinda said. She hadn't changed either. She *still* looked like an old gypsy woman, wearing a long dress and a headscarf that concealed her hair. "Come with me."

Emily looked around with interest as Madame Rosalinda led her down the corridor. She'd never been allowed into the Sixth Year dorms, not even to see Aloha. The Sixth Years guarded their privacy, she'd been told. Younger students tried to sneak in, of course—it was an old tradition—but most of them wound up being turned into frogs or kicked out by the Sixth Years. It was vanishingly rare for *anyone* to get an invitation into the dorms.

They looked very similar to the Fifth Year dorms, she noted, but the common room and study chambers looked larger. Magic hung in the air, including a handful of protective charms she didn't recognize. Emily felt them inspecting her as Madame Rosalinda stopped in front of a gold-edged door at the far end of the corridor. A touch of her finger opened it, revealing a large suite. Emily followed her into the suite, shaking her head in disbelief. It looked like a luxury hotel.

"These are the Head Pupil quarters," Madame Rosalinda said. She jabbed a finger around the suite. "You have a large bedroom and bathroom in there, a private office there... even a small kitchen, if you wish to cook for yourself. Draw supplies from the kitchens downstairs and bring them up. You're the only one allowed to enter these rooms without special permission, but you can invite whoever you like. You also"—she pointed to the office—"have a private door. Students who want to see you can visit without having to walk through the dorms."

"It's too much," Emily said.

"Every other student has a large bedroom to themselves," Madame Rosalinda informed her. "It's one of the perks of surviving five years in school."

"Thanks," Emily said, dryly.

She peered into the bedroom. It was easily large enough for two or three people—the bed alone was large enough for two people to share comfortably—and the bathroom was even bigger. She'd never had a private bathtub before, not at Whitehall. She had the sudden urge to undress and take a soak for the next few hours. It was a luxury she'd grown to love over the past five years.

"You can also arrange for the floor to be swept and the bedding to be changed by the staff," Madame Rosalinda added. "But you would be well advised to do it for yourself."

Just to keep from getting lazy, Emily thought.

"Thank you," she said. "But it seems too large..."

"You're the Head Girl," Madame Rosalinda said. "You *are* expected to work for this, you know."

"Yeah," Emily said. "I know."

Chapter Four

E MILY AWOKE, SLOWLY.
The bed was comfortable, too comfortable. It tempted her to close her eyes again and go back to sleep, even though she knew she had to get up. There were no windows in the bedroom, but a glance at the clock told her it was nearly ten bells. She'd have to get up in a hurry if she wanted to get breakfast. If she didn't make it down to the dining room in time, she'd have to beg the kitchen staff for a plate of toast and eggs.

Or make it myself, she thought, as she sat upright and climbed out of bed. She'd stocked the small kitchen with milk, bread, eggs and a handful of other items liberated from the main kitchen. She was an indifferent cook at best—she'd never mastered the skill—but she could do scrambled eggs on toast if she wanted. *I could keep myself fed up here.*

She walked into the bathroom, showered quickly and donned another long dress. It felt odd to be living in the suite, as if she was a guest in her own quarters. The wards hummed around her as she walked into the kitchen, growing stronger as she approached the walls. She made a mental note to check on them when she had a moment, if she could ever find enough time to slip down to the control center below Whitehall. She'd repaired the foundational wards last year, after their near collapse, but she was in uncharted territory now. Generations of grandmasters had added so many different pieces of spellware to the wards that she wasn't sure what half of them did.

Frieda is coming back today, she reminded herself. Her younger friend had been on work experience, priming herself for Fourth Year. Emily had missed her when she'd been cramming to retake the exams. They'd hoped to meet up, but it hadn't been possible. *I'll see her later today.*

She boiled a pot of water, silently cursing the lack of any modern kitchen equipment. She'd never lived in a truly modern house, stuffed with labor-saving gadgets, but she'd had electric mixers and can openers. Here, she had nothing beyond hand-powered tools, unless she wanted to take the time to learn or design household spells. It constantly astonished her just how much work went into cooking on the Nameless World. King Randor's chefs—and the cooks at Whitehall—worked like demons, just to keep the castles *fed*. They didn't even have desiccated *coffee*!

Or Kava, she thought, as she poured herself a mug. *I have to grind the beans myself.*

She took a sip. It tasted foul, thick and stronger than normal. She drank it anyway as she walked into her office and sat down at the desk. The wards seemed to slide back from her mind, suggesting the office had fewer protections than the rest of the suite. No doubt trying to break into the Head Pupil's office was *also* a tradition. God knew she'd tried to break into every other office in the school.

The papers in front of her mocked her. She'd racked her brains to think of something—anything—that might be better than the dueling club and contest, but nothing had come to mind. Small projects wouldn't interest Gordian—and wouldn't leave a mark on the school—while bigger projects would require far too much work. She just didn't have the time to handle them. Lady Barb had been right, she suspected. Gordian would help her with the dueling club because it was what he wanted her to do.

And it might leave a mark on the school anyway, she thought, ruefully. *Just not in the way he wants.*

She took another sip as she glanced through the files. Whitehall's *last* dueling club had been closed down after a series of accidents, back when Hasdrubal had become Grandmaster. He had believed, according to one report, that the accidents hadn't been anything of the sort, but there hadn't been any proof one way or the other. There had been protests from some of the other tutors, yet they hadn't been able to convince him to rethink his decision. Emily didn't blame him. Dueling wasn't remotely safe.

And the sergeants have fewer accidents, she reminded herself. *Hardly anyone gets killed.*

She kept reading through the reports—and outlining a set of procedures for the club and contest—until the wards vibrated, informing her that Frieda had just passed through the school's outer protections. Emily stood and hurried out of the suite, heading down the stairs to the entrance hall. A small number of older students, mainly Fifth and Sixth Years, were already flowing into the school, preparing to start the next level. As Emily walked past them, she made a mental note to organize a meeting with the Fifth Years before the First Years arrived—she'd have to ensure they knew how to mentor their students. Frieda was just walking into the hall.

"Frieda," she called.

"Emily," Frieda called back. "I missed you!"

Emily half-ran over to her as Frieda dropped her trunk on the floor and opened her arms for a hug. She looked different, Emily noted; her dark hair was hanging down, rather than tied up in her trademark pigtails. Her face was pale—as always—but softer, somehow. The red dress she wore was tight around her bust and hips, outlining her curves rather than revealing her bare flesh. And she wore a golden amulet around her neck and a similar bracelet on her right wrist.

Frieda wrapped her arms around Emily, tightly. "I've got so much to tell you," she said, quietly. "Did you pass your exams?"

"Head Girl," Emily said.

"I *knew* it." Frieda winked. "I was betting on you, you know."

"Good thing I didn't turn it down," Emily said. She hadn't known that people were betting on her, either. "We'll get your trunk upstairs, then we'll have a chat."

Frieda grinned and picked up the trunk. "They had me working in an alchemist's shop in Celeste for a couple of months, then assisting a charms master for two weeks," she said, as they made their slow way up the stairs. "It was a good time, really. Better than school."

Emily smiled. "Really?"

"I had to work hard, but at least I got paid." Frieda tapped the amulet around her neck. "What do you think?"

"Very showy," Emily said. She'd never really been comfortable with jewelry. It had taken her far too long to get used to wearing the snake-bracelet. She'd never been able to forget she was wearing it. "Where did you get it?"

"One of the lads I met had a brother who was apprenticed to a jeweler," Frieda explained, cheerfully. "He was happy to give me a discount, if I helped him with a couple of his projects."

Emily smiled. "Do I want to know?"

Frieda shrugged. "He had a few ideas about how magic could slide into metalwork. They came to nothing, but I was happy to help him."

They reached the dorm and made their way down to Frieda's room. Madame Beauregard was standing by her office, issuing orders to students and stewards alike. She shot Emily a sharp look, then nodded as Frieda led the way into her bedroom. It was bare; the beds unmade, the bookshelves empty. Emily hurried down to the storage lockers to pick up a selection of bedding while Frieda opened her trunk. Madame Beauregard made a disapproving sound as Emily walked back, but said nothing. Emily suspected the Head Girl wasn't *meant* to help younger students with their bedding.

"I made this for you." Frieda held out a small necklace, a white crystal dangling from a silver chain. "There's a very basic protection spell worked into the crystal."

Emily took the necklace and examined it, thoughtfully. The chain was perfect, too perfect to have been made by hand. Or maybe she was wrong... she'd seen some pretty elegant pieces of work produced without magic, back in Zangaria. Magic was woven carefully into the chain, tiny runes channeling background magic into the crystal. The charm pulsed faintly against her bare skin, allowing her to test it. Frieda had done an excellent job. The spell would give her some additional protections against outside threats.

"You shouldn't have," Emily said.

"There's quite a market for those," Frieda said, ignoring her. "My master was trying to talk me into coming to apprentice with him formally, after Fourth Year. He said I had a talent."

"You do," Emily said. She meant it, too. *She'd* never had any real skill at making pieces of art, but it was obvious Frieda *did*. "How long did it take you to make it?"

"Hours." Frieda grinned broadly as she picked up the bedding and started to make her bed. "It took a couple of weeks to master the skills to make the chain, then enchant the crystal itself. I broke three crystals before I managed to insert it properly. My master said he'd done worse when *he'd* been in training."

Emily nodded. The protective charm wasn't *that* complex, but inserting it into the crystal would have been tricky. She'd had problems mastering it herself, back when she'd been learning how to cast and anchor wards. Frieda had done *very* well. The charm wasn't very flexible—and someone could probably break through it, if they had enough power or skill—but it would be useful. She'd have to blend it into her own protections before she could wear it properly.

But I will, she thought. *It's beautiful.*

Frieda chatted happily as she made her bed, then started to unpack the trunk. Emily sat on one of the other beds and listened as Frieda recounted stories about spending three months in a magical community. It sounded as though she'd had a whale of a time, Emily decided, feeling an odd flicker of envy. *She'd* never spent time in a magical community, unless one counted the time she'd spent in Beneficence. And she'd been a guest, not a student on work experience.

"There was a girl who could make the most beautiful toys," Frieda said, sounding rather impressed. "She hadn't had any formal training—she'd never been to school—but she was still a skilled enchanter. Her parents have been making toys and tools for *years*. I was hoping to talk her into making something for me, but she didn't have time. She really should move to Beneficence, if the city has recovered by now. She's got a handful of siblings who can take over the family business."

She smiled. "And then there was a boy who kept talking me into taking long walks..."

Emily grinned. "A boyfriend?"

"We just fooled around." Frieda's fingers touched her cheek, gently. "I..."

She paused, just for a second. "You're Head Girl," she said. An unpleasant smile spread across her face. "You can send *Caleb* to be caned."

Emily flushed. "I don't think that's allowed..."

"Of course it is," Frieda said, briskly. Her face darkened. "He deserves it, doesn't he?"

"No," Emily said. She wasn't sure if she meant it or not. There were times when she wanted to be angry, really angry, at her former boyfriend. "We are talking again, now."

"Hah," Frieda said.

Emily opened her mouth to point out that she could send *Frieda* to be caned too, then stopped herself firmly. She had no intention of abusing her power, unlike Master Tor or Master Gray. And besides, she could handle her problems herself. She and Caleb would just have to work together long enough to pass their exams, then... if they still had problems, they could part on good terms.

"It sounds like you had a great time," she said. "But you do realize that Fourth Year is going to be hard."

"The hardest," Frieda agreed. "But I'm looking forward to it."

She produced a pile of books from her trunk and dumped them on the bookshelves. Most of them were freshly-printed magical textbooks, but a couple were blue books. Emily groaned inwardly, knowing Frieda had just placed her in an invidious position. Blue books were banned at Whitehall, no exceptions. If she confiscated them, Frieda would be mad at her; if she ignored them, Gordian would point out she wasn't doing her job. Either way, she'd lose something...

"Take those books out of here before term starts," she said, pointing to the blue books. "Or you'll get us both in trouble."

Frieda looked embarrassed. "... Sorry."

Emily sighed. She'd read a handful of blue books, but none of them had been particularly decent. They'd read more like bad fan fiction, crammed with IKEA erotica, than anything else. There were only so many times one could read them without feeling they'd read the exact same story a dozen times over. *She'd* known they were poorly written and staggeringly unrealistic even *before* losing her virginity.

"Just keep them out of sight," she said. "Take them to the house, if you want."

"I'll keep them out of your sight," Frieda promised.

Emily sighed, again. "I don't think you'll have time for reading them," she added. "You'll have to do a joint project..."

She saw a flash of hot anger cross Frieda's face. "Celadon is useless. I should never have paired up with him!"

Emily blinked, alarmed. "What's *wrong* with him?"

"Oh, we had a plan to go on work experience to get the training we needed to complete the project," Frieda said. "And then he started coming up with new ideas of his own."

"That's not a bad thing," Emily pointed out. "You don't want to do all the work..."

"He wants to change everything, even after we spent the summer working on our skills," Frieda snapped. "And he didn't listen to a single word from *me*!"

Emily looked up. "Frieda, what's wrong?"

"He won't listen to me," Frieda said. Her face darkened. "He just won't *listen*!"

Emily sucked in a breath. "What are you actually trying to do?"

Frieda hesitated. "Are we allowed to tell you?"

"I think so," Emily said. She hadn't talked about *her* joint project, but it had wider implications than anyone apart from her and Caleb had realized. "I'm just not allowed to actually *help* you."

"We were working on using rare materials to design a whole new generation of alchemical tools," Frieda said. "It was something that grew out of the New Learning, a concept that might..." she trailed off and knelt down beside the trunk, then started to dig through it. "I'll see if I can find you the papers."

"Leave that for the moment," Emily said. "What does he want to change?"

"We had a plan for crafting the tools," Frieda said. "And now he wants to change it!"

Emily cocked her head. "How do you know his way isn't better?"

"Because he didn't suggest it to me," Frieda, sounding furious. Magic crackled over her fingertips. "He *told* me. Just... wrote and said we were going to be changing everything. I don't even know everything he wants to do!"

"I see," Emily said. "When he gets here, why don't you sit down with him and work through it, piece by piece? If his idea is truly better, you can use it."

"And then he gets all the credit," Frieda pointed out.

"No, he doesn't," Emily said. She could see Frieda's point, but it didn't work like that. "He would only get all the credit if he did all the work. He's not talking about dumping you, is he?"

"He doesn't seem to *need* me," Frieda muttered. "Emily, what happens if he *does* shove me out of the project?"

"I don't think he can," Emily said. The joint project was meant to be *joint*. Neither Celadon nor Frieda would get high marks if their partnership failed, even if their work was pure genius. And, somehow, they'd managed to get through the first stage without going down in flames. "You have to work together to complete the project."

Frieda scowled. "And what stops him from doing all the work?"

"You," Emily said. "At the very least, you have to know what's going on."

"I don't know if I do." Frieda's face twisted as she closed the trunk and stood. "I don't think he listens to a single thing I say."

"You were exchanging letters and chat notes, right?" Emily asked. "You'll probably get on better face to face. Sit down with him, go through what he wants to do, run a few basic experiments and then... and then, decide how you want to proceed. If things *really* fall apart, you can probably talk to your tutor."

"He'll probably blame me," Frieda said, sourly. "Professor Thande doesn't *like* me."

"You don't blow up enough cauldrons." Emily stood and nodded to the door. "It'll be several hours until dinner, so come for a swim. Or a walk. It'll make us both feel better."

She smiled. "And you can help me think of something we can do instead of a dueling club."

Frieda blinked. "What?"

Emily explained, quickly.

"But that would be fun," Frieda said, when Emily finished the explanation. "I'd *love* to duel."

"I fought in two *real* duels," Emily pointed out. "They weren't *fun.*"

"You're also a champion," Frieda said. "Aren't you?"

Emily shrugged. Casper had beaten her in a duel before his death. She assumed the title had fallen to the next person in line, rather than returning to her. No one had tried to challenge her since Casper's death, if nothing else. *That* meant she'd probably fallen a *long* way down the league table. But it wasn't something that bothered her.

"Come on," she said, instead. "Let's go for a swim."

Chapter Five

EMILY HAD HOPED—DESPITE FRIEDA'S ENTHUSIASM—TO FIND SOMETHING THAT WOULD serve as an alternative to the dueling club, but a week of brainstorming and research turned up nothing remotely practical. Some of her ideas had been tried before, while others would have required too much effort to make them work. She simply hadn't been able to find anything that would satisfy the requirements without demanding too much from her.

"At least *this* way you can be sure of getting willing helpers," Frieda pointed out, as they waited outside Gordian's office. "A homework club wouldn't raise quite so much enthusiasm."

"I suppose," Emily said. She wished, not for the first time, that someone else had been elected Head Girl. It wasn't as if she'd *wanted* the post. There *had* been class presidents back home, but the role had been purely ceremonial. The schoolchildren certainly hadn't had any real authority. "You'd think they'd *want* help with their homework."

"No one wants to *do* homework," Frieda said.

Emily had to agree. She'd never met a student who *liked* doing homework, even if they considered the subject to be fascinating. And, on Earth, she'd had problems finding a place to *do* homework without encountering her stepfather. Having an older student help her with her homework—at Whitehall—might have made life easier, but it wouldn't have made it any more enjoyable. Besides, students were supposed to learn to manage their own time. A homework club—even one that wasn't compulsory—wouldn't teach them skills they'd need for future life.

But it might have made sure they actually got their homework done, she thought. But then, anyone who didn't get it done would be in real trouble.

Her lips quirked—she'd heard students argue, earnestly, that their homework had eaten the dog. The door opened. Madame Griselda stood there, eying Emily and Frieda as if they were something unpleasant she'd scraped off the sole of her boot. Emily looked back at her, wondering what Gordian's secretary had against her. But then, Madame Griselda seemed to be unpleasant to *all* the students. Perhaps she felt the school could be organized perfectly if all the pesky students went elsewhere.

"Lady Emily," Madame Griselda said. "The Grandmaster will see you now."

"Thank you," Emily said.

She sighed. She'd had the morning free—insofar as she'd spent it doing *more* research than schoolwork—but she had an orientation meeting with the rest of the Sixth Year students in an hour. She wasn't even sure which tutor would serve as their Year Head. The note she'd received when classes resumed, detailing her first week, hadn't said. She was fairly sure it wouldn't be Master Tor, but there were too many other possible candidates.

"I'll see you this evening," she said to Frieda. "Have fun."

Frieda looked downcast. "I have to read through *his* latest set of proposals." A flicker of anger crossed her face. "Is it too much to ask that *he* makes up his mind?"

"Probably," Emily said. She and Caleb hadn't had so many problems, had they? But then, students were expected to show they could think for themselves, not single-handedly solve magical conundrums that had baffled older and wiser minds. Even drawing out a new line of enquiry would be more than anyone was *expected* to do. "You don't *have* to stick with him after the project is completed."

"You did," Frieda said.

Emily felt her cheeks heat. She'd been confident enough in the joint project that she'd agreed to apply for extra credit, rather than putting the whole concept aside until after she and Caleb graduated. It had been a risk, but she'd had faith in her ability to turn the project into something viable. And besides, it would have allowed her—it *had* allowed her—to spend more time with Caleb. It was clear that *Frieda* wouldn't be dating Celadon anytime soon.

"I didn't have to," Emily said. "Nor do you."

Madame Griselda cleared her throat, meaningfully. Emily winked at Frieda, then turned and walked into Gordian's office. It was empty, but a door was open at the far end, a door she was *sure* hadn't been there before. Was Gordian experimenting with manipulating the school's interior dimensions? Or had it merely been concealed behind a haze of powerful charms? After everything that had happened last year, it would be a long time before anyone—Emily included—wanted to meddle with the school's interior. The risk of triggering another collapse was too great.

"Emily," Gordian called. "Come on in."

Emily walked to the new door and peered through. The compartment looked like a comfortable study, complete with armchairs, a small wooden table, a pot of Kava on the sideboard and a warm fire burning merrily in the grate. A handful of portraits hung from the walls, one marked as Master Whitehall. Emily smiled when she saw it. Lord and Master Whitehall—most history books didn't seem to realize that *Lord* and *Master* were combined—hadn't looked anything like *that*. The man in the painting looked like someone had crossed Dumbledore with Gandalf and added robes at least five hundred years out of time. The next picture—Grandmaster Bernard—*might* have been more authentic. She had no idea what Bernard had looked like as an older man.

No sign of Julianne, of course, she thought cynically. Whitehall's daughter—and Bernard's wife—had practically fallen out of the history books. *And no mention of me either.*

Gordian followed her gaze. "I was meaning to ask you how close they were to reality." He sounded friendlier, for once. "Is that really *him*?"

"That isn't Lord Whitehall." Emily studied the portrait for a long moment. "I don't think he would have aged into *that*."

"Times change, people change," Gordian said, his voice oddly reflective. "Others stay the same."

He cocked his head. "I was hoping to discuss history with you at some later date," he added, after a moment. "And there are a handful of historians who would be very interested in your story."

Emily frowned. Gordian was the only one who knew she'd gone back in time and played a vital role in the founding of Whitehall School. She hadn't told anyone else, not even her closest friends. The last thing she wanted was to encourage magicians to start experimenting with time travel, despite the fact that her equations insisted it wouldn't be easy to navigate without a nexus point and a checkpoint. Random jumping through time would be incredibly dangerous.

And Gordian has his own reasons to keep it quiet, she thought. *He wouldn't want to admit that I can take control of the school's wards. It would undermine his position as Grandmaster if everyone knew I could overrule him.*

"I thought you wanted to keep it quiet," she said. Professor Locke's dream of long-lost spells had never materialized, but there *were* secrets in the past that should be left there. Demons and DemonMasters, for one. And Manavores, whatever they'd been. She'd seen signs of their presence at Heart's Eye too, back when she and Casper had sneaked into the fallen school. "It would give people ideas."

"The historians would be under oath not to disclose anything without clearing it with me first," Gordian assured her. "Your name would never be mentioned."

Emily wasn't so sure. It was hard to tell just *what* clue would allow someone to untangle the whole story, even though time travel wasn't even a *concept* in the Nameless World. Or perhaps it was, in a sense. Going *forward* in time wasn't impossible, as long as one had the power. It was getting *backwards* that was impossible.

Without a nexus point, she reminded herself. *And even if they had a nexus point, they'd find it hard to navigate...*

"Perhaps I could talk to them later," she said. She understood the urge to dig up the past, even though there were some secrets *definitely* better left buried. "But it would be hard to prove anything."

"We will see," Gordian said. "We haven't even *begun* to explore *all* the tunnels below Whitehall."

"That would be dangerous," Emily warned. "We don't know *what* we might do."

"Or what else might be on the verge of going wrong," Gordian said. "I can't even use the wards to scan below the school. Can you?"

Emily shook her head. The lower levels hadn't *quite* been excluded from the wards, but the spellware that monitored the school didn't work down there. She suspected the surveillance spells had been designed and implemented after the lower levels had been sealed off and forgotten. Whoever had designed them hadn't known to look below the open levels.

"We'll be very careful," Gordian said. "But we do have to know what might be under us."

Emily nodded, reluctantly. Whitehall's spellwork had lasted for nearly a thousand years, but she could understand Gordian's concern. Something might have been steadily going wrong—or falling out of alignment—for all that time. Or Lord Whitehall might have buried a basilisk under the school. She didn't think that was likely—he'd have had more sense—but it was a possibility.

"Just be careful," she said. "And leave the wards alone."

"We will," Gordian assured her. "Who knows how many more books and records are hidden below, just waiting for us to find them?"

Emily shrugged. As far as she knew, there had only been one cache of books. But if Master Wolfe had somehow been active *after* his presumed death, there might be more. He—or someone—had left a cache in Beneficence, after all. Why wouldn't he have hidden one in Whitehall?

Because it would be the first place anyone would look, if they knew who'd written the books, her own thoughts answered her. He'd certainly have fewer problems hiding them here.

"It might come to nothing," Gordian said. "But we have to search the lower levels thoroughly."

He motioned for her to sit down. "Please, be seated. Would you like a mug of Kava?"

Emily hesitated. She'd really drunk too much caffeine over the last few hours. But etiquette demanded that he offer and she accept. It was a way of saying she was welcome, even if she wasn't.

"Yes, please," she said, finally. It wasn't as though it was *that* late. "Milk, no sugar."

Gordian rose and poured her a mug. "I trust you spent the week productively," he said, as he passed it to her. "Did you find an alternative to the dueling club?"

"No, sir," Emily said. It galled her to admit it, but all of the *practical* ideas had been done before. A couple of failed ideas had been reasonably promising, yet she doubted Gordian would have let her try to make them work. He'd say they'd already failed once and he would be right. "Nothing I found would be workable in the time I have."

Gordian's lips twitched, as if he'd scored a point. Emily silently conceded he had.

"Very good," Gordian said. "And you have drawn up the rules?"

Emily reached into her pocket and produced a small notebook. "For the club itself, I modeled the structure on the kingmaker and fencing clubs. Members will be ranked according to wins, losses and draws... insofar as there *are* draws. I've copied the rules from the dueling league, with the principle exception of no lethal combat. Ideally, the members will *not* be seriously injured in dueling."

"That might be tricky to enforce," Gordian said. "The monitors might not catch any illicit moves."

Emily nodded. No one—apart from Sergeant Miles—had realized she'd deliberately given Casper an opening, when she'd dueled with him. Unless the others *had* realized and kept their mouths shut... no, she couldn't imagine Master Grave letting Casper prance about in celebration if he hadn't won fairly. The man was a stickler for the rules. Casper himself certainly hadn't known.

"The arena will be spelled to keep combat as safe as possible." She knew *that* wasn't going to be easy. Small injuries happened all the time, no matter what the tutors said or did. Whitehall certainly wasn't at risk of being sued if a student cut his finger or scraped her knee. "I was thinking that preparing the arena would make a useful project for some of the older students."

"And give you some practical experience," Gordian said, slowly. He nodded in apparent approval. "I believe Professor Armstrong would be happy to assist you. You're still with him this year, aren't you?"

Emily nodded. She'd passed her wardcrafting exam, somewhat to her surprise. Professor Armstrong wasn't known for letting his students get away with anything. The theoretical part of the exam had been bad enough, but the practical side had been worse. She'd had to stand in the center of her own wards and watch, helplessly, as the examiners blasted away at them with powerful spells. She was honestly surprised they'd lasted long enough for her to pass the exam.

"I have another year with him," she confirmed.

"I'm sure he will assist you." Gordian cocked his head. "You may also wish to work with Professor Lombardi. The arena *must* come up to the league's standards."

"I will." Emily sighed, inwardly. *That* was going to be a great deal of work, even if she could shovel some of it onto her fellow pupils. Coming to think of it, she'd *definitely* have to get Professor Lombardi involved... perhaps even Sergeant Miles. The Dueling League's rules were very specific. "I wasn't planning to have students join the league."

"They'll *want* to join the league," Gordian said. "And the less they have to unlearn, the better."

Emily resisted the urge to roll her eyes. The Dueling League had never struck her as particularly logical. She'd fought two formal duels in her life, one of which had catapulted her to the top while the other had knocked her all the way down to the bottom. And yet, no one had questioned her right to the championship. They'd merely started making plans to challenge her after she left Whitehall.

They won't be doing that now, she thought. *My ranking is no longer worth taking.*

She pushed that thought aside. "The contest will consist of three rounds. For the first one, everyone who wins their duel will proceed; for the second, we'll keep dueling until we end up with a handful of candidates. And then they'll battle it out for the championship."

"You'll be knocking anyone who has a bad day out of the running," Gordian pointed out, dryly. "There'll be complaints."

"It depends on how many people want to duel," Emily said. Frieda had been enthusiastic, but she didn't know how many others wanted to compete. The Sixth Years were going to be very busy over the coming year. Caleb and the Gorgon certainly wouldn't want to waste time... Melissa *might* want to take part, but she had a lot of work to do. "If we only have a handful, we won't really need to run three separate rounds after all."

"Magicians will *want* to compete," Gordian said. "Don't you?"

Emily shook her head. *She* hadn't wanted to compete. Nor had Lady Barb. *Casper* had, she supposed, but he was the only one she'd met who'd been genuinely enthusiastic. Even Master Grey had soured on dueling, though he'd been too prideful to give up his ranking without a fight. She wondered, absently, if Jade or Cat had ever been interested in dueling. It was something she'd have to ask Alassa, the next time they talked. Jade certainly had the skill to be a good duelist.

"Others will want to compete," Gordian said.

He leaned back in his chair. "I'll expect you to have the club organized within a month of term starting. You can set the contest dates as you see fit, but I advise you to wrap the third round up well before the final exams. Your classmates will probably try to lynch you if they have to choose between the duel and their exams."

Emily nodded. *She* wouldn't want to take part in a contest while *she* was preparing desperately for her final exams either. She certainly wouldn't have chosen to take part in a contest *instead* of her exams, but she could understand—she supposed—why some of her classmates would feel differently. Backing down—or out—was often seen as worse than standing up against insurmountable odds. It explained some of the odder moments of military and magical history. Better to die bravely, they reasoned, than be branded a coward.

"I'll try to wrap it up midway through the second term," she said. Hopefully, she could abandon the whole concept afterwards and concentrate on her exams. "By then, the club should be running on its own."

"Very good." Gordian gave her a look that suggested he knew *precisely* what she was thinking. "I'll be announcing your election as Head Girl this afternoon. After that, you'll be speaking to the Fifth Years tomorrow..."

Emily sighed. She wasn't looking forward to that, either.

"You defeated Shadye," Gordian said. "I'm sure speaking to younger students won't be *that* bad."

"Hah," Emily muttered. She was already dreading speaking in public. Alassa could do it, easily. *She* couldn't. "Shadye didn't want me to *speak* to him."

Gordian nodded. "How *did* you beat him, anyway?"

Emily refused to allow the question to throw her. Gordian was hardly the first person to *ask*, although she'd always suspected Grandmaster Hasdrubal knew more of the truth than he'd bothered to admit. She'd always hidden behind the Sorcerer's Rule and refused to answer, even though she feared that was coming to an end. Dua Kepala had guessed too much of the truth.

But she wasn't going to tell Gordian. Not yet.

"I harnessed the power of a dying star," she said. It was true. Technically. "And I crushed him with it."

Gordian's eyes darkened. "I'll see you in twenty minutes. *Do* try not to be late."

Emily rose. "Yes, sir."

Chapter Six

EMILY SPOTTED A HANDFUL OF UNFAMILIAR FACES AS SHE WALKED INTO THE SIXTH YEAR common room and took a seat on the sofa. Most of the students were known to her—by name, if nothing else—but there were a couple of newcomers who had to repeat their final year at Whitehall before graduating. A couple of others she knew were missing, having failed too many of their exams to be given a chance to retake them. They'd be back in Fifth Year...

At least they'd know how to mentor students, she thought. And they'd be aware of the pitfalls from last year.

She leaned back and looked around the room. Caleb was standing by the bookshelf, reading a book so intently that she *knew* he wasn't taking in a single word. Cirroc stood beside him, his eyes flickering from face to face. He shot Emily a sharp look when their eyes met, as if he blamed Emily for Caleb's silence. Emily groaned inwardly, then ignored him. There had been too many rumors about her breakup with Caleb for her peace of mind, even if it *had* been almost a year ago. The whole story had been blurred into rumors about whatever had happened in Beneficence, emerging—as always—as something that bore very little resemblance to the truth. She supposed she should be grateful. Given time, anyone who knew the truth could probably devise a god-spell of their own.

"Emily," a soft voice said. Emily looked up as the Gorgon sat down next to her, the snakes on her head hissing softly. Cabiria leaned against the armrest, looking as pale as ever. She and the Gorgon had become friends, Emily recalled. They had quite a bit in common. "I hope you had a good holiday."

"It could have been worse," Emily said.

It was true, she supposed. Compared to some of her earlier summer holidays, spending weeks revising before retaking her exams was almost restful. And besides, having Lady Barb and Sergeant Miles all to herself had done wonders for her comprehension. "Yours?"

"I was back in the Gorgon Lands," the Gorgon said. "My parents kept me busy all summer."

Emily nodded. "You'd be quite close to the Desert of Death," she recalled. "Did you have any trouble with roving orcs?"

"Not really," the Gorgon said. "But we did have some trouble with military patrols."

"They probably thought you were hiding the orcs," Cabiria said. "Bastards."

"Yes," Emily agreed.

She frowned as Melissa entered, followed by Jacqui and Cerise. Melissa's former cronies glanced around the room, their eyes lingering on Emily for a long moment, then headed straight for the sideboard to pour themselves drinks. Emily wondered, absently, how they'd managed to pass their exams, although she had to admit they were both formidable magicians. They'd kept their distance from Melissa—and Emily—since Melissa had been disowned by her family, seemingly concerned about how *their* families would react if they continued the friendship. Emily couldn't help wondering what it meant that they'd accompanied Melissa to the common room.

Perhaps nothing, she thought, ruefully. *We were all invited here, weren't we?*

They made a striking couple, she had to admit as she watched them leaning against the wall. Jacqui was black, with dark eyes and white hair; Cerise was blonde, her hair curled into ringlets that fell around her shoulders. They'd both had their black robes tailored to show off their figures, even though it was technically forbidden. Emily couldn't help wondering if they'd be ordered to change the first day they walked into a classroom. Wearing revealing clothes wasn't permitted in class. No doubt they'd try to argue that they weren't actually revealing any bare skin below their necklines.

Melissa took a chair and nodded, politely, to Emily. She'd spent the summer with her husband, Emily recalled. She hoped Markus had had *time* to spend with his wife. His last set of letters had spoken of chaos in Beneficence, of savings wiped out and riots on the streets despite the best efforts of the bankers and councillors. It might be years, he'd warned, before the city recovered from Vesperian's Folly and the Fists of Justice. The only upside was that the rules had been updated to ensure no one else could start a Ponzi scheme.

Which probably won't stop someone smart enough to find the loopholes and ruthless enough to exploit them, Emily thought, crossly. *They can't close everything without making it very hard to establish a business and turn a profit.*

She nodded back to Melissa, then resumed her survey of the room. Caleb was still pretending to read, but most of the others were chatting amongst themselves. She felt a twinge of the old regret—she'd never been good at socializing, not in large groups—and pushed it aside, sharply. Being isolated wasn't that bad, was it? It wasn't as if she wanted to chat about pointless social pleasantries.

The wards shifted as Gordian strode into the room, followed by Master Tor. Emily sat upright, momentarily confused. Master Tor couldn't be their Year Head, surely? He'd been their *last* Year Head. Coming to think of it, he'd been her Year Head back in Second Year too. She'd never really liked him and she was fairly sure the feeling was mutual.

Her lips twitched as the chatter died away. *He must be pretty sick of us by now.*

"Welcome back to Whitehall," Gordian said, without preamble. His voice echoed in the quiet room. "You'll be pleased to know that I won't keep you long."

Emily kept her face expressionless with an effort. She'd heard that before—they'd *all* heard that before—and she'd believe it when she saw it. Gordian might not be as fond of the sound of his own voice as some of the others she'd met, but she was sure he'd taken the opportunity to pontificate as much as possible. If nothing else, he wanted—he needed—to stamp his authority on the school.

"First, the staff met last week to elect a Head Pupil." Gordian looked directly at Emily. "It was decided that *Emily* would serve as Head Girl for the year."

Emily felt herself flush as everyone looked at her. She forced herself to look back at Gordian, even though she wanted to hide. Caleb and Cabiria looked pleased, at least; Jacqui and Cerise didn't look particularly happy. Melissa and the others didn't seem to want to reveal their feelings. *Emily* might not have wanted to be Head Girl, but she was grimly aware that it made her practically unique.

"As such, Emily will also serve as Head of Sixth Year," Gordian continued. "I trust you will show her the same level of respect you'd show to any of your other Year Heads."

Emily felt her blood run cold. She hadn't anticipated *that*. It certainly hadn't been included on the list of official duties. Aloha hadn't mentioned it to her either, although they hadn't really had time to sit down and talk about being Head Girl. Perhaps Gordian was trying to do her a backhanded favor. She'd *told* him she wanted to be a teacher, after all. Serving as a Year Head *would* look good on her resume. It wouldn't be a purely ceremonial post either.

They won't need that much help, she told herself, firmly. *They're not firsties.*

Gordian paused long enough to allow that to sink in, then continued.

"Sixth Year is the hardest year, as some of you are already aware," he added. "I expect each and every one of you to concentrate on your studies as much as possible. Those of you who spend time partying instead of studying will *not* impress your future masters, if you want apprenticeships. Nor will you pass your exams. You will be required to demonstrate a grasp of the material *far* in excess of what you have done over the past five years—yes, even *last* year. There are very few masters who will *willingly* take on an apprentice who has not shown a willingness to learn and master the material.

"I advise you to put your studies first. Those of you who have personal concerns should put them aside for the year. Those of you who *like* partying should wait until you have passed your exams before returning to self-indulgence. And those of you who cannot act like adults should leave the school now. This is your last year of schooling. If you fail to take full advantage of it, you will fail.

"In the outside world, you would already be considered adults. Here—now—you will *also* be considered adults. You will be held to account for mistakes—and malice—in a way you may find strange and even unbelievable. Those of you who act badly will not be caned, nor will you be given detentions. You will be suspended, perhaps even expelled. And if you are expelled, in this year, you will not be permitted to return. You will have great difficulty finding a place at another school of magic."

Emily swallowed, hard. She wasn't the only one. Several students looked pale, as if they were hastily rethinking their plans. They'd grown used, perhaps, to being treated as overgrown children, in a world where a child of ten could be hanged as an adult. Now... now they would be treated as adults.

Then act like an adult, she told herself, firmly. *And they can act like adults too.*

She sighed, inwardly. How the hell was she supposed to be Head Girl—and run the dueling club—when she was *also* supposed to be keeping up with her studies? She *could* shuffle *some* of the work onto other students, if she got volunteers, but she didn't think she could put enough of it onto others to make a difference. Passing her exams was going to be a nightmare. What could she do, she asked herself silently, to get out of the post? Nothing came to mind.

And there are others who would have loved the job, she thought. *I didn't want it.*

"I could go on for hours," Gordian said. She dragged her attention back to him. "I could list entire *volumes* of things you shouldn't do, things that will get you kicked out of school. But I won't, because I—we—expect you to use common sense. Those of you who think it's funny to play puerile pranks on your fellow students can either rethink your approach or waste all your hard work over the last five years at school. You will face, for the first time, long-term consequences for your actions. Think carefully before you act."

Emily nodded. *That,* at least, she understood, even approved. Students at Whitehall were fond of playing terrible pranks on each other, pranks that were rarely punished. She'd been told, more than once, that it was better for students to learn to defend themselves than have the teachers protect them, but she'd never approved of it. Now, at least, the Sixth Years would think twice before pranking each other.

Not that we'll have the time, she thought. *We'll be far too busy to play games.*

"There are some other matters that require attention," Gordian said, calmly. "One of them is that our Head Girl"—he nodded at Emily—"will be setting up a dueling club and running a contest. You are all welcome to take part, if you wish, both as duelists and assistants. I believe the Head Girl will handle registrations after the first week. Emily?"

Emily took a breath. She *hated* speaking in public. Gordian hadn't even warned her she *would* be speaking in public. She'd met people who had a talent for off-the-cuff remarks, but she wasn't one of them. And the twenty-four people looking at her—twenty-six, counting the tutors—wouldn't hesitate to remind her of any missteps or mistakes.

"I need at least three assistants," she said, slowly. She'd planned to approach a handful of students privately, but it seemed that was no longer an option. "I'll also be passing sign-up sheets around later in the week. If any of you wish to duel, you'll be welcome to sign up; if any of you want to assist, please let me know in the next couple of days."

There was a pause. "Very good," Gordian said, his voice artfully bland. "Are there any questions?"

Cirroc waved, cheerfully. "What happens if you get too many assistants?"

"I will spread the workload out as much as possible," Emily said. It was hard to keep the irritation out of her voice. Sergeant Miles wouldn't be pleased if Cirroc—or Johan or Mathis—joined the dueling club. They'd have too much to unlearn. "I'll need to recruit some assistants from the lower years, just to ensure some continuity."

"I'd like to assist," Cirroc said. "Anyone else?"

Jacqui gave Emily a sweet smile. "I'd like to assist too," she said. "I do have a dueling badge, if you're interested."

"*Emily* beat Master Grey," Melissa said, her voice edged. "I was there."

"And she lost to a mere apprentice," Jacqui pointed out, snidely.

Caleb shifted, uncomfortably. "There was nothing *mere* about my brother."

Emily looked down at the ground. Casper's death had weakened her relationship with Caleb, even before it had been destroyed. She wished Casper hadn't died, she wished... she pushed the thought aside, sharply. There was no point in wishing for things she knew she couldn't have. Casper had died bravely and well. She knew that would have made him happy.

And Casper had graduated from Stronghold and become an apprentice, she thought. *And that marked him as a competent magician.*

Gordian smiled. "Can we have a third volunteer?"

"I'll do it," Cerise said. "I may not know much about dueling, but I *am* a good wardcrafter."

Emily looked from Cerise to Jacqui. She had the uncomfortable feeling that she'd been outmaneuvered, somehow. She didn't trust *either* of them very far, if only because they'd hexed Emily and her friends while Melissa and Alassa had had their stupid little feud. But they *were* competent magicians and she needed them. If there were no other volunteers, she wouldn't have a choice. She couldn't do everything herself.

They didn't know I'd be elected, she thought. *Did they?*

It didn't seem likely, she decided, as Gordian ran through a list of rules and regulations for older students. The nomination and election had been held at the end of the holiday, with everyone involved sworn to secrecy until the prospective candidate had been notified. It was possible Jacqui and Cerise had *guessed*, she thought, but how could they have been *certain*?

They would have known I failed my exams, she reminded herself. *And they know I'm not the most popular student in my year.*

She gathered herself. Maybe she was just being paranoid. Jacqui and Cerise had every reason to want to be involved, if only because it would look good on their resumes. They'd be able to talk it up, when they were interviewed by prospective masters. And if they sabotaged the club, she could handle it. It wasn't as if she cared *that* much about it.

"The first year students will arrive in two days," Gordian said. "Classes will restart the following morning. You will have access to the library from today, so I advise you to brush up on your studies and make sure you're ready to hit the ground running. This is your final year. You must *not* waste it."

He smiled. "If you have any further questions, you may address them to the Head Girl," he added. "I believe her door is always open."

Emily ground her teeth, silently. She was obliged to have office hours—and post them on notice boards all over the school—but she knew they would just cut into her spare time, such as it was. If no one came, she supposed, she could sit there and get on with her own work, yet... she had a feeling it wasn't going to be that easy. *She'd* never approached the Head Girl for help, not in her office, but other students might have a different view.

"I'll post office hours in the next few days," she said, finally. Her face flushed as a handful of snickers ran around the room. She had no idea what she was going to do, if she was faced with a problem she didn't know how to solve. Perhaps she could just dump it in Master's Tor's lap. "But I am going to be very busy."

"Very good." Gordian looked from face to face. "Thank you for listening."

He turned and walked out of the room, Master Tor following like a duckling hurrying after its mother. Emily's fingers played with the bracelet on her wrist for a long moment as chatter broke out again, her mind torn between staying in the common room and hurrying to the library. There would be new books there, freshly printed...

She rose and headed out of the room. Caleb followed her.

"Emily," he said, sounding nervous. "Can we talk?"

Emily glanced at her watch. She didn't *want* to talk to him, not now. Things were just too awkward. The only good thing was that she was fairly sure *Caleb* hadn't wanted to be Head Boy. He'd certainly never expressed interest in the post.

"Perhaps later," she said. "Frieda and I were going to go up the hill this evening."

"Tomorrow afternoon, then?" Caleb said. "It's important."

Emily honestly wasn't sure she wanted to be alone with him. She knew it wasn't wise, but her body was reminding her just how much she'd enjoyed everything they'd done together... once they'd gotten over the fumbling, of course. Part of her wanted to drag him into her bedroom, even though she *knew* it was a bad idea.

"Tomorrow," she said, finally. Perhaps they could meet in the library. "Is it private?"

"Yes." Caleb's face reddened. "Sorry."

"It's all right," Emily said. "I'll see you in my office, after lunch."

"Thank you," Caleb said. "And congratulations."

"Hah," Emily muttered.

Chapter Seven

STEPPING INTO THE FIFTH YEAR COMMON ROOM FELT A LITTLE LIKE STEPPING BACK IN TIME. It hadn't been *that* long since Emily had been a Fifth Year student herself, even though she hadn't spent *that* much time in the common room. A pair of familiar faces greeted her, but the remainder were strangers. In hindsight, perhaps she should have paid more attention to the year below her. But when had she had the time?

Never, she thought. She placed the folders she was carrying on the sideboard as all eyes followed her. *I never had the time.*

She leaned against the wall and listened to Gordian giving the Fifth Years a short speech. It was, more or less, what he'd told Emily and *her* class last year, although he avoided any snide references to students on probation. Or, for that matter, to the oaths she was still meant to take. She couldn't help wondering just how long he intended to let the matter rest. Perhaps he was still hoping for something that would allow him to summarily expel her from Whitehall.

Which would be interesting, she thought. She could feel the wards at the back of her mind, just waiting for her to reach out and make contact. *He can't make me leave if I don't want to go.*

She sighed, inwardly, as the speech came to an end. Gordian was in one hell of a spot, one he wouldn't be keen on admitting to anyone else. He was supposed to be the supreme authority in Whitehall, yet he *wasn't*. *She* could overrule him, if she wished. Except... she wasn't sure how far her command over the wards actually stretched. She was *a* founder, not *the* founder. And so much had been added, over the years, that a skilled wardcrafter could probably impede any attempt she made to take control of the wards.

"The Head Girl will now talk to you about the mentoring scheme," Gordian finished. "Lady Emily?"

Emily resisted the urge to play with her bracelet as she stepped away from the wall. The Fifth Years turned to look at her; some admiring, some suspicious, some simply doubtful that *she* could be the dreaded Necromancer's Bane. Emily couldn't help wondering precisely *what* they'd expected, although she had a pretty shrewd idea. Between the statues, the paintings, and the ballads, it was a minor miracle that anyone believed *she* was Lady Emily.

Because everyone knows that Lady Emily is ten feet tall and breathes dragon-fire, Emily thought. *And could pass for Honor Harrington on a bad day.*

She cleared her throat with an effort, then glanced down at her notes. Aloha had spoken from the heart, but *Emily* couldn't do that without losing track of *something*. It was important to cover all the right details, *without* confusing them or making it seem impossible. Frieda had advised her to imagine the audience naked, but it hadn't helped. *Emily* felt naked as she stood in front of them.

I suppose it would get their attention, the cynical part of her mind noted. *But they wouldn't take me very seriously.*

"Some of you were raised in magical households or had magical tutors," she said. "You were taught everything from which fork to use at dinner to when and where you could use searching spells without mortally offending your host. By the time you arrived at Whitehall, you knew everything you needed to know to blend in with your new environment. You even knew enough of the fundamentals of magic to speed through the basic classes and proceed to the higher ranks."

She paused. "That isn't true for all of you. You were raised in isolated households or non-magical households, where you were *not* taught anything you might need to fit into magical society. My father"—she paused to allow them to remember who her father was supposed to be—"certainly didn't teach *me* the fundamentals, let alone how to behave in school. I had some trouble because of it."

A low rumble of surprise ran through the room at her frank admission. It was true, but she wouldn't have hesitated to make it up if necessary. There wasn't a stigma against newborn magicians—like Imaiqah and Frieda—yet they *were* at something of a disadvantage until they learned the basics. Alassa, at least, had been given *some* tutoring in etiquette, even if she'd chosen to ignore it. And while Emily normally paid as little attention to the social graces as she could get away with, she had to admit that some of the formal etiquette was rooted in cold practicality. A student who failed to master it would *always* be at a disadvantage.

"The purpose of the mentoring scheme is to ensure that all of our *new* students are prepared as quickly as possible for magical life," she continued. "You are required to assist them in learning everything from the magical basics to etiquette, at least for the first couple of months. The vast majority of your mentees won't *need* you after that, although we hope you will continue to listen to them and assist when necessary. If nothing else, you'll have the basics of a patronage network of your own when you leave Whitehall."

She glanced down at her notes as she heard a rustle running around the room. It wasn't *that* likely to be a *useful* patronage network, but there was no way to know for sure. Emily would bet good money that Tiega and Jasmine—two of the students she'd mentored last year—would become something spectacular, if they survived their education. And two more of her mentees had powerful family connections. Who knew *what* they'd become in the next couple of decades?

"We are aware that this will mean taking time out from your studies," she added. "Last year, we discovered that the demands on our time were minimal past the first three months—I only had a handful of requests for assistance after I returned to Whitehall. If you *do* find that you are spending more of your time assisting the younger students than you can afford, come find me and we'll sort it out. We don't want the students becoming *dependent* on you."

"Her door is always open," Gordian said.

Emily swallowed several nasty responses that came to mind. So far, she hadn't had any interruptions, but she knew it was just a matter of time. The remaining students would return to Whitehall tomorrow and classes would resume. After that... she suspected she'd be very busy. She'd already planned interviews with Professor

Armstrong and Professor Lombardi to begin work on the arena. She honestly wasn't sure how she'd manage to balance *all* of her new responsibilities with her studies.

Perhaps I should have taken Void up on his offer, she thought. The apprenticeship offer—an *unconditional* offer—was at the bottom of her trunk, hidden behind a series of obscurification charms. *But I didn't want to leave Whitehall.*

She looked from face to face. "Do you have any questions?"

A young man with a shaved head eyed her challengingly. "Why is this even necessary?"

Emily stared at him, evenly. *I just answered that question, you idiot.*

She controlled her annoyance. "Apart from students raised in magical households, who are taught the basics from a very early age, far too many students come to Whitehall with only a very sketchy idea of everything from the rules and regulations to the reasons for their existence," she said with icy patience. Master Tor had said the same thing, word for word. She'd used a memory charm to make sure she recalled it correctly. "Some students understand the dangers from the start, others have to learn the rules as they go along—and sometimes they only learn a rule when they get in trouble for breaking it."

She paused. "Does that answer your question?"

The young man gazed at her for a long moment. Emily looked back at him, knowing better than to back down. Sergeant Miles and Lady Barb had told her, time and time again, that she would be tested, her authority challenged. Showing weakness would be held against her. It wouldn't make any difference, she'd been assured, if she was male or female. Anyone who wanted to push the boundaries would challenge her.

"Yeah," he said. "But can't they learn on their own?"

Emily smiled. "And what sort of results would they get if they tried?"

Grandmaster Hasdrubal *had* argued that students should learn on their own. Emily understood the logic, but she didn't agree with it. Gordian, whatever else could be said about him, had a point. *She'd* been hellishly ignorant when she'd been sent to Whitehall, even though her discoverer was supposed to ensure she received a full briefing on how to handle the school before sending her there. Void, for whatever reason, had barely told her anything before summoning a dragon to fly her to Whitehall.

And I didn't even get whatever allowances are made for newborn magicians, she thought, sourly. *Everyone thought I was his daughter.*

"It might be fun to throw ingredients into a caldron and see what happens," a young girl said.

"You might be lucky if you were *only* sent to see the Warden," Emily said. Professor Thande took a lax view of health and safety, but even *he* would be appalled if someone threw ingredients into a caldron at random. The prospect of an explosion would be alarmingly high. "I'm sure the healers would enjoy fixing the damage—if they could."

She looked from face to face, silently trying to gauge who understood and who would be a problem. The newborns would probably understand better, she thought, although it was hard to pick them out from the rest. Four years in Whitehall had eroded all the tells. Even the ones who didn't have a family name might have had magical contacts and training before they came to Whitehall. She'd just have to hope most of them at least *tried* to take care of their charges.

"There are two other things I need to make clear," she said, "before I give you the paperwork and assign you to your students. First, you are *not* being given servants or pets. You are expected to treat your mentees like little brothers and sisters, but you are *not* allowed to get so close to them that you don't let them flourish into decent magicians. You will assist them in growing. You will *not* do the work for them. Nor will you put them to work on *your* behalf."

She allowed her voice to harden. "If any of you abuse your charges, I will make sure you regret it. You will be severely punished—at best—if you mistreat them. I will do everything in my power to make sure you are expelled."

"And I will back her up," Gordian said, quietly.

Emily kept her face under tight control. She had no idea if she *could* get someone expelled, although she could probably deny someone access to Whitehall itself if she fiddled with the wards. But then, she *was* practically plagiarising from Master Tor's speech. He'd said the same thing, in similar words. And she thought he'd meant it too.

"If you have problems understanding where the line is drawn, come speak to me," she added, carefully. "But if you cross that line, you will be severely punished. Do you understand me?"

She waited for them to nod, then went on.

"The second point is that you *will* have limited power to assign punishments," she said. She knew *she'd* done it, even though she hadn't *wanted* to do it. Sending someone to be caned had never sat well with her. "You can give them everything from lines to a trip to the Warden. If you abuse this power—and you *will* be tempted—you will face the same punishment yourself, only worse. Those of you who issue unnecessary or excessive punishment will regret it. I will make sure of it."

There was a long pause. Emily gave them a moment to let it sink in, then leaned forward.

"Are there any more questions?"

"Just one," a dark-skinned boy said. "How much help are we actually allowed to give them?"

"You are expected to show them how to find the answers for themselves," Emily said. "If they ask a question about how dragon scales react with unicorn dung, you can point them to *1001 Alchemical Combinations* or *Florid Foliage Files*... even *Basic Potions for Imbeciles*, all of which can be found in the library. You are *not* to give them the answers, no matter how much they beg and plead. Your objective is to help them develop their scholastic skills, not make them go away."

One of the boys snorted. "But what about our study time?"

"If you have problems coping, come to me," Emily said, patiently. "We'll do a review two months into the program. We'll sort out any problems then."

She held up a hand. "I know it won't be easy, at first." She held up a set of papers, silently thanking Aloha for her foresight. The end-of-year reports had included outlines of all the problems the mentors had faced. "My year had problems too, some of which are listed here. If you have other problems, we'll deal with them."

"You will," Gordian said.

Emily looked down at the papers. "I've assigned students at random." She didn't think Aloha had put any more thought into *her* assignments. "If you happen to be *closely* related to any of the firsties, swap that student for someone else. The idea is to avoid family ties as much as possible."

"A student of the same sex," Gordian added. "I don't want boys mentoring girls and vice versa."

"Yes, sir," Emily said. "If you have any questions about the other material in the folders, please don't hesitate to ask."

She handed out the folders, then dismissed the Fifth Years. It was mid-morning, yet she still felt tired. Sweat was prickling on the back of her neck. Speaking to so many students, even issuing orders rather than holding conversations, was practically painful. She hadn't found it *that* hard to walk into a necromancer's lair, despite the near certainty of death. And yet, she'd done it.

"Reasonably well done," Gordian said. "You covered all the basics. You could have been a bit more assertive in places, but your reputation will probably give you some cover."

"Thank you, sir," Emily said.

She really *did* feel tired. If it hadn't been less than an hour until lunch, she would have thought seriously about taking a shower and perhaps a nap. Frieda had tried to talk her into going walking again, after lunch, but Emily didn't have the time. She had to meet Caleb too. God alone knew what *he* wanted.

"You'll be there when the First Years arrive," Gordian said. "Make sure you're wearing your formal robes *and* badge."

Emily sighed. The Head Girl wore white, apparently. *She* wasn't allowed to wear sorcerer's black, even the traditional robes of a Sixth Year student. She'd probably be allowed to get away with not wearing it outside formal functions, but she was scheduled to attend a number of them over the coming months. Being Head Girl was already more trouble than it was worth.

And I've only been Head Girl for a week, she thought, balefully. *How bad is it going to be after the first month?*

She shrugged, inwardly. The mentoring program had slowly decreased in importance after the first couple of months, although the near-collapse of the entire school had probably helped. She hadn't had *that* many questions after she'd returned from Beneficence, even though she *had* made time to have tea with her mentees every month. She'd have to do it again, just once. She owed it to her charges to check up on them one last time.

But the Head Girl has far too much to do, her own thoughts mocked her. *She has to give the speech at Final Feast, as well as everything else in-between.*

Gordian cleared his throat, loudly. Emily jumped.

"I'm sorry," she said. "I was miles away."

"I could tell," Gordian said, with heavy sarcasm. "Make sure you get back in time to greet the firsties. You'll need to set a good example for everyone else."

"Yes, sir," Emily said. "I know."

She sighed. She had no idea what Caleb wanted, unless it was to discuss their work. But she didn't think so. He wouldn't have been shy about *that*, not after they'd rebuilt enough of their friendship to work together.

It's going to be a long year, she thought. *And it's only just begun.*

"This will be the most important year of your education," Gordian warned. "You do *not* want to mess it up."

Emily nodded, slowly. "I'll do my best, sir."

"That's all I ask." Gordian's voice was pleasant, but there was a hard edge hanging in the air. "You are not expected to succeed in everything."

Really, Emily thought. *You would be pleased if I failed.*

Chapter Eight

If Emily were honest, she'd have to admit that she could grow to like her office very quickly. It was large enough to store a considerable selection of reference books and school tomes, and secure enough that she felt reasonably safe working on some of her private projects at her personal workbench. Indeed, with a little effort, she could turn it into a personal spellchamber, although she suspected that wasn't a good idea. It would have been far too revealing to anyone who looked closely.

And if it hadn't come with the Head Girl responsibilities, she acknowledged as she felt someone tapping on the door, it would have been perfect.

She sighed inwardly as she linked to the wards, commanding them to open the door. Caleb stood on the far side, looking oddly nervous. He'd grown his hair out, Emily noted absently, and he was wearing a shirt and trousers instead of his robes. She felt a flicker of... *something*... as she remembered him holding her, an odd wistfulness she brushed aside with grim determination. They were better off just being friends. And if they couldn't overcome the awkwardness by the end of the year, perhaps they'd be better off being apart.

"Emily," Caleb began. He *sounded* nervous too. It was something personal, then. Caleb had always been more enthusiastic talking about magical theory and spellwork than anything more personal. Spells weren't embarrassing, after all. "How was your summer?"

"I spent most of it preparing for the exams," Emily told him. It was hard to sound welcoming when she wasn't sure *what* she felt. "Come on in and close the door behind you."

Caleb entered, taking one of the smaller chairs. Emily sat down at her desk, silently glad it was between her and Caleb. It wasn't much of a barrier—she knew a dozen spells that could reduce it to atoms—yet it put *something* solid between them. It was yet another reminder that there was no way they could go back to being just friends without some bumps along the way.

I don't know how Imaiqah managed to have so many boyfriends, she thought. Imaiqah had had more lovers than every other girl in the year put together, as far as Emily could tell. She found a boy, spent a few weeks with him and then broke up and moved on. *But then, she didn't have to work with any of them.*

She met his eyes, trying not to think about his arms around her. "How is your family?"

"Recovering." He shook his head, slowly. "Father is on the new city council; mother's practically taken over Sorcerer's Row, now that some of the former residents have moved away. That won't last, she says, but it keeps her occupied. She's been talking about trying to attract more magical talent to Beneficence."

"That would be interesting," Emily said. She wasn't sure it was a good idea—too many magicians too close together tended to lead to fights—but Sienna presumably knew what she was doing. "And the city itself?"

"A mess," Caleb said. He shifted, uncomfortably. "Oh, things look to have returned to normal—on the surface—but there's an undercurrent of fear running through the streets. We lost quite a bit of investment immediately after the Fists were defeated, even though your bankers remained in place. I daresay Cockatrice picked up a lot of our deserters."

Emily shrugged. Imaiqah sent her regular reports, but Emily hadn't had the time to read them. She'd been too busy with her studies. She trusted that Imaiqah would use the chat parchments to alert her to anything that required immediate attention. An influx of trained craftsmen from Beneficence wasn't a problem, not in Cockatrice. There was no shortage of work for them if they were willing to stay permanently.

King Randor might worry about immigration, she thought. *But he's unlikely to put up with any nonsense.*

She shook her head, inwardly. Ideas were spreading all over the Allied Lands, changing and growing as they were fitted to local conditions. The attempted assassination of King Randor and his sole daughter—his sole legitimate child—had merely been the tip of the iceberg. Who knew what would happen when republicanism and socialism, if not communism, really took off? The basis of power in the Nameless World—the aristocracy of might and magic—was already being questioned. There was no way the kings and princes could put that particular genie back in the bottle.

Because they can't counter it, she mused. *What does give them the right to rule?*

"I'm sure the locals don't mind," she said, out loud. Cockatrice and the other cities within the barony had a constant influx of newcomers, mainly runaway peasants from the nearby estates. Most of them rapidly blended into the city's population and vanished. *She'd* certainly never been interested in hunting the immigrants down and returning them to their former masters. "There's always work for willing hands."

Caleb smiled, weakly. "There is."

Emily leaned back in her chair, wishing—suddenly—that they were talking about their project. Or magical theory. Or something that didn't feel as though they were tap-dancing over an emotional minefield. She hadn't had any problems working with him over the last year, had she? She'd thought those feelings were dead and buried. But she hadn't spent any time outside work...

We used to go on dates, she reminded herself. She'd never thought she would enjoy it, but she had. *And now we don't.*

She nodded to the sideboard. "Kava?"

"Please," Caleb said, sounding relieved.

Emily rose and walked to the sideboard, trying to keep her emotions under tight control as she poured the drinks. And yet, the mere act of preparing Kava the way he liked it *hurt*. Imaiqah had once told her that men were useless when it came to dealing with emotions, but *Emily* didn't feel any more competent at controlling *hers*. She'd thought, once, that she'd never have a boyfriend, let alone a real relationship with a man. And yet, when she'd been offered the chance, she'd jumped right into it... she hadn't thought, she knew. She'd gone too far, emotionally if not physically.

Perhaps that was Imaiqah's secret, Emily wondered. She'd kept sexual pleasure separated from her more intimate emotions.

She passed Caleb the mug and returned to her desk. Caleb sipped his drink gratefully, but she knew he was stalling for time. She'd known him long enough to be sure when he was reluctant to broach a particular subject. Her imagination provided too many possibilities, ranging from their joint project to their former courtship. She didn't think *his* parents would want him to try to restart the courtship, but what about the rest of his family? House Waterfall might just feel they had a say in his relationships, after all.

"It wasn't easy for any of us," Caleb said. She knew, from experience, that he was slowly circling the subject at hand. "Casper's death shook the family, followed by... well, everything else that happened. Marian's betrayal..."

"She wasn't in her right mind," Emily said. She'd had enough experience with mind-warping magic to know how dangerous it could be. "I didn't think anyone *knew* about her."

"No one outside the family knows the truth, save for you and Frieda," Caleb said. "Mother was careful to warn us to keep it to ourselves. The council... father fears they are still looking for scapegoats."

Emily sighed. Janus was dead, killed by his false god. Very few of the other Fists of Justice had survived the mobs, when their grip on the city was shattered. Anyone who *had* survived had probably fled by now, knowing they'd be brutally murdered when—if—their secret came out. She just hoped they hadn't taken Master Wolfe's papers with them, if they hadn't been lost. It would probably be better, all things considered, if they'd been destroyed in the final battle.

And if the council can't fix the city's problems in a hurry, she thought sourly, *they might try to put a scapegoat on trial just to hide their failure from their people.*

"I won't breathe a word of it," she said. She felt a stab of raw sympathy for Caleb and his family. They were sitting on a secret that could see them lynched—or forced to flee their hometown. And it wasn't really their fault. Subtle magic had a way of twisting people until black was white, up was down and right was wrong—or vice versa. "Is that what you wanted to ask?"

Caleb shook his head. "Emily... Marian is coming here."

"To Whitehall?" Emily *had* heard something about that, but it had been months ago. "She's going to be a firstie?"

"Yes," Caleb said. "She's coming here."

Emily frowned, inwardly. Marian blamed—had blamed—Emily for Casper's death. Emily recalled, all too clearly, just how unpleasant Marian had been. And yet, Marian had *already* been affected by Justice and his followers. It was impossible to tell how much of her unpleasantness had been *hers* and how much had been shaped by subtle magic. Even Marian herself wouldn't be able to provide a real answer. Her moral compass and her ability to monitor it had shifted.

"Mother and father didn't think she could handle Stronghold, not after... well, everything," Caleb added. "There was some suggestion she would go to Laughter, but she missed the cut-off date. Mother even considered holding her back for a year, just to give her more time to recover..."

Emily leaned forward as his voice trailed off. "How *is* she?"

"She's been getting better, apparently," Caleb said. "I mean... most of the time, she's normal. Just like I recall from before... before Casper's death. But there are times when she suddenly starts crying for no apparent reason. We've worked our way through most of the tangles in her mind, but we think some are left."

"Ouch," Emily said. A person who'd been warped by subtle magic would have problems when they were forced to confront the difference between their mental conception of the world and reality. Their train of thought might as well run into a brick wall. Some people never recovered from the experience. "Have you discussed this with the Grandmaster?"

"I believe mother spoke to him at some length." He paused. "But you know how little he can actually *do*."

Emily nodded, shortly. The Nameless World had no concept of mental health treatment. There were certainly no psychologists. Anyone with a mental problem was expected to work their way through it on their own or be driven away, if they posed a danger to everyone else. She understood the logic—treating unstable magicians might make them all the more dangerous—but it had never sat well with her. Subtle magic wasn't the only kind of abuse that could result in long-lasting trauma. Marian was on her own.

"I don't know how I can help," she said, slowly. There was no way she could reinvent the science of psychology, even if she hadn't held most of its practitioners in contempt. The school counselors she'd encountered had been universally useless. "What do you want me to do?"

"Just... be nice to her," Caleb said. "And don't hold her actions against her."

"I won't," Emily said. "But I can't turn a blind eye to misbehavior."

"I know," Caleb said. "I just wish... I wish she could take another year to get better."

Emily nodded in agreement. People *didn't* recover that quickly from trauma. *She'd* had enough problems recovering from subtle magic and *she* hadn't been anything like that badly affected. The bouts of mental incomprehension and confusion hadn't lasted long enough to force her to retake the year. But Marian had been twisted until she'd betrayed her own family, staunchly convinced she was doing the right thing. It would take her years to get over it.

And the taboo on treating mental disorders makes it hard for her family to help her, she thought, grimly. *Sienna must be desperate for Marian to fix herself before it's too late.*

"I won't hold her accountable for anything that happened before now," Emily promised, slowly. "But like I said, I can't turn a blind eye to misbehavior."

She sighed as she realized just how much trouble this was likely to cause. Marian had said some pretty awful things to her, back in Beneficence. She could ignore them if they were said in private, even after Caleb's sister arrived at Whitehall, but not if they were said in public. She'd *have* to insist on punishment, which wouldn't endear her to Marian any further... not, she supposed, that it mattered. She wasn't going to marry Caleb, after all.

"I wouldn't expect you to," Caleb said, looking relieved. "We do want her to get better."

Emily didn't blame him. There were people, she knew all too well, who would consider Marian to be little more than a maddened beast who needed to be put down. A magician who was already mentally unstable... why wait until she embraced necromancy or the darkest arts to stop her? And yet, Marian was a sixteen-year-old girl, not a monster. Old enough to be treated like an adult, by the standards of the Nameless World, but not an irredeemable criminal.

"I want her to get better too," she said. "I'm sure she will."

Caleb nodded, gratefully. Emily kept her thoughts to herself. She didn't *hate* Marian. She just wanted as little to do with her as possible. Thankfully, she probably wouldn't be expected to interact with Marian on a daily basis. She had no idea who'd been Head Girl when *she'd* been a firstie. Jade had been a prefect, if she recalled correctly, but Head Girl? For all she knew, it had been a Head Boy.

I'll have to have a word with whoever mentors her, she thought. In hindsight, she should have made the connection between the name on the list of firsties and Caleb's sister, but she hadn't looked too closely. She'd just matched mentors to mentees at random. *If there are problems, that person can talk to me about it first.*

She sighed. *That* was going to be a problem too. The last thing anyone needed was rumors getting out. Marian's betrayal wouldn't have to become public knowledge for her fellow pupils to get wind of her problems. And then they'd start picking at that sore until Marian recovered or snapped completely. Emily made a mental note to make it absolutely clear to Marian's mentor that word was *not* to get out, but she knew it might be pointless. Someone in First Year might notice the problem and then all hell would break loose.

"I will do what I can to make it easy for her," she said. "But you know it won't be *that* easy."

"Yeah." Caleb shook his head. "Is it wrong of me to want to protect her?"

Emily felt a flicker of envy. She'd never had a brother, never had anyone to look after her... would her life have been better, she wondered, if she'd had an older brother like Jade or Caleb or even Casper? Or would their overprotectiveness have been stifling? Frieda had had older brothers, brothers she refused to talk about. But it was clear she'd hated them. It hadn't been an easy life in the mountains.

"I don't think so," she said, finally. "But you do need to let her stand on her own two feet."

"If she can," Caleb said.

Emily shrugged. Marian was *sixteen*. There were places on the Nameless World where she would be married by now, perhaps even raising her first child. She was certainly not a child herself, as far as the outside world was concerned. And if she wanted to be a magician, she would have to learn the basics herself. There was no way to cheat on the exams, not in Whitehall. Anyone who hadn't mastered the material was unlikely to get very far.

"Keep an eye on her," she said. "But she won't be able to advance if an overprotective big brother keeps jumping in whenever she has a problem."

"Casper never did that for me," Caleb said. "He... preferred to rub my nose in my own mistakes."

"Which probably didn't help," Emily said. *That* explained a great deal about Caleb, coming to think of it. "But you don't have to do the opposite."

"Thanks," Caleb said.

Emily relaxed, slightly. "I've got to write a short speech for the firsties," she said. Gordian had dropped it on her, as well as a hundred other tasks. "What do you think I should tell them?"

"Don't tell them the truth," Caleb advised. "They'll run for their lives."

"Hah," Emily said. She'd been nervous when *she'd* walked into Whitehall for the first time, even though a whole new world had been opening up in front of her. "Should I tell them the school was nearly destroyed three times in the past five years?"

"Four times, if you count the Mimic." He smiled. "It would probably not be a good idea to tell them *that*."

"Probably," Emily agreed. "But what should I tell them?"

"Work hard, do well; party hard, fail spectacularly," Caleb said. "Short, succinct and completely true."

Emily giggled. She had to admit he had a point.

"And you'll be *loved* for giving a short speech," Caleb added. "The Commander at Stronghold was very much in love with the sound of his own voice. We stood for *hours* while he babbled on and on and on and..."

"Oh," Emily said. "What did he say?"

"I don't know." Caleb winked. "I wasn't listening."

Chapter Nine

THE FIRSTIES LOOKED... *YOUNG.*

Emily had thought the same *last* year, when she'd watched the First Years make their way into Whitehall's Great Hall for the first time, but *this* time the effect was far more pronounced. Eighty-two students, the youngest being sixteen... they shuffled into the hall, too nervous to speak a single word. Emily's eyes flickered over them, silently picking out the ones who'd grown up in magical families or had learnt something about magic before they went to school. They were the ones who didn't seem *that* daunted by their surroundings.

She stood on the raised stage, next to Gordian and Master Tor, and waited while the room slowly filled. Some of the students were already using levitation spells to maneuver their trunks to the stairs or—perhaps more practically—ordering servants to transport their trunks to their room, while others were struggling to move their trunks into the hall. It didn't seem to occur to them to use magic, or to ask others to cast the spells, or even to order one of the servants to do the heavy lifting. That, if nothing else, suggested they came from poorer households. People who grew up without being waited on hand and foot found servants a little creepy.

Alassa can issue orders as she pleases, Emily thought. *But I still find it strange.*

She shook her head. Alassa had a small army of servants, ranging from the young girl who brushed her hair to the manservant who carried her bags everywhere. None of them seemed to find anything *odd* about the whole setup. Hell, there were people who expected Emily to have an even *bigger* army of servants. Having servants was a sign of wealth and power...

Emily sucked in her breath, grimly. Some of the younger students were too thin, suggesting that they'd grown up in peasant households. Others had scars and other wounds that had been allowed to heal naturally, rather than by magic. They'd have nothing in common with the rest of their families, she knew all too well. By the time they left Whitehall, they'd probably have lost touch. Frieda had certainly lost contact with *her* family.

Imaiqah didn't, Emily thought, as she sought out Marian. *But she was a special case.*

Caleb's sister stood alone, a little apart from the remainder of the students. Marian had always been healthy—Sienna would never have underfed her children—but Marian looked thin and scrawny, somehow. Her long blonde hair fell around her shoulders, thinner than Emily remembered. There were no visible marks on Marian's face, but there was something in her expression telling anyone who cared to look that she'd seen terrible things. Her blue eyes were haunted by the past.

She looks like she came from a village, Emily thought. She shivered, remembering the first time she'd met Frieda. *She looks as though she doesn't know what to do.*

Marian looked up. Emily looked away, half-hoping Marian didn't see her stare as a challenge. But the girl standing apart from her future classmates didn't look as though she had the energy to shout and scream, let alone throw wild accusations.

Emily would almost have been relieved if Marian *had* shouted at her. Gordian would not have been pleased—there was no way Emily could have covered it—but it would have showed that Marian still had spirit. Instead, she seemed to have withdrawn completely.

She needs help, Emily thought. *But there's no one here who can give it to her.*

Gordian stepped up to the podium and tapped it, once. A wave of magic fanned out through the air, silencing the handful of firsties who'd begun to whisper to their friends. Emily smiled as she tried to assess their reaction to the simple spell, noting the ones who seemed alarmed by the casual use of magic. *They* were probably unused to magic, she told herself firmly. They'd have to learn to use it as casually as breathing. Brute force might solve some problems, but it wouldn't find favor at Whitehall.

Nor would asking someone else to do the work, she reminded herself. *Even older students are expected to do their own work.*

"A thousand years ago, Lord Whitehall and his followers determined to set up a place where young magicians could be schooled in magic," Gordian said. "They built Whitehall Castle and laid the groundwork for what would become Whitehall School. Over the years, Whitehall developed a reputation for turning out some of the most proficient sorcerers in history, men and women who were heirs to a tradition of practical magic. *You* are the latest students to enter the castle, but the eyes of history look down on you."

Emily kept her face carefully blank. No one knew who'd *really* built the castle, not even her. It had been empty for generations before the Whitehall Commune arrived to take possession and tap the nexus point. But otherwise, Gordian was correct. The seeds Whitehall had sown—with her help—had blossomed into a proud tradition. She'd never felt any real pride in her school on Earth—it had been a shitty building filled with shitty teachers and worse students—but Whitehall was different. The students and tutors knew themselves to be part of something greater.

It helps that students can be punished or expelled for bad behavior, she reminded herself, wryly. There had been students at her old school who should have been expelled, but had been allowed to remain instead. *The staff are in full control.*

"Some of you have grown up with magic," Gordian added. "Some of you have never seen a single spell until you were tested when you turned fifteen. Either way, we will teach you to develop and control your magic. You will spend four years learning the basics, honing your skills and teasing out your specialities. And then, if you choose to remain, you will spend two more years focusing your powers and preparing for an apprenticeship.

"This will not be easy. Those of you who have grown up with magic will, perhaps, be surprised to discover how hard it can be. You will be required to comprehend the fundamentals of magical theory as well as memorizing and casting spells—those of you who do *not* comprehend will always be at a disadvantage when it comes to testing and using your magic outside the school. Many of you will feel like giving up—some of you *will* give up—but those of you who push onwards will find it very rewarding."

He held up his hand. A series of lights darted out of his fingertips and danced up and down his arm.

"This is a party trick, a spell that requires little power, yet none of you will be able to cast it until you master the fundamentals," he told them. The lights reached his head and floated above his hair. He paid them no mind. "Some of you will already be able to cast more powerful spells. And yet, very few of you will be able to calibrate and recalibrate your spells on the fly. A true magician—a true *sorcerer*—is one who can alter and adapt his spells at will. *That* is what we will teach you.

"The tutors are here to help. They will teach you the basics and warn you of the dangers. And yes, there *will* be dangers. Magic is not *safe. Listen* to them. There isn't a person on the staff who doesn't have at least *ten* years of experience with dangerous magic. You'll want to experiment—every student in Whitehall has wanted to experiment—but *learn* the dangers before you begin. The warnings are not there to keep you from having fun. They are there to keep you from making dreadful mistakes that might get others—and you—killed."

And the warnings are all written at the front of the book, Emily thought, wryly. *There's no excuse for missing them.*

Gordian paused, his eyes sweeping the room. Emily wondered, absently, just what he saw when he looked at the younger students. Potential? Students who could become great? Or liabilities who had to be coaxed through the basics before they could turn into something useful? Offhand, she couldn't recall Gordian ever taking a class for a full term. He'd stepped in when a teacher couldn't be present, but he hadn't been a full-time tutor.

Maybe he has, she told herself. *What was he doing between graduation and now?*

"Master Tor will explain to you the basic rules and regulations," Gordian concluded. "I don't care who or what you are, nor do I care who your parents are. If you break the rules, you will be punished. And if you break the rules in a manner that injures or kills another student, or risks the school itself, you will be expelled. Do *not* test me on this. It will not end well."

Emily winced. *She'd* been lucky not to be expelled, back when *she'd* been a firstie. If she *had* killed Alassa, she *would* have been expelled... and triggered a civil war. Master Tor had made it clear, later, that *he* would have expelled her in Second Year if the Grandmaster hadn't overruled him. In hindsight, Emily had to admit he'd had a point.

Master Tor took the stand and started to speak. Emily had to fight to keep her face impassive as he droned on and on. For someone who looked an awful lot like Captain Picard, the nasty part of her mind noted, he certainly didn't have any talent for making short and inspiring speeches. No one came thousands of miles to listen to Master Tor giving a speech.

She forced herself to keep an eye on the firsties instead, silently noting who was paying attention and who'd wandered off into their own little world. A couple of girls who looked almost like twins—she would have thought they *were* twins, if magical twins weren't completely unknown—whispered quietly, despite the silencing spell. A boy beside them stared at the stage, challengingly. The older boy next to him rolled his eyes; he caught Emily's gaze and looked away, hastily. No doubt he didn't want to be noticed *that* much. Emily smiled as she glanced at Marian. Caleb's sister was looking away, her eyes flickering from place to place. She clearly wasn't listening to Master Tor.

It's not easy to blame her, Emily thought. *He just keeps saying the same thing over and over again.*

She pushed the thought to the back of her mind as Master Tor finally came to an end. The firsties looked relieved as he surrendered the podium to Gordian, who *also* looked a little relieved. Luckily, their first classes would probably go over all the important details again, complete with graphic examples of what happened to students too stupid to listen to the warnings before they started casting spells. Emily's palm twanged suddenly, reminding her of all the times Professor Lombardi had struck it with a ruler. Better the pain, he'd told the class when he'd started, than the problems caused by a poorly-written spell gone wrong.

"And now our Head Girl will explain the mentoring program to you," Gordian said, nodding to Emily. "Lady Emily?"

Emily heard a rustle as she took the podium and peered down at the younger students. *That* was a mistake. Some of them looked awed—they'd heard of her, then—while others looked doubtful. *Emily* wasn't a common name—as far as Emily knew, she was the *only* Emily in the Nameless World—but she still didn't *look* impressive. The firsties hadn't even seen her in the corridors or working in the library. They probably believed all the stories without question.

As long as they don't believe the really weird stories, Emily thought. The stories that suggested she'd beaten Shadye using advanced—and forbidden—sex magic should have been unprintable. But bards had been singing songs extolling the power of love over necromancy ever since Shadye's death. She'd cringed every time she'd heard the tamer lyrics. *I don't know what I'll do if they believe them.*

She met Marian's eyes, just for a second. She'd expected a challenge, but instead... Marian looked depressed, too depressed to believe in a better future. Or any future at all. There was a loneliness in her eyes that tore at Emily's heart. *She'd* been depressed too, once upon a time. She hadn't climbed out of it until Shadye had kidnapped her and Void had sent her to Whitehall.

Marian will do better here, she told herself, firmly. *If nothing else, she's a long way from her parents.*

She composed herself as quickly as possible, remembering the rules for public speaking. In hindsight, she should have practiced more. Speaking to her friends—or even to a handful of Fifth Years—wasn't so bad, not compared to the firsties. There were nearly a hundred pairs of eyes looking back at her, an alarming number glowing with hero worship. She didn't think she could live up to her legend. They wanted a heroine, not... not her.

"Whitehall is a very different environment from your homes, wherever you come from." She tried to project her voice as much as possible, keeping her eyes fixed on the far wall. There was no way she could speak if she met their eyes. She'd never make a natural politician. *They* could make crappy ideas sound good, just by pitching them. "None of you have any real idea of what studying here is going to be like."

She paused, allowing her words to sink in. "Each of you will be assigned to a mentor," she continued, after a moment. "That mentor—an older student—will advise you, if you need advice; support you, if you need support. You can go to them at any time you like, if you have a question that needs answered. They will be able to advise you on anything from approaching your tutors to comprehending basic spell notation. Think of them as your elder brothers and sisters.

"They will not do your homework for you, but they will show you how to do it. They will not fix your mistakes, but they will show you how to avoid making them in the future. They will not *speak* for you, if you have problems with your tutors, but they will help you understand the problem so you do not make the same mistake over and over again. They will, in short, help you to come to grips with life at Whitehall.

"Life here can be wonderful. You'll learn about magic and make new friends, play games and study hard. But it can also be difficult. You are away from your families for the first time in your lives, living with other students who are often very different from you. *Life* here is different. The mentors will do their best to help you get through the transition as quickly as possible. Listen to them, learn from them... and if you have any problems, come speak to me. I will try to help."

She took a breath. "Each and every one of you has already been assigned to a mentor. When you are dismissed, go into the next hall and link up with your mentor, who will explain the basic rules to you. After that... how much use you choose to make of your mentor is up to you. If you think you already know everything—if you feel prepared to move ahead without delay—you don't have to speak to your mentor again. If not... remember your mentor is giving time up for you. Do *not* waste their time.

"And, once again, welcome to Whitehall."

She stepped back, gratefully. Gordian took the stand, said a few brief words and then dismissed the firsties into the next hall. Emily followed, watching as students thronged about, checking lists and finding their mentors. Aloha had used a simpler system, she recalled, but she'd thought it was too random. And then she'd realized separating out the students wasn't easy.

My system was random too, she thought. *I just thought I was trying to be clever.*

Her eyes sought Marian and found her, standing shyly next to Jacquelyn. Jacquelyn was Jacquelyn of House Firestorm, if Emily recalled correctly; she was a pretty girl who hadn't impinged on Emily's radar. But then, she hadn't had time to research the Fifth Years in any depth. Perhaps, in hindsight, that had been a mistake. Jacquelyn would see too much—know too much—about Marian for anyone's peace of mind. If she took what she'd seen to her family...

I'll have to have a word with her, Emily told herself. She *had* told the Fifth Years they were expected *not* to talk about their mentees, certainly not to anyone outside the school, but she hadn't demanded any formal oaths. *If I speak to her tonight, she'll be warned before it's too late.*

"You did reasonably well," Gordian said, coming up behind her. Emily twitched. She hadn't sensed him coming. "A little unsteady at first, but good afterwards. Perhaps a course in public speaking...?"

Emily sighed. "I never wanted to speak in public." Alassa could do that, if she wished. But then, she had no choice. The Crown Princess was meant to speak in front of the Assembly every three months. "How many speeches do I have to give?"

"You're a public figure," Gordian said, amused. She couldn't help noticing that he hadn't actually answered her *real* question. "You'll give *many* speeches throughout your life."

He gave her a droll smile. "Learn."

And that, Emily knew as she watched him walk away, was good advice.

She just wasn't sure she could take it.

Chapter Ten

"THEY'RE LETTING *HER* IN THE SCHOOL?"

Emily sighed as she walked up the mountain trail. Perhaps it had been a mistake to tell Frieda that Marian had entered Whitehall. But Frieda would have recognized Marian the moment she laid eyes on the younger girl. And, unlike just about everyone else, Frieda knew what Marian had done. She'd been far less forgiving than anyone else too.

"She wasn't in her right mind," Emily said. She smiled as a gust of warm air struck her, brushing through her hair. "She can't be blamed for what she did."

"She also nearly managed to get us all killed," Frieda pointed out, sharply. "And she *did* manage to destroy your... *relationship*... with Caleb."

Emily sighed, again. "That wasn't wholly her fault. Caleb and I... we were having problems, even before our final fight."

"Which wouldn't have happened if she hadn't betrayed us," Frieda said. "She should be kicked out of her family, not sent to Whitehall."

"That wasn't our choice," Emily said. "And I don't blame Sienna for wanting to take care of her daughter."

She glanced at Frieda's hard face and knew she wouldn't be believed. Frieda had grown up in a mountain village, where family was all. Betraying the family wasn't a harmless little prank like arson, murder and jaywalking. There could be no greater sin in a world where family was often all that stood between you and darkness. Willing or not, Marian had called into question the building blocks of House Waterfall itself. Frieda couldn't forgive Marian for her betrayal, not when it had almost cost her everything. She couldn't understand, either, why Caleb and his family were prepared to keep Marian with them.

"She betrayed her mother and father," Frieda insisted. "That doesn't deserve forgiveness."

"I could cast a spell on you that would make you say or do or believe anything I wanted," Emily pointed out. Sergeant Miles and Lady Barb had made her memorize a number of dominance spells, warning her only to use them *in extremis*. "Would that make you responsible for whatever I made you do?"

Frieda looked away. "She wasn't controlled directly, was she?"

"She lost her way." Emily reached out and squeezed Frieda's shoulder. "She's a firstie—you're a grown-up Fourth Year. You won't have to see her or speak to her or have *anything* to do with her."

"Unless she joins the dueling club," Frieda muttered.

Emily shrugged. *That* wasn't likely to happen. Marian had looked scared of her own shadow. It was hard to understand *why* Sienna had allowed her daughter to leave the house, although... perhaps Sienna's parenting style had only made matters worse. Emily could appreciate having a mother who actually cared, but Marian might have felt differently after she'd been saved from certain death. She certainly might not have the strength to endure her mother's care for long.

"If she does, you can cope with it," Emily said, firmly. "And if she doesn't... well, you don't have to do anything with her anyway."

She turned right as they reached the top of the path, using a spell to push aside the concealment spell someone had placed on the bush years ago. It faded without a fight, to her private relief. The spell would have resisted more forcibly if someone had beaten them to the hollow. They made their way down a hidden path, then stopped as they reached the cliff. Below them, Whitehall shone in all its glory. Emily closed her eyes, feeling the magic spiraling around the school. The nexus point was tamed, but she could still feel it beating against her soul.

This place was drenched in magic a thousand years ago, she thought. The forest had been full of magical creatures, almost universally dangerous. Dragon's Den hadn't been founded for another five hundred years, after the Empire. *Now... only a magician would sense anything out of place.*

She opened her eyes and sat down on the grass. Caleb had taken her to the hollow more than once, back before Whitehall had started to collapse in on itself. They'd made out on the grass, kissing and hugging and exploring each other's bodies as the sun beat down and insects buzzed through the air. Now... she shook her head, telling herself not to be silly. Falling in love and falling out of it was just part of life. And she didn't really regret what she'd done.

Frieda sat next to her. "Classes start tomorrow," she said softly, one hand toying with her necklace. "Are you looking forward to them?"

"Yeah," Emily said. Some of her classes were new. Others... she hoped the tutors realized how much work she'd done, between the war and retaking her exams. Whitehall wasn't obsessed with GPA, but failing the first set of exams reflected badly on her. "I need to speak to the professors afterwards."

"You're Head Girl," Frieda pointed out. "You can go see them any time you like."

Emily nodded. She *could* have gone... if she hadn't been concerned about disturbing the tutors. They had everything from lesson plans to retaken exams to review before term actually started. Lady Barb had even told her the first week of term was always a nightmare for the tutors. And *that* was before a particularly stupid student could find a new and inventive way to injure or kill himself in front of the entire class.

"I'll see them tomorrow, hopefully." She smiled. "Master Tor has me in his Ethics of Magic and Politics class."

"Ouch," Frieda said. "It would probably be better just to keep your mouth shut."

Emily shrugged. Master Tor *had* been quite informative, back in Second Year. Law had never really interested her, beyond trying to figure out why some of the odder— and stupider—laws on the books had ever been written in the first place. Most of them had remained in force long after their original purpose had become immaterial, if there had been a reason in the first place. But she supposed it was important to know what might be considered a crime before it was too late.

"I'll try to pay attention," she said. She wasn't sure *what* Master Tor could tell her about ethics, but she supposed she'd find out tomorrow. "Did you catch up with Celadon?"

Frieda's face darkened. "Yeah," she said, as she unslung her backpack and tore it open. "He was useless, as always."

"You didn't say he was useless *last* year," Emily reminded her, carefully. "I thought you were working well with him."

"That was before he started trying to change everything." Frieda produced a notebook and thrust it at Emily. "Have a look!"

Emily took the notebook, tested it for unpleasant surprises and then opened it. Students at Whitehall *normally* secured their notebooks, just to make it difficult for someone to steal their work, but Frieda hadn't bothered. Emily made a mental note to remind her she was back at school now, then started to work her way through the diagrams. Celadon had been busy. He'd taken the original idea—which Frieda had copied down last year—and changed it beyond recognition.

"There are some good thoughts here," Emily mused, as she worked her way through the notebook. "A couple of them are quite innovative."

Frieda gave her a nasty look. "He didn't check with me about *any* of them," she snapped, angrily. "He didn't even *ask* before he filed changed papers with our supervisor!"

Emily looked up. "He told them you were changing everything?"

"*Yes.*" Frieda looked down. "He didn't even bother to *tell* me in his damned letters!"

"Oh," Emily said. She didn't blame Frieda for being steamed. If Caleb had done that to her, back in Fourth Year, she would have been furious too. She wouldn't have minded if he'd found a new way to tackle the project, but she'd have wanted to check it—and make sure she understood it—first. "Weren't you required to countersign it?"

Frieda looked blank. "I..."

"Check that," Emily advised. If Frieda hadn't countersigned, she couldn't be blamed; if she had, she might be in some trouble. No one was supposed to sign or countersign until they understood the underlying theory. Who knew *what* questions a suspicious supervisor might ask? "They'll expect you to make a progress report in a couple of months."

"Fuck." Frieda clenched her fists, angrily. "I don't even know where to begin!"

Emily studied the notebook for a long moment. Celadon had decided to combine charms, alchemy and crystallomancy to produce a set of alchemical tools that would make potion brewing considerably easier. Or so he'd said, according to the first set of notes. He'd talked Frieda into working out how magic flowed through different materials, then into planning a set of practical designs. Emily had a sneaking suspicion that some of the smaller devices wouldn't work well—they'd explode if the magic level rose too sharply—but she had to admit it was innovative. The combination of charms and alchemy was particularly clever.

"You think it's a good idea, don't you?" Frieda rose and started to pace. "Why does *everyone* think he's always right?"

Emily didn't look up. "You helped to devise the first set of plans, didn't you?"

"Yes," Frieda said. "And those plans have now been scrapped."

"I see," Emily said.

She found herself utterly unsure how to proceed. She understood *precisely* why Frieda was so upset. How could she claim a share of the marks if *he'd* done most of the work? Celadon had done nearly *all* of the theoretical work, as far as Emily could tell. He'd certainly done *all* the theoretical work for the second set of designs. And yet, most of his modifications appeared to be *better*. That could not be denied.

Not easily, she corrected herself. *But it would be pointless.*

"Sit down," she said. "Do you actually understand what he's done?"

"No." Frieda sat down heavily, crossing her arms under her breasts. "I can't follow half of the equations. His spell notations are..."

"Poor," Emily finished.

She frowned as she skimmed through the final pages. Her handwriting wasn't *that* good, but Professor Lombardi had drilled the importance of writing clearly and concisely into her skull, forcing her to write entire sections out again and again until he deemed them readable. She wondered, absently, just how Celadon had managed to avoid those lessons. Perhaps he'd been careful to write properly in class, perhaps he'd been good enough to get a free pass...

Or perhaps he's trying to conceal something, she thought, darkly. She'd read countless reports where the grains of truth had been buried beneath a collection of polite, but ultimately meaningless, nonsense. It had taken her weeks to explain to her subordinates at Cockatrice that she wanted facts—including bad news—rather than obsequious toadying. *There might be all sorts of gaps in his logic.*

"If this is his work," Emily said slowly, "he certainly should be capable of explaining it to you."

Frieda looked pained. "Are you sure?"

"Yes," Emily said. "*Anything* can be broken down into bite-sized chunks."

She sighed, inwardly. Frieda was very far from stupid, but she was *far* more interested in practical magic than theoretical studies. She mastered charms, hexes and incantations with terrifying speed, yet it took her *days* to grasp even the simplest theoretical concept. Someone who wanted to snowball her *could* snowball her, if they worked at it. There was certainly nothing to stop them.

"You haven't signed off on it," she said. "Tonight—" she glanced at the setting sun and changed her mind "—tomorrow, go to him and ask him to break it down for you. Explain what he's done, explain what he wants to do... explain everything. And if he can't explain it, insist on going back to the original set of plans. You *have* to understand what you're doing before you get interrogated by the supervisor."

Frieda flushed, darkly. "He'll say I'm stupid."

"You are *not* stupid," Emily said. Frieda was in *Martial Magic*. She was surprised that Celadon had the nerve to suggest she was stupid. "Not understanding something doesn't make you stupid."

"Hah," Frieda said. "I don't understand what you saw in Caleb."

Emily shrugged. "I don't understand what Pandora sees in Mathis either."

"He's handsome," Frieda said. "And his parents are *very* wealthy."

"True," Emily agreed, dryly. If there was *one* thing she'd picked up from Alassa's stint on the marriage market, it was that money and land could make *anyone* look attractive. Ugly daughters and charmless princes were still courted with great enthusiasm. She found it hard to believe that any of the resulting marriages were actually happy, but stranger things had happened. "Do you *like* Celadon?"

Frieda glowered at her. "He's a conceited little git!"

"It must be love," Emily teased. "When's the wedding?"

"*Never*," Frieda snarled. "I... I should never have agreed to work with him."

"You *were* getting on fine last year," Emily said. She couldn't help feeling a flicker of disquiet. Had something happened between Frieda and Celadon? Frieda could take care of herself, physically, but emotionally? "What happened?"

"We were, until he decided to change everything." Frieda reached for the notebook and glowered at it. "What was he *thinking?*"

"Perhaps he was trying to find a better way to do things," Emily mused. *She* liked trying to find new and better ways to do things. "Or perhaps..."

"I don't *know*." Frieda's voice rang with frustration. "I don't *know*."

Emily looked at the distant school, thinking hard. She *could* take the notebook and work her way through it, trying to understand what Celadon had written. There was nothing to keep her from understanding it—or determining that it wasn't *meant* to be understood. If Celadon had written a great deal of nonsense—or even ill-defined spellwork—she should be able to figure it out. But he'd have to be out of his mind to do it deliberately. The supervisor would not be amused. Celadon would, at best, have to repeat the year.

Or worse, because he'll have ruined Frieda's work as well as his own, Emily thought. *She might have to retake the year too. His punishment will be very unpleasant.*

She sighed. She didn't really have time to do anything of the sort. There was no way she could check each and every piece of spellwork, not in less than a day or two. And there were too many other demands on her time. The Gorgon or Cabiria—or Caleb—wouldn't have much time either. Besides, Frieda would sooner fail than ask Caleb for help. She'd never warmed up to him.

"Get him to explain it to you," she said, as another gust of warm air washed across the hollow. Dark clouds were already forming over the Craggy Mountains. It looked like a thunderstorm was on the way. "And if he can't, you can file an official complaint."

Frieda gave her a sharp look. "Wouldn't that be tattling?"

"This isn't someone turning you into a frog as you walk down the corridor, minding your own business," Emily said. "This is something that threatens your academic standing."

She smiled, ruefully. Five years ago, she would have been horrified at the thought of being turned into a frog; *six* years ago, she'd known it was impossible. Now... tattling wasn't encouraged at Whitehall—students *were* meant to sort out their own problems—but pranksters and bullies were *not* meant to impede their victim's studies. Anyone who tried would be in deep trouble, when they were caught. Frieda had every right to complain about Celadon if he—deliberately or otherwise—screwed up her marks.

"He just makes me angry." Frieda glared down at the ground. "I bet *Caleb* didn't make you angry."

"Not that often," Emily said. "We did have arguments over how to proceed, but we didn't snap and snarl at each other."

She cocked her head. "If the two of you *really* can't work together, you need to find other partners. Now."

"No one else will want me." Another flicker of anger crossed Frieda's face. "Or him. They all have their own partners."

Emily winced. Frieda might be right. The only reason she'd been partnered with Caleb—after missing half of Third Year—was that he'd been forced to retake a year. If he hadn't, she didn't know *what* would have happened. She might have had to retake a year herself, just so she had a partner, or try to complete the project on her own. But that would probably have been an automatic fail.

"You're not being judged on your spellwork alone," she said. It was true, particularly for students who were exploring more conventional avenues of magic. "You have to learn to work with him. And he has to learn to work with you. If you can't get him to see sense, you need to get your supervisor involved."

She glanced up, sharply, as she heard thunder crashing over the mountains. "We'd better get down quickly," she said. "It won't be long before it starts raining."

"I've seen worse," Frieda said. "In the Cairngorms, we wouldn't bring the sheep in for *this*."

Darkness fell rapidly as the storm moved towards them. Emily cast a night-vision spell and looked around. In the faint light, the trees and bushes were starting to take on a vaguely sinister aspect.

Emily rose. "We're not in the Cairngorms." She'd only been to the Cairngorms once, but she hadn't liked it. Frieda's life had been hellish before she'd been discovered by a roving magician and taken away. "And the rain might turn to snow very quickly."

She held out a hand. "Shall we go?"

Chapter Eleven

Emily hadn't been sure what to expect when she first walked into Master Tor's new classroom. A traditional room, with rows of desks and chairs, or something a little more informal? His *last* classroom had been *thoroughly* traditional. But this one was startlingly informal. A handful of comfortable chairs arranged in a circle, a number of groaning bookcases, a pot of Kava on the sideboard, a fire burning merrily in the grate... it could easily have passed for a living room, a place where a family might relax after a long day. She took one of the seats as Cabiria and the Gorgon followed her into the room, reminding herself to be sharp. Master Tor didn't like her much.

Cabiria nudged her. "Half the class seems to have vanished," she said. "Where have they gone?"

"There's only nine chairs," the Gorgon pointed out. Her snakes shifted uncomfortably as she took a seat close to the fire. "The others probably decided not to take this class."

Emily frowned. "I thought it was compulsory."

"It is," a familiar voice said. Emily looked up as Gordian strode into the circle and took one of the remaining seats. "But we cannot accommodate all twenty-five of you at once."

The Gorgon cleared her throat. "Sir, I was under the impression that Master Tor would be the teacher in this class..."

"It was decided that I would take the class instead," Gordian said, coolly. Emily caught a flicker of displeasure in his eyes. It was hard to escape the sense that Gordian didn't like the Gorgon any more than he liked Emily. His predecessor had been seen as astonishingly liberal for allowing a gorgon to study at his school. "Master Tor is otherwise occupied."

He leaned back into his seat, crossing one leg over the other. "The others *should* be here in two minutes. For future reference, the door will be locked two minutes after class begins. Anyone who fails to arrive by then will be denied entry and marked absent for the period. There will be no further warning."

And no way to alert the others to hurry, Emily thought. *They won't have heard the warning.*

Cirroc walked through the door, followed by Jacqui and Cerise. There was no sign of Caleb, to her private relief.

She sighed, inwardly, as the last of the students arrived. Gordian taking the class boded ill, she was sure, even though it wasn't a *practical* subject. Master Tor could hardly have *ordered* his direct superior to take the class, could he? But then, she'd checked. Gordian had very little experience of actually *teaching*. It was possible that he'd decided to try to fill in the gaps as much as possible. She supposed he deserved respect for that, if it was true. She'd met too many people who were staggeringly ignorant of their own ignorance.

But you couldn't get away with it indefinitely at Whitehall, she reminded herself. *Bluffing doesn't work when you're expected to show competence at all times.*

Gordian waved a hand at the door. It shut with an ominous *bang*.

"Thank you for coming," he said. "This class is Ethics in Magic and Politics. Those of you who noted that there was no reading list—and had the sense to ask Master Tor—already know this is *not* a class in the traditional sense. I will be operating a discussion group, rather than lecturing you for the next two hours."

His lips curved into a cold smile. "I'm sure you will find that something of a relief."

Emily wasn't so sure. She enjoyed discussions and debates, one on one, but she'd never been comfortable speaking in front of a group. It was too easy to make a mistake, then have everyone call her on it. She'd addressed the firsties, but there hadn't been any audience participation. They'd been too awed or nervous to question her.

And Gordian will probably enjoy pointing out my mistakes, she thought, sourly. *So will some of the girls.*

"Let's start with an obvious question," Gordian said. "What *are* ethics?"

"A code of conduct," Cirroc said.

Gordian looked faintly displeased. Emily wondered, sardonically, if he'd planned to make *her* answer the question. Or maybe he'd expected them to put up their hands and wait to be called on before they opened their mouths. Clearly, *he'd* never taken a discussion group before. She couldn't help wondering if he'd taken the class himself, back when *he'd* been at Whitehall. Perhaps it was a relatively new innovation.

"Close," Gordian said. "Ethics are a framework of thought that define *right* and *wrong.*"

He paused. "How many of you think it is wrong to *steal?*"

Emily put up her hand. So did most of the class.

"Gorgon, you don't agree." Gordian's nose twitched, as if he'd smelled something disgusting. "*Why* don't you agree?"

"If my daughter was starving, I would steal to feed her," the Gorgon said. Her snake-like eyes gazed at Gordian, daring him to disapprove. "I would take the risk, knowing the only alternative was watching my child die."

Gordian looked at her for a long moment, then nodded curtly.

"A good answer," he said. "Ethics—as a framework of thought—are flexible. It is *wrong* to steal for oneself, but *right* to steal for someone else. Thoughts?"

"I wouldn't like it if someone stole from *me*," Mathis said. "They might be stealing food from *my* daughter."

"That's true," Gordian agreed. "Something that looks reasonable to one person might look very unreasonable to another."

"But what happens if the person could afford to spare the food?" Melissa offered. "If I was starving myself, I wouldn't want to lose the food. But if I was swimming in plenty, I could spare the food without a qualm."

"It would still be *your* food." Jacqui sneered. "Don't *you* get to make the choice of what happens to it?"

"A valid point," Gordian said. "Here is a different question. Should a thief who steals to enrich himself be treated more severely than a thief who steals to feed his children?"

Emily shrugged. She'd never seen any suggestion that the Nameless World cared one whit for social justice, in any of its forms. Thieves were thieves, whatever their cause; they were put in the stocks, or enslaved, or even executed... there was no mercy, no matter their motives. And she could understand the logic, even if the punishments repulsed her. Far too many communities lived on the brink. A thief could push them over the edge.

Which doesn't excuse lords and ladies living high while peasants starve, she reminded herself, grimly. *They would kill men and rape women just for a little sport.*

"It's still theft," Jacqui said. "There's no misunderstanding here, sir. A person who steals from another *knows* he's stealing from another, whatever his... reasons. They have to be dealt with harshly."

"Yeah," Prunella agreed. "They could just *ask* for the food."

Emily snorted. She couldn't help herself. Prunella had grown up in a magical family and gone straight to Whitehall. She'd never starved a day in her life. She'd certainly never lived as a peasant or even a powerless aristocratic girl. There was no way she could comprehend the gulf between the peasants and the aristocrats, let alone the mundanes and the magicians...

Gordian gave her a sharp look. "Do you have something to contribute, Emily?"

"A starving peasant *could* go to the lord of the manor to ask for food," Emily said. It was hard to keep the disdain out of her voice. "But he'd be lucky if he was only laughed at. His lord and master wouldn't lift a finger to help."

She sighed. The aristocracy considered the peasants subhuman. They were more concerned about their horses and dogs than the hapless men and women who toiled on their estates, wretched serfs fit only to hew wood and draw water. Emily had never understood it—even if they hated the peasants, starving them to death was self-defeating—but it was a fact of life. A starving peasant who begged for help was more likely to be beheaded than fed.

"Yes, he might," Gordian said. "But would refusing help be *ethical?*"

"Yes, it would," Jacqui said. "The peasant has no claim on his master."

Emily scowled. She'd been told, more than once, that a feudal chain of obligations ran up from the lowliest peasant serf to the monarch himself, that the nobility had obligations to the peasants... but she'd never seen any proof. The nobles of Zangaria seemed to believe they had no obligations at all to their peasants, not even to help keep them alive during famine. The only time she'd seen the aristocracy concerned about the peasants had been when the peasants had started to run off to the big cities. They were prepared to move heaven and earth to recover a runaway peasant, but not to make any concessions that would convince the peasant to stay on the estate. The whole system was shitty.

"And if that is so," Gordian asked, "does the master have any claim on the peasant?"

He held up a hand before anyone could answer. "We'll return to this topic later," he said, firmly. "Right now, we are discussing magic. What *are* the ethics of magic?"

"To know when to use and when not to use magic," Melissa said. "And when magic can be used for power."

Gordian nodded. "Power—and magic is a form of power—brings responsibility," he said, seriously. "Why do you think we teach you here?"

"Efficiency," Cirroc said. "Instead of one teacher trying to teach one student, you teach twenty or thirty of us at once. We pick up the basics so our future masters don't have to hammer them into our heads."

Emily wasn't so sure. The master-apprentice relationship had its advantages as well as its disadvantages, but so did the educational system. On one hand, it could impart a great deal of knowledge relatively quickly; on the other, it limited the amount of individual attention each student could receive. Emily was fairly sure that *she* would have progressed far faster at school—in both worlds—if she'd been the sole focus of her teacher's attention. But, on the other hand, she probably wouldn't have gotten away with anything.

"That's not a bad point," Gordian said. "But it isn't the one I want to discuss now. Anyone else?"

"Uniformity," Melissa offered. "A cert from Whitehall has a fixed value, sir. Anyone who takes me on as an apprentice knows what I did to earn the cert. He doesn't have to put me through my paces to discover the limits of my knowledge."

"That's also true," Gordian said. "But there's a different point."

The Gorgon leaned forward. "You allow magicians from all over the Allied Lands to get to know one another," she said. "Everything from friendships to patronage networks go through Whitehall."

"There *are* other schools," Gordian said. "But you're right. Uniformity *is* important. It just isn't the point I have in mind."

Cabiria nudged Emily. "Then what *does* he have in mind?"

Gordian proved to have sharp ears. "You tell me, young lady."

"You want us to come to believe that we are all magicians," Cabiria said, a hard edge in her voice. Her early life had been blighted by the belief she wouldn't develop magic when she reached puberty. "That whatever our origins, we have magic in common."

"Again, not a bad answer," Gordian said. "But it isn't the one I want."

Emily glanced at Cabiria. Her pale cheeks darkened, just for a second. Perhaps it was as close as Cabiria could come to a flush.

"There is a more fundamental point to Whitehall's existence than anyone, even Cabiria, mentioned," Gordian said. "In Whitehall, you grow up surrounded by your fellow magic-users. Anything you can do, they can do too. You can turn someone into a frog, or freeze them in place, or force them to recite doggerel... but they can do it to you too. There is nothing *special* about you here. You are just one of many.

"That isn't always true in the outside world. A lone magician in an isolated region can wind up dominating an entire village—or worse. The sole possessor of *power*— true power—can crush any opposition, as long as they are careful not to attract attention. How much damage could you do, as students? Think how much you could do to people helpless to stand against you."

Emily swallowed. A couple of months at Whitehall had taught her enough magic to do *real* damage. She'd had the advantage of having ideals—and a mindset—that came from Earth, but that hadn't made her uniquely destructive. Someone who'd grown up among people who couldn't stop her, someone who had every reason to think they were superior to everyone else, might go mad with power. Or they might have set out to avenge themselves on their former tormentors. If Frieda hadn't left her village, after developing her magic, would she have turned it into her own personal fiefdom? Or would the villagers—including her family—have killed her in self-defense?

"When you leave Whitehall, next year, you will leave with enough magic and power to make yourselves unchallengeable, save by your peers," Gordian added. "What will you do with that power?"

"I don't know," Jacqui said. "But it will be my choice."

"Yes," Gordian agreed. "And what will you choose?"

He looked from face to face. "Ethics in magic is all about how you choose to use power. And you *have* power—have no doubt about that. Here, you are surrounded by your peers; there, you are the sole person with power. What will you do with it?"

Cirroc's eyes narrowed. "Sir... why would I go live somewhere without other magicians?"

"Perhaps you *want* unchallenged power," Gordian said. His dark eyes gleamed. "Perhaps you *want* to live a life without limits."

His eyes met Emily's, just for a second. "Perhaps you *want* to be accountable to no one, to answer to no one, to take orders from no one. Or perhaps you have always secretly wanted power and now you have the ability to claim it."

Emily kept her face expressionless. Better to reign in hell than serve in heaven?

She wondered, as Gordian's eyes moved on, if he was talking about her—or Void. The idea of being a Lone Power, of being strong enough—in magic—that no one could tell her what to do was attractive. She could admit that, privately. If someone else held power over her—power to tell her what to do, power to *make* her do what they wanted her to do—they could turn abusive. And if there was no higher court she could appeal to—to beg for help—there would be nothing she could do. Who could she count on to *always* put her interests first?

But I might also go mad with power, she thought. Lady Barb had told her quite a few horror stories about sorcerers who went mad, even if they never crossed the line into necromancy or demon-summoning. *If I lost my moral compass, how would I know I was crossing the line until it was far too late?*

"Many years ago, there was a young man who was treated badly by everyone he knew," Gordian said, brutally. "He was kicked and beaten by his peers, ignored by his parents... there wasn't a young woman in the village who didn't mock him for an ugly gnome. And he *was* ugly. He was weak and feeble and useless and they kicked him around for sport.

"And then he developed magic. He enslaved his village. He killed or transformed most of his tormentors, then turned the young women into his adoring love-slaves.

He might have enjoyed a long and happy reign over his village if he hadn't started to build himself an empire by invading *other* villages. He was killed..."

Gordian paused. "Now tell me... was he in the *right?*"

Emily hesitated. On one hand, everything the young man had done had been awful. There was no way she could condone it. And yet, the villagers had treated him badly too. Didn't they deserve some punishment? But hadn't he gone far too far?

"Maybe he had a point," she said. "But he went too far."

Gordian lifted his eyebrows. "And what point is going too far?"

"I have no answer," Emily admitted. She recalled the age-old definition of pornography and smiled. "But I'll know it when I see it."

"He should have just left," Jacqui said. "He had power. He could have come here or gone to one of the other schools... even apprenticed himself to a village druid or apothecary. He didn't have to stay there, grubbing in the mud and rutting with peasant girls. His power should have lifted him up. Instead, he dragged it down."

"A valid point," Gordian said. "Should he have left?"

"There was nothing for him there," Cirroc said.

"Except revenge," Mathis pointed out. "Didn't they deserve to be punished?"

Melissa shot him a challenging look. "I don't think *you* got punished for turning my shoes into slugs."

"You jinxed my hands to the wall," Mathis countered. "Who punished the villagers for treating that poor boy like shit?"

Gordian cleared his throat. "The world is rarely as black and white as we like to pretend. And it is astonishing how many seemingly simple problems can become complex."

"It's astonishing how many people can *make* simple problems complex," Melissa muttered.

"Quite right," Gordian agreed. "But the world very rarely admits of simple solutions."

Because there's always someone who loses out, Emily thought.

"For homework, I want you to think about what *you* would do in that situation." Gordian rose, just as the bell began to ring. "And I'll see you all next week."

Chapter Twelve

EMILY WAS STILL MULLING IT OVER AS SHE FOLLOWED CABIRIA AND THE GORGON DOWN TO the common room to get a glass of water, then up to the wardcrafting classroom. What would *she* have done, if she'd grown up in a village where she'd been savagely abused? What would she have done if she'd acquired the power to make her tormentors pay? What would she have done, she asked herself grimly, if she'd had her magic when she'd been living with her stepfather? Would anyone have blamed her for driving him out? Or turning him into a small hopping thing? Or even killing him outright?

Someone who wasn't there probably would, Emily thought. She knew Frieda had been abused and Alassa had been neglected, but she didn't really comprehend how bad it must have been. *They'd think I went too far.*

She sighed, inwardly. Objectively... there was no *objectivity*, not when abuse was concerned. One might argue that regular beatings were better—or worse—than a constant torrent of emotional abuse, but the victim wouldn't care. She'd just want the abuse to stop, whatever it took. If she'd had her magic on Earth, she wouldn't have hesitated to drive her stepfather out of the family. It wouldn't have mattered to her if some people thought she'd overreacted. All that mattered was putting an end to the abuse.

But I wouldn't go any further, she told herself. *Would I?*

"Welcome back," Professor Armstrong said. "I trust you remember my warning from last year?"

Emily nodded. She liked Professor Armstrong, more than she cared to admit. He was a towering man, with long red hair and a long red beard that hung down to his chest. His face was scarred and pockmarked, his hands were large enough to make her feel uncomfortable, yet there was an odd gentleness about the way he moved that reassured her. She didn't blame him in the slightest for warning his students that lateness would not be tolerated. He had too much material to cover in too little time.

"I want you to sort yourselves out into groups of three," Professor Armstrong added. "Make sure you pick a pair of partners you can work with. You'll be doing a lot of work with them over the next few months."

"Emily," Cabiria said. "Over here?"

Emily hesitated, then hurried over to join Cabiria and the Gorgon. She'd worked with Caleb last year, but she didn't think she could do it again, not even when there would be a third person in the group. There would be too much drama. She didn't *think* they had to do another group project, but there was no point in taking chances. Besides, she got along with Cabiria and the Gorgon. Most of the other students didn't like them that much.

"Very good." Professor Armstrong waved a hand at the blackboard. It filled, rapidly, with a complicated spell diagram. "In the previous year, we looked at establishing anchored wards against external threats, with a particular concentration on protecting your house and your private rooms. I trust you took the opportunity to practice over the summer?"

Emily nodded. Lady Barb and Sergeant Miles had forced her to practice time and time again, then talked her through the basics of ward-etiquette. Putting up a temporary ward to protect your bedroom was fine—even if you were sleeping in another person's home—but establishing a permanent ward was far less acceptable. Emily had puzzled over it until she'd realized that a permanent ward would interfere with her host's wards, perhaps weakening them from the inside. She wouldn't care to get the blame for someone breaking into a house and wrecking the place.

"My parents were very proud of me," Cabiria muttered. "But they refused to test my wards."

"This year, we will split our attention," Professor Armstrong informed them. "First, we will be studying nestled wards, how you can place one ward seamlessly inside another to expand its function; second, we will be looking at wards designed to monitor the interior of your houses and—if necessary—react badly to misbehavior. Those of you interested in a career in wardcrafting might want to pay *very* close attention. We'll only be touching on the basics, but you need to master the basics before you go onwards."

Emily exchanged glances with the Gorgon. Neither of them were likely to study wardcrafting in detail, let alone seek a wardcrafter apprenticeship, but it was *better* to construct your own wards rather than rely on someone else. Besides, she had too many secrets to conceal. Lady Barb had given her a whole series of practical lessons in ward maintenance, but she was uneasily aware she probably couldn't ward a whole house from scratch. It was something she'd need to master before too long.

"I have given you several warnings before." Professor Armstrong's eyes swept the room. "This one, perhaps, is one of the more *important* warnings. We will be using blood, later in the year, to anchor and personalize your wards. I expect you to remember the rules for handling blood and follow them to the letter. Anyone who doesn't recall them should brush up on them before the end of the week. Carelessness in handling your own blood tends to find its own punishment."

"How true," Cabiria muttered.

Emily nodded. She'd learnt *that* lesson five years ago. She took extreme care with her own blood, even when she cut her finger. It wasn't paranoia, either. A skilled mage who obtained—somehow—a sample of her blood could use it against her, easily. If Shadye could do it, she had no doubt another magician could do it too. She would have preferred not to use blood magic at all, if it could be avoided.

But a ward that isn't tied to me won't be so effective, she thought, glumly. *I won't be as attuned to it as I need to be.*

She pushed the thought out of her mind and started to take notes as Professor Armstrong launched into a long and complicated lecture. As always, he took complex subjects and broke them down into bite-sized chunks—giving her time to parse out each and every segment—before demonstrating how they went together. Emily knew, from bitter experience, that turning theory into practical reality wouldn't be easy, but it was still important to understand the theory behind the nestled wards. She'd crafted anti-magic wards before, even overpowered them, yet her work had been crude. A skilled magician might have been able to overwhelm them.

"You'll notice that the lower section of spellwork here"—Professor Armstrong pointed to a complex set of spell notations—"defines the lower level of magic. Magic *below* that level simply doesn't activate the spell. Why might that be so?"

Caleb stuck up a hand. "Because you'd start draining personal wards if you didn't set a lower limit," he said. "You might even drain a magician's reserves."

"Correct," Professor Armstrong said. "Outside a prison, it is *very* rare to see wards designed to drain a magician completely. Even *in* a prison, it is generally considered preferable to use potions to keep a magician from using magic. Why? There is a very real risk, if you do, that you'll accidentally *kill* your captive. The disadvantages of *that* should be obvious."

"Depends on the captive," Cirroc said.

"Anyone dangerous enough to warrant *that* level of security would be executed out of hand or stripped of his magic," Professor Armstrong said. "There would be no great advantage in keeping him alive."

He glanced at the blackboard. "The spellwork here"—he tapped the diagram—"is designed to react to active spellwork. When the ward senses the magic, it automatically starts to redirect and absorb the spellwork. It *doesn't* try to break up the spellwork because the results of *that* can be dangerously unpredictable. It also doesn't try to absorb *all* the magic because...?"

"It might overload the local ward structure," Caleb said. "If the ward is dislodged, it'll collapse."

"It depends on how firmly the ward is anchored," Professor Armstrong said. "There are designs that allow magic to be vented into the air or dumped into the bedrock, but they have their advantages and disadvantages. We'll look at those later."

He smiled. "But enough of that now," he said, nodding to the blackboard. The diagram changed, becoming something far simpler. "For the moment, I want you—in your teams—to construct these two wards. You will not find it easy."

Cabiria reached into her desk and produced a hearthstone. "Why does he need *three* of us to put the ward together?"

Emily frowned. She could understand why a team might be required to ward an entire house, but a tiny hearthstone? *One* of them would have enough problems; *three* of them would just keep getting in each other's way. There was no way they could do it as a team. She tapped the hearthstone, making sure it was inert before they began. Perhaps they were meant to take turns.

"If you set up the first ward, we can watch carefully and make unhelpful remarks," the Gorgon said. Her thoughts had clearly been heading in the same direction. "We might see what you do wrong."

"The trick is getting it right the first time." Cabiria sketched out a runic diagram, carefully weaving the two wards together. "How does that look?"

"Very strong," the Gorgon said. "But if one ward comes down, the other will collapse too."

Emily nodded in agreement. There was no way the ward would last indefinitely. It was too weak, even after it was properly established. *She* thought the wards shouldn't be so closely connected. The inner ward wouldn't help tie the outer ward in place.

"I think we'd have worse problems if someone battered down the outer ward," Cabiria countered. "Why do we need a sensing ward if someone is crashing through the walls?"

"It would be a little bit redundant," Emily agreed.

"You'd also lose *all* sensing wards," the Gorgon said. "You wouldn't be able to track someone trying to sneak into the house."

"Point," Cabiria said. She winked. "But you have to learn to walk before you can run."

Emily watched, carefully, as Cabiria set up the ward. It was an order of magnitude harder than the ward lines they'd crafted last year, she noted; the inner ward had to be perfectly positioned or it weakened the outer ward. She couldn't help thinking, as Cabiria struggled to balance the two wards, that it would be easier to separate them. But that would have disadvantages of its own.

"Someone who casts a full-scale cancelling spell is going to bring your edifice crashing down," she pointed out. "And you might not be able to counter it in time."

"You can tune the wards to resist cancelling spells," Cabiria pointed out. Sweat trickled down her face as she held the wards together. "Otherwise *everyone* would be using them to break through wards."

"You'd need a lot of power too," the Gorgon added. "Particularly if you wanted to cancel a household ward."

"True," Emily agreed. Could she cast one with a battery? It was certainly worth trying at some point, just to see what happened. If it worked, she'd have a secret weapon up her sleeve. "I wonder..."

She broke off as Cabiria's ward collapsed into a flickering mass of spellwork that vanished a second later. Cabiria snapped out a swearword, then picked up the hearthstone. It was cracked and broken, utterly beyond repair. Emily shook her head in amused disbelief. She'd never seen *that* happen before.

"You tried to force the ward into place," Professor Armstrong said. Emily looked up. He was standing in front of the table, studying the hearthstone. "You need a delicate touch."

"I thought the wards would work together," Cabiria said. "Why *didn't* they?"

"Because the wards aren't static," Professor Armstrong said. "And you didn't account for that when you planned the spell."

He turned and walked away. Emily exchanged a look with the Gorgon, then picked up a piece of paper and started to write out her own spell diagram. If Cabiria's spell had failed because the nestled wards couldn't cope with their own fluctuation, perhaps she could keep them further apart and only link them in a handful of places. Perhaps, if she was *very* careful, she could oscillate them both...

"This should be workable," Cabiria said. She'd been scribbling notes too. "If I limit the power surge..."

"The ward needs a certain level of power to survive," the Gorgon pointed out. "You'd be starving it of power."

"Try to limit the intake." Emily finished her own diagram and reached for a new hearthstone. "Let me see what I can do..."

She concentrated, muttering the spells under her breath as she built up the wards. The first ward went together perfectly, but the second started to flicker out of control almost as soon as it was in place. It just wouldn't stay still. Emily cursed, fighting to hold it together, but they seemed to be intent on collapse the moment she took her eyes off it. Fixing it in place seemed impossible. And then the *first* ward started to collapse too.

"Bugger," she muttered, as the spellwork finally disintegrated. "What happened?"

"I don't think your foundations were secure," the Gorgon said. "Let me try."

Emily nodded and watched as the Gorgon went to work. *Her* spellwork was a little more stable—she'd seen Cabiria and Emily both fail—but it refused to last more than five minutes without constant maintenance. It was better than hers, Emily acknowledged without rancor, yet it was useless. There was no way anyone could constantly monitor and maintain their household wards if they hoped to do anything else at the same time.

This would be so much easier with a nexus point, she thought, sourly. *A vast source of power would let me build all the individual wards I want.*

"It's nearly time for lunch," Professor Armstrong said. His voice echoed around the room, calling their attention to the front. "None of you succeeded. Don't feel too bad about it, please. Very few sorcerers manage to get two wards working together on their first try."

He paused long enough to let that sink in. "You will need to work hard to develop the fine touch you'll need to put multiple wards into place," he added. "It is not something you can master overnight. I would be surprised if any of you manage to master the basics by the first half-term. Practice, practice and practice some more."

Emily rubbed her head. She could feel a headache coming on.

"I'll see you all again, tomorrow," Professor Armstrong said. "Dismissed."

The Gorgon tapped Emily's shoulder as she rose. "Coming to lunch?"

"I have to speak to the professor," Emily said. "But I'll see you down there."

"Emily," Professor Armstrong said. He eyed her as she rose. "What can I do for you?"

"I have to set up a dueling club, then run a contest," Emily said. She cursed the whole concept under her breath. A day of schooling and she already felt overworked. "I was wondering if I could ask you for help setting up the arena."

Professor Armstrong gave her a sharp look. "Are you asking me to set it up for you or to teach you *how* to set it up?"

"To teach me," Emily said. She would have liked to pass the job to someone else, but she doubted anyone would volunteer to do it for her. "And also to make sure it's safe."

"Dueling is not *safe*," Professor Armstrong said. "You should know that, young lady."

Emily nodded, remembering when Master Grey had burned to ash... when *she'd* burned Master Grey to ash. The stench had haunted her for weeks afterwards, lingering in her nostrils no matter how many showers or baths she took. Even the training duels at Mountaintop had not been safe. There was no way to *make* them safe without twisting the whole concept beyond repair.

"I would be honored to help you." Professor Armstrong smiled. "It will serve as a practical lesson, perhaps. There are students who could benefit from such instruction."

"Me included," Emily said. She could always use the practice. Besides, she'd been taught to go back to the basics every time she didn't understand something. "But I don't want to risk lives."

"I won't let a mistake get past me," Professor Armstrong said. "But I will make you pay for any errors that might be life-threatening."

"I have no doubt of it," Emily said.

Professor Armstrong gave her a droll smile. "I should be free on Saturday. We can do it then."

Emily winced. She'd made plans to go to Dragon's Den with Frieda. But those plans would have to be changed. There was no way Professor Armstrong would change *his* timetable for her. Head Girl or not, she was still a student. She couldn't make demands of her professors.

"That should be fine," she said. The volunteers would have to be alerted, of course. She'd tell them over lunch. "What time?"

"I think an early start would be good," Professor Armstrong said. "After breakfast?"

They're going to hate me, Emily thought. *But they did volunteer to assist.*

"That should be fine," she said, again. "And thank you."

"Thank me with some hard work," Professor Armstrong said. "I want you to pass your exams. That glitch in your last set of papers could have killed you."

"I know," Emily said.

"Luckily, you made up for it," Professor Armstrong added. "You might not be able to do *that* again."

He smiled. "Go for lunch," he said. "And I'll see you tomorrow."

Emily nodded and left.

Chapter Thirteen

IT FELT ODD, EMILY DECIDED, TO SHARE LUNCH WITH CABIRIA AND THE GORGON, RATHER than Caleb or Frieda. She wasn't sure why that was the case—she'd shared lunch with Alassa and Imaiqah all the time—but it was. Perhaps it was the fact that they had clearly opened their friendship to include her—three outcast girls instead of two—or perhaps it was the fact that they both talked more about their studies than anything else. But she couldn't help feeling grateful to them too. It was a sign, perhaps, that she wasn't *completely* isolated from her peers.

Just most of them, she thought, glancing along the table. Maybe I should have talked more to the others before Alassa and Imaiqah left.

She shook her head in annoyance, dismissing the thought. There was no point in crying over spilt milk. The students had developed friendships and study groups since they started at Whitehall and there was no room for an interloper. She was lucky that Cabiria and the Gorgon had decided to invite her to sit with them. Her eyes swept the room, picking out students she knew. Most of the Sixth Years were chatting away in their little groups—she spotted Caleb sitting next to Cirroc and Mathis—and clearly trying to recover from the first day back at school. The only person missing was Melissa, who might have decided to go to the library instead of eating. Emily hoped she'd have enough sense to make sure she didn't go hungry. There was a great deal of practical magic in healing.

The bell rang as she sipped her juice, reminding her that she was meant to be on her way to Soul Magic. She put the glass down and took a moment to center herself—her memories of soul magic weren't good—and then bid Cabiria and the Gorgon farewell. They waved her off, then returned to their conversation with nary a break. Emily couldn't help feeling oddly isolated as she walked through the door and out into the corridor. She was alone in a crowd of students.

And being Head Girl doesn't help, she thought, as younger students scurried to get out of her way. *They all think of me as one of the tutors.*

She sighed, inwardly, as a cluster of Second Years ran around the corner... and practically screeched to a halt when they saw her. They'd been playing freeze tag in the corridors, Emily noted, as she pretended not to see them. It was a fun game, for younger students. She wondered, absently, if she should have tried to introduce a formalized version of freeze tag as a project, rather than dueling. It wouldn't have been *that* hard to come up with a list of rules and plan a contest. God knew three-fourths of the student body had played it over the last few years.

A couple of female students scattered, leaving behind a third frozen into an embarrassing position. Emily rolled her eyes and silently cast the counterspell, shaking her head in amusement as the young girl squeaked and ran as if the devil himself was after her. Did she expect punishment for being frozen? She'd hardly be the first person to be frozen in Whitehall. Or did she expect Emily to be a bitchy upper-class student? It wasn't *common* for senior students to socialize with their juniors.

She watched the younger student vanish down the corridor, then slowly climbed the stairs towards the upper levels. The wards hummed around her, growing stronger as she reached the healing section. It was unusual for anyone to enter, Emily recalled, without a long-term plan to become a healer, even though there were few prospective candidates. The requirements were just too demanding. Even if they failed the exams, they'd still be bound by the oaths. It would make it hard—very hard—for them to take up another career.

The painting on the wooden door—a snake, eyeing her unpleasantly—came to life as she approached. Emily could feel the wards poking and prodding at her, making sure she was exactly who she claimed to be. She braced herself, feeling as if she was being watched from up high, a second before the feeling vanished. The door opened a moment later, the snake hissing quietly as Emily walked into the classroom. An elderly lady, so frail that Emily couldn't help thinking a gust of wind would blow her over, was sitting at a table. The rest of the room looked more like an examination chamber than anything else.

Emily looked around, interested despite herself. The walls were dominated by diagrams of the human body, showing everything from veins and chakras to skeletons—male and female. She couldn't help being fascinated by a set of hand-drawn diagrams that were more detailed than anything else she'd seen in the Nameless World, even though she wasn't sure she wanted to know how the healers had garnered that kind of knowledge. Smaller diagrams discussed the life cycle of a human, the reproductive and menstrual cycle, the innermost workings of the brain and a dozen other subjects. She was tempted to ask if she could stay and study them. Healing had never really interested her—she didn't have the patience, let alone the dedication—but knowledge was always useful...

The elderly woman cleared her throat. Emily turned back to her, suddenly aware that she was being very rude. The woman—the tutor, Emily assumed—looked frail, but there was a strength about her that suggested she was no pushover. Her bushy white hair rested atop a face covered in wrinkles, yet still projected determination and power. Emily could *feel* the magic curling around the woman, barely visible under her wards. *This*, she realized numbly, was a magician in absolute control of her magic. Even Lady Barb allowed flickers of her power to leak out when she was upset or angry.

"Lady Emily," the woman said. Her voice was strong, too. "I am Samra. I am a Healer, a Mistress of Soul Magics and a Mistress of Charms. Do you wish to see my qualifications?"

"No, thank you," Emily said. There was something in Samra's voice that practically *dared* her to ask for proof. It was hard to escape the feeling that Samra didn't *want* Emily in her classroom. She hadn't even invited Emily to sit down. "I don't think you'd be here if you weren't qualified."

"I would be elsewhere, if I could," Samra said, her voice tart. "The Grandmaster has made it clear to me that you are to be tutored in Soul Magic, without taking any binding oaths. I am not pleased about this. There would be nothing stopping you from abusing your knowledge."

She met Emily's eyes. "Healers swear such binding oaths to *keep* them from abusing their powers. Even for one such as I, the temptations are sometimes too much to handle. I accepted the oaths because I feared what I might become, if I abused the power in my hands. If it was up to me, you wouldn't be taught Soul Magic. Or anything, without the oaths."

Emily swallowed. Her throat was suddenly dry. Aurelius of Mountaintop had taught her a handful of healing spells, then given her a rough introduction to Soul Magic. She hadn't even scratched the surface of the possible, yet... she understood just how easily some of the spells could be abused. She didn't blame Samra for being worried. Healers had far more power perversion potential than a doctor on Earth.

"I understand," she managed, finally.

"Understand this." Samra pointed a long finger at Emily's chest. Emily had to fight the urge to take a step backwards. "Healers are not allowed to kill. A Healer who *does* kill signs her own death warrant. Her oaths would kill her before the wheels of justice caught up with her. That is a form of judgement. A Healer *cannot* knowingly break her oaths.

"If you abuse the magic I will teach you, I will *kill* you. I will accept the judgement of my oaths and go to my death knowing that you will no longer be able to pervert my teachings. And I will do it with magic that even your *father* would find hard to defend against, if he realized he was under attack before it was too late."

She rose, slowly. "Do you understand me?"

"Yes," Emily managed. She knew enough about Healers to realize it was no idle threat. Her defenses were good, but Healing magics—when perverted—were almost impossible to stop. And if Samra was willing to sacrifice her own life to kill Emily, it would merely give the magic extra punch. "I understand."

"Good." Samra walked around the desk and headed to another room. "You have a great deal to learn before I can put you in a class with other trainees. If you don't learn the basics, you'll get nothing—at best—from the class."

Emily sighed to herself—she'd heard *that* before—as she followed Samra into the next room. It looked like a study, complete with bookcases and a pair of comfortable armchairs. Soft light shone down from high overhead, somehow warm and welcoming even though she couldn't sense the source. Samra picked up a small mirror and held it out to her. Emily took it, puzzled. It was a small handheld vanity mirror, no larger than a hairbrush. Alassa had been fond of carrying one just to check her hair. If someone hadn't carved a handful of runes into the gold edge and more into the handle, she would have dismissed it as something along the same lines.

"Know thyself," Samra said, as she sat in one of the chairs. "And understand this— you will *not* share anything you discover about your classmates with *anyone*. Or I will kick you out of the class and do everything in my power to get you kicked out of the school."

"And what if they discover things about me?" Emily turned the mirror over and over in her hand. "Truths I would sooner keep secret?"

Samra gave her a nasty look. "We all swore oaths. Whatever we learn through soul magic, whatever a patient tells us in confidence... we keep it to ourselves. I could not discuss your affairs with *anyone* without my jaw locking closed. It is not a pleasant experience. Nor is it possible to hide what I tried to do."

Emily made a face. Melissa had cast a mouth-sealing spell on her once, back when she'd had a pointless feud with Alassa. It had been horrific, even though she'd been able to breathe through her nose. Imaiqah had been able to undo the spell, but a Healer probably wouldn't have that option. They'd have to go to another Healer and seek help, which would expose what they'd tried to do. Their peers would not be impressed.

Samra pointed to the mirror. "Hold it up in front of your face and admire yourself," she ordered. "Now."

Emily lifted the mirror, feeling oddly embarrassed. She'd never been particularly vain, not when she'd never wanted to be attractive. Her stepfather had been bad enough even when she'd been a scrawny girl in third-hand clothing. Any lingering traces of vanity she'd had when she'd arrived at Whitehall had vanished when she'd met Alassa. The princess's perfection was just overpowering.

"Look at your features," Samra said. "And concentrate."

"On what?" Emily tilted the mirror. "My nose?"

"On your face," Samra said. "Concentrate."

Emily sucked in her breath. Her hair framed her pale face, a face too long and too sharp to be conventionally attractive. Or so she'd always thought. It had never crossed her mind that someone might find her attractive, not in any way she'd *want* to be found attractive. She'd been surprised when Jade and Caleb expressed interest...

They said my face had character, she thought. Alassa had said it too, insisting that Emily would be beautiful if she put more effort into her appearance. *And they didn't think it was a bad thing.*

She studied her own appearance, unsure what she was meant to be looking for. Her eyes seemed shadowed, somehow; her pale face seemed to blur, her lips thinning... she seemed older, all of a sudden. Her head felt... she wasn't sure *how* it felt. It was translucent, as if she could see her thoughts throbbing through her head and....

A stab of pain tore through her head. She screamed, throwing the mirror aside. Her head spun, as if she'd suddenly fallen backwards or... she wasn't sure *what* she was feeling. It was suddenly very hard to focus. Her thoughts were a tattered mess.

"That's not uncommon," Samra said.

Emily opened her eyes, unsure when she'd closed them. Her eyes felt as if someone was stabbing knives into her eyeballs.

"Very few people master it on the first try," Samra continued.

Emily felt sick. Her head throbbed with pain. She had to swallow, hard, before she was sure she wasn't going to throw up. Her entire body felt limp, as if she'd run for miles before collapsing in a heap. She wasn't even sure she could muster the energy to sit up and find the mirror. A vague part of her mind prattled on and on about seven years of bad luck. In the Nameless World, it was quite possible that wasn't a superstition.

"Oh," she managed. "What happened?"

"In order to use soul magic properly, you have to know yourself." Samra stood— Emily breathed a sigh of relief when she saw the mirror in Samra's hand—and walked over to the sideboard. When she returned, she was carrying a glass of water. "Drink this, then ready yourself to try again."

Emily sipped the water, eying the mirror as if it were a deadly weapon. Perhaps it was. The pain had been agonising, even though it only lasted for seconds... perhaps longer. Her head no longer felt as though a hundred elephants were trying to stampede through her thoughts, but she still felt fragile. She wasn't sure she *wanted* to try again.

It was hard to speak. But she had no choice.

"What... what is that?" She waved a weak hand at the mirror. "What are we doing?"

Samra eyed her as if she were a particularly interesting specimen on the dissection table. "I told you," she said. "Know yourself."

"I don't understand." Emily forced herself to sit upright. "What *is* this?"

"When you look into a regular mirror, you see your face," Samra said. "When you look into *this* mirror, you eventually see your soul. You look at yourself from the outside, as it were, and learn things about yourself that you never really knew. Once you know yourself, you can proceed to the next step, which is peering into someone else's soul."

"Gordian used..."

"*Grandmaster* Gordian," Samra corrected.

"Grandmaster Gordian used soul magic on me last year," Emily said. She wondered, absently, if Samra had advised him. "He helped Frieda look into my mind."

"A step born of desperation," Samra said, sounding coldly disapproving. "It was not a wise thing for him to do. Even with your consent, the risks were high. I would not have authorized it in his place."

"I volunteered," Emily said.

"That doesn't make it right," Samra said. "Soul magic is **dangerous**. If you take it lightly, you can destroy your mind—or someone else's mind."

She held out the mirror. "Again," she said. "And again, until you know yourself."

Emily hesitated. "Why do I need to know myself?"

"When you are physically naked in front of another person, and he is naked too, there is still a clear line between you and him," Samra said. "Even in the throes of sexual congress, when he is deep inside you and pumping hard, you are still two separate people. He will pull out of you, eventually, without difficulty. You and your lover are not the same person."

She paused. "Using soul magic, on the very lightest level, is like being naked in front of someone else. But as you go deeper, you run the risk of blurring into their magic and soul. The most intensive sexual experience has *nothing* on it. They are totally vulnerable to you, but you can also be influenced by them. And if you don't know yourself, you will never be able to tell what's you and what's them."

"So I might come out thinking I'm a boy," Emily said.

"Yes," Samra said, flatly. "Or worse.

"You will be able to tell, once you know what you're doing, if someone has been... influenced... or not. I believe that is what Gordian wanted to check. If I'd been there... I would have insisted on doing it myself. Frieda didn't have direct contact with your mind, but the risks were still considerable."

"I trust Frieda," Emily said.

"Frieda would not have *wanted* to hurt you, I am sure," Samra said. "Many of the men who hurt women and vice versa don't want to hurt them either. But saying or doing the wrong thing at the wrong time can cause hurt that cannot be mended, even with the best of intentions. And that's just in the regular world. In soul magic, the slightest misstep can be disastrous. You cannot hide from the truth in your own head."

Emily kept her face blank. She'd met a number of people who did just that, as far as she could tell.

"Now." Samra indicated the mirror. "Let us try again, shall we?"

Chapter Fourteen

"YOU DIDN'T DO TOO BADLY, FOR YOUR FIRST TIME," SAMRA SAID, AN HOUR LATER. "YOU'LL need practice, of course, but you're getting there."

Emily barely heard. Her head was throbbing with intense pain. Sheets of fire seemed to be crashing through her mind, as though her very thoughts were burning. If it was this painful just to look at herself, she couldn't help wondering how anyone lasted long enough to gain a soul magic mastery. It was hard to imagine someone as frail as Samra surviving such brutal treatment. But then, she wouldn't have been an old woman when she was in school.

"It does get better," Samra said. "Right now, you're trying to twist your head to look down your back."

"I can't twist my neck to look down my back," Emily pointed out, crossly. The headache was slowly fading, but her entire body was now aching. "It's physically impossible."

"It's a very limited metaphor," Samra acknowledged. "Your magic—your insight—doesn't *want* to look at yourself. Naturally, it is resisting."

"As if I was trying to perform surgery on myself," Emily said. Sergeant Miles had taught them a great deal of battlefield medicine, but he'd made it clear that they weren't to try to heal themselves unless there was no choice. "My body rebels against it."

"Your mind, yes." Samra shrugged and reached into her pocket, producing a small vial of potion. "Go back to your room and get into bed, then drink this. It'll help you sleep."

Emily took the vial and eyed it, warily. It was unmarked. "What is this?"

"A strong sleeping draught," Samra said. "Make sure your wards are up. You don't want to be awoken ahead of time."

I have to eat dinner, Emily thought. And yet, she didn't *want* to eat dinner. Sleep sounded very attractive, all of a sudden. She could sleep, then cook something on her own stove... even slip down to the kitchens. She was Head Girl. She could even ask the cooks to send something to her room, if she wished. *I...*

"Thank you." She rubbed her forehead, wishing the pain would go away. "When... when do we meet again?"

"Thursday, I think," Samra said. "Come to my office after your last class. The sooner you master the basics, the better. You'll have to work hard to catch up with the others."

Emily groaned. "Does it get easier as we go along?"

"I'd say it gets *different*," Samra said. "Soul Magic is *never* easy."

She nodded to the door. "I'll see you later. Goodbye."

Emily took the hint and headed to the door, pocketing the vial as she walked through the outer classroom. Melissa and a dark-skinned girl Emily didn't recognize were sitting at the table, working through a large medical textbook. Emily couldn't help feeling a moment of respect for Melissa, if she'd been studying soul magics as well as healing. She was clearly stronger than Emily realized.

She's always been very sure of herself, Emily thought. Melissa had possessed the nerve to defy her entire family, including her fearsome grandmother. Emily wasn't sure she'd have been able to do that, if she'd fallen in love with someone the family considered unsuitable. *And she's taken on one hell of a challenge.*

Melissa looked up. "Did you have a good first lesson?"

"It could have been better," Emily said. Her lips twitched. She supposed it could have been worse. "How did you cope?"

"It's like push-ups," Melissa said. "The more you do them, the easier they get."

Emily had to smile as she walked through the door and down the stairs. Sergeant Harkin had been horrified, utterly horrified, when she'd started Martial Magic and he'd seen how few push-ups she'd been able to do. She'd been forced to do more and more until her arms were aching, but she had to admit that it *had* gotten easier—slowly. Aloha hadn't been too pleased either, even though she'd been starting out too. Emily had made her look bad.

Which wasn't entirely my fault, Emily thought. *I didn't ask to be put in that class.*

She was nearly at the dorm level when she felt the school's wards pulse in alarm. She tensed, reaching out with her senses to touch the wards. Someone was using magic further down the corridor, someone was using magic that brushed against the unspoken limits. She hesitated, wondering if she could direct someone else to deal with the problem, then cursed under her breath as she realized no one else was within range. There certainly didn't seem to be any tutors nearby.

Gritting her teeth, she forced herself to stride down the corridor. Someone was jeering—and others were laughing—ahead of her. There was a cruelty in the tone that told her what she would see, even before she rounded the corner. A young boy—a firstie—was hanging from the ceiling, his eyes wide with terror. Three other boys stood under him, pointing and laughing. A girl leaned against the far wall, looking as if she wanted to run, but she was too scared to take that first step. Emily realized, to her shock, that it was Marian.

She cleared her throat. "What do you think you are doing?"

The boys—the bullies—turned to look at her. They were firsties too, but they were clearly not unused to magic. Emily had no difficulty, now, in picking out the signs that they'd been raised in magical families. If nothing else, they'd managed levitation and sticking charms in their first week of formal schooling.

Their eyes went wide when they saw her, their bodies shuffling as if they were unsure whether they wanted to challenge her or run for their lives. Emily glared at them, fighting to keep her anger under control. She'd seen too many bullies in her life, people with the wealth, power and social capital to convince authority figures to overlook their transgressions. Even in Whitehall, where one could hardly wave a wand without hitting someone with powerful connections, the popular bullies could get away with almost anything...

Not now, she thought. She hadn't wanted to be Head Girl, but if they gave her the power she was going to use it. *Not with me.*

The leader took a half-step forward. Emily met his eyes, silently daring him to defy her. He was handsome enough, she supposed; he was too handsome to be entirely natural. His black hair framed a face that was utterly unmarked by life. It was bad manners to check if someone was using a glamour, but she could sense faint traces of magic covering his face. He hadn't applied the glamour properly.

"We were just showing the new bug how important it is to master his magic." He sounded as though he was trying to seem assured, as if it had never crossed his mind that there might be something wrong with his conduct, but he didn't have the presence to pull it off. "Being stuck to the ceiling will..."

"Injure him quite badly if the spell fails and he can't catch himself in time," Emily finished, sharply. Falling three meters to a hard stone floor would result in broken bones, at the very least. "And can you be sure you can catch him before he falls?"

"New bugs have to learn," one of the other firsties said. He wore a face that was surprisingly adult. Emily tried to sense a glamour, but felt nothing. Either he was a far superior magician or that was his real face. Emily didn't know which prospect was more disconcerting. "My father told me..."

"*You're* a new bug," Emily pointed out, sharply. "And your father isn't here."

"We have a duty," the first bully said. "And..."

Emily forced herself to tamp down on her anger. "No, you don't," she said. "Go see the Warden, all three of you. And afterwards, you might want to reflect on just what would have happened if he *had* fallen to the floor."

The firsties looked rebellious. "Are you not going to beat us yourself?"

Emily flared her magic. "Would you rather I stuck you to the ceiling and left you there until you fell?"

She felt a flicker of heavy satisfaction as they stumbled backwards in shock. Flaring one's magic was raw intimidation, nothing else. Firsties—even ones who'd had some training before coming to Whitehall—couldn't have hoped to match her power. She could have taken all three of them with one hand tied behind her back and they knew it. Perhaps they didn't think much of her appearance. She knew she didn't have the presence of Aloha, let alone Lady Barb. But they'd respect her power.

"Go," she ordered.

The bullies turned and fled. Emily looked down the corridor—Marian had vanished while she'd been focused on the bullies—and then up at their victim. He was easy to read, even for her; he was torn between relief that she'd saved him and shame that he'd needed help. At least he probably wouldn't be ashamed of being saved by a *girl*. The magical community wasn't particularly sexist.

Because sorceresses can be just as good as sorcerers, Emily thought. She remembered Julianne Whitehall and smiled. Teaching Lord Whitehall's daughter the basics of magic had planted a seed that had flowered into something great. *And we have an even playing field.*

She cast a series of charms, lowering the victim gently to the floor. He rolled over the minute he landed and stood, looking as though he wanted to bolt too. Emily didn't blame him for being unsure. No one respected *weakness* at Whitehall. And no one would care that three on one was obviously unfair.

"You didn't have to do that," he muttered.

Emily snorted. "You would have preferred to fall to your death?"

He looked sullen. His eyes flickered around, as if he wanted to look at anything but her. "They... they just *picked* on me."

Emily studied him for a long moment. He wore firstie robes, of course, but he didn't *look* as though he'd grown up wearing them. Coming to think of it, wearing robes outside class was a pretty solid indicator he didn't have anything else to wear. And the pockmarks on his face suggested he hadn't had access to any magical healing. His build and general demeanor was only the icing on the cake. She would have bet good money that he'd grown up in a mundane community.

"Dickheads like that don't need an excuse to pick on people," she said. She'd known too many people like the bullies in grade school. They'd find a social outcast and drive him to despair—or suicide. "They just want to have fun."

He wilted. "Is that what it's always going to be like? People *picking* on me?"

Emily swallowed hard, trying to think of an answer. She'd known too many people who'd been on the brink of despair too. They were isolated and alone, ignored by those in power... there was nothing they could do to fight back. All the stories about victims learning martial arts and thrashing their bullies were just... stories. And yet, hadn't *she* done it? She'd learnt enough magic to defend herself...

"It depends," she said. "You have magic, don't you?"

"I can't get it to work properly," he said. "It just refuses to *work!*"

"It takes practice," Emily said. How long had it taken her to cast her first spell? "You wouldn't be here if you didn't have magic."

She reached out and patted his shoulder. He cringed away.

"You wouldn't be here if you didn't have magic," she repeated, silently kicking herself. She hadn't liked to be touched either, back when she'd been his age. "I know—they know more spells than you. But you can master other spells and use them to fight back."

She took a step back and studied him. "Let me guess. You grew up in a village, perhaps on a farm. Your parents were peasants or landed tenants. Right?"

"Yeah," the boy said.

Emily met his eyes. "And you didn't really have any hope of climbing up the ladder. To you, there was *no* ladder. You were never going to leave the farm, let alone marry the local lord's daughter..."

He stared at her in disbelief. Emily hid her amusement with an effort. The peasants and aristocrats were so far apart, socially, they might as well live in two separate worlds. No lord would *ever* consider giving his daughter to a peasant. Hell, he'd be reluctant to marry his daughter to a wealthy merchant, even if the merchant had enough money to pay the family's debts.

And I once tried to explain Sofia the First to Alassa, Emily reminded herself. *She didn't get it.*

"Things are different here." She felt her head starting to throb again and gritted her teeth. "You *can* rise, if you work at it. Learn magic and *use* it. I guarantee you that the gulf between you and them is *not* impossible to cross, if you work hard."

"No one will help me," the boy said, mournfully.

It's been two days, Emily thought. *They can't have poisoned everyone against him already, can they?*

She pushed the thought aside. She'd seen bullies do just that, back on Earth. It was rarer in Whitehall, but not completely unknown. If she hadn't been lucky enough to share a room with Imaiqah...

I could teach him, she thought. *But I don't have time.*

The thought caused her a stab of guilt. He *needed* help. But she barely had time to do everything else she needed to do. And besides, he didn't need a guardian angel. No one would respect him if the Head Girl or his mentor was constantly watching him, protecting him. He needed someone who would show him how to develop his powers and master enough spells to defend himself. Someone like...

"There are people in Second Year who will help you," Emily said. She'd been meaning to have lunch with her former mentees. "Ask some of them for help. They'll remember going through the same experience themselves. Believe me, they *won't* be impressed by any of the dickheads."

He looked up. "Really?"

"Yes, really," Emily said. "Take my word for it."

She leaned forward. "How many spells do you think I knew when I came here?"

"Hundreds," the boy said.

"None," Emily corrected. "My father didn't teach me any spells."

He didn't look as though he believed her. Emily didn't blame him. Magical parents would often teach their kids the basics, just to give them an edge when they reached Whitehall. Everyone had certainly *expected* Void to do that for Emily. Very few people realized that he'd never had the chance.

"But... you're the Necromancer's Bane!"

"Yes," Emily said. "And I didn't learn any magic until I was your age."

He swallowed. "They're not going to be happy, are they?"

Emily shrugged. "They're going to have problems sitting down for a couple of days," she said. The Warden wouldn't go lightly on firsties. "But it could have been worse and they know it."

She took a step backwards. "You have a chance to rise in the world. Yes, they have an advantage. But it isn't a big enough advantage to keep you from rising to meet them—or going higher. There's a boy I know—a master magician—who married into royalty. And he's powerful and skilful enough to kick my ass. You could do that too."

The boy looked doubtful. "Really?"

"Yes." Emily nodded towards the stairwell. "Go to the library and start studying. Find someone who can and will teach you. Or let them walk all over you for the rest of a very short and miserable life. Good luck."

"Thanks," the boy said.

Emily watched him go, suddenly feeling very tired. Had she done the right thing? She knew the boy—it struck her that she hadn't even asked his name—was not going to have an easy time of it. But there was no choice. She couldn't protect him indefinitely, even if she'd wanted yet another responsibility. What would he do when she left Whitehall?

At least he has a chance, she told herself. A person *couldn't* rise in the world if they were born on a farm, not if they wanted to *stay* on the farm. Running off to the city was about the only escape valve the peasants had. *And he might become something great.*

She rubbed her forehead as she walked down the corridor. It was possible that someone would complain about how she'd handled the situation. Older students weren't supposed to intervene while the younger students sorted out the pecking order. It was even possible that she would be punished for meddling. But she'd never liked bullies. Sooner or later, the dickheads would try their games on someone powerful enough to make them pay a very high price for stupidity. Better they learnt to be careful now than later.

And it might make them better people, she told herself. *Who knows?*

She felt the vial in her pocket as she reached her office door and paused. The sign-up sheet for the dueling club was already filled, with more names written on the stone below. It looked as though over a hundred students were interested in joining, mostly from second or third year. Frieda's name was right at the top.

So much for having a small club, she thought. She should have known better. Casper had wanted to win the champion title, after all. He'd risked his life to win. *But at least it will teach some of them how to defend themselves.*

Sure, her own thoughts added. *And it will teach others how to pick on the weak.*

Chapter Fifteen

THERE HAD BEEN A TIME, EMILY ACKNOWLEDGED RUEFULLY, WHEN THE WEEKEND HAD BEEN a genuine chance to rest. She could spend her free time in the library, if she wished, or leave the school for an afternoon. Dragon's Den wasn't *that* interesting a place to go, now that she was used to it, but it was something different. And there was always the prospect of going walking in the mountains, weather permitting. Only a complete idiot would go walking in the mountains when a thunderstorm turned the paths into muddy swamps.

Now, as far as she could tell, there wasn't any chance to rest at all. When she wasn't in class, she was in her office; when she wasn't in her office, she was desperately trying to keep up with her homework or catch some sleep while she had a chance. Three days of schooling had left her feeling like a nervous wreck, praying for the weekend as she forced herself to push onwards and do her duty. But the weekend offered no respite. She had to work on the dueling club.

She couldn't help feeling a flicker of resentment as she walked out of the school and headed around the arena. It was a bright, sunny day, the sort of day she should have spent walking the mountains or swimming, but instead she had to work. Gordian—for better or worse—hadn't wanted her to disassemble the *ken* arena and replace it with a dueling circle. Instead, she—and Professor Armstrong—would have to set an arena up from scratch.

Which will at least give me some more practical experience, she thought. Professor Armstrong had invited the other Fifth and Sixth Years to help too. *And it won't be a complete loss.*

The field near the arena was normally used for sunbathing and weekend barbeques when it wasn't being used for practical exercises. It was nothing more than a grassy lawn, regularly maintained by students in detention. Now, Professor Anderson had started to lay wardstones in a neat circle, carefully outlining *precisely* how the spells had to go together for maximum safety. The handful of students who'd managed to beat Emily to the lawn were taking detailed notes. Professor Armstrong had hinted that the exercise might turn out to be very useful when exam season rolled around again.

Emily shivered, despite the warmth, as she saw the circle slowly taking shape. The last time she'd seen a full-scale warding circle, she'd faced Master Grey in a fight to the death. It still chilled her to think how close she'd come to death, how easy it would have been for him to kill her if she hadn't caught him by surprise... she gritted her teeth as she rounded the circle, careful not to cross the line. The wardstones weren't charged—yet—but she knew better than to develop bad habits. A person who stepped across a charged line might be hurt or trapped if they weren't careful.

"Emily," Professor Armstrong said. He held out a sheet of parchment, covered in spell notation. "I trust this meets with the Head Girl's approval?"

Emily took the parchment and worked her way through it, carefully. Head Girl or not, she was *still* subordinate to the tutors. Professor Armstrong would *not* be pleased if she took him for granted, let alone spoke to him as if he were a servant. Besides, this *was* an exercise, as far as he was concerned. There *would* be a glitch, somewhere in the diagram. And she had to find it before they tried to implement it.

"There isn't enough of a safety ward here," she pointed out, finally. "And I don't see how the two wards here and here"—she tapped a lower section—"interact."

"Poorly." Professor Armstrong gave her a droll smile. "Are there any other points of interest?"

Emily worked her way through the diagram again, but found nothing. It was true that the flaws in *some* spellwork only became apparent when the spell was actually tried, yet there shouldn't be anything too complex about a warding circle. The theory was simple, even if the implementation was tricky. And there shouldn't be anything about the grassy lawn that would throw all their calculations out of sync.

"You're drawing power from the nexus point," she said, finally. "Is that wise?"

"We use something similar for the arena," Professor Armstrong said, jabbing a finger back towards the giant structure. "This one actually draws on much *less* power."

Emily frowned, making a mental note to check the outer edge of the school's wardstones before she returned to Heart's Eye. Someone—perhaps Whitehall and Bernard, but more likely someone history had forgotten—had added wardstones to the edge of the school grounds, giving Whitehall's masters an astonishing degree of control over the whole area. It made her wonder what else had been forgotten over the years—or what might have been deliberately lost. Whitehall's founding wasn't the only era that was poorly recorded, for all sorts of reasons. *Something* had happened during the fall of the Empire that had been wiped from all records, at least the ones she'd been able to read.

But the circle will be powered by the nexus point, she thought. *We shouldn't have any difficulty keeping it safe.*

Professor Armstrong raised his voice. "We put the wardstones in place," he said, his words booming around the field. Nearly every Sixth Year student had arrived, as well as half of the Fifth Years. "I want each of you to check that they're in the *right* place."

Emily sighed, inwardly, as she took her copy of the spell diagram and went to work. Each of the wardstones had to be placed in *exactly* the right position or the ward network would start to collapse, even with the nexus point providing enough power to overcome any minor flaws in the network. Professor Armstrong wouldn't let them get away with allowing the nexus point's raw power to save them from their own mistakes. There weren't *that* many nexus points in the Allied Lands. Most sorcerers had to rely on their own power to put their wards in place.

"This one is out of place," Caleb called. "Can I move it?"

"Check and double-check," Professor Armstrong ordered. "And *then* move it."

Emily felt sweat running down the back of her neck by the time the entire network of wardstones was checked, time and time again. It had been a mistake, she decided, to wear a shirt and trousers rather than a summer dress... or even charmed robes. Some of the other students had clearly shown more foresight. Melissa was in a long dress, while Jacqui and Cerise both wore short skirts. Emily scowled at them, wondering who they were trying to impress. They looked more like girls from Earth than the Nameless World.

Perhaps they're just trying to be practical, she thought, as they moved on to checking the embedded spells. The day was growing hotter as the sun beat down. *It's too hot today.*

"Very good," Professor Armstrong said. He was smiling, coldly. Emily hoped—prayed—that they'd caught all the problems. "If you'll all step back from the wardstones...?"

Emily stood next to him and watched as he started the first set of incantations. They'd acquired an audience, she noted. Gordian, Master Tor and several other tutors, including a scowling Sergeant Miles. *He* didn't look pleased. Emily didn't blame him. Dueling had about as much in common with sorcerous warfare as a pedal bike had in common with a car. She supposed it *would* teach reflexes and quick thinking, if nothing else.

I'll have to talk to him, later, she thought. She wasn't in Martial Magic any longer. She'd completed both years, well before the usual time. *And see what he thinks of this.*

"We will now channel power into the wardstones," Professor Armstrong said, after ordering everyone to step well back from the circle. "If something is wrong, we'll find out now."

Emily braced herself, the words of a protective spell on her lips as she felt the magic field suddenly twist. The wardstones came to life, glowing with a brilliant light as the wards took on shape and form. And then one of the wardstones turned a sickly color, a second before it exploded violently. Students scattered or raised shields of their own as pieces of debris flew in all directions. The remainder of the wards crashed out of existence a moment later.

"And that," Professor Armstrong said into the silence, "is why you check everything repeatedly before you risk activating the wards."

"You could have gotten someone killed," Caleb protested. He sounded shocked. "If someone had stood too close..."

"If someone had tried that in their house, the consequences would have been a great deal worse," Professor Armstrong said, his voice utterly unrepentant. He picked up a spare wardstone and carried it over to the circle. "I want you all to check the circle, once again."

Emily sighed and did as she was told. They hadn't found anything last time, something that worried her more than she cared to admit. Professor Armstrong had over three *decades* of experience as a wardcrafter. It didn't surprise her that he could have sneaked a tiny flaw past his class—he hadn't rebuked them for missing it, which was telling in itself—but it made her wonder what else she might miss, over the years. A tiny little spell, in the right place, could be horrendously destructive.

She stepped back when they finished and looked around. The audience had grown bigger. She saw Frieda standing with a couple of other girls, eyeing the new circle with interest. Frieda looked worn down, somehow. Emily silently promised herself that she'd take Frieda to Dragon's Den—or somewhere—as quickly as possible. *She needed a break too.*

And that will be sometime next year, she thought, as Professor Armstrong began charging the wardstones again. *At this rate, I'll be busy for months.*

She tensed as the wardstones came to life, expecting a second explosion. Nothing happened, even as the individual wards fell into place. She felt a flicker of admiration for Professor Armstrong's work. She—and her teammates—had worked hard, but they hadn't managed to get a ward network to stay up for more than a few minutes. It took more precision than any of them could muster.

"Very good," Professor Armstrong said. He glanced at Emily. "Is there anything wrong with the wards?"

Emily leaned forward, reaching out with her senses. The ward network seemed stable, just waiting for someone to step into the circle. It wasn't as strong as the wards she remembered from either of *her* duels, but that was intentional. There was no way *she* was denying herself—or the referee—the ability to step into the circle and put a stop to the duel. She wasn't going to allow the students to fight to the death.

"No," she said, finally.

She half expected to have a dozen problems pointed out to her, but instead Professor Armstrong merely pointed a finger at the wards.

"You can test them, now," he said. "Just be careful which spells you use."

Emily nodded and walked forward. The magic fizzled in front of her—she felt her hair trying to stand on end—as she stepped through the ward. It wasn't painful, like some of the other wards she'd encountered, but it was impossible to miss. *No one* could step across the line by accident. The gentle repulsion was enough, by itself, to keep anyone out unless they were *very* determined.

Silence fell, the second the wards snapped closed behind her. No one could shout advice to the duelists, save for someone keyed to the wards. Emily had insisted on that, back when she'd drawn up the list of requirements. The last thing she needed was an argument between two duelists over who would have won, if they hadn't been distracted. Professor Armstrong could speak to her, but no one else. She'd have to make sure that the other referees were keyed to the wards before the club started.

Lifting a hand, she cast a simple hex. The flicker of green light flashed across the circle and struck the wards, vanishing harmlessly in a brilliant flash. Emily had considered tuning the wards so that spells were reflected, ricocheting in all directions, but she'd dismissed the idea after she'd realized that it would make life too complicated. Better to have the wards absorb the spells than anything else. She concentrated, then cast a stronger spell. The wards glowed brightly as they absorbed it.

Not bad, she thought. *And now...*

She took a moment to gather herself, then cast a cutting spell. It was rarely used in duels, if only because it was easy to deflect if the target saw it coming. Besides, if it hit unprotected skin it would be lethal. But now... she smiled, thinly, as the spell refused to form properly, raw *mana* flaring around her as the wards broke up the spellware. A gong sounded, a second later. She'd just cast an illegal spell.

"I am very disappointed in you, Emily," Professor Armstrong said, artfully. He sounded amused. "Tut, tut. What sort of example are you setting for our younger students?"

Emily felt her cheeks heat, even though she *knew* he wasn't serious. She'd had to test the wards, after all. She cast two more illegal spells, silently monitoring how the wards reacted to her magic. It might be possible to overpower them, she decided, but it would be tricky to do it without the referees noticing. They'd have a chance to intervene.

"It works," she said, after one final test. "Thank you."

She strode forward and pushed through the wards. They resisted for a second— normally, contestants weren't allowed to leave the circle until the duel was over— and then parted, allowing her to walk through. The sound of students chattering loudly struck her like a physical blow. She shook her head, tiredly, as she walked up to Professor Armstrong. He looked pleased.

"Very good," he said. "Perhaps the others would like to test it too."

Gordian walked up to Emily as Cirroc, Jacqui and Cerise made their way into the circle and started throwing spells at each other. "When do you plan to start?"

Emily kept her face impassive as she turned to face him. "I was thinking tomorrow evening," she said. At least she'd have a *chance* for some rest. "Everyone gets the same welcoming lecture, then we start teaching spells."

"Very good," Gordian said. "And the first round of the contest?"

"Several weeks, at least," Emily said. She wondered, sourly, just how many miracles Gordian *expected* from her. "I want everyone to get used to the rules before we start the contest itself."

"Very good," Gordian said.

Emily shrugged as the Grandmaster turned and walked away. A Fifth or Sixth Year was going to win, she was sure. It was absurd to expect a firstie to beat a Sixth Year student in a duel. Maybe at Kingmaker, maybe at cards... but not in dueling. She'd probably have to come up with a prize for each year. Or maybe she'd just leave that for whoever ended up being elected Head Pupil *next* year.

She leaned back and watched as Cirroc, Jacqui and Cerise danced around the circle, tossing spells around with abandon. At least they seemed to be having fun. Perhaps she could pass some of the job onto them, once the club was underway. She'd have a preliminary meeting with them first. They'd all have to be clear on the rules before the club assembled for the first time.

"You'll have control of the wards," Professor Armstrong said. "Just be careful to check them every week."

"I'll make sure of it," Emily said.

She looked at the crowd. Frieda was still there, looking tired. Tiega and Adana stood close to her, looking eager as they chatted to their fellow Second Years. Jasmine stood a little apart, her eyes shadowed. She hadn't had an easy time of it last year, Emily recalled. Even after she'd faced her punishment for her games, her fellows hadn't warmed up to her.

We have to lie in the beds we make, Emily thought. It was true everywhere, particularly at Whitehall. *And sometimes we can't recover from our mistakes.*

"Be careful," Professor Armstrong said. "And good luck."

He walked away. Emily watched him go, noting how many students decided that his departure meant the end of the show and followed him. The coaches to Dragon's Den would be leaving soon, if they wanted to go down to the town. Emily glanced at her watch, wondering if she had time to go herself. Thankfully, she hadn't been charged with escorting the younger students. *That* was a tutor's job.

Frieda walked up beside her, one hand playing with her bracelet. "What are you doing now?"

Emily felt a stab of bitter guilt. She hadn't had time for Frieda over the last few days. Frieda was meant to be studying, but Emily had the distant impression that it hadn't been going well. Fourth Year was always hard, even though most of the students *didn't* have a tutor who was literally planning to kill them. Failing their exams could cost them the chance to go on to Fifth Year.

"We can go down to Dragon's Den, if you want," Emily said. "Just give me a moment to speak to the others first."

Frieda's face lit up, then fell. "The coaches are going now. You don't have time."

"I can teleport," Emily said. Her *house* was in Dragon's Den. She'd teleported there several times over the last year. "It won't be hard to get there at all."

Chapter Sixteen

"NOTHING EVER CHANGES HERE, DOES IT?"

Emily looked around. Dragon's Den hadn't changed *that* much over the last five years. It was still a midsized cluster of houses and shops, surrounded by a low wall. She could pick out a handful of new shops, including a couple of printers, but otherwise the town hadn't benefited *that* much from the New Learning. Anyone unlucky enough to be born in Dragon's Den would be condemned to follow in their parent's footsteps unless they developed magic or moved away.

"They've cleaned up the streets," Emily said. "That's one change, isn't it?"

She smiled at the memory, even though it wasn't a pleasant one. Dragon's Den had smelled foul, the first time she'd visited. The streets had been covered in grime. That was one very definite advantage of the New Learning. Everyone knew about the importance of keeping their streets clean. Horse dung was swept up at once and carted off to be turned into fertilizer, while anyone stupid enough to urinate or defecate in the streets was put in the stocks or brutally beaten by the street patrol. It wasn't something she liked, but she had to admit it was effective. The mortality rate in Dragon's Den had gone down sharply.

"I suppose," Frieda said. "Where do you want to go eat?"

Emily shrugged. "Pick a place," she said, as they turned onto the restaurant row. "Where do you want to go?"

She looked up and down the street as Frieda struggled to decide. Dragon's Den had always been one of the more cosmopolitan cities on the Nameless World, if only because of its close proximity to Whitehall. It was probably one of the few places away from the coast where opening up a foreign restaurant was a profitable enterprise, although *that* was changing as the New Learning spread from place to place. She couldn't help smiling in amusement as she saw a pizza restaurant right next to a burger bar. The foods *she'd* introduced were spreading widely.

A shame they'd already thought of sandwiches, she thought, wryly. *That might have spread even faster.*

"There's a small restaurant here." Frieda indicated a building that looked like a fancy cottage, weirdly out of place in Dragon's Den. It was surrounded by a small garden, packed with a dozen wooden chairs and tables. The handful of visible patrons looked to be enjoying their food. "Shall we go?"

Emily shrugged and followed her through the gate. A young serving maid picked up a pair of menus, then led them to an empty table. She looked to be around ten, Emily decided, making a mental note to pass her a tip when her seniors weren't looking. The Nameless World didn't have child labor laws. If someone's parents owned a restaurant, they'd be expected to help wash the dishes and serve the food as soon as they were old enough to do it safely. And if she'd been sold into service instead...

Better make very sure no one sees her get the tip, Emily reminded herself. *They'll try to take it from her if they know she has something worth stealing.*

Frieda sat down, wincing slightly. Emily lifted an eyebrow. "What happened to you?"

"Professor Lombardi didn't appreciate my brutal candour," Frieda said. She shifted, uncomfortably. "He thought I was being cheeky."

"Ouch," Emily said. "And were you?"

Frieda made a face. "I don't think he understood the difference between pointing out the flaw in someone's work and being cheeky," she said. "He wasn't pleased."

"He probably wouldn't have been." Emily looked down at the menu. "What do you want to eat?"

"Whatever," Frieda said, looking downcast. "I just want to get away for a while."

Emily eyed her, concerned. "What's the matter?"

"Too much work, too little time," Frieda said. "And a pointless argument with Celadon, last night."

"Fourth Year is hard," Emily agreed, softly. "I wish I could tell you it gets easier."

"You were dating what's-his-face," Frieda pointed out. The *non sequitur* caught Emily by surprise. "Celadon hates my guts. And everything else about me."

Emily made a face. "Why haven't you spoken to your advisor?"

"I did." Frieda shifted, again. "That's what got me caned."

"Oh," Emily said. "Professor Lombardi is your advisor?"

She wondered, suddenly, just what had happened at that meeting. She'd assumed that Frieda had been cheeky in class, not afterwards. It wouldn't be the first time a tutor hadn't seen the funny side and assigned punishments all around. But if an advisor meeting had gone bad... she gritted her teeth, trying to decide if she should speak to Professor Lombardi. But... that would probably not end well. Frieda was supposed to learn to stick up for herself.

"Yeah," Frieda said. "He's a pain in the ass."

Emily studied the menu, choosing to ignore that comment. There were only seven dishes listed, rather than the dizzying array of choices she recalled from Earth. But then, without freezers and microwaves, restaurant owners were very limited. It was a minor miracle that they could serve as many as seven dishes. Perhaps they had a magician on staff who could cast preservation spells. Or maybe they owned a preservation chamber.

"I'll have the roast beef and potatoes," she said, passing the menu back to the serving girl. "Frieda?"

"The fish," Frieda said. "And bring me a beer too."

Emily eyed her in alarm. "A beer?"

Frieda reddened. "Maybe some juice instead," she said. "Emily?"

"Juice for me too," Emily said. She had no intention of touching alcohol if it could be avoided. It might be the safest drink in the Allied Lands—for anyone who couldn't cast spells to clean water—but it was dangerous. "Have you been drinking?"

"Just a little, when I went out with the other apprentices," Frieda said, sullenly. Her fingers played with her bracelet as she looked down, seemingly unwilling to meet Emily's eyes. "Is it that bad?"

"Yes," Emily said. She remembered her mother and shivered. There was no way she was going to let Frieda ruin her life like that. "Drink is a poor servant and a bad master."

"Hah," Frieda muttered. "Can I still eat the fish?"

"Be careful," Emily advised.

She felt embarrassed, but she kept her face impassive as the serving girl curtseyed and retreated. Emily had never been fond of eating fish away from the oceans—it was hard to be sure how fresh it was when it arrived in Dragon's Den—but she supposed there were rivers and lakes nearby. The restaurant wouldn't last long if it made a habit of poisoning students from Whitehall. Besides, food hygiene was another part of the New Learning. A cook who didn't wash his hands after going to the toilet would be drummed out of town.

"I know Fourth Year isn't easy," she said, finally. "But you do have to carry on."

She leaned forward. "Are you taking *all* the classes?"

"All of them," Frieda confirmed.

"Then maybe you should consider dropping a couple," Emily suggested. "Are you actually planning to be a healer?"

Frieda shook her head. "I want to be a combat sorceress." Her face twisted, suddenly. "No one will ever laugh at me again."

"Maybe they wouldn't," Emily said, with the private thought that no one had ever laughed at Lady Barb. "But you don't need healing to try to become a combat sorceress. You could drop it tomorrow."

"But I *like* healing," Frieda protested. "What about alchemy? Or charms?"

Emily shook her head. "You'd need them both if you wanted to be considered for an apprenticeship," she said. "I don't think anyone would want to take you if they had to drill those subjects into your head too."

"You could ask *Jade* to take me." Frieda looked up. "Or someone else you met during the war."

"Jade has other duties," Emily pointed out.

She smiled at the thought. Being Alassa's husband and Prince Consort was a full-time job, but King Randor had made Jade a Baron as well. On one hand, it *had* boosted Jade into the aristocracy so he could marry Alassa; on the other, it was something of a poisoned chalice. The Barony of Swanhaven had been rebellious. It had even killed the legally-appointed baron. Matters had calmed down now, but even so...

"You could ask Cat, I suppose," Emily added. She didn't know how many of the other apprentice combat sorcerers had thought well of her. "But he'll still want you to be qualified by the time he takes you on."

Frieda looked downcast. "I wish... I wish it was simpler. I don't even know how to cope with Celadon."

Emily sighed. "Did you ask him to break it down for you?"

"He said I should understand," Frieda said. Her voice was bitterly frustrated. "And I *don't*. I don't know how his plans work, let alone how to explain them. I'm going to fail!"

"It's only the first week," Emily said. She wondered, again, if she should have a word with Professor Lombardi. It wasn't easy to get sorcerers to work together, but it sounded as though the relationship between Frieda and Celadon had turned poisonous. "Have you considered asking to be released?"

"There's no one else searching for a new partner," Frieda said. "And if we did, we'd still be in trouble."

Emily made a face. The project wouldn't *just* be graded on their work, although that was a large part of it. They'd be graded on how well they managed to work together, blending ideas from both of them into a coherent whole. If Celadon did all the work, they'd only get half-marks at best; if Frieda left, neither of them would pass. And even if Celadon managed to salvage what was left, he'd still be marked down. There was no way the tutors would allow someone to swap partners without practically restarting the project from scratch.

"You could always threaten him," Emily pointed out. "If you leave the project, he'll be fucked."

Frieda smiled. "And not in a good way." Her face fell. "But I'll be fucked too."

Emily did the calculations in her head. Assuming that Frieda got *nothing* for the joint project—which was likely—she'd need to do *very* well in her exams to have a hope of passing Fourth Year. Failing the joint project would probably cost her the chance to proceed onwards to Fifth Year. Hell, she'd have to ally herself with a third-year student... who might wind up screwed if Frieda wasn't allowed to retake Fourth Year. It was a terrible mess.

"That's something you should bear in mind," she said. "You *do* have leverage over him too."

Frieda's face darkened. "I don't feel as though I do. What happens if he tells me to go?"

"Then you can complain to your advisor or see if you can work out an agreement with a third student." Emily gritted her teeth. Grandmaster Hasdrubal had made arrangements for *her* to work with Caleb over the summer between Third and Fourth Years, but *Gordian* wasn't likely to be so accommodating. Maybe if they picked the *right* third year... she shook her head. She didn't know any of the third years personally. "At the very least, you can spread the blame a little."

She looked down at her hands as the food arrived. The roast beef looked delicious, something she would never have been able to have on Earth. It would have been far too expensive for her family, even if her mother hadn't spent her welfare checks on drink. She still found it hard to believe how many roast animals Randor and his court could eat at a single sitting. They ate enough meat and fish—and vegetables—to feed an entire city for a month. Conspicuous consumption was part of a monarch's job, she'd been told, but it still made her feel uneasy.

"I never ate fish, back home," Frieda said, wistfully. "It was rare, and..."

"You don't have to go home now, if you don't want to," Emily pointed out. She remembered Gordian's assignment and leaned forward. "Do you *want* to go home?"

"They hated me," Frieda said. Her face darkened, suddenly. Her anger was almost a palatable force. Emily could feel her magic crawling over her skin, demanding release. "I want to go home, I *want* to make them *hurt*..."

She softened. "And I never want to see any of them again."

Emily reached out gently and pressed Frieda's hand. "You don't have to see them again, ever," she said. The sudden flash of anger had been disturbing. "You don't have to go back to Mountaintop either."

"I wouldn't." Frieda looked up at Emily. "Thank you. For everything."

"You're welcome," Emily said. The naked adoration in Frieda's eyes was enough to make her uncomfortable. Frieda had jumped ahead by leaps and bounds ever since coming to Whitehall... no, ever since meeting someone who actually wanted to help her. "You are doing well."

"I don't *feel* as though I'm doing well." Frieda rubbed her arms. "I work hard in class—and do everything Sergeant Miles tells me to do—but I still feel as though I'm drowning. How do you cope?"

Emily hesitated. *She* felt as though she were drowning too. And yet, there was no way she could stop.

"You sort out what you have to do, and then you do it," she said, finally. "And you isolate what you *don't* have to do and put it aside for later."

"I wish it was that easy," Frieda said. "I might have taken on too much."

"Then you have to admit it now, before you get too far into the new year." Emily took a sip of her juice. It tasted sharp against her tongue. "You really don't want to burn out."

Frieda looked grim. "I don't want to give up either. But Celadon..."

Emily considered—briefly—attempting to mediate. But Professor Lombardi would consider it an unjustified intrusion into his sphere. And it would be, unless she asked him first. Which would be a vote of no confidence... she shook her head, annoyed. If *she* was in his shoes, *she* would have been glad of the help.

I'm just the Head Girl, she thought. *And Gordian would not be impressed if I did his job.*

"You have faith in yourself," she said, firmly. "And make him tell you *exactly* how his diagrams work."

She ate the meal slowly, savoring every bite. Whitehall's food was very good—it was one of the techniques used to convince common-born students to forget their roots—but home-cooked food was often better. The cook had probably been told secrets from her mother which had been passed down in an unbroken line from some distant matriarch. Or maybe it was a *male* cook. She smiled at the thought. It was funny how cooking for one's wife was seen as unmanly, on the Nameless World, but cooking for business was not.

"The fish is good," Frieda said. "Why don't they cook it like this at school?"

"It's probably a matter of scale," Emily said. She'd asked the same question about healing potions. Poaching a single fish would be easy, she supposed; poaching enough fish to feed the entire student body would be a great deal harder. Brewing enough potions to sell them cheaply would be even worse. "I don't think they'd be able to do this for everyone."

"Not everyone eats fish," Frieda pointed out. "Idiots."

Emily nodded, although for different reasons. She'd never been allowed to be fussy, not on Earth. Ramen noodles, baked beans... cheap, crappy and very unhealthy food. Her fellows at school had moaned about the school dinners, but Emily had cleaned her plate and gone back for seconds every day. Maybe it *had* come from the lowest bidder. It was still better than eating nothing. The idea of refusing to eat just because someone didn't like the taste was absurd.

Frieda never got enough to eat, either, she thought. *She knows better than to waste food.*

"It doesn't matter," she said. She caught the serving girl's eye and waved. "You can come here every weekend, if you like."

"Only if you come with me," Frieda said. "There's no fun in eating alone."

Emily lifted her eyebrows. "You don't have anyone who'll go with you?"

"Not really." Frieda looked down at the table. "No one I want to spend time with, at least."

"Oh," Emily said. "What will you do when I leave?"

Frieda stared at her. "I don't... you don't have to leave."

"I wish I didn't have to leave," Emily said. It was true. Whitehall was the first place she'd considered a real home. But she had an apprenticeship in her future. "What will you do when I go?"

"I don't know," Frieda said. "But I'll think of something."

Emily paid the bill, then passed the serving girl a silver coin. It was one of the newly-minted coins from Beneficence, with a stable value. Oddly, it would actually be worth *more* if it was sold as a curiosity, rather than used for currency. But that wouldn't last as more and more minted coins entered circulation.

"It was very good," she said, as she rose. "And thank you."

"Thank you." The serving girl curtseyed formally, then picked up the plates with practiced ease. "Please come again."

Emily smiled. "We will."

She looked at Frieda. "Come on. There's still some daylight. We can go shop before we go back to the school."

"Sure," Frieda said. She still looked down. "Why not?"

Chapter Seventeen

"REMEMBER WHAT WE DISCUSSED," EMILY SAID, AS THE DOORS OF THE GREAT HALL OPENED. "And stick to the rules."

Cirroc nodded, affably. Jacqui and Cerise looked artfully blank. Emily eyed them both suspiciously—they'd been surprisingly quiet when she'd outlined the rules—and then looked away. Dozens—perhaps hundreds—of students were flooding into the Great Hall. It looked as if a third of the student body wanted to join the club. Emily couldn't help wondering, despite herself, if Gordian had a point. There was definitely a *demand* for a dueling club.

She sucked in her breath as she surveyed the students. Two-thirds of them had followed instructions and donned shirts and trousers before coming, the remainder wore everything from robes to dresses. Emily glanced at some of the latter and decided they'd come to encourage their boyfriends rather than taking part themselves, if only because anyone wealthy enough to buy a dress wouldn't have any problems buying a cheap shirt and second-hand trousers. There were families who objected to girls and women wearing male clothes, but they tended not to have magic. *Magical* families put learning ahead of almost anything else.

And what happens in Whitehall stays in Whitehall, Emily reminded herself. Magicians enjoyed a certain level of freedom from sexual mores, particularly when no one outside the school knew what they'd done. *No one is going to talk about it when they go home.*

She climbed onto the podium and looked down. Frieda stood with a group of Fourth Years, her eyes fixed on Emily. Several of the students she recalled mentoring last year stood near the front, chatting happily amongst themselves; others were strangers, students she couldn't even recall passing in the corridors. There were fewer Fifth and Sixth Years... she was oddly saddened to realize that Caleb had decided not to attend. It would have been awkward, but she could have relied on him to be sensible. She wasn't sure that was true of some of the others.

Cirroc wants to be a dueling master, she thought. *He's got every incentive to make the club work.*

The thought made her smile as she gathered her magic, drawing their attention to her like moths to a flame. Perhaps, after a month or two, she could pass most of her dueling club duties to Cirroc. He *wanted* the job, after all, and it would look *very* good on his resume. A dueling master would definitely see it as a plus, even if a combat sorcerer would have doubts. She could make a reasonable case that passing control to him would actually have beneficial effects in the long run.

Gordian might not buy that argument, she reminded herself. *And he has the final say.*

She cleared her throat. "Welcome to the first session of the dueling club," she said, using a simple spell to amplify her voice. She made a mental note to thank Sergeant Miles for teaching her the spell, even though she'd thought it useless at the time. "How many of you are actually here to duel?"

Nearly all the students—including some of the girls in dresses—held up their hands. Emily resisted the urge to roll her eyes. Perhaps someone could fight in a dress, if the whole scene was carefully choreographed by a dedicated director—but it wasn't something she would care to try for herself. Sergeant Miles would have had quite a few sharp things to say, she thought, if *she'd* turned up in a dress. He'd probably make her run laps or swim in it, just to teach her that impractical clothing could be dangerous.

They'll learn, she told herself, firmly.

"Those of you who are *not* here to duel, please go to the back of the room," she ordered, putting her thoughts aside. "We're going to run through the rules first, which I expect you to obey. Anyone caught breaking the rules will be kicked out and *not* allowed back."

A low rustle ran through the crowd. Emily found it hard to care. She didn't want any accidents—or serious injuries—on her watch. Gordian *might* just have given her the job in the hopes she'd do something to blot her copybook spectacularly. Or something might happen anyway. Even a basic duel could lead to broken bones or spell damage that proved alarmingly resistant to treatment.

"We will fight our duels until one party is unable to continue," she said. "We will *not* intentionally fight to first blood, nor will we battle to the death. Spells that might cause serious injury are *not* to be used, whatever the circumstances. You are *not* to bring wands, staffs or any other charged objects into the dueling circle. And if someone throws up their hands and surrenders, that surrender is to be honored."

She ran through the other rules, ignoring a handful of discontented mutters. It wasn't illegal, in a duel, to make someone's clothes fall off, but it was rare. A *real* duelist wouldn't take the risk, knowing that while he was casting something effectively harmless, his opponent might be trying to cast something nastier. But she'd chosen to ban such spells, along with a handful of cruel pranks. They might turn out to be valid tactics in *her* duels, making it harder for the duelists to adapt to the real world.

"Anyone who breaks these rules will be kicked out," she warned, again. "And they will not be allowed to return."

She took a breath. "We will hold the first round of the actual *contest* a week before half-term. Those of you who want to take part will have until then to put your name down for the first round. You can *withdraw* your name up until the moment I start assigning partners, at which point you will be recorded as having forfeited the match if you withdraw. The remainder of the rules can be found on the notice board outside my office or in the common rooms. Make sure you read them before you put your hat into the ring."

There was a long pause. "We won't be going outside *just* yet," she said, as she snapped her fingers. A number of circles appeared on the floor. She smiled at their astonishment, although she knew that Gordian and Professor Armstrong had set up the wards beforehand. "If you have some experience in casting spells, we will now divide you into teams which will be supervised by my assistants; if you don't, I'll teach you some of the basics now."

Cirroc stepped forward. "Everyone with experience, over here," he bellowed. "Now!"

Emily concealed a smile as the group slowly split in two. Cirroc and the others had by far the largest group, if only because anyone who'd survived a year at Whitehall *would* know a number of defensive spells. She watched them for a long moment, then turned her attention to the firsties. They stared back at her with varying degrees of awe and fear.

"I'm going to teach you the basics," she said, as she led them to a corner. "You'll need to go to the library to learn more spells and practice, always practice, to develop your skills in combat. Some spells which sound ideal are actually useless in a real duel."

She smiled, thinly. Sergeant Miles had talked about sorcerers who'd tried to be clever, only to have someone more *practical* blast them through a wall while they were trying to cast their brilliant spells. Or have his head bashed in with a brick, in one particularly humorous example. It was better to be practical than brilliant, in a fight. A brilliant man could overlook the flaws in his brilliant plan until they caught up with him.

Gathering herself, she talked them through a very basic set of spells. They were largely harmless, although she doubted that anyone without magic would agree. A magician might take being turned into a frog or frozen solid in stride, but a mundane would find the experience terrifying. *Emily* had found it terrifying, years ago. Now... it was just part of her life.

"The basic shield has some advantages over an embedded ward," she said, demonstrating the spell. A translucent disc appeared in front of her. "Its weakness, however, is that a solid blow against the magic can force you backwards or even knock you over, even if the blow isn't strong enough to break through. It also won't cover *everything*, which means that someone can still sneak a spell through your defenses."

She ran through a couple of other spells, then looked at the other groups. Older students were snapping off hexes and jinxes at each other with a great deal of enthusiasm, while Cirroc, Jacqui and Cerise moved from circle to circle, correcting technique or offering advice when it seemed to be needed. Emily couldn't help noticing that most of the students had paired off against other students in their year, although there were some exceptions. Both Frieda and Tiega were hurling hexes at students a year older than them. Emily wondered, absently, what would happen if they were paired up. They both had a desire to overcome their pasts and succeed.

"The shield keeps shattering," one of her students said. "I can't get it to solidify."

Emily dragged her attention back to him with an effort. "You're not pushing enough power into the spell," she explained. "You want to envisage it as a solid wall, not as something insubstantial."

Cirroc wandered over to join her. "It's going to be a while before we can get them outside," he said, cheerfully. "The rules haven't *quite* bedded in yet."

"I suppose," Emily agreed. Far too many students would have been taught to reach for the dangerous spells first. "Take care of the firsties for a while, okay?"

"Of course," Cirroc said.

Emily nodded, then strode off to watch the others. A number of younger students were lining up in front of Cerise to have various spells removed, ranging from a pig's snout to a full-body transformation. The remainder were dueling with more intensity; Frieda was still sparring with her opponent, even though he was a year older. What she lacked in finesse, Emily noted, she made up in raw power and determination. Blood trickled down her cheek, but she didn't seem to care. And her opponent didn't seem to be able to match her.

"Keep dodging," Jacqui called.

Emily turned to see Jacqui supervising a pair of third year students.

"You don't want to waste power on defending yourself," Jacqui added.

Emily rolled her eyes. *That* wasn't the only problem. The two students were treating the duel as a ballet, rather than an actual fight. They were both showing off, wasting magic in a manner that would have cost them the duel if their opponent had been more interested in winning than looking good. The only good thing was that one of the duelists had transfigured her dress into a pair of trousers.

She shook her head. Sergeant Miles would be furious if someone played games like that in Martial Magic—and she didn't want to *think* about Lady Barb's reaction. The two students were just playing games, bouncing spells around... they'd lose, and lose badly, in the contest, if they chose to take part. But instead...

Jacqui looked up at her. "They're having fun. And they're at least smart enough to keep moving."

Emily nodded, shortly. It *was* better to dodge a spell rather than waste magic blocking, deflecting or casting the counterspell. But *she* could envisage a dozen spells—half of them non-lethal—that could have won the duel in an instant, if her opponent didn't react with lightning speed. And yet... she sighed, inwardly. One didn't win a chess match by sweeping one's opponents to the floor, any more than a football player was allowed to win by bringing a battleaxe onto the field. Victory only counted if it was won by the rules.

But not in a real fight, Emily thought. Lady Barb had hammered that into her head, time and time again. *When everything is at stake, the rules go out the window.*

Jacqui headed off to watch another duel. Emily kept watching the first set of duelists until one of them finally managed to score a lucky hit, turning her opponent into a snail. It was all Emily could do to refrain from pointing out all the mistakes, starting with treating the entire match as a game. But she supposed it *did* teach them to cast spells in a hurry...

A thunderclap shook the room. Emily spun around, raising one hand in a casting pose, as she felt the wards *scream* in alarm. Her ears rang. Tiega stood in the center of a widening circle, Jacqui standing next to her and her opponent lying on the ground... Emily ran forward, pushing some of the younger students out of the way. Tiega's opponent looked dazed, but otherwise unhurt. Tiega herself looked torn between relief and fear.

"I slammed a force punch into his shield." Tiega glanced at Jacqui, then back at Emily. "I didn't expect *that* to happen."

"I advised her to put some more oomph into it," Jacqui said, quietly. "It helped her to win."

Emily took a firm grip on her temper. Slamming a force punch into a shield would have been a gamble, even for a far more powerful magician. If the shield *hadn't* broken, the blowback would have thrown Tiega right across the hall. But the shield had clearly broken, which had injured her opponent...

She forced herself to keep her face blank, even though she wanted to glare—and scream—at Jacqui. Her advice hadn't been *bad*, for a duel, but it had risked causing serious injury. And *that* could have been *very* bad for Tiega. Emily turned and knelt beside the stunned third year, checking for injuries. There were none, as far as she could tell. His shield had clearly absorbed or deflected *most* of the blast.

He should have angled the shield, just a little, she thought. It would have redirected the force punch rather than trying to block it outright.

She found herself torn. Part of her *wanted* to tell Tiega off, but she *hadn't* caused any serious injury... and she *had* won. And part of her wanted to tell Jacqui off instead. Even a relatively harmless spell could cause injury if it was overpowered. She'd faced necromancers who overpowered their spells. She wouldn't take anything lightly just because it was a simple first-year spell.

"*Don't* do that again," she said, finally. She wondered if she should come up with a list of forbidden spells, then dismissed it as pointless. A rules lawyer would argue that a potentially dangerous spell was legal if it wasn't on the list. She looked up at Jacqui. "See me afterwards."

Jacqui gave her a completely sweet, completely fake smile. "Of course, My Lady."

Emily eyed her for a long moment, then checked her watch. It had been over an hour since she'd thrown open the doors. Most of the younger students looked tired, unsurprisingly. They'd been expending magic at a fearsome rate. Even the older students were starting to look a little worn down. They were more used to placing demands on their magic, but most of them had never fought in a duel. Frieda's opponent looked utterly drained.

"Stop casting spells now," Emily said, using magic to boost her voice. The remaining duelists stepped back, watching their opponents nervously. "I hope you all enjoyed yourselves—" there was a brief, if tired cheer "—and you'll be glad to hear that supper will be served in the dining hall. Go there and eat something before going back to the dorms for a shower and a rest."

She paused. "The club will meet twice a week from now on," she added. Gordian had wanted *three* meetings a week, but she'd turned him down. "If you want to come again, remember the rules; if someone new comes along, they'll have to be taught the rules ahead of time. And anyone who breaks the rules will not be allowed to return."

The doors opened. She watched the duelists leave, then turned to Jacqui. "Tell me," she snapped. "What the hell were you thinking?"

Jacqui looked back at her, evenly. "I told her how to win!"

"At the risk of doing her opponent an injury." Emily allowed her anger to flow into her voice. "And at the risk of being kicked out."

Jacqui shrugged. "People are injured all the time."

Cerise snickered, behind her.

"The wards would have prevented a *serious* injury, would they not?" Jacqui asked.

Emily felt her blood boil. "And would you be prepared to bet your life on it?"

"*I* wouldn't have used a flat-edged shield to defend myself," Jacqui said, sharply. "*My* shield would have deflected her spell."

"She does have a point," Cirroc said. He sounded oddly irked. "Like it or not, there will always be a chance of someone being hurt."

"He did recover quickly," Cerise put in.

"Yes, he did," Emily conceded. "And next time, we might not be so lucky." She met Jacqui's eyes. "If you want to do something *dangerous*, you can do it on your own time," she snapped. "Here, we are trying to minimize the danger."

"Which will not prepare them for a *real* duel," Cirroc objected.

Emily felt a hot flash of anger. She didn't *know* Cirroc that well, but he *was* one of Caleb's friends. And he *did* have interests of his own. A watered-down dueling club—and contest—would be less impressive than something that could pass for a *real* duel.

But she didn't care. "We are trying to minimize the dangers," she repeated. "Do I make myself clear?"

"Of course," Jacqui said. Her voice was very sweet. "I understood you perfectly."

Chapter Eighteen

E MILY HAD HOPED, AGAINST ALL REASON, THAT THE DEMANDS ON HER TIME WOULD EASE OFF a little as days turned into weeks. Gordian and the other tutors couldn't *keep* discovering new things she had to do, could they? But it seemed that every day brought a new problem needing the Head Girl's personal attention, from homesick firsties to older students in detention who needed to be supervised. There was barely any time for Emily to relax, let alone go walking with Frieda or talk to her friends through the chat parchments. Her life seemed to have devolved into an endless series of classes, duties and naps... naps that were often interrupted by the *next* urgent matter. If Gordian was *trying* to keep her busy and out of trouble, she reflected, she had to admit he was succeeding. She had hardly any time to herself.

"I wish we'd been able to meet earlier," she said to Caleb. It was the first time they'd been together for two weeks. They still had a private workroom for their project, but they hadn't been able to use it. Or at least *she* hadn't been able to use it. "I just keep getting overloaded."

"It wasn't your fault." Caleb looked rueful. Every time they'd planned a review session, something had come up. "I hear you're a soft touch, for a Head Girl."

Emily gave him a sharp look. "Compared to who?"

"Apparently, Aloha was a great deal stricter." Caleb grinned at her. "And Roberson would send younger students to the Warden if they even looked at him funny. Or thrash them himself, when he was in a foul mood."

"Bastard," Emily said. She'd grown used to corporal punishment, but she had no intention of ever administering it herself. "Is being *soft* a bad thing?"

"It depends on how much you let people get away with." Caleb smiled, rather thinly. "My mother never let us get away with anything."

"Your mother would make a very good teacher," Emily said. She swallowed the urge to point out that Sienna wasn't a perfect mother, although she *was* far better than *Emily's* mother. "But there's a fine line between being authoritative and dictatorial."

"Or being kind and being soft." He opened his folder and held out the paperwork. "Do you want to put the project on hold, for the moment?"

Emily looked at him and felt a sudden rush of affection, mingled with concern. "Are you sure?"

Caleb looked back at her. "No," he admitted. "We're not *dependent* on completing the project—not now—but we will risk being marked down."

"Or being called quitters," Emily muttered. She'd thought that applying for extra credit was a good thing. The project *had* taught her a great deal about runic tablets *and* virtual spellware. She'd used what she'd learnt in Old Whitehall and, later, in Heart's Eye. "Can your marks survive?"

"I would need to do *very* badly indeed to risk having to retake the year," Caleb assured her, after a moment. "If, of course, they would *let* me retake the year."

Emily nodded. Caleb had *already* retaken a year, although a charitable mind would probably point out that he hadn't actually completed the year he'd had to retake. Being injured so badly he'd lost the use of his hands for several months had made it impossible to continue, after all. But Gordian might well refuse him a *second* chance to retake a year. It would be harder to argue for sympathy, this time.

"The project can be put aside for a year or two," Caleb said. "Or taken elsewhere..."

"We can work on it at Heart's Eye," Emily said. She *still* wanted to found a university, damn it. Surely, she and Caleb could put their past behind them and cooperate. "We might *need* it there."

"Along with quite a few other things," Caleb said. "Who actually *owns* the city near the school?"

Emily shrugged. She didn't *think* the city was hers. In any case, it had been abandoned years ago. The inhabitants had either been forced to flee across the desert or sacrificed by the necromancers. As far as she knew, no one had returned to the ruined city since she'd killed the necromancer. There probably wasn't anything there worth taking. The necromancers and their servants would have stripped the city bare long ago.

"I doubt anyone will return there in a hurry," she said. "The desert will make it hard for them to support themselves, at least for a while."

"I thought you said the desert would retreat," Caleb said.

"I think it will take years," Emily said. She'd restarted the nexus point, but she had no idea how long it would take for the land to come back to life. The Desert of Death was thoroughly unpleasant, choking the life out of any communities unlucky enough to be close to the edge and expanding in all directions. If that had changed... she knew it might be years before anyone saw any improvement. "We'll just have to wait and see."

Caleb nodded. "Are *you* all right with putting the project aside, for the moment?"

Emily hesitated, unsure how to answer. It *did* feel like giving up, even though they'd long-since completed the *compulsory* requirements. Most projects weren't *that* innovative, but *her* project... she'd had high hopes for the future, particularly after she'd put their work to practical use. The thought of stopping—at least for a year or two—wasn't one she wanted to contemplate. But, at the same time, she was being worked to death. She supposed she was lucky that *Caleb* was being reasonable about it.

"I think I don't have the time to do it properly," she said. Caleb could do all the work, if he wanted, but then he'd get all the credit. Frieda had the same problem, only worse. She *had* to complete her project. "Do *you* mind?"

"I can survive," Caleb said. "And the project isn't really something I can show to a potential master."

"True," Emily agreed.

Caleb reached into his folder and produced another sheet of paper. "We have to fill this in, then give it to Master Tor. I don't think *you* can approve this, can you?"

"I doubt it," Emily said. Technically, they should go to their advisers, but she'd never tried to replace Lady Barb. She hadn't *wanted* to replace Lady Barb. And Grandmaster Hasdrubal had been *Caleb's* adviser. Master Tor would be able to approve their request or point them to the person who could. "I just hope Gordian doesn't cause trouble."

"He really doesn't like you, does he?" Caleb shook his head, slowly. "Did he even make you take the oaths?"

"No," Emily said. She hadn't been too displeased—she certainly wasn't going to *ask* to take the oaths—but it was a curious omission. "Why?"

"They come with mutual obligations," Caleb reminded her. "I suspect he isn't eager to assume them himself, either."

Emily nodded. "I suppose." She took the sheet of paper and read it, quickly. There were no multiple-choice questions. Whitehall expected its students to demonstrate comprehension and contextualization at all times. Even now, they were expected to put forward a comprehensive reason *why* they should be allowed to back out of their extra credit project. "What happens if he refuses to allow us to quit?"

Caleb smiled. "We do nothing. And we get zero marks. It won't ruin our graduations unless we fail everything else too."

"Maybe," Emily said.

She looked down at the paper, wondering what it would do to her grades. She wasn't obsessed with getting the highest marks—she'd been convinced that her GPA was useless on Earth—even though high marks at Whitehall *were* a form of validation. Aloha had been both Head Girl and valedictorian. Emily doubted *she* would do so well. Melissa *might* have the best shot at the title, unless politics intervened. Caleb probably had a good shot at it too. Unless Gordian decided to hold the project against him...

"It might cost you your chance to be valedictorian," she said. "Are you sure?"

Caleb shrugged. "I don't need it."

Emily smiled, remembering—again—why she'd liked him. It was tempting to reach out and pull him to her, even though she knew it would be a mistake. She could kiss him and then... and then what? After everything they'd done together, could they just have fun? She knew it wouldn't work out...

No, she told herself, firmly.

She kept her expression blank as she tried to figure out what to write. Blaming the whole mess on Gordian was tempting, but it was unlikely to get them very far. Citing time commitments *might* work... she sighed, realizing that Gordian might hold that against her too. But he hadn't bothered to warn her that she might be made Head Girl. The thought had never crossed her mind. If she'd known it was a possibility, she might have held back on any extra credit projects until she found out the truth.

"You *could* tell them we had a messy break-up," Caleb said, a hint of pain in his words. "Or maybe just say that we have too many other commitments."

"The latter, perhaps," Emily said. Her voice sounded harder than she'd wanted. A break-up wouldn't be accepted as an excuse, particularly as they'd worked together in the latter half of Fifth Year. "And we might as well commit to finishing the project later."

"Which won't be in Whitehall," Caleb said. "I don't think he'd care."

Emily shrugged. Their project had potential. If Gordian had looked at their notes—*really* looked at them—he might see it too. Coming to think of it, he was the only person who might realize just what their project had seeded, nearly a thousand years ago. And yet, to him, their project had to be just one of many extra credit projects. It was hardly important enough for him to study.

Which will cost him, she thought. *Unless he decides to watch my work closely.*

She wrote out a brief paragraph explaining the problem, then held it out for his inspection. It wasn't much, but it would have to do. Gordian might *just* let it pass without comment. Or Master Tor might make the decision himself. Master Tor might be working for Gordian, but he wouldn't want to give up too much of his power by passing the buck to his superior all the time. It would undermine his position in the long term.

Everyone has interests of their own, she recalled Lady Barb saying, years ago. *And if you understand them, you can manipulate them.*

"I think it sounds convincing," Caleb said. "But I'm not on the Grandmaster's shit list."

"You might be," Emily said. "You"—a handful of possible words danced across her mind—"dated me. For a time."

Caleb reddened. "True."

They sat together in awkward silence. Emily wondered, again, just how Imaiqah had managed to handle her string of boyfriends. Perhaps she'd never really grown attached to any of them. She'd opened her legs—Imaiqah had been *very* frank when they'd discussed it—but she'd never opened her heart. Emily found that hard to imagine. She couldn't *kiss* someone—let alone go all the way—unless she cared about him. And she had—she did—care about Caleb.

But caring means you get hurt, when things go wrong, she told herself. *And you have to pick up the pieces afterwards.*

"I'll take the note to Master Tor," Caleb said. "Unless you want the job."

Emily shook her head. Better not to remind Master Tor that his least favorite student was the other person involved in the project. Maybe he wouldn't bother to glance at their names before approving it. Or maybe she was clutching at straws. Whatever his faults, Master Tor wasn't stupid. Gordian wouldn't have tolerated a stupid tutor.

Caleb leaned back in his chair. "Have you been spending more time with Frieda lately?"

"Not enough," Emily said. She'd barely *seen* Frieda over the last few weeks. "Why?"

"She's been acting... odd... lately." He sounded reluctant to say much of anything. "Snapping at people, tossing hexes around in the corridors... she got into a real fight with another student a couple of days ago. And she keeps glaring at me whenever she *sees* me."

"She's not having an easy time," Emily said, slowly. She didn't want to talk about Frieda with Caleb. Frieda didn't *like* Caleb—she had *never* liked Caleb—and Emily suspected the feeling was mutual. "Fourth Year isn't easy."

"That doesn't excuse her acting like a little brat," Caleb warned. "How many times can someone get in trouble before she gets kicked out?"

Emily hesitated. "I don't know."

"Me neither," Caleb said. "Emily, people are *talking*. Perhaps you should try to find more time to spend with her."

Emily's eyes narrowed. "Talking about *what*?"

"About you." Caleb glared down at the workbench. "I don't hear much, because they know we were... were lovers. But I hear whispers. People are talking about you."

"They always have," Emily said. She would have preferred to pass unnoticed. But Void had blown that possibility out of the water when he'd arranged for her to ride a *dragon* to Whitehall. "There have always been rumors..."

"These are worse," Caleb said.

He paused. "Have you even *bothered* to visit the bookstores in Dragon's Den?"

Emily shook her head, suddenly unsure if she wanted to hear what he was going to say. The bookstores in Dragon's Den were crammed with novels, blue books and little else, certainly nothing of value to a magical student. She'd read a handful of what passed for novels in the Nameless World, but most of them hadn't been very good. It would be a while before the Nameless World produced its own Tolkien, let alone Asimov, Heinlein and Susanna Clarke.

"There are books about you and some of your friends," Caleb told her. "They're worse than the ones we saw in Beneficence."

"I don't want to know," Emily said. She hadn't seen anything about *her* in Beneficence, but there had been a number of obscene semi-libels about Alassa. King Randor would have a heart attack, perhaps literally, if he ever read them. Emily didn't know who benefited by writing such crap, but she was fairly sure they didn't mean any good. "Caleb..."

"There are broadsheets questioning everything you've done," Caleb said. "And people are reading them."

Emily sighed. "There are people who believe that I used the power of love to destroy Shadye," she snapped.

"And people who believe you're a necromancer yourself," Caleb added. "Or someone who might pose a *worse* threat than all of the remaining necromancers put together."

"Madness," Emily said.

"Perhaps." He met her eyes. "Did Void *really* make you walk around naked until you learnt to materialize clothing?"

Emily felt her temper flare. "You know perfectly well..."

She caught herself. "Is that what they're saying?"

"Yes," Caleb said. "And that is one of the tamer things."

Emily sucked in her breath. In a way, it was a backhanded compliment. A skilled magician would have difficulty materializing clothes. Conjuring them into existence was hard enough, but locking them in place was harder. She doubted she could do it now, as a student in her last year at school. There was no way a *child* could do it, certainly not regularly. And yet, it was also a deliberate dig at her.

And Void, she thought.

"Fuck," she said, finally. "What else?"

Caleb hesitated.

Emily glared. "*What else?*"

"That you had affairs with Alassa, Imaiqah and Frieda," Caleb said. "That you and Jade were lovers before you gave him to Alassa. That you copied ideas from other magicians and merely claimed credit for them. That you... that you did things with King Randor to get a barony. That you..."

Emily held up a hand. "Enough."

"Someone has been spreading lies about you," Caleb said. "And it started fairly recently."

Not that recently, Emily thought. She felt her cheeks flush with embarrassment. If she had to hear one more ballad about herself, she was going to show the poor minstrel *precisely* how Shadye had died. The most popular ballads were the ones that bore no resemblance to the truth. *But if someone has been building on it...*

"Fuck," she said, numbly. She wasn't sure how to handle this new problem. "What do I do?"

Caleb shrugged. "Concentrate on doing a good job," he suggested. "And ignore everything else."

"Hah," Emily muttered.

"But try to spend some time with Frieda," Caleb advised. "She probably needs a friendly ear. And maybe a kick up the backside."

"I'll try." Emily rose, feeling irked. She could hex anyone who insulted her to her face, but it was harder to fight back against an anonymous enemy. The only thing in her favor was that it was unlikely anyone senior would pay too much attention to rumors. Anyone who was anyone had their own sources of information. "And thanks, I suppose."

"You're welcome," Caleb said.

He looked down, just for a second. "I know... I know things ended badly," he added. His voice was very quiet. "But..."

Emily felt cold. Was he going to ask her out again? And what would she say if he did?

"If you need a friendly ear, I will listen." Caleb met her eyes. "I can't promise much, but I will listen."

"Thank you," Emily said. She felt another rush of affection. Perhaps there was hope for their friendship after all. "That means a lot to me."

Chapter Nineteen

"**Y**OU'RE NOT CONCENTRATING," SAMRA SAID, SHARPLY. "FOCUS!"

Emily gritted her teeth as she looked back at the mirror. It hadn't been a pleasant couple of days. Caleb had been right. No one had said anything to her face—unsurprisingly—but she'd caught a lot of sidelong glances from younger students. Most of the Sixth Years seemed above it, yet both Jacqui and Cerise had been questioning her orders and rules in the dueling club often enough to make her want to throw in the towel and give them the job.

"It isn't easy to focus," she said. She'd looked for Frieda, but her younger friend had been nowhere to be found. There hadn't even been time to arrange a meeting during dueling club. "I need to..."

"Stop whining," Samra said. "Focus!"

Emily sighed and looked at herself in the mirror. Her reflection seemed sharper, somehow; her eyes seemed tired, oddly unfocused. She stared until she felt the image starting to blur, strange sensations spinning around her until she felt as if she was looking at her body from the outside. Her heartbeat was thumping all around her, a steady *thump-thump-thump* that kept her focused on her body. She could see herself...

... The vision blurred around her, as if she was trying to present herself in a way she could comprehend. Her mind was a library, a vast repository of knowledge; her thoughts were librarians, moving from shelf to shelf. She smiled softly, remembering the days she'd considered becoming a librarian. There weren't many people she missed, back on Earth, but the librarian in her hometown was one. She'd let Emily stay until closing hour and never asked any inconvenient questions. Emily would forgive a great deal in exchange for peace and privacy. The woman had been a gem...

... Her thoughts spun backwards and forwards, clearly visible. The oath she'd sworn to the Unseelie Court was still there, just inactive. She shivered, knowing that one day that debt would come due. She owed them... *something*. She just hoped she wouldn't have to make the choice between doing something terrible and letting the oath kill her. It was difficult, very difficult, to break a sworn oath and survive. It was impossible to do it and *know* you'd done it...

... She saw herself, clearly. The truths and the lies, things she didn't mind sharing and things she wanted to forget, the attractions she didn't want to admit, the revulsions she knew she should never have felt, all the little compromises she'd made... she *knew* herself. She stood in front of herself, mentally naked. Her thoughts hummed, suggesting little improvements... she pushed that thought aside, hard. Meddling with her own mind might be utterly disastrous. It was certainly not something to try...

Emily pulled back, opening her eyes. When had she closed them? She wasn't sure.

"That was... that was odd." She lifted a hand and studied it, just for a moment. It looked oddly translucent, as if her skin had turned to jelly. She blinked, hard. The illusion vanished. "I... I *saw* myself."

"And now you know what everyone else knows about you," Samra said. "You can't hide from yourself any longer."

Emily thought she understood, but she wasn't sure. Yes, she'd been attracted to people she shouldn't have been attracted to; yes, she'd been repulsed by people for petty reasons, reasons she was ashamed to admit...

When one is guided by emotion, one must understand the reason behind one's emotion, she thought. Lady Barb had said that, years ago. *But one must understand that an emotional response is not necessarily an invalid response.*

"I think so," she said, doubtfully. She could feel her own thoughts pulsing inside her head, as if she'd acquired a second heartbeat. It was an odd, somewhat unpleasant sensation. "Do I have to do it again?"

"Not for a while," Samra said. "Those who seek to obtain a soul magics mastery—or even practice soul magics regularly—look in the mirror every day, just to ensure that they don't lose touch with their thoughts. But you probably shouldn't do it unless you intend to use soul magic."

Emily felt oddly cheated. "Is that it? I mean... are we done?"

"No." Samra met Emily's eyes. "Do you remember what I told you about abusing the magics?"

"You said you'd kill me," Emily recalled.

"Yes." Samra made no visible move, but the door opened anyway. "Melissa has volunteered to allow you to practice on her. She feels she owes you something. And if you betray her secrets, I will kill you."

Emily looked up as Melissa strode through the door. The redhead looked as though she was trying to project an air of confidence, but even *Emily* could see she was having second—or perhaps third—thoughts. There was an... *edginess* in her movements that worried Emily more than she cared to admit. Alassa's old rival wasn't precisely a friend, perhaps, but she wasn't an enemy either.

"You will attempt to see *her* mind." Samra rose in one smooth motion. "Melissa, be seated."

Emily swallowed. "You don't have to do this..."

"Yes, she does," Samra said. "*Someone* has to do this. And Melissa volunteered."

"It's all right," Melissa said. "You'll be fine."

Emily eyed Samra darkly. The tutor stared back, silently daring Emily to say something that could—that would—be held against her. *She* could have volunteered, Emily thought, but even *that* would have been a risk. The secrets in Melissa's mind would be much less damaging than the secrets in *Samra's* mind, if Emily abused them. Emily had no doubt that Samra *would* try to kill her, if she tried to abuse what she learned, but a smart magician would know better than to assume success. It was better to limit the possible fallout than take a chance on being able to put the genie back in the bottle.

She met Melissa's eyes, feeling another flash of respect. Melissa knew the dangers, knew how much could go wrong... and she was going to do it anyway. She was going to strip naked in front of Emily—metaphorically, if not literally—and let Emily inspect her mind, knowing that far too many of her secrets might be revealed. Maybe she did owe Emily something, after everything. It was still one hell of a gutsy move.

"Thank you," she said, quietly.

"You know how to touch your own mind now," Samra said. "Focus on that sensation, then reach out and touch Melissa."

Emily wondered, sourly, if they were going to mind-meld—then closed her eyes, focusing on her own mind. The sensation came easier now, without blinding headaches. Samra had been right to tell her that practice made it better, although she still disliked it. Her thoughts were *hers*, marked as hers...

"Reach out and touch Melissa's hand," Samra ordered. "Or her forehead, if you like."

Emily opened her eyes, trying to keep in touch with her thoughts. The sensation threatened to fade as she reached towards Melissa, as if she couldn't keep her eyes open *and* feel herself think. She closed her eyes again as she touched Melissa's hand, suddenly *very* aware of Melissa's presence. Her thoughts beat against the air, thrumming so loudly that Emily was surprised she was the only person who could hear them. And yet, there was still a barrier between them. She could no more read Melissa's thoughts than Melissa could read hers.

She shivered, realizing—to the very depths of her soul—just how dangerous soul magic could be. Truth spells and potions couldn't force someone to bare themselves completely, but soul magic could. She knew she should push forward, she knew she should try to reach into Melissa's mind, but she didn't *want* to. The sense that she was doing something fundamentally wrong was growing stronger by the second.

"You're not moving," Samra said. "Glide into her thoughts."

Emily swallowed several sharp responses and concentrated. Mental communication and combat was all about how one represented themselves, at least on the mental plane. She wasn't bound by the normal limits, not when the encounter was in her mind. It was easy, suddenly, to imagine herself as a ghost, leaning forward and sliding into Melissa's mind...

... Her thoughts were suddenly very loud, a tangled web of words, feelings and factoids that battered against Emily's mind. She pulled back hastily, gritting her teeth as a torrent of images lanced into her mind: Fulvia casting a spell, a grim-faced Caelian telling her that she'd have to get married, her own face wiped clean of everything save her eyes... Markus, his eyes bright with lust as he walked towards her...

Emily pulled back, hard. The memory had been so strong that she wasn't sure it was Melissa's, rather than hers. She'd never slept with Markus—she *knew* she'd never slept with Markus—and yet it was hard to escape the impression that she *had*. Melissa's embarrassment boiled around her, the emotions driving other memories towards Emily's mind. Markus and Melissa had clearly worked their way through every sexual position they knew and then invented some more.

"Concentrate," Samra said. "I wish you to find a particular thought."

Emily braced herself, then glided back into Melissa's thoughts. Another torrent of images roared at her, each one carrying its own baggage. Fulvia staring down at a tiny Melissa, terrifying her; an older boy, screaming in pain... Melissa waking up in pain, only to feel relief—even joy—when she discovered the blood on the sheets. A ceremony had followed, a welcoming into womanhood. Emily couldn't help feeling a flicker of envy. *Her* first period had been a nightmare. She'd had to go to the school nurse for advice.

The roaring grew louder. Images blurred together; Alassa and Imaiqah, Jacqui and Cerise, Markus... Emily fought to hold on to something—anything—but it was like being caught in a tidal wave. She couldn't keep her thoughts together any longer...

Something slapped her face, hard. Emily staggered, breaking contact. Her head swam, her body falling... she caught herself, somehow, before she fell out of the chair. Melissa was suddenly gone, as if she'd never been there. Emily had to peer through suddenly sore eyes to make sure that Melissa was still alive. Her jaw ached, hard. She hadn't felt so sore since someone had slapped her...

Someone *had* slapped her.

"You lost yourself," Samra said. "A few minutes more and you might have been lost forever."

Emily touched her cheek. "You slapped me?"

"I had to get you back," Samra said. She didn't sound repentant. "Believe me, the alternatives were worse."

"She slapped me too, once or twice," Melissa said. She sounded tired. "I'm sorry you had to see everything."

Emily cringed, mentally. She'd seen... too much. Even now, even after being yanked out of Melissa's mind, it was hard to escape the sense that it had been *her* who'd made love to Markus. Or had been hexed by Fulvia... she shuddered, knowing she could no longer dislike Melissa. She'd been through her own particular brand of hell.

"I won't tell anyone," she said. She wondered just how much strength it must have taken for Melissa to sit there and let Emily ransack her mind. There hadn't been any attempt to drive Emily out, let alone engage in mind-to-mind combat. Emily wasn't sure she could have done it, even knowing that her secrets would go no further. "You have my word."

"Markus and I are married," Melissa said. "People *do* understand we're not playing with wands."

Emily nodded. She didn't know what the saying meant—something akin to playing doctor, she assumed—but she understood. And yet, she'd learnt far more about Markus and Melissa's sex life than she'd ever wanted to learn. Everyone would know they were sleeping together, but... but they wouldn't know the details. And they didn't need to know the details.

"You'll have to do it again," Samra said. "You didn't manage to even *start* looking for that particular thought."

Emily gave her a sharp look. "You could have told me *what* thought."

Samra smiled, mischievously. "And you didn't think of trying to extract it from Melissa's mind?"

"No," Emily said.

She looked down at the floor, feeling guilty. She'd been *told* what she'd had to do, but *nothing* she'd been told had come close to the truth. Perhaps there was no *way* to prepare her for soul magic, save by experimenting under controlled conditions. Nothing Samra could have said would have conveyed the true intensity of the experience. Her words might just have made Emily a little complacent. *That* would have been disastrous.

"I don't want to do this again," she said.

Samra slapped her hand against the chair. "You don't have a choice," she snarled. Her sudden anger made Emily recoil in shock. "You've been given these classes, over my strong objections, even though you refused to take the oaths! You don't get to withdraw now you've discovered that it isn't as easy as it looks!"

Melissa touched Emily's arm. "It's alright," she said. "I really don't mind."

Madness, Emily thought.

"You'll be back here in two days for our *next* session," Samra said, firmly. "And I shall expect a much better performance."

She rose. "Pull yourself together, then get out," she ordered. "Melissa, see me in an hour. I need to discuss your research paper with you."

Melissa winced. "Yes, Mistress."

Emily wilted. Her bones suddenly seemed to be made of jelly. "I'm sorry," she mumbled, quietly. "I..."

"I knew what I was agreeing to." Melissa made a face. "Just wait until you try to touch minds with a boy."

"I don't want to," Emily said. She knew she sounded petulant, but she didn't really care. "I saw too much of you..."

"You'll see worse," Melissa said. "They had me on walkabout during the hols, Emily. I saw... I saw nightmares."

Emily believed her. *She'd* seen all sorts of unpleasant sights on *her* walkabout. Men who'd been injured, but unable to afford medical attention; women and children who'd been beaten or abused by their husbands or parents, yet unable to run. A genuine healer-in-training would probably see worse. No, there was no *probably* about it. She touched the bracelet on her wrist, remembering the horrors Mother Holly had unleashed. Maybe Melissa hadn't encountered a necromancer. She would still have seen far too much of man's inhumanity to man.

"Thank you," she said. She knew she *should* be grateful. It just felt far too much like having someone thank her for hurting them. "What... what was that ceremony I saw?"

Melissa frowned. She didn't seem to wonder *which* ceremony. "Didn't your mother ever arrange one for you?"

Emily shook her head, wordlessly.

"It was the moment I became a woman." Melissa smiled, ruefully. "My mother and the other women held a ceremony, welcoming me to womanhood. I was no longer a child, but a young woman of House Ashworth. I was seated at the adult table and..."

Her face darkened. "Fulvia wasn't pleased, I think. She should have been delighted, but she wasn't. She was brooding all through the ceremony she was supposed to lead. I never understood why."

Emily frowned. She didn't pretend to understand how the complex ties of blood and magic bound magical families together—or what had happened to allow House Ashfall to break off from House Ashworth—but she thought she understood some of the implications. Melissa's rise to womanhood meant that she was in line to inherit the family—or she had been, before she'd been disowned. Given time, Melissa might have challenged Fulvia's control. Perhaps that was why Fulvia had sought to marry her off as soon as possible.

And then dispose of Melissa, once she produced an heir, Emily thought. Gaius had betrayed the Allied Lands. She had no doubt he would have betrayed Melissa too. *Fulvia's position would be secure.*

"Just be glad she's out of your life," Emily said. It was unlikely Melissa and Fulvia would cross paths again, now that Melissa had been disowned. "Have you heard anything about her?"

"No one talks to me, these days." Melissa looked wistful, just for a second. "I don't hear much from home. The last I heard, the witch had vanished. Maybe she dropped dead in a ditch somewhere."

Too much to hope for, Emily thought. Fulvia was old, but she was also powerful. She certainly had enough magic to rejuvenate herself, if she wished. A change in face, a change in name... it wasn't as if Fulvia would have any trouble earning money, if she didn't have something stashed away for a rainy day. *Someone like that wouldn't die so easily.*

Melissa rose. "I would suggest, if I were a healer, that you use the mirror again before you leave. If not... well, most of my memories should fade from your mind fairly quickly, before they really take root. The handful that remain shouldn't stand up to examination. You *weren't* making love to Markus and you know it."

Emily covered her face. "I'm sorry..."

"A couple of years ago, I would have been utterly humiliated," Melissa said. "Now... well, I understood what I was agreeing to when I volunteered. And... well, I have been inside other minds too, when I was being trained. You'll see others too."

She winked. "Just remember not to pry *too* much. Some memories are *very* disconcerting."

"They're *all* disconcerting," Emily said.

"You and I have a lot in common," Melissa said, briskly. She winked. "Wait until you try to read someone who has something different between his legs."

Emily flushed, helplessly.

Chapter Twenty

"MY FAMILY WROTE TO ME TO ASK IF THE RUMORS WERE TRUE," CABIRIA SAID. "I ASSURED them that you were *not* in the habit of using dark magic."

"Thank you," Emily said. She'd been reluctant to accept Cabiria and the Gorgon's offer of a study date in the library, but she had to admit it was a welcome change. The study room was private, yet roomy enough to allow all three of them to work without getting in each other's way. She looked at the Gorgon. "Did *you* hear any rumors?"

"My people do not pay attention to rumors," the Gorgon said, primly. Her snakes hissed in unison. "And nor should yours."

"My people *do* pay attention to rumors." Cabiria shot Emily a reassuring look. "But I like to think that my family listened to me."

Emily sighed. She'd heard too much over the last few days. Rumors spreading through the school, passed from student to student with no discernible origin point. She'd even confiscated a handful of printed pamphlets that made a whole series of unsubstantiated and thoroughly unpleasant allegations concerning her and her friends. One had outright accused her of plotting to declare herself the empress of mankind. No one with any common sense should have believed them, but most of the charges were maddeningly difficult to disprove.

If I had time, she thought. *And I don't.*

She'd never really cared about popularity, even at Whitehall. Her early life had left her with no taste for being part of the in-crowd. And yet, the constant rumors were slowly wearing her down. No one should believe them, yet... the stories were still spreading. Someone was throwing mud at her, hoping that some of it would stick. It was frustrating. She was starting to wonder if she should take the whole matter to Gordian and ask for help. He might not like her, but she *was* Head Girl. It wouldn't do Whitehall any good if her reputation was tarnished so badly.

"Don't worry about it," Cabiria said. "Do you think you're the first person to become the focus of disgusting rumors?"

"No," Emily said. Cabiria *had* been the focus of rumors too, although hers hadn't been *quite* so nasty. "But this feels *personal*."

"It probably is," the Gorgon said. "Who benefits from smearing you so badly?"

Emily shrugged. The necromancers gained, but... it was unlikely they would have thought of launching a smear campaign. Most of them could barely comprehend anything above brute force, although Dua Kepala had proven himself depressingly subtle. But then, his technique for balancing madness with power was unique, as far as she knew. None of the other necromancers had shown such relative sanity.

Her lips twitched. *Gaius* would have thought of it, she was sure. He'd tried to spike her drink in camp, hoping to watch her making a fool—or worse—of herself. *He* would have been alive to the possibilities of smearing her name. But Gaius and his sworn companions were dead. Who *else* benefited?

She tossed the possibilities over and over in her head. King Randor might not be her greatest fan—not now—but he wouldn't launch a smear campaign. And his enemies would be leery of slandering her. They knew *Emily* had been the one who'd introduced the New Learning and liberalized government in Cockatrice. Emily knew she was popular there, even if she also knew not to take it too seriously. It would have been difficult to be *worse* than the previous baron. He'd spent so much time deflowering young maidens, with or without their permission, that she honestly wondered when he'd found the time to plot a coup.

And someone from Zangaria wouldn't be able to get papers and rumors into the school, she thought. Perhaps broadsheets from Zangaria would reach Dragon's Den—she was fairly sure some of them did, even though they were probably out of date—but there would be no way to guarantee getting them to Whitehall. *They'd need someone in the magical community to help.*

She closed her eyes for a long moment. Gordian? It seemed unlikely. He might not like her, but... she *was* Head Girl. Her disgrace would reflect badly on him. But how many enemies did she have? Aurelius was dead. Zed had ample reason to forget his petty grudge against her. He wouldn't let Mountaintop's staff seek revenge, either. Master Highland? She knew she had something he wanted, but smearing her name was an odd way to *get* it. Fulvia? No one had seen anything of her since her fall from grace. Perhaps she was the most likely suspect...

A memory flashed across her mind, bringing with it a wave of shame and fear that wasn't hers. Fulvia had never beaten her children and grandchildren. She'd hexed them, instead. *Melissa* had been hexed... Emily swallowed, banishing the memory as best as she could. No *wonder* Melissa had been so determined to escape the vindictive old crone, even if it meant being disowned by the rest of her family.

Or it could be someone I don't know, she thought. Someone who didn't want to reveal himself, someone who didn't want to confront her directly... perhaps someone who wanted to weaken or discredit her. *I've put a lot of noses out of joint.*

Cabiria cleared her throat. "My family asked if I'd like to invite you to the estate," she said, seriously. "What *are* your summer plans?"

Emily shrugged. Void had offered her an apprenticeship. She'd always assumed she'd go straight to him after graduation, although she hadn't thought about it *that* much. Merely *getting* to graduation was starting to look difficult. Maybe she'd visit her friends in Zangaria, if she could clear it with King Randor. Or maybe just go to bed for a week.

Matters in Zangaria are far from settled, she thought, recalling Alassa's last letter. *King Randor won't want me to visit until things have calmed down a little.*

"I have no solid plans," she said. "Aren't *you* aiming for an apprenticeship?"

"It depends on my marks." Cabiria sighed. "I don't know if any master will take me, not after..."

"You'd think they'd be curious," Emily said. "How many children are born without magic?"

"Millions," Cabiria said. Her face was suddenly very cold. "But they're never born to magical families."

Emily nodded. Magic was *strong*. The child of a magician would be a magician himself. It was one of the reasons so many people had assumed that Void had fathered her. The magic might weaken, but it didn't vanish. And yet, Cabiria had been born without magic. She'd been a freak until—somehow—she'd developed magic. No one was quite sure why. Cabiria's uncle had done something to help her, but what? No one knew that either.

"I'll think about coming," she said. "But I don't know *what* will happen after graduation."

"You'll be fine." the Gorgon smiled, wanly. "You could always visit the Gorgon Lands."

"I thought they discouraged outsiders," Emily said.

"My clan would welcome you," the Gorgon said. "And the other clans would be *painfully* polite."

Cabiria giggled. "That bad, huh?"

"Worse," the Gorgon said. "They'd be *very* painfully polite."

Emily smiled, despite herself. *Painful* politeness was a way of saying that someone wasn't welcome, without actually coming out and *saying* that someone wasn't welcome. There was no room, on the face of it, for someone on the receiving end to take offense, although she doubted it worked out *quite* so well in practice. The aristocracy of Zangaria had turned politeness into a weapon of social war.

"Perhaps," she said. She *was* curious. She'd never been to the Gorgon Lands. She had always planned to explore more of the Nameless World—there was no reason *she* had to stay still, even if most people rarely went beyond the next village or two—and it was something she could do over the summer, if Void didn't want her immediately. "But we'll have to talk about it after graduation."

"Come see us first," Cabiria said. "My cousins would like to meet you."

"Would these be your *handsome* and *unattached* cousins?" The Gorgon winked at Emily. "I thought they were already engaged to be married."

Cabiria had the grace to blush. "I've got five cousins," she clarified. "Only two of them are currently engaged."

"And the other three want to meet Emily," the Gorgon teased. "My, oh my. *Whatever* could they want?"

Emily blushed. "I can't imagine."

She shook her head as Cabiria giggled. There was a part of her that would *like* a new relationship, but one with fewer strings attached. Things wouldn't have grown so... sticky... with Caleb if he hadn't opened a formal courtship. Meeting Cabiria's cousins, after graduation, wouldn't be quite the same as dating someone in Whitehall. She didn't think they'd be allowed to date in peace...

Particularly as I haven't met them, she thought, wryly. She was not rushing into another courtship. *They might be sweet on the outside, but monstrous on the inside.*

"My parents also want to meet you," Cabiria said. "They want to discuss magical theory and other matters."

Emily frowned. "What *sort* of magical theory?"

"They didn't say," Cabiria told her.

"Oh," Emily said.

Her thoughts raced. What did Cabiria's parents know? Did they know anything? Her innovations, as far as anyone knew, were strictly mundane. She'd never told anyone, save for Lady Barb, about the batteries or the nuke-spell. Unless... had they caught wind of the virtual spellware? It was possible they had obtained a copy of Caleb's original proposal, written while Emily had been in Second Year. Gordian might even have sent them a copy of the updated proposal...

Or maybe they just want to introduce me to their nephews, she thought. *Who knows what...?*

She looked up as someone tapped on the door, sharply. Cabiria made an odd noise. They were Sixth Years, senior students... no one could turf them out of a study room. The door opened a minute later, revealing Jacqui. She seemed oddly amused.

"I caught an older student pranking younger students," she said, her eyes alight with malice. "I thought the Head Girl should take care of it personally."

Emily rose, slowly. *No one* played pranks in the library. The librarians took a dim view of anything that interfered with studies. Even speaking too loudly could result in punishment—or, at worst, a ban that made it impossible for a student to complete the year. Whatever had happened, it had happened outside the library. And that meant...

Her eyes narrowed. Jacqui wasn't a tattletale. Whitehall disapproved of tattletales, not when students were expected to overcome their problems on their own. And Jacqui probably wouldn't give a damn if younger students were pranking each other, even if it was technically forbidden. It wasn't her job to keep the younger students in line.

"They're in the lower corridor, by the statue of Terrance the Tamer," Jacqui added. "You'd better go before they manage to escape."

Emily gave her a sharp look and then strode out of the study room. She could feel Jacqui's eyes on her back as she walked through the door and down the stairs, heading straight for the statue. Ice was starting to congeal in her chest, a presentiment of disaster. The wards were flickering alerts, trying to summon the nearest tutor. Emily wondered, sourly, why someone hadn't beaten her to the scene. Jacqui must have run to the library, just to find Emily. And yet, she hadn't *looked* to be out of breath...

Emily rounded the corner and stopped, dead. Frieda stood there, frozen by magic. Two younger students—both Second Years, judging by their robes—were also frozen. Emily felt a flicker of relief as she realized that neither of them were her mentees, then winced as she saw the frogs—also frozen—on the floor. She closed her eyes for a moment, trying to sense the different magical signatures. Jacqui had laid down an impressively comprehensive freezing spell, but it was Frieda who'd cast the other spells. And she'd cast them on Second Years...

Shit, Emily thought, numbly.

Jacqui's spell snapped. Frieda stumbled forward, then collapsed to the floor as her muscles cramped violently. The others fell too, gasping in pain. Jacqui had used a cruel spell, part of Emily's mind noted. She'd locked up their muscles rather than simply freezing them in place. It wasn't an easy spell to break, but still... Frieda *should* have been able to break it before Emily arrived. Unless...

"She turned them into frogs," one of the younger students cried. "She..."

Emily glanced at Frieda, who was pulling herself up into a sitting position, then looked at the frogs. They stared back at her, beseechingly. Emily sighed as she cast the counterspell, wondering if she was doing them any favors. But Frieda had used a transfiguration spell that was cunningly designed to be hard to remove, from the inside. It wasn't quite fixed in place—something that would have landed Frieda in *real* trouble—but neither of the victims could escape. Emily groaned as they returned to human form. They, *too*, were Second Years.

She gazed at Frieda, who looked back at her defiantly. What had happened?

"Go back to your dorms," Emily ordered the Second Years. She glanced at her watch. "Stay there until dinner, then go eat."

"But..."

"Go," she repeated. "Now."

She looked at Frieda. "Come with me."

The wards pulsed against her mind as she led Frieda into a nearby classroom. They hadn't recorded *everything* that had happened, merely the brief exchange of magic. Emily was torn between relief—the staff couldn't monitor their words—and concern. Whatever had happened, it looked bad for Frieda. She was a Fourth Year. Picking on Second Years was beneath her. It would also land her in hot water if anyone else found out.

Jacqui did find out, Emily thought. *What happened?*

She cast a handful of privacy wards, then met Frieda's eyes. "What happened?"

"They were talking about you," Frieda said. "One of them said..."

Emily winced as Frieda's voice trailed off. Of *course* one of them had mouthed off. Frieda wasn't the sort of person to let an insult go by, not given her upbringing. And it hadn't even been an insult about Frieda herself.

Frieda looked down. "They deserved it."

"You're two years older than them," Emily pointed out, carefully. It was hard to reprimand Frieda. She was a *friend*. "They shouldn't stand a chance against you."

"They're all in the dueling club," Frieda said, tartly.

"Which is meaningless," Emily countered. "You know as well as I do that the older students dominate the arena."

"I kicked what's-his-name's ass," Frieda snapped.

"That's because he got careless." Emily cleared her throat. "Playing freeze tag with younger students is one thing. Hexing them in the corridors is quite another."

"They insulted you," Frieda insisted, stubbornly. "I taught them a lesson."

"Perhaps not the right lesson." Emily gritted her teeth. There had been times, back on Earth, when she would have sold her soul for the power to silence her critics. The rational side of her mind pointed out that it wouldn't have gained her anything, but she had to admit that it would have felt good. "Frieda, you can't go picking on younger students. You *know* that!"

Frieda wilted. "Are you really that angry at me?"

Emily sighed. "What's the problem? What's the *real* problem?"

"I don't understand it." Frieda stamped her foot on the floor, suddenly looking younger. Much younger. "Everything he says. I don't understand it!"

"Celadon," Emily realized. The frustration in her friend's tone was striking. "Is he not trying to explain things to you?"

"He *says* he's trying." Frieda started to pace, one hand playing with the bracelet on her wrist. "But I don't understand!"

She spun around, her plaits dancing through the air. "I don't understand and we're running out of time and..."

Emily forced herself to think. Frieda and Celadon would be required to make a presentation to the staff, either during or after half-term. If Frieda *really* didn't understand what she was talking about, it would become obvious very quickly. Was Celadon deliberately sabotaging his own project? That would be insane. He'd lose marks too... at best, he'd scrape through the year. And at worst, he'd be denied the chance to repeat the year.

She held up a hand. "Tell you what," she said. "Half-term is in two weeks. I should have some free time over the holidays. We'll sit down together and go through the project together. If *I* can't make head or tails of it, we'll go to your supervisor and request that you be assigned a new partner."

Frieda shot her a worshipful look. "That would be *great!*"

"Maybe," Emily said, dryly. Professor Lombardi would not be pleased. There was a fine line between assisting and doing the work and she had a feeling she might be about to cross it. "But you can't go around assaulting younger students."

"They deserved it," Frieda said. "Emily, they said..."

"It doesn't matter what they said," Emily told her, knowing that Frieda wouldn't understand. She'd grown up in a society where insults *had* to be punished. "I don't want you to hex them anymore."

"Oh." Frieda looked down. Her voice was suddenly very quiet. "Are you going to punish me?"

Emily hesitated. "No," she said. Frieda was going through a bad patch. And Jacqui knew Frieda had been hexing younger students. "But you should probably keep that to yourself."

"I'll scream every time I sit down," Frieda promised.

"I think that might be overdoing it," Emily said. "Just try to look a little subdued."

Chapter Twenty-One

"IT'S BEEN AN INTERESTING SIX WEEKS." GORDIAN SIPPED HIS KAVA, THOUGHTFULLY. "Would you not agree?"

Emily kept her face expressionless. Gordian had summoned her two days after the incident with Frieda, inviting her to his private chambers and offering her a drink. She supposed that meant she wasn't in trouble, although she had no idea what it *did* mean. Gordian could hardly be blind to the rumors flowing around the school. He might choose to consider them beneath his dignity, but he'd still be aware of them.

Aloha didn't have these problems, Emily thought, resentfully. The badge on her chest felt heavy. She wondered, tiredly, just how bad it would be if she resigned. Cirroc was clever, handsome and popular. She was sure he'd be chosen in her place. *If I'd known I was going to be elected...*

"Yes," she said, finally. "I've been very busy with my studies."

Gordian nodded, slowly. "And running the dueling club and everything else a Head Girl has to do. I trust you've been finding it an interesting insight into life as a tutor?"

Emily tried, hard, not to show any reaction. "Do tutors have to do *everything?*"

"No," Gordian said. "But they *do* have to mark essays as well as patrol the corridors, supervise detentions and whatever other duties I see fit to assign."

He leaned back in his chair, lifting his head until he was peering down his nose at her. "Which leads neatly to another point," he added, dryly. "Why *didn't* you punish Frieda for bullying younger students?"

Emily blinked in surprise. She hadn't expected *that* question. "I told her off," she said, carefully. She wondered, suddenly, if Jacqui had tattled on her. Or if Gordian had been monitoring Frieda for reasons of his own. Or... maybe she was just being paranoid. But *someone* had started a smear campaign against her. Gordian might be trying to keep an eye on Emily as well as her closest friends. "I believed that was enough punishment."

"I'm sure Frieda was scared straight by your telling-off," Gordian said, his tone as dry as dust. "You have an *obligation* to punish students for breaking the rules. Tell me... would you have *told off* another student? Or would you have sent them to the Warden? Or administered the punishment yourself?"

"I believe I would have handled the matter as I saw fit," Emily said. She had to fight to keep her hands from shaking. She'd stumbled into... something. "I don't believe there's a single way to handle *all* such incidents."

"And yet you sent a trio of bullies to face the Warden only a few short weeks ago," Gordian said. His voice suddenly hardened. "Whitehall's rules work, Lady Emily, because they are enforced evenly. We do not pretend to care if someone comes from the very highest levels in society or if they were born in a pigsty. We treat them all equally. Frieda's crime was far worse than those idiotic firsties, yet you saw fit to give her a lesser punishment. Why?"

Emily gritted her teeth as she tried to think of an answer. The hell of it, she suspected, was that there *wasn't* a good answer. Frieda had been guilty of a serious offense. There was no way around it. And *Emily* had barely done anything about it. Gordian was right. Her telling off—which had been nowhere near as unpleasant as the lectures Emily had endured from Lady Barb or Sergeant Miles—wasn't a real punishment.

"I believed that other factors were involved," she said. "I..."

"And none of those factors matter," Gordian said, flatly. "What matters is that you saw fit to let her get away with it."

"I didn't," Emily said.

Gordian snorted. "A matter of opinion. And *everyone's* opinion is that you showed favor to your friend."

Emily felt her temper begin to crack. "What would *you* have done?"

"*I* would have sent her to the Warden," Gordian said. "And if *I* had felt unprepared to handle it, I would have turned the matter over to a tutor."

"No tutor showed up," Emily said, icily. She told herself, firmly, to keep her temper under control. "Where were they?"

"Outside, mostly." Gordian cocked his head. "You're making excuses for your failure, Lady Emily."

Emily forced herself to stare back at him, as evenly as she could. Was she about to be dismissed from her post? It would be something of a relief. She wouldn't mourn the office, not when it came with duties she was ill-prepared to handle. Cirroc or Melissa or someone who actually *wanted* the job could have it. She could finish her studies and graduate in peace.

Gordian reached into a desk drawer and produced a large scroll. "Have you ever seen one of these before?"

"No, sir," Emily said. She felt a flash of disappointment. Was she *not* being dismissed? "I... I don't think so."

"It's a permanent record." Gordian touched his hand to the wax seal, his lips moving soundlessly as he murmured a charm. Emily couldn't make out the words, but the wax seal dropped off a second later and fell into Gordian's hand. "We rarely show them to anyone but the parents or guardians of the student in question. Eventually, they become a matter of public record."

Emily frowned. She'd assumed she had a permanent record, but she'd never seen it. Had Void? Or any of the other tutors? A spy in Whitehall might be able to read it... she shrugged, dismissing the thought. Her permanent record wouldn't include anything that would make a reader raise their eyebrows. She doubted Gordian had written anything about Emily's influence over the wards where someone else might see it.

"This is your friend's record." Gordian removed a pair of nasty-looking hexes from the scroll, then held it out to Emily. "Have a look."

Emily hesitated. "Am I *allowed* to look?"

"I am authorized to share these with anyone, if I see fit," Gordian said. "And besides, you *are* listed as one of Frieda's guardians."

"I am?"

"Yes." Gordian pushed the scroll towards her. "You're listed as an unattached guardian."

Emily took the scroll and opened it, slowly. She wasn't sure she *wanted* to look. It felt as though she was invading Frieda's privacy, even though she knew Gordian and the other tutors could—and did—read the scroll whenever they liked. Her fingers felt oddly uncertain as she placed the scroll on the table, skimming the first set of lines. Someone—Lady Barb or Grandmaster Hasdrubal—had definitely listed Emily as one of Frieda's guardians.

Third in line, after Lady Barb and Sergeant Miles, she mused. Lady Barb had never mentioned being Frieda's guardian. Emily had never considered the possibility. But *someone* would have had to take on the role, after Frieda left Mountaintop. It was more of a surprise that *Emily* had been included on the list. Baroness of Cockatrice or not, the magical community wouldn't see her as an adult until she left school. *That will make life interesting, if I ever have to use the title.*

She looked up. "Sir... what do you want me to see?"

"The records for her Fourth Year," Gordian said. "You might find them... interesting."

Emily eyed him suspiciously, then opened the scroll still further. Frieda had done well in her third year, she noted, but she'd been marked down repeatedly for her theoretical work. Her Fourth Year—only six weeks into the year—was marred by over thirty disciplinary notes, including nine trips to the Warden. Emily swallowed, hard, as the meaning dawned on her.

"Frieda's behavior has gone downhill," Gordian said, putting it into words. "*Sharply* downhill, I might add. There is no record of someone else earning *quite* so many thrashings in such a short space of time. The vast majority of students don't earn so many thrashings in all *six* years. Not handing in her homework, talking back to her tutors, fighting with her classmates... she's *really* gone downhill."

Emily felt her heart sink. "I..."

"There is a very good chance that her marks will fall below acceptable levels by the time we reach the second half-term," Gordian said, his voice carefully controlled. "I have reviewed some of her work personally. It has a number of mistakes that she should have been able to avoid, even as a younger student. I am not impressed."

"I didn't know." Emily swallowed, hard. "What... what happens if her marks stay low?"

"It would depend," Gordian said. "If there was a good chance that she wouldn't be able to complete the year, regardless of her performance on the exams, she would normally be offered a chance to retake the year. But her behavior has been so poor over the last few weeks that I would hesitate to allow it."

"She... she wasn't that bad with me," Emily said. "I..."

But Frieda hexed a pair of younger students, her thoughts pointed out. *And she's still unable to come to grips with her joint project.*

"That is not my concern," Gordian said. "What *should* be your concern is that you are... associated... with Frieda."

"She's my friend," Emily snapped.

"And people judge you by the friends you keep." Gordian tapped the scroll, meaningfully. "*This* friend is on a rapid course towards expulsion, Lady Emily. And she might bring you down too. You do *not* want people thinking you treat her any differently from anyone else."

"Because that would be *so* uncommon here," Emily snarled. She took a long breath, forcing herself to calm down. "I don't know how to handle it."

"I suggest that you tell her to shape up before it's too late," Gordian said. "And if she doesn't, I would advise you to dump her. Her behavior reflects on you. If she's bad, she'll make you look bad too."

"I'm not going to dump her," Emily said.

"Then she might bring you down with her too." Gordian took the scroll and started to roll it up. "We generally discourage friendships between students in different years, Lady Emily. This is why."

Emily fought down a couple of nasty responses. She and Caleb were friends—and they'd been lovers—but they'd been in the same year, when they'd met. Frieda was two years younger than Emily, a gap that the vast majority of the student body would consider insurmountable. And yet, no one had said anything when Emily had spent time with Jade, back in her first year...

We were in Martial Magic together, she reminded herself. *And the sergeants would have taken a dim view of any hanky-panky.*

"I'll talk to her about it," she said. "But..."

"It isn't uncommon for the less... academically-inclined students to have problems as they move up in years," Gordian said. "That is understandable. Sometimes, repeating a year is the best thing for them. But I cannot tolerate bad behavior on this scale. Frieda is not just hurting herself, Emily. She's hurting others."

"I understand," Emily said.

"I would advise you to have nothing more to do with her," Gordian said. "But you wouldn't listen, would you?"

Emily felt a hot flash of anger. "Are you always so... so callous?"

"I'm old enough to know that some people are beyond help," Gordian said. "And such people are always going to drag you down, if you let them."

He put the scroll back in the drawer, then slammed it closed. "I have heard from the Dueling League," he added. "They'll be sending observers to the first round."

"Oh." Emily wasn't ready to pretend enthusiasm. Maybe, next term, she could dump the club on Cirroc. "Did they accept the planned rules?"

"For the moment," Gordian said. "They'll want us to change them later, I think. Our students will acquire bad habits."

"*More* bad habits," Emily said, before she could stop herself.

Gordian gave her a sharp look. "You feel that we are teaching students bad habits?"

"Dueling and fighting are two very different things," Emily said, unwilling to back down from the unspoken challenge. "The club isn't preparing students to fight."

"But it *is* laying the groundwork for our return to the interschool dueling contests," Gordian said. "In times such as these, Emily, it is important for the schools to work together. *Your* position as dueling champion could have opened many doors, if we had a position in the league."

"Until I lost it," Emily said.

"It would have been enough," Gordian said.

Emily shrugged, expressively. It hadn't been *easy* to hold back, when she'd been dueling with Casper. Giving him an opening, even a tiny one, had been harder. Everything she'd been taught had called for drawing on all of her power and pounding him into the ground, to kill him before he killed her. She'd run a colossal risk just to let him hold the title for a few wonderful days.

And he was killed in combat, she thought. *He never had to defend his title in the arena.*

"I expect you to make sure we put on a show," Gordian added. "Put the best of the duelists in the ring, then pit them against one another. Make it *spectacular.*"

And if someone gets seriously hurt, Emily thought sourly, *will you consider that spectacular too?*

"I'll do my best." She already had over ninety students who wished to compete in the first round. Thankfully, the ones who were more interested in having fun than winning had chosen not to take part. "But time really is not on my side."

"I saw your application to abandon your extra credit project," Gordian said. "Do you really want to quit now? You put in a great deal of work over the last two years."

Emily resisted, barely, the urge to scream. He sounded as though he was trying to be helpful, but she was sure he wasn't. A *helpful* man wouldn't have encumbered her with so much extra work that she was trying to find ways to pawn it off on her fellow students. Perhaps she could talk Melissa into manning the office, one day per week. Or Caleb. They'd both be better at talking to young students than she was.

"I don't have the time to do justice to the project," she said, flatly. "We decided we'll pick it up later, when we're less busy."

"Or pass it on to someone else," Gordian said. "Have you considered that?"

"Not yet," Emily said. The thought was tempting, but she didn't want virtual spellware to get out of her hands. Someone without scruples could *really* misuse it. "It's ours, sir."

"Quite understandable," Gordian said.

He made a show of looking at his watch. "Before you go, there is one final matter. A trio of historians are planning to visit over the half-term. Their original intention was to explore some of the tunnels and examine the documents you recovered, but I believe they'll want to speak with you about what you saw."

Emily frowned. "*All* of it?"

"Not *all* of it," Gordian said. "But you could tell them enough to fill in some of the blanks."

"Maybe," Emily said. She wondered if it was worth trying to bargain. She'd talk to the historians if Gordian let her put Cirroc in charge of the dueling club. But she had a feeling that would get her nowhere. "I kept meaning to read some of those documents myself."

And look for others, she thought. *If Master Wolfe had—somehow—survived and made his way to Beneficence, might he have concealed other documents below the school? What else might be down there?*

"A good idea," Gordian said.

Emily looked down at the table, considering the problem. History was *important.* And yet, it was in the past. She wasn't sure *what* would happen if the truth—or even part of it—came out. Would the magical community be *really* bothered if it learnt that Lord Whitehall hadn't been some insane combination of Dumbledore, Gandalf and Q? Or would there be a reopening of interest into some more dangerous questions? What had *really* happened when Whitehall had been founded and why? Who'd *really* been there?

"It depends on time," she said, finally. "I have a great deal of work to do."

And I did promise to help Frieda, she added, silently. *Perhaps if we can get over the major problem, she'll calm down.*

"Talk to me about it first," Gordian said. "We don't want to tell them everything."

Emily nodded. The truth would only upset people.

And start them experimenting with time travel too, she thought. The spells weren't actually that complex, but any would-be time traveler needed a nexus point and a way to navigate. It would be impossible for anyone to succeed without both, as far as she knew, yet that wouldn't stop sorcerers from trying. *And who knows what will happen then?*

"I advise you to be careful," Gordian warned. "People *are* watching you."

"I know," Emily said.

She rose. "I'll see you at the contest," she said. "And I hope you enjoy it."

"I'm sure I shall," Gordian said.

Emily walked out of the room, feeling her thoughts and emotions churning. Something had to be done about Frieda, but what? Emily wasn't even sure she knew what was going on. There *had* been a girl on Earth who had gone downhill rapidly, but her parents had been going through a messy divorce at the time. *Frieda* hadn't seen her parents for nearly four years.

Find her and ask, Emily told herself, firmly. *Then you can decide how to proceed.*

But when she looked for Frieda, her younger friend was nowhere to be found.

Chapter Twenty-Two

IF EMILY HADN'T KNOWN BETTER—AND SHE WASN'T SURE SHE *DID*—SHE WOULD HAVE WONdered if Frieda was avoiding her. Frieda took classes as normal, thankfully, but when she wasn't in class she was walking the grounds or wandering through the mountain paths on her own. Emily couldn't tell if Frieda was ashamed of her conduct or angry at Emily for giving her a mild telling off, but it didn't matter. She was surprised, four days later, when Frieda showed up for the first dueling contest.

Emily saw her with the others and sighed, inwardly. There was no *time* to have a private chat, not now. Seventy-eight students were waiting on one side of the arena, holding their tokens in their hands and clearly impatient for matters to begin; Gordian, a handful of tutors and the dueling league representatives were standing on the other side, chatting quietly amongst themselves. Emily couldn't help wondering if *she* was the subject of some of those discussions. A number of representatives had been glancing at her with more than passing interest.

She looked up at the clear blue sky and sighed. It was a perfect day, a minor miracle given how rapidly the weather near Whitehall could change from brilliant sunshine to a freezing snowstorm. If she had been free, she would have walked the mountains herself—perhaps invited Frieda along so they could talk outside school— or even strolled down to Dragon's Den. Instead...

"You all read the rules." She waved her hand in the air, triggering the tokens. The spell was simple enough, linking two students together at random. There was no way to avoid the simple fact that the older students were likely to dominate, but at least the younger ones would have a *chance* to move on to the second round. "Find your partners, then line up in front of the dueling rings. Do *not* step into the circle until you are ordered to do so."

She smiled, inwardly. Professor Armstrong had checked and rechecked the original dueling circle, then forced her and the other students to add a whole series of dueling rings. It had been practical work Emily would have enjoyed if she hadn't been all too aware that *lives* depended on their wardcrafting. Professor Armstrong had promised her that he wouldn't allow a *real* mistake to go through, even if it meant someone ending up in trouble, but she knew how easy it would be for *something* to go wrong. Too many spells were about to be exchanged in close quarters.

"In order to progress, you have to win at least two out of three duels," she reminded them, as the younger students shuffled about, trying to find their partners. Next time, Emily promised herself, she'd just pick couples herself, even though there would probably be complaints that the selection process wasn't truly random. "Those of you who win all *three* will have higher marks as you go into the second round."

She glanced at Cirroc, Jacqui and Cerise. Cirroc looked excited—he'd been disappointed when Emily had told him he couldn't take part himself—but Jacqui and Cerise looked as if they were waiting for something. Emily eyed them suspiciously, trying to convince herself that neither Jacqui nor Cerise was stupid enough to try anything in front of a dozen tutors and three outside representatives. And yet, she was *sure* that Jacqui had deliberately manipulated events so *she* had to deal with Frieda. The snide suggestions and constant interruptions suggested that Jacqui thought *she* would make a better Head Girl.

And I'd give her the post, if I could, Emily thought, wryly. *It isn't really a reward for anything.*

"Make sure they follow the rules," she told her assistants. She hadn't seen any more blatant attempts to push the limits, but she had a nasty feeling it was just a matter of time. "And *don't* let them hurt each other."

"Of course," Cirroc said. He didn't sound impressed. "We'll look after them."

Emily scowled at him, then walked to the first dueling circle. Adana stood there, facing a second-year boy Emily vaguely remembered as being one of Caleb's mentees, last year. He looked nervous when he saw Emily, his face falling sharply. Emily wondered what was bothering him—the storm of rumors had somehow managed to get even *more* intense over the last few days—but whatever it was, she was sure it wasn't important. She would be a fair and impartial referee and that was all that mattered.

"Into the circle," she said. Behind her, she heard whizzes and bangs as two contestants began their duel. "When I blow the whistle, you may begin."

Adana looked confident, Emily noted. She was Melissa's cousin, if Emily recalled correctly; she'd been taught a number of dueling spells—and self-defense spells—when she'd come into her magic, before she'd been sent to Whitehall. Emily would not have cared to face her as a firstie, even though it hadn't taken long for *Emily* to pick up a number of spells of her own. Adana lacked Tiega's undoubted skill—and vindictiveness—but she was still formidable for her age. Her opponent didn't look anything like so calm.

Emily blew the whistle. Adana opened the duel by hurling a massively overpowered transfiguration spell at her opponent, who jumped out of the way rather than try to block it directly. It was a smart move, Emily noted, as he launched a set of needle-hexes back at Adana. Even if he *had* managed to block the spell, Adana would have had a clear shot at him before he managed to recover and return fire. Perhaps the duel wouldn't be as one-sided as she—and Adana—had assumed...

Someone has definitely been teaching Adana, she thought. The younger girl fought with a mixture of skill and cunning, hunching down and expanding her wards to provide a smaller target. Her opponent was larger, but he made up for it in speed. He might lack Adana's collection of spells, yet he was smart enough not to give her an opening. And yet, he also lacked a certain ruthlessness. *I wonder if...*

Adana whooped as she snuck a spell through her opponent's defenses. Emily winced inwardly at the shock on the young boy's face, an instant before his body shrank and became a mouse. He scuttled away at speed, but it was clear that he couldn't continue the duel. Emily waited for ten seconds to see if he could free himself from the spell, then blew her whistle.

"Well done," Emily said, as Adana released the spell. The boy snapped back to normal. "Go wait for your next duel."

She met the boy's eyes as Adana strode off, waggling her hips in a manner that would probably have earned her a particularly unpleasant hex from her great-grand-mother. "You didn't do badly," she said. "But you're not casting your spells fast enough."

"Thank you," the boy said, sourly. "I tried..."

"Sometimes, that is all you can do," Emily said, as reassuringly as possible. He hadn't broken and run, had he? That counted for something. Sergeant Miles would probably have approved. A brave man could be trained. A coward was better off well away from the battlefield. "Good luck with your next duel."

He nodded and walked off. Emily took a moment to note that both Frieda and Tiega had made it through their first duels, then turned her attention to the next pair of duelists. She winced, openly, the moment she saw them. A firstie and a Fifth Year? The outcome was practically pre-ordained. She was tempted to order them both to find other partners, but the selection process had been random. Perhaps she should have put her thumb on the scale.

"I'm not going to give up," the firstie said.

"I wasn't expecting you to give up," his opponent countered.

Emily sighed and blew the whistle. The duel shouldn't have lasted more than a handful of seconds. And yet, the firstie had guts, if not brains. He kept moving, ducking low and jumping high... he even attached himself to the wards, firing hexes down at his opponent's head. Emily made a mental note to recommend him to Sergeant Miles. The firstie lost—his opponent finally managed to hit him with a gust of freezing air, then locked him in place—but he'd put up an impressive fight. It was hard to say who'd truly won the duel.

Particularly as the odds were so unbalanced, she thought, as the two opponents left. It hadn't escaped her notice that there was a greater gap between the two contestants than there had been between Frieda and her victims. *Doing so well with the odds so heavily slanted against you definitely counts in your favor.*

She shook her head, then supervised the next set of duels. Some of them surprised her—the opponents were imaginative and flexible—while others were boring, nothing more than hexes being exchanged like tennis balls until one side slipped up and lost. She suspected that some of the latter duelists were in for an unpleasant surprise when they faced someone a little more imaginative. Frieda would have smashed them flat, even when they were older and more experienced. But then, *losing* was a great teacher. Sergeant Harkin had told her that time and time again.

And he ensured that I lost, Emily recalled. Her magic had been pitiful compared to the older students, back in her first year, but her hand-to-hand combat skills had been worse. She had improved, over the years, yet she knew she would never match Jade or Cat. *I learnt never to let a stronger man get within arm's reach of me.*

She muttered a spell to amplify her voice as the final duels came to an end. "Those of you who want to withdraw, hand in your tokens," she ordered. "The rest of you, get a drink and catch your breath. We'll be starting the next set of duels in ten minutes."

Gordian walked over to her, his face utterly blank. "Not bad so far," he said, curtly. "They"—he nodded towards the representatives—"seem to like it. They're just wondering why you don't have a ranking ladder."

Emily shrugged. "First, we're starting from scratch." She'd considered duplicating the league's ranking system, but it had never struck her as particularly clever. Besides, too many students would have to start out ranked at the bottom. "And second, we have too many duelists to go through in too little time."

She smiled as she glanced at Frieda. It was nice to see her younger friend looking happy again, although they were going to have a serious conversation relatively soon. Frieda wasn't going to go anywhere for half-term, was she? Emily made a mental note to catch up with Frieda after dinner, then turned her attention back to Gordian. The Grandmaster was reviewing the results, nodding happily to himself.

"We'll probably have to hold separate contests for each year," she said, as she read the results. She'd been right. They *were* weighted in favor of the older students. "But you can do that next year."

Gordian nodded. He wouldn't have *Emily* next year... the thought caused her a pang, even though she knew she'd be coming back one day. She hadn't abandoned her dream of teaching. It was an odd career, she'd been told, but it was the one she wanted. And besides, she was good at one-to-one tutoring.

I might start teaching at Heart's Eye instead, she mused. Gordian would be relieved. He wouldn't have her in his hair any longer. *And then I can set my own class sizes.*

She glanced at her watch, then blew the whistle. A number of duelists had backed out, she noted; she reset the tokens, then watched the contestants take their places. There was no chatter this time, just a grim determination to get ahead. She felt a moment of sympathy for anyone who wasn't good enough to stand their ground, then pushed it aside. It was a sport, not war. And it wouldn't keep them alive, if pressed.

It might, she told herself.

Gordian stood beside her, completely silent, as the first pair of students marched into the dueling ring. They were both Fifth Years, Emily noted; they fought like experienced magicians, rather than duelists. The line between legal and illegal spells was brushed over a dozen times in the first two minutes alone, forcing her to make split-second decisions between blowing the whistle and letting it stand. She couldn't help thinking, judging by the way they hurled spells at each other, that there was something deeply personal in it. Perhaps they *really* didn't like each other. By the time one of them was blown back against the wards, hard enough to stun him, they'd exchanged so many spells that the ring was on the verge of collapse.

"Not bad," Gordian said, as Professor Armstrong hastily checked the ring. "Not bad at all."

Emily said nothing. The next set of duelists stepped in as soon as Professor Armstrong declared the ring safe, then went at each other with bitter determination. They'd both learnt from the last set of duels, Emily decided. She'd seen them standing still before; now, they were moving to dodge spells instead of trying to deflect them. She mentally commended them for showing a little more imagination, then sighed as one of them finally lost. They still didn't have the skill they needed to win.

Gordian tapped her arm as the loser stumbled out of the ring, followed by the winner. "Do you wish you were with them?"

Emily shook her head. Dueling had never struck her as *fun*. She'd learnt the basics at Mountaintop, but she'd considered it just another contemptible sport, no different from football or basketball. The jocks who were good at it were feted, allowed to get away with murder if it was what it took to keep them on the team. And then Master Grey had tried to kill her...

"I'd be happy if I never saw another dueling circle," she said. "I don't like dueling."

Gordian gave her a surprised look as the last of the duels came to an end. Twenty-nine students had won one or both of their duels; the remainder, the ones who had lost both, exited the field. Emily hid a smile as a number of them headed straight for the showers, rather than staying behind to cheer everyone going into the third round. If she'd been that hot and sweaty, she would probably have done the same.

"It's a way to prove that you are the best," Gordian said. "Isn't it?"

"I don't *want* to prove that I'm the best." Emily nodded towards the dueling ring, where Professor Armstrong was testing the wards again. "I just want to *live*."

Gordian frowned, but said nothing as the final set of contestants assembled. Emily *had* agreed that students who won both of their matches could move ahead to the second round, but only two of them—Adana and an older student she didn't know—had taken advantage of the opportunity. Everyone else was lining up, looking ready and willing to resume the dueling. Emily glanced from face to face, seeing the same grim determination everywhere.

This isn't just a game to them, she told herself. *This is... a chance to prove themselves.*

She winced, inwardly, as Frieda and an older student stepped into the ring. If she'd had time, she would have called one of the other supervisors... but Gordian was standing right next to her, watching. Emily cursed under her breath, wondering just what she'd do if Frieda stepped over the line. Or even the other student. She knew from grim experience that *someone* could slip a spell past the referees, if they were careful. If she saw something and Gordian didn't—or vice versa—it could easily get her in trouble.

"Good luck," she mouthed. "And..."

She blew the whistle. Frieda launched her first spell at once... no, *two* spells fired off so closely together as to make them seem one. Her opponent tried to block it and was knocked backwards for his pains, although his shield was strong enough to deflect most of the magic and absorb the rest. He retaliated with a set of spells of his own; Frieda dodged and ducked, hurling spells towards him as she moved. Emily felt Gordian tense beside her as Frieda cast a prank spell, followed by one of the nastier—and yet legal—hexes. Her opponent yelped in pain as the prank caught his arm, then threw back a ward-cracker. Frieda grunted, then launched herself forward. Emily sucked in her breath as Frieda slammed her wards into her opponent's.

"Ouch," Gordian said.

Emily nodded in grim agreement. It wasn't—*technically*—illegal, but it was borderline. She half expected Gordian to call Frieda on it. Instead, he watched as magic cascaded around the two duelists, Frieda pushing her cracking wards right into her opponent's face. Emily wanted to scream at her to stop—if something went wrong, both of them would be injured—but she couldn't form the words. And then there was a flash of light as her opponent flew backwards, landing badly. Frieda lifted her hand and stunned him before he could recover...

"Very good," Gordian said.

Emily glanced at him suspiciously, then at Frieda. There were scars on her face and blood was trickling down her cheek... and yet she looked unbowed. And the cold satisfaction on her face made her look completely different. For an insane moment, Emily wondered if it really *was* Frieda...

"Congratulations on your victory," Gordian said to Frieda, his voice flat. "I trust this will improve your mood."

I hope it will make her feel better too, Emily thought, as she watched Frieda stumble out of the ring. Someone had busted her knee in an earlier duel. *But we still need to talk.*

Chapter Twenty-Three

"WHY IS IT," FRIEDA ASKED, "THAT THEY CALL HALF-TERM THE *HOLIDAYS?*"

Emily smiled. They stood together in the battlements, watching a line of coaches making their way down to Dragon's Den and the world beyond. Nearly two-thirds of the student body were heading home. Whitehall felt empty, now they were gone. Emily welcomed it, even though she knew she had a considerable amount of work to do. Most of the lower years were leaving and *they* were the ones who gave her the most trouble.

They need help, she told herself. *And I'm the one who's supposed to give it to them.*

"I imagine they plan to do as little work as possible," she said wryly, putting the thought aside. "And they will pay for it, when they come back."

She glanced at Frieda, who was waving to a handful of students driving down to the gates and out onto the road. She'd had a talk with Frieda, after the duel, but she wasn't sure if Frieda had paid any attention. It wasn't *easy* to keep an eye on her younger friend when they had different classes and responsibilities, yet it was clear that Frieda *was* having problems. Emily had seen too many half-hidden cross faces and angry sighs—and overheard too many snide comments—to think otherwise.

"At least we don't have any classes," she added. "You and I need to sit down and go over your work."

Frieda looked rebellious. "Can't we spend a couple of days resting first?"

"Perhaps," Emily said. Dragon's Den would be quieter now. They could go to the house, if they wanted, or even just go for a meal. "But I'd sooner get to grips with the problem before it's too late."

She shook her head. The last two weeks had been nightmarish, as tutor after tutor struggled manfully to cram information into student heads. The tutors had been growing more and more irritable too; she'd been snapped at twice, while other students had been even less lucky. Professor Armstrong had given them two days to work on the practical side of wardcrafting, then set a whole series of theoretical exercises that had left Emily's head spinning by the time half-term finally rolled around. She didn't think a *single* Sixth Year student was leaving the school, even for a weekend. There was too much work to do.

And I don't have much time to work with Frieda, she mused, as they started to walk towards the dorms. The wards felt quieter now too, reflecting the reduced student body. It was something of a relief. They sank into the back of her mind when she wasn't thinking about them, but they tended to emerge the moment she remembered them. *I have too much work of my own to do.*

"Celadon is staying too," Frieda said, mournfully. "Do I *have* to work with him?"

"Yeah," Emily said, absently. A younger student was hurrying towards her, waving his arms in the air. She tensed, unsure what to expect. "I'm afraid you do."

The student skidded to a halt, breathing heavily. "Ah... um... Lady Emily, the Grandmaster requests your presence in your office."

Emily frowned. "*My* presence in *my* office?"

"Yes, My Lady," the student said, still struggling for breath. "He says he'll meet you there."

Emily exchanged glances with Frieda. She was fairly sure Gordian could enter her office, if he wished—the wards would let him in unless she configured them to block him—but it was a severe breach of etiquette. Legally, the Grandmaster could go wherever he wanted; practically, he'd be unwise to invade his staff's quarters without a very good excuse. Emily might not be staff, *technically*, but the rule still held. Magicians valued their privacy. The staff was reluctant to search student dorms and trunks without good reason. If nothing else, it would cause problems with the student's parents.

"I'll go there." She made sure to memorize the student's face, just in case it was a prank of some kind. "Thank you."

"I could come with you," Frieda offered, as the student hurried away. "You might want a witness."

Emily hesitated, then shook her head. "You go to the library and catch up with your studies," she said, firmly. "I'll find you afterwards and we'll go walking."

She watched Frieda go, then walked up the stairs to her office door. Gordian was standing outside, accompanied by two men in plain robes. One of them looked old enough to be *Samra's* father, with short white hair and a wry smile; the other was only a few years older than Emily, with bushy black hair and a neatly-trimmed beard. She glanced from one to the other, wondering who they were. She didn't recall seeing either of them before.

"Lady Emily," Gordian said, formally. "Please allow me to introduce Brothers Akanke and Oscine of the History Monks."

"A pleasure," the older man said. "Oscine and I have heard much about you."

"Thank you," Emily said. She cursed Gordian under her breath. Had he *meant* to blindside her? "I bid you welcome to my office."

She opened the door and led them into the chamber, wishing she'd had a chance to clear up the mess. The table was covered with papers, ranging from lists of duelists to notes she'd taken in class. She motioned for them to sit down—she wished she'd had a chance to obtain some comfortable chairs too—and then poured Kava. They'd take the mugs, even if they didn't want a drink. It was a way of showing they were welcome.

Even if they are not, Emily thought. The only History Monk she'd met had been Master Locke—and his obsession with Old Whitehall had nearly led to utter disaster. *This could prove awkward.*

Gordian sat down and crossed his legs, leaning back as casually as if he owned the room. "I trust you are *aware* of the History Monks?"

Emily nodded. They were a religious sect charged with recording history as it happened, then analyzing it. They'd been established shortly after the Empire itself, when they'd worked for the Emperor directly, but they'd fallen on hard times since the Empire had been destroyed and replaced by the Allied Lands. In theory, they were supposed to be completely objective; in practice, she'd heard they'd found it impossible to maintain their neutrality. It was astonishing just how many times history had been rewritten, according to Professor Locke, to accommodate a local tyrant or to support some aristocrat's claim to disputed lands.

"We believe it is vitally important that we come to understand what happened in the past." Akanke gave her a genuinely warm smile. "As I believe Brother Locke informed you, far too many records have been lost or destroyed over the years. Even our *dating* system is a mess. It is hard to place hundreds of events within their proper context."

"And it is thus impossible to construct a detailed historical narrative," Oscine added. He had a gruff voice, oddly accented. "We cannot say, in all honesty, just how long it was since Lord Whitehall founded the school."

"Nine hundred and seventy-two years," Emily said. A demon had told her that, which made it automatically suspect. But demons weren't allowed to lie. "That is... I believe that to be true."

Akanke leaned forward. "We were given to understand that you obtained some... historical knowledge because of your work with Brother Locke. We *are* sworn not to discuss certain details until enough time has passed to make them irrelevant."

Emily looked at Gordian, who nodded.

And that leads to a different question, she thought. *Do I trust them or not?*

She agonized over it for a long moment. She'd witnessed history when she'd fallen back in time. She'd been *there* when Lord Whitehall founded the school. Her observations could unlock dozens of secrets, perhaps place vague records or historical notes in their proper context. And besides, convincing historians that there had been no great magics in the past—magics that had long since been forgotten—would be no bad thing. Professor Locke's quest for forgotten magic had driven him insane.

"I was there," she said, simply.

Akanke showed no visible reaction. Oscine looked disbelieving. Emily didn't blame him. Extraordinary claims required extraordinary evidence. Her control over the wards would be enough, she supposed, except that would be far too revealing. *Gordian* wouldn't want her to discuss that, would he? She couldn't blame him, either.

"Really," Oscine said.

"Yes," Gordian said. "I can confirm it."

Emily smiled, then launched into a brief explanation. She glossed over her own involvement as much as possible, but she was careful to mention Bernard and Julianne as well as Master Wolfe and Lord Whitehall. Julianne *deserved* to be remembered, if only as the first formally-trained female magician. Emily talked briefly about the Curse—and how it had been overcome—then how the castle had turned into a school.

"It was attacked by dark forces," she finished. "I wound up using a pocket dimension to return home."

That was a lie, but it was one she had to make. She didn't want to talk about demons, let alone what she'd done to get home. The Books of Pacts she'd brought to the future had been carefully hidden, beyond the reach of mortal man, but she didn't want to encourage them to go looking. There was no way to know if the books were still dangerous after nearly a thousand years. To demons, timeless creatures, a thousand years might as well be a second.

And there is always a sting in the tail, Emily thought. Lord Whitehall had banned demons from the castle, eventually. He'd known the dangers, even if younger and less experienced magicians had sought shortcuts to power. *The demon wouldn't have asked me to take the books for fun.*

She put the thought aside for later contemplation as the two monks asked question after question, poking and prodding at her memories to establish a coherent timeline. Emily wished, again, that she'd had a chance to prepare for the interview. Most of what she'd told them was true, but there were details she really *didn't* want to discuss. Demon summoning wasn't unknown, yet the techniques were largely forgotten. The last thing she wanted was countless magicians experimenting with demon-based magic.

"So," Oscine said. "Who built Whitehall?"

Emily shrugged. "All I know is that the castle was built and abandoned years before Lord Whitehall turned it into a school." The more she thought about it, the more it struck her as odd. Whitehall had been strikingly isolated, even by the standards of the time. There hadn't been any settlements within two or three days walking distance. She had a feeling that the castle had been largely forgotten before Lord Whitehall rediscovered it. "Perhaps they had an accident with the nexus point."

"Perhaps," Akanke agreed. "There *are* other castles from that era."

"And we know who built most of them," Oscine pointed out. "Whitehall, however, is largely unique."

"Or the builders were killed, after they completed their work," Emily said. Alassa had once told her, quite calmly, that her father had executed several hundred workmen after they'd finished their job. A king's secrets had to be preserved, whatever the cost. "Whoever built the castle might have wanted it to stay secret."

"It's still odd," Akanke said. "Building a castle is not an easy task. The logistics alone would be daunting."

Emily had to agree. "Even accommodating the workers would be a problem," she said. "I don't think there were any settlements within walking distance."

"The nexus point was there," Gordian pointed out. "Castles are normally built to hold territory and defend chokepoints. The nexus point alone would be worth any price."

"Of course, Grandmaster," Akanke agreed.

"There *might* have been a settlement," Oscine put in. "But if it was abandoned, it wouldn't be long before it returned to the soil."

"True," Gordian said.

Emily nodded. The towns and villages she'd seen had a striking air of impermanence about them, as if constant maintenance was the only thing that kept them from decaying into rubble. It wasn't entirely uncommon to see deserted villages in the countryside, villages that had been abandoned by the inhabitants when they'd decided they were no longer viable. The cities and castles would last longer, but even *they* would be worn down by time. It was easy to believe that Dragon's Den might have—unknowingly—been built on a long-forgotten settlement. A fair-sized town might have vanished completely between the castle's completion and Lord Whitehall's arrival.

"We thank you for your time, Lady Emily." Akanke smiled. "It is our intention to study the documents that were discovered last year."

"And to search for others," Oscine said.

Emily glanced at Gordian. His expression was artfully blank.

She thought, fast. She'd reviewed all the documents while she'd been hiding in the tunnels under the school, waiting for her timelines to reintegrate. There were some secrets she would prefer to keep hidden, but Gordian had already reviewed them. Besides, they were largely useless to anyone without a nexus point.

And the rest are really nothing more than historical curiosities, she thought. Lord Whitehall and Master Wolfe had been powerful and smart, but they hadn't learnt from generations of previous magicians. *There weren't any long-lost magics after all.*

"I think you will find them interesting," she said. Discouraging others from searching for non-existent secrets would be a good deed, even if there were many who would find it disappointing. "And I don't know if there were any other documents stored under Whitehall."

"None of our inspections have found any," Gordian put in. "But we believe we have barely scratched the surface. There are tunnels and hidden chambers that have yet to be searched."

Emily winced, inwardly. There were thousands of protective and concealment spells woven into the tunnels. Professor Locke would never have found the control chamber without her, although neither of them had realized it at the time. Back then, the idea that *she* had helped found the school would have been laughable. They'd certainly had no reason to think that *she* had permission to go where she liked.

But anything could be concealed under the school, she thought. *And we wouldn't know anything about it until we stumbled over the hidden chamber.*

"We do intend to look," Akanke said. "I trust that will meet with your approval?"

"As long as you stay out of the control center," Gordian said. "We decided to leave that well alone."

He looked at Emily. "Perhaps you would care to escort them?"

Emily shook her head. "I don't have time." She wondered, briefly, if she could convince Gordian to let her pass the dueling club to Cirroc. If he wanted her to talk history with the history monks, something else would have to be put aside. "I'm going to be busy until after graduation day."

Another thought struck her, making her wince. It had been nearly a *year* since she'd set foot in the underground complex, let alone made her way to the control center. She certainly *hadn't* bothered to check for other hidden compartments. In hindsight, that might have been careless. Whitehall and Bernard might have lacked her knowledge, but they'd also been less reluctant to tamper with the nexus point.

There might be a hundred sealed chambers below the school. Perhaps she should find them before anyone else.

And the control center should be checked too, she thought, grimly. It wasn't something she wanted to discuss with Gordian. Grandmaster or not, she didn't trust him that far. *I should see to it before anything else.*

"I'll arrange for a couple of my staff to escort you," Gordian said, addressing Akanke. He didn't seem unhappy that Emily had declined to do it. "We can start tomorrow, if you wish."

"That would be fine, I believe," Akanke said. "We can spend the rest of the day compiling our notes. If we could borrow the office..."

Emily was caught between amusement and offence. "This is my office," she said, dryly. Did they think she'd let them kick her out of her own office? "But there are study rooms you could use."

Gordian raised a hand to conceal a smile. "I've had the pair of you assigned to a guest suite," he said. "There are offices attached, which you are welcome to use. And I look forward to the pleasure of your company for dinner."

Oscine shot Emily an apologetic look. "That would be suitable. And thank you."

"I'll take you to them personally," Gordian said. "Emily, thank you for coming on such short notice."

"You're welcome," Emily lied. She was going to be second-guessing herself for the rest of the day. *And* she was going to have to sneak down to the catacombs. Frieda would probably want to come with her, too. Emily wasn't sure that was a good idea, but at least it would keep Frieda out of trouble. "If you don't mind, I have work to attend to."

Gordian bowed. "Of course. I'll send you a message if they require any further assistance."

"We will want to discuss some secondary matters," Oscine grunted. He put out a paw-like hand and shook Emily's, firmly. "But we thank you for your time."

Emily nodded, keeping her face expressionless. She'd considered becoming a historian, once upon a time. *That* dream hadn't lasted, but she still had great respect for historians. Writing down what had really happened was *important*. And yet, she wasn't sure *what* would happen if some version of the truth got out. Too many people would start asking too many questions about where the truth had come from. The only real consolation was that there weren't any long-forgotten super-magics lurking in the past.

Unless you count demons, she thought. *But the modern world doesn't need them.*

Chapter Twenty-Four

"**Y**OU NEVER TOOK ME DOWN INTO THE TUNNELS," FRIEDA MUTTERED, AS THEY WALKED down the stairs to the armory. "Is it anything like the tunnels under Mountaintop?"

"It's very different," Emily said. It was safer now, but she still felt tense as she approached the hidden door. The staff, including Gordian and Sergeant Miles, would be at dinner, yet there was still a risk of getting caught. "Give me a moment to work on the defenses..."

She closed her eyes, reaching out to touch the wards. Gordian had been busy, she noted; he'd drawn on the school's wards to conceal the entrance to the catacombs, but he'd also added a series of independent wards of his own. Her eyes narrowed as she studied them, wondering just what Gordian had in mind. The wards weren't anchored to the school, let alone drawing power from the nexus point. Putting them in place must have cost Gordian a considerable investment in time and magic...

And the only person they could be keyed against is me, Emily thought. She cursed under her breath, wishing—suddenly—that she'd kept a closer eye on the entrance. Anyone *else* would be deterred by a normal set of wards. *Gordian wanted to be very sure he'd know about it if I went into the tunnels.*

The wards were impressive, she admitted sourly. She could draw on the school's wards and break them through brute force, but she was fairly sure that would set off any number of alarms. Gordian would hardly have missed *that* possibility. Instead, she carefully worked her way into the ward network—drawing a trickle of power from the school—and froze the wards in place. It wasn't perfect—she was grimly aware that the history monks *were* planning to visit the catacombs, which meant that Gordian would have to let them in—but it would have to do.

She opened her eyes. "Come on. Let's go."

Frieda smiled as they slipped past the frozen wards and down the tunnel. Emily had expected to have to cast light-globes or night-vision spells, but the eerie radiance followed them as they reached the bottom and stepped into the catacombs. Someone had been busy. The dust she recalled from the previous year was gone. She peered up and down the corridor as she sensed trickles of magic plummeting towards the nexus point. It looked as though someone had been exploring.

"Keep very quiet," she muttered to Frieda. She'd explored some parts of the catacombs, but she'd left other parts strictly alone. "We don't want anyone to know we're here."

She drew on the wards as they made their way down to the hidden library. Someone had *definitely* been busy. The walls had been swept clean of dust, allowing the runes and diagrams to be copied... she tensed as she caught sight of a complex runic diagram, positioned neatly above a drawing of a Manavore. *She'd* drawn up the power-draining runes, back in the past. Someone had copied them down and hidden them as a warning to future generations. And someone *else* had copied them down.

The thrumming of the nexus point grew louder, throbbing in time with her heartbeat. It wasn't a physical sound, more like something beating against her magic. It was all she could do to think as the sensation pounded into her thoughts. She tried to use the wards to peer ahead, but it was like trying to look into the sun. There was too much stray magic flowing through the system for her to see through the charms.

Frieda caught her arm. "Look!"

Emily turned. A chamber—a large chamber—had been turned into a sleeping room. A number of blankets lay on the stone floor, while bags and food supplies had been placed against the far wall... it looked like someone was on a camping trip. She peered inside, trying to determine how many people were living under the school. It was hard to be sure—the chamber appeared deserted—but she would have guessed that at least five men were using the chamber. And there were *hundreds* of similar chambers under the school. Were they all occupied?

She cursed under her breath. *What the hell is going on?*

"Watch the door," she ordered. "And get ready to cast an invisibility spell."

She slipped into the chamber and looked around. If there were notes lying about... she saw nothing, save for a handful of blue books and a couple of magical texts. She picked up the nearest blue book, just in case it had been charmed to conceal something more interesting, but a glance at a couple of random pages told her that no one had bothered. A pair of unrealistic sex scenes... whoever was under the school, she told herself as she replaced the book where she'd found it, had to be very bored.

Sergeant Miles had taught her how to read a campsite, years ago. She looked around, silently noting the absence of bras or other feminine clothing. They were men, probably. The handful of visible clothes certainly backed that up. But then, there could be a *female* campsite on the other side of the corridor. She took one last look, reluctant to start opening bags unless there was no other choice. A trained magician would have booby-trapped his bag, just to make sure no one stole from him. She'd done it herself while she'd been in the army camp.

Gordian's been busy, she thought, as she slipped back to the door. *No one could have gotten under the school without the Grandmaster's permission.*

Her mind raced. Gordian had told her that he'd sealed the catacombs. He'd lied to her. And that meant... what? What *were* these people doing under the school? Checking to make sure there *wasn't* a monster buried under Whitehall? Or something more sinister? She forced herself to put the matter aside for later contemplation as she met Frieda's worried eyes. If they slipped further towards the control center, the odds of being caught would go up sharply.

And Gordian will need to clear these people out before the history monks start exploring, she reminded herself. *Unless he plans to pass them off as staff...*

"We need to sneak closer to the control center," she said, very quietly. "Get ready to turn invisible."

She listened for a long moment, then inched down the corridor, keeping her senses peeled for magical traps. It wasn't *too* likely that anyone would booby-trap the passageway, but it was better to be careful. The constant presence of the nexus point throbbed against her mind, yet she could hear nothing else. She could practically *sense* the spellware Master Wolfe and Lord Whitehall—and Emily—had devised to control the nexus point...

Something moved, further down the corridor. Footsteps echoed up, towards them. Emily tensed, then pulled Frieda into an alcove and cast a glamour, drawing on the wards to make it stronger. Anyone who didn't already know they were there shouldn't notice them, she told herself firmly. The nexus point would make it harder for anyone to spot them if they were looking with magic.

Harder for us to see them too, Emily thought. *We have to be careful.*

Two men strode into view. They wore long robes and wardcrafter badges, carrying devices Emily didn't recognize in their arms. A third man followed, holding a large notebook and a small wooden wand. Emily kept herself as still as possible, knowing that the slightest movement might draw their attention. And yet, she wanted to know what was in that notebook. What were the men *doing* under the school?

Understanding clicked. *They're studying the nexus point,* she realized. *And the spellware we created to take control.*

She watched the three men stride into the distance as she fought down a sudden rush of sheer rage. Gordian had *lied* to her. He was tampering with the nexus point. Or, at least, studying the nexus point in hopes of *finding* a way to tamper with it. Perhaps he wanted to lock her out of the school's control network... he could, perhaps, if he found a way to get himself classed as one of the founders. Emily had always assumed that Lord Whitehall had done just that to any founder who'd declined to play ball, in later years. God knew that some of the early deserters had nearly brought the Whitehall Commune to its knees.

As soon as the men were out of sight, she led the way further down the corridor, adjusting the glamour to provide some concealment. People *saw* things close to a nexus point. If she was lucky, anyone who caught a glimpse of them would decide it was just another trick of their mind. And if she wasn't... a dull anger burned in her breast. She would almost have welcomed a confrontation, even if it would have pitted Frieda and her against an unknown number of fully-trained magicians. Gordian had *lied* to her.

He'll definitely have to move them out before it's too late, she thought, as she reached the control center. *How many of the staff know he's got a team working down here?*

Two men were inside the control center, monitoring the spellware as it drew on the nexus point to maintain the school. Emily eyed their backs for a long moment, then glanced around the chamber. They'd been *very* busy, she noted. It looked as though they'd filled over a dozen notebooks with observations. She had no idea how long it would take them to untangle the web of spells that made up Whitehall—a number of grandmasters had clearly made their own modifications before the chamber had been buried and forgotten—but she didn't think it would take *that* long. Gordian would hire the very best. And he had access to her notes on virtual spellware...

She ground her teeth in sudden frustration. Gordian could have—he would have—shared her notes with his researchers. Given access to the nexus point, it would only be a matter of time before they unlocked its secrets. Hell, for all she knew, Gordian had only kicked the research program into high gear after she'd taken control of Heart's Eye. He had ample reason to be... *concerned*... about the ill-understood spell-ware holding his school together. And if he feared what she could do with her control over the wards... she knew he wouldn't hesitate to lock her out, if he could.

Emily led Frieda away, down a set of corridors that had also been thoroughly cleaned. The map room—including the immense world map that showed a completely unknown continent—had been turned into another research center, with notebooks and study materials scattered everywhere. Other chambers had been given a sweep, then left to gather dust once it was clear there was nothing to be learned there. Emily understood, rather sourly, why Gordian hadn't raised more objections to the history monks exploring the lower levels. If there was anything hidden by the wards, anything hidden so well his men couldn't find them, the monks wouldn't find it either.

And he can just move his researchers out for a few weeks, she thought. *Who knows? It might even give them a rest.*

Frieda caught her arm. "What was *that*?"

"That was the control center," Emily said. "And..."

She broke off. There was no one she could talk to about this, not even Frieda. Or Lady Barb or Sergeant Miles... perhaps she would have confided in Void, if he'd been around, but she didn't have the slightest idea how to contact him. He moved around a lot. A letter might reach him in a week... or months. And even if she did contact someone, anyone she asked would want to know why she hadn't told them about her trip to the past.

Because I thought it needed to be kept secret, she told herself.

She closed her eyes for a long moment, studying the collection of wards and concealment charms that pervaded the lower levels. Someone had *definitely* been busy, inserting their own pieces of spellwork... it was hard to know *when* they'd done it—it was possible that it predated her arrival at Whitehall—but she couldn't help finding it ominous. Gordian would know better than to touch the spells holding Whitehall's pocket dimensions in place—she was sure of that—yet that left him plenty of room for mischief. Given time, he might be able to take the whole network over...

"Fuck," she muttered.

Frieda snickered. "Language."

Emily ignored her. She was trying to think of what to do. It was sheer luck she'd stumbled onto Gordian's plan, yet she had no idea how to react. She could sabotage his modifications, but she didn't have complete control over the school's wards. Too many grandmasters had added too many modifications for her to be *entirely* sure what would happen if she tried. Whitehall wasn't intelligent, not as she understood the term, but it was definitely a learning system. God alone knew how it would react if she and Gordian engaged in a battle for control.

It might recognize me as the last surviving Founder, she thought. Professor Locke had told her stories of prospective masters who'd battled for control, but she had no idea how many of the stories were actually true. *Or it might recognize him as the legally-appointed Grandmaster. Or it might turn on both of us.*

"We have to get out of here," she said, grimly. There was no point in searching for any more documents, not now. Anything Gordian hadn't been able to find could stay there, for the moment. "Come on."

She kept her senses primed as they made their way slowly back to the entrance. Now she knew what to look for, it was easy to spot more and more powerful charms inserted into the spellwork. It was a brilliant piece of work, she had to admit, combining functionality with plausible deniability. Every charm had a mundane use as well as a blatantly hostile one. She doubted she could construct an ironclad case against him in a court of law, if she ever had to try. He could just accuse her of being paranoid.

And he might be right, she thought. *He needs to understand how his school actually works.*

"We should explore further," Frieda said. She didn't sound discouraged by everything they'd seen. The risk of getting caught didn't seem to bother her either. "How far down do the tunnels go?"

Emily shrugged. She didn't know who'd carved the tunnels, let alone warded them. They'd been in existence, partly, before Lord Whitehall had arrived. That secret had definitely been lost in the mists of time. And then someone else had turned the school into a pocket dimension, years *after* Whitehall. Who knew what had happened then?

They reached the top of the tunnel and entered the school. Emily unfroze the wards, taking a moment to check them before hurrying Frieda to the showers. They weren't covered in dust—she still shuddered when she recalled the dusty chambers from last year—but there was no point in taking chances. It was better that Gordian believe they'd gone for a walk in the mountains—and come back hot and sweaty—than work out where they'd actually gone before she was ready to confront him. Or... she didn't know *what* she'd do. And there was no one she could ask for advice.

"Don't tell anyone what we saw down there," Emily warned, as they stepped into the changing room. She breathed a sigh of relief when she realized it was deserted. She'd never liked changing and showering in front of others, even girls. "If anyone asks, we went walking."

"Of course." Frieda undressed rapidly, dropping her shirt and trousers on the bench before hurrying to the shower. "I know better."

Emily smiled, then frowned as she saw the marks on Frieda's bare back. "What happened to you?"

Frieda froze. "I had a... disagreement... in martial magic," she said, finally. She started moving again, heading into the shower. Emily couldn't help noticing that there were fainter marks on her buttocks and the back of her legs. "The other students weren't pleased with me."

"Oh," Emily managed. She was no expert, but the bruises looked relatively new. Patches of her skin had clearly been broken, then healed. "What happened?"

"We had a frank exchange of views." Frieda rubbed a red mark on her leg. "I lost."

Emily stared at her back. She'd heard that some martial magic classes took matters into their own hands if a student was dragging the rest of the class down, but she'd never believed it was real. God knew *she'd* dragged down her class's marks, back in first year... the sergeants wouldn't have intervened if the rest of the class had decided to give her a beating. Barrack room lawyers had no place in the military, she'd been told. Maybe Jade had intimidated the others into leaving her alone...

Or maybe Frieda is having even worse troubles, she thought. Some of the bruises looked *nasty*. Emily hated to think of what would happen if they got infected. *What happens if she doesn't improve?*

"I think we'll start going over your work," Emily said firmly, as she removed her own clothes and stepped into the shower. The warm water felt good, even though the changing room showers were deliberately underpowered. "And then you and I will sit down with Celadon."

"You don't have to," Frieda said. She sounded desperate. "Really..."

"I think this has gone on long enough," Emily said, flatly. "And it really needs to stop."

Chapter Twenty-Five

EMILY HAD HOPED, AS THE HALF-TERM WORE ON, THAT *SOME* KIND OF SOLUTION TO ONE OR both of her problems would present itself. Perhaps she could figure out just what Gordian was doing—she'd watched the historians and several others make their way down into the tunnels, now she knew what to look for—or help Frieda solve her problems. But neither one seemed willing to be solved. Gordian kept himself to himself, while Frieda seemed to veer wildly from being the playful girl Emily had befriended to a trigger-happy witch. The changes were so striking—and so sudden—that Emily found herself considering the possibility of outside interference, but—when she checked—she found nothing.

She couldn't help being grateful that her Head Girl duties shrunk with most of the students on holiday, as she'd had so little time to herself. Her studies were suffering too, even though the Gorgon and Cabiria were trying to help her. There was only so much their notes could do. Between her own work and trying to help Frieda, she felt as though she was running out of time. She was honestly tempted to take Void up on his offer and leave Whitehall, without bothering to sit the exams. But it would feel like giving up.

And Gordian might be trying to drive me out of the school, she thought, as she sat in her office and worked her way through yet another set of notes. She needed to finish them before Frieda and Celadon arrived for their appointment. Professor Lombardi had given her two sets of detentions to supervise the following day, leaving her wondering just what she'd done to upset him. *Who is actually being punished?*

She sighed, remembering Alassa and Jade's last letter. There was trouble in Zangaria, real trouble. And yet it was so maddeningly imprecise! Rumors of rebellious peasants, rumors of civil war... barons and aristocrats arming while King Randor worked to build up his army... nothing seemed to have come out into the open yet, but it was just a matter of time. Emily was starting to wonder if she was seeing a joint offensive—one aimed at her, one aimed at her friends—although she had to admit it might just be coincidence. The problems in Zangaria had started a long time before anyone had heard of her.

I probably just made them worse, Emily thought.

She sighed. She probably had. The broadsheets alone—and reading and writing—allowed rumormongers to spread the word much further than they could by word of mouth alone. She wasn't blind to the irony. Frieda had shown her a handful of papers containing the most scurrilous rumors about her relationship with four young men she barely knew. She wasn't sure if she should be impressed by the unknown writer's imagination or horrified. A couple of the sexual positions he described were probably impossible without strong magic or grievous bodily harm.

There was a knock on the door. She pushed a handful of her papers into the drawer—cleaning up was something else that had taken a backseat to her work—and waved a hand in the air, casting an opening charm. It was something that would have awed her five years ago, even though it was a very simple spell. She couldn't help

wondering what Alassa or her other friends would make of Earth. Technology had
made life so much easier that most of the inhabitants didn't know how lucky they
were.

The grass is always greener on the other side of the hill, she thought, as Frieda and
Celadon entered the office. Celadon was carrying a leather folder under one arm. *And
no one realizes what they have until they lose it.*

She rose as the door closed behind them, nodding politely to Celadon. He bowed
in return, a formal bow that told her everything she needed to know about his origins. Someone who'd been taught magical etiquette had either grown up in a magical
household or had been given a great deal of tuition. The former seemed more likely.
His magic was clearly present—she could sense it, even at a distance—but carefully
controlled.

Celadon pressed one hand to his heart. "I greet you, Lady Emily." His voice was
formal, tinged with an accent that reminded Emily of Markus. "I pledge to hold my
hand in your house."

Emily studied him for a long moment. He was handsome, she supposed, but in
a vague kind of way. His face was just a *little* too soft, his short hair just a *little* too
blond... he held himself in a manner that suggested formal etiquette lessons, rather
than military training. He wore a pair of black trousers and a white shirt that had
probably cost him a great deal of money, but was carefully tailored to allow him to
move freely. There was no sword at his belt, yet the way he held himself suggested
there should be. It was hard not to feel a flicker of dislike. Celadon had never been
truly tested in life.

"I thank you," Emily said, with equal formality. She didn't miss the resentful look
Frieda shot at Celadon's back. "Please, be seated."

Celadon bowed again then sat, resting his folder on his lap. Frieda stood behind
him, ramrod straight; her hands clasped behind her back. Sergeant Miles had been
teaching her, Emily reminded herself. There was nothing *technically* wrong with
her posture, nothing a senior officer could take exception to, but it clearly signaled
her displeasure. Emily didn't miss the message, yet... she didn't know if *Celadon* had
picked up on it. Frieda wasn't just unhappy, she was *pissed*. And, perhaps, reaching
the end of her tether.

Emily met Frieda's eyes, silently willing her to sit down, then sat. Celadon looked
back at her, his bright blue eyes not quite meeting hers. *That* too was magical etiquette, she reminded herself. Forcing eye contact was a challenge, of sorts. Maybe
not one that would lead to a duel, but definitely one that could lead to trouble. Frieda
remained standing, her hands out of sight. Emily hoped—prayed—she wouldn't do
anything stupid.

"Frieda has requested that I go over your joint project with you," she said, flatly.
"Professor Lombardi has raised no objections."

She kept her face under tight control. Professor Lombardi hadn't been pleased
when she'd asked permission, although he'd granted it without more than a handful of vague warnings and instructions. She could talk to them, she could attempt

to meditate their disagreements, but she couldn't do the work *for* them. Learning to work with other magicians was part of the point, he'd said. Emily couldn't help feeling grateful that she and Caleb hadn't had so many difficulties when *they'd* been working together.

Celadon opened his folder. "I will talk you through it," he said. Emily felt a flicker of annoyance at the assurance in his tone. If he spoke to Frieda like that, he was lucky she hadn't already hexed him into next week. "Our original project was to find ways to improve channeling magic into potion brews. As you know, an alchemical brew requires a certain amount of magic to work..."

"I *should* know that," Emily interrupted. His tone wasn't winning him any friends. If nothing else, common sense should have warned him that Emily *had* passed all of her fourth-year exams. "Do you have a point?"

Celadon had the grace to blush. "Controlling the influx of magic is one of the hardest aspects of alchemy. A relatively simple potion might forgive you if you push in too much magic, but a far more complex potion will not. There are even some potions that will turn to sludge if you give them too little magic, yet explode violently if you give them too much."

"A common problem," Emily said. "I believe you managed to convince Professor Lombardi that it was worth trying...?"

"We did," Celadon said. "He accepted our presentation last year."

Emily looked at Frieda, who scowled. "And then... what?"

Celadon produced a sheet of paper. "Our original work was relatively simple: a combination of stone, iron and crystal fingers... ah, tools. We just called them *fingers*. They would allow a preset amount of magic to flow through, then burn out."

"There'd be blowback," Emily said.

"The magic could be reabsorbed or dispelled," Celadon said. "It would have worked, Lady Emily. The *real* drawback was that each *finger* could only be used once."

"It would get costly," Frieda said. There was a hint of desperation in her tone. "But they would have worked."

Emily nodded, slowly. She doubted *Frieda* had been the one to have the original idea. Frieda was imaginative, but not *innovative*. And yet...given an idea, she could run with it.

"I see," she said. Cost *would* be a problem, although Whitehall's budget was larger than Cockatrice's. And she could see a handful of other problems too. Professor Lombardi might like the idea, but Professor Thande would be horrified. Magicians wouldn't be able to learn precise control over their magic if they used tools. "So... what happened?"

Celadon smiled, a little shyly. "I found a way to make the fingers reusable. If there was a careful charm worked into the wood, I found, the magic would cut off *without* destroying the finger. But..."

"He didn't consult me about it," Frieda said. Her hands were out of sight, but it was clear she was flexing them. "He didn't even bother to tell me that he'd had an idea until he'd done all the work!"

"It's a good idea," Celadon said. For the first time, Emily heard *passion* in his voice. "You *know* the problem, you know we need a solution and you won't *listen!*"

"I do listen," Frieda snapped. Emily sensed her magic flare. "You're not answering..."

Emily cleared her throat, loudly. "Celadon," she said. "Talk me through your idea, step by step."

Celadon blinked. "I keep trying," he said. "And..."

"Do it for me," Emily said. "Keep it as simple as possible."

"Hah," Frieda muttered.

Emily shot her a quelling glance, then looked at Celadon. "Begin."

Celadon took a breath. "As you know"—Emily was starting to hate that phrase—"you can use wood to store spellware and channel magic," he said. "Wands work, put simply, because magic flows through the wood and into the embedded spell, triggering the spell. They're seen as a bad habit because magicians can forget how to cast the spells for themselves."

"True," Emily said. "And, *later,* you can tell me how you plan to evade that problem."

"I worked out a spell regulator that basically limits the amount of magic that flows through the wand." Celadon produced a sheet of paper and held it out to her. "It is a fearsomely complex piece of magic, but quite understandable."

Emily gave him a sharp look. His tone was just one step below objectionable, but she knew it would grate on Frieda. It grated on *Emily* and *she* hadn't encountered *quite* so much condescension in her life. *Everyone* had looked down on Frieda, once upon a time. Now...

"The excess magic would be drained into a simple light spell," Celadon continued. "And the light would alert the caster that they no longer needed to expend magic."

Emily took the sheet of paper and slowly worked her way through the spell diagram. It *was* a complex piece of magic, she had to admit. The notation made it clear that Celadon had put it together from scratch, even though some aspects were similar to spells she'd cast in her first two years as a magician. She felt a flicker of respect, even though *Celadon* was starting to grate on her. Very few magicians would have thought of a flow regulator, let alone a magical valve. They would have considered the whole concept pointless.

Her blood ran cold. A valve... she'd designed a valve for her batteries. But it wasn't quite the same. Her valve discharged all the magic in the battery at once. Celadon's concept was better, if it could be scaled up... she worked her way through the spell diagram carefully, testing and retesting every segment. It should work, if someone had the power and precision to cast the spell. Doing *that* would not be easy.

She looked up at him. "Can you cast this spell?"

"I believe so," Celadon said. "It *should* be workable."

"Theoretically," Emily said.

She sighed, inwardly. She understood now. Celadon *had* come up with something new—something brilliant—and had run with it, rather than checking with his partner. And Frieda hadn't been able to follow the spellwork, which had led to her getting angry and then Celadon had gotten angry too...

Frieda might not be able to cast the spell, Emily thought, numbly. She wasn't sure *she* could cast the spell, certainly not on the first try. *Can* Celadon *cast the spell?*

She looked down at the paper for a long moment, trying to think. Frieda *hated* to appear stupid. Emily didn't blame her for that, not even slightly. But Frieda had also been illiterate only three years ago. It was easy to see why she might be behind her classmates, now the deficiencies in her education had finally started to catch up with her. And instead of understanding the problem and seeking help, Frieda was lashing out...

And Celadon was probably a bad choice for Frieda's partner, her thoughts added. *He doesn't have the background to understand her weaknesses, let alone help her to overcome the limitations of her education.*

"It isn't a bad piece of work," Emily said. She did her best to ignore the betrayed look Frieda shot her. "But you really do have to simplify it."

"I have simplified it as much as possible," Celadon said. "The spell *cannot* work as a collection of smaller charms. It would break up under the first influx of magic. There is no way to break it down further."

"Which would make actually *casting* the spell a nightmare," Emily said.

She rubbed her forehead. The whole situation was a nightmare. Celadon had stumbled across something brilliant, yet—if he couldn't convince his partner to work with him—the joint project was going to crash and burn. Perhaps she should urge him to stick with the original version, the one Frieda understood... except there had been too many limitations in the project. Gordian and the senior tutors might class it under the heading of 'awesome, but impractical.' Frieda and Celadon *might* get some marks for it, but...

"You need to actually cast the spell," she said, "or you have nothing more than a theory."

"I was planning to practice next term," Celadon said. "It only takes one of us to cast it..."

Emily sighed. *Gordian* would insist on *Frieda* being able to cast it too. And he'd be right, damn him. A spell that could only be cast by a handful of magicians was of limited value.

"Go to the spellchamber," she ordered, firmly. "I want you to practice casting the spell until you succeed. If you can't cast it by the end of half-term"—she made a show of looking at the calendar—"in two days, you need to rethink your project."

"Yes, My Lady," Celadon said. There wasn't even a *trace* of sarcasm in his words, but Emily narrowed her eyes anyway. "I'll report to you as soon as I succeed."

"Good." Emily nodded to the door. "Go."

Celadon rose and bowed, then turned and walked out the door. Emily watched him go, then looked at Frieda. The hatred was clearly visible on her face. She might have listened to Emily—or another older student—but not to someone who was no older than her. Emily could understand why. Celadon was no different, at heart, from the well-bred students who'd tormented Frieda at Mountaintop. Even if he *was* different, *Frieda* certainly wouldn't see him that way.

"Sit down," Emily said, flatly. "You *were* very rude to him."

Frieda shrugged. "He's been very rude to me," she said, as she sat. "Can he cast the spell?"

Emily sighed. Frieda wasn't going to like what Emily had to say.

"If he can, then he's come up with something that will earn you both high marks," she said, reluctantly. Celadon's work *would* need to be fine-tuned. But she didn't know if Frieda could do it. "He hasn't done a bad job..."

"You *agree* with him?" Frieda's face twisted with anger. "After everything, you *agree* with him?"

"I think his work needs to be tested, but his ideas are sound." Emily fought to keep her voice level. "If we break it down and examine each piece, section by section..."

Frieda rose. "He didn't *ask* me," she snapped. Magic flickered around Frieda's fingertips as her voice rose hysterically. "He went ahead and did it without asking me and I don't understand and you say he's right!"

"If he can get the spell to work," Emily said. It would have been easier to talk to a girl she *didn't* know personally. She and Frieda had shared too much for Emily to speak sharply to her younger friend. "If he can, you need to learn it too..."

Frieda clenched her fists. "Are you saying he's *right?*"

"I'm saying you have to find out if he's right," Emily said. "I..."

"You mean he's right," Frieda said. The betrayal in her voice was almost a physical blow. "You think he's right..."

She turned and stalked towards the door. "Leave me alone," she snapped. Magic flared through her words, brushing against the wards. "Just... leave me alone!"

And then she was gone.

Chapter Twenty-Six

E MILY STARED AT THE CLOSED DOOR IN SHOCK.
   She could have stopped Frieda. Even without the wards, she knew a dozen spells that could have stopped Frieda in her tracks. And yet... she had been too shocked to muster them. She'd expected argument, she'd expected... she hadn't expected Frieda to shout, or to storm out like a teenage girl.

She is a teenage girl, Emily thought. She reached out to touch the wards, then stopped herself. *She...*

Emily looked down at her hands. She didn't know what to do. Nothing she could think of seemed appropriate, not after Frieda had stormed out. She could do anything from summoning Frieda back to giving her a few days to get over it, yet none of her ideas seemed useful. Frieda had changed over the last year. Emily had no idea how to make it better.

You can't do the work for her, she told herself. Perhaps she should seek out Sergeant Miles and ask for advice. Or write to Lady Barb. They were listed as Frieda's other guardians, weren't they? Perhaps *they* should step in... although it was rare for parents to be directly involved in Whitehall. Students were expected to sort out their problems for themselves. *But what can you do?*

She groaned, tiredly. She'd hoped to either prove that Celadon was wrong or convince Frieda to listen to him. But she hadn't had the chance. Celadon might not even be able to turn his theory into reality... if he couldn't, Frieda and Celadon were running out of time. They'd have to go back to their original plan and make it work before they faced their supervisors. And even if he could, Frieda would need to *understand* the spellwork to pass the exam. No one would condemn her for not coming up with the idea herself, but they'd certainly object if she couldn't explain or build upon Celadon's work.

Fuck, she thought. She rubbed her eyes, trying to *think*. But no magical solution came to mind. *What the hell do I do?*

There was a knock on the door, sharp and authoritative. Gordian, then. Or maybe one of the male tutors... she waved a hand in the air, opening the door. Gordian had probably come to check on progress or... or something. He didn't *know* she'd been down to the catacombs, as far as she knew, but he might suspect something. Or maybe he just wanted to nag her about starting the second round of the dueling contest.

"Emily," Caleb said.

Emily looked up, surprised. Caleb—*not* Gordian—stepped into the room. She smiled, feeling a wave of relief. Caleb had sisters. He could advise her... if she asked him. And she *could* ask him. They might no longer be lovers—and their friendship was more than a little strained—but she didn't think he'd deliberately sabotage her. He'd never been that kind of person.

Caleb raised his eyebrows. "Are you alright?"

"No," Emily said. She wondered, vaguely, what she looked like. There was a mirror in the washroom... she pushed the thought aside, sharply. She didn't have *time* to worry about her appearance. "Frieda and I just had a fight."

"Ouch." Caleb sat down on the chair Celadon had vacated and gazed at her. "What happened?"

Emily gathered herself, then ran through the entire story. She wasn't sure she believed her own words. Frieda had always been... *emotional*... but she'd never expected the younger girl to lose her composure so badly. Or to shout at *her*. Frieda had had her differences with other students—and Caleb—but she'd always been friendly with Emily. Emily had valued her uncomplicated friendship more than she cared to admit.

Caleb winced when she'd finished. "Did you check for any outside influence?"

"Yeah," Emily said. Casting *those* spells without Frieda noticing hadn't been easy. "No spells or potions to make her more... aggressive."

"Nothing that showed up, at least." Caleb stroked his chin. Emily couldn't help thinking that he looked like a younger, clean-shaven version of his father. "Did you check her room?"

Emily sucked in her breath. Nanette—Lin—had used subtle magic to keep people from noticing her, way back in Emily's Second Year at Whitehall. It had worked, too. And yet... she'd heard that Grandmaster Hasdrubal had modified the wards to sound the alert if someone *else* tried to use subtle magic outside the classroom. Gordian wouldn't have cancelled that, would he?

Except subtle magic helps keep the school together, she thought, darkly. The detection spells might be completely useless.

She closed her eyes for a long moment. It went against the grain to walk into Frieda's room without permission. She would have felt like a trespasser. And yet, she *was* Head Girl. She had authority to enter the dorms at will, even the *male* dorms. No one would question her looking for Frieda in her bedroom. The rune on her chest would respond to subtle magic, even if it wasn't aimed at her. And then...

It might have escaped detection, she thought. *Or the spells might have been jiggered to let it work without sounding the alert.*

She thought, fast. The only person who could have ordered the wards not to sound the alert was Gordian. He was the only person—save for her, perhaps—who could have ensured the housemothers didn't catch a whiff of subtle magic. And yet, she found it hard to imagine him taking such a risk. He'd be in *deep* trouble if the truth got out. Frieda might be a nobody, as far as the magical community was concerned, but she was hardly the only student at risk.

Better check, she thought. *And then decide what to do.*

Caleb was speaking. She dragged her attention back to him.

"I'm sorry," she said. "I missed that."

He gave her a long-suffering look. "What about her time of the month?"

Emily snorted. "It hasn't been her time of the month for two months straight!"

She shook her head. Frieda would have been given potions to help her cope, like all of the other girls in Whitehall. She'd have a little discomfort every month, but nothing that would interfere with her schooling. Whoever had invented those potions, Emily had decided long ago, couldn't possibly be honored enough. The magical community should have come up with a whole new series of awards, just so they could be presented to her.

"Then she might simply be cracking under the workload," Caleb offered. "She'd hardly be the first student to have problems in Fourth Year."

"I know." Emily shook her head. "I don't know what to do."

"Mother would give her some time to calm down, then force her to go over everything piece by piece," Caleb said. "But Frieda has to come to grips with this herself."

Emily felt a sudden stab of envy, mingled with bitter resentment. How nice it would have been to have a mother who *cared*! Sienna was strict, but at least she *cared* about her children. And she'd worked hard to help her youngest daughter recover after the... incident... in Beneficence.

"I know," she said. "But at this rate, she's going to fail."

She's going to be expelled, her thoughts added. How much trouble could a student get into before the tutors decided to expel her? Master Tor had clearly thought *Emily* should be expelled, way back in Second Year. *Gordian won't let her retake the year— he won't let her retake the Fourth Year—when she's caused so much trouble.*

"Then you have to make her get over herself," Caleb said. "Or *let* her fail."

Emily shrugged, then rose. "We'll check her room," she said. Taking Caleb along would raise eyebrows, but she had the feeling she'd need a witness. And besides, she trusted his instincts. "And then we'll decide what to do."

The corridors felt oddly empty as they walked through them and down the stairs. A number of portraits had been removed for cleaning, leaving blank spaces on the walls. Others had been replaced with older portraits, paintings of magicians who'd lived and died hundreds of years ago. She couldn't help thinking, as she caught sight of a particularly shifty looking magician, that the portrait had been painted after its subject's death.

That wouldn't be a surprise, she thought, bitterly. *None of the portraits of me look anything like me.*

She heard a number of students playing in the distance as she led the way into the fourth year dorms. Someone—probably Madame Beauregard—had fiddled with the wards, allowing the students to mingle. It was half-term, Emily recalled. The handful of younger students who'd remained in Whitehall could play with their elders, even if their elders wouldn't be seen dead with their juniors during term-time. True friendships that crossed the year-line were rare. Emily couldn't help thinking that the age gap between Frieda and herself was actually greater than almost any other friendship in Whitehall.

Her eyes narrowed as she stopped outside Frieda's door. Someone had stuck a copy of one of the pamphlets outside, fixing it to the wood with a sticking charm.

Emily cancelled the charm, glanced at the parchment and then crumpled it in her hand. Another set of lies and libels... she promised herself, if she ever found out who was carrying them into Whitehall, she would not be *gentle*.

It has to be someone who stayed over, Emily thought. She tapped on Frieda's door and waited, counting the seconds under her breath. Frieda had roommates, but Emily couldn't recall if they'd stayed in Whitehall for half-term. *And there aren't* that *many suspects.*

No one opened the door. Emily motioned for Caleb to stay back, then pushed the door open gently. The wards parted at her touch, allowing her to step inside. She peered forward, half- expecting to be caught by a hex, and looked into the room. It was deserted. Frieda's bed was a mess, clothes and blankets hurled in all directions; the other two beds looked strikingly neat, as if they'd been made up before their occupants went home. They probably had. Madame Beauregard had been known to carry out surprise inspections, just to make sure the rooms were clean and tidy.

Good thing she didn't check this room, Emily thought. *Being forced to make and remake her bed a hundred times wouldn't do anything for Frieda's state of mind.*

She took a long look around the room, making sure there wasn't anything embarrassing in plain sight, then beckoned Caleb inside. It was a risk—Madame Beauregard would *not* be pleased if she caught them—but there was no choice. Emily touched the rune on her chest, feeling nothing, as Caleb closed the door behind him. There was no subtle magic at all.

"They warded their beds thoroughly," Caleb said. "That's not a good sign."

Emily nodded. All *three* beds bristled with wards and protective hexes, ready to sting or freeze or transform any unwary intruders. Emily had long-since developed the habit of warding *her* bed, even in Whitehall, but Frieda and her roommates had been excessively paranoid. There were so many protective hexes that an unwary caster might wind up being caught in his own trap. Emily turned her attention to their trunks and sucked in her breath, tightly. The trunks had been heavily warded too.

And that means they're fighting all the time, she thought, grimly. *She'd* never warded her bed so thoroughly, even when she'd had disagreements with her roommates. The implications weren't good. *They don't trust Frieda to leave their stuff alone while they're on holiday.*

She shivered. Frieda was many things, but she was no thief. God knew a *real* thief would be beaten to death in the Cairngorms, or mutilated and then sent out to die in the cold. Emily couldn't imagine Frieda stealing anything... but she *could* imagine the younger girl setting a booby-trap on someone's trunk. A moment of carelessness was all it would take for the trap to spring. And then...

"We could unlock some of the wards," Caleb said. "But rebuilding them afterwards would be a challenge."

"Or impossible," Emily said. There were so many hexes built into the protective wards that she didn't think she could rebuild them, not without leaving something out. It would be a great improvement, but it would also be a red flag to whoever had crafted the wards in the first place. "I think they cast far too many spells to protect their bed."

Caleb snickered. "Getting out of bed in the middle of the night to go to the toilet would pose a challenge."

Emily nodded. The occupants could use a chamberpot, she supposed, yet they'd still be risking accidental contact with their own wards. An advanced student could key the wards to allow them to pass unmolested—it was what she'd done, back in her suite—but she doubted Frieda was at that level. It only added to her sense that something was badly wrong. No one would make life so inconvenient for themselves without feeling they *needed* the additional security.

She stepped around the beds, careful not to brush the wards, and walked into the bathroom. It was identical to the rooms she'd used for the last five years: a shower, a toilet, a washbasin and a towel rail. A handful of spells glittered in the air as she entered, but a quick check revealed that they, too, were standard. Frieda would have thought it was heaven, Emily reflected, as she tested for subtle magic. The bathroom was sheer luxury compared to the toilets in her village. And yet, it was the bare minimum as far as Earth was concerned.

Nothing, Emily thought.

She gritted her teeth as she walked back into the bedroom, reaching out with her mind to touch the wards. She'd expected to find that Gordian—or someone—had tampered with them, but there was nothing beyond a basic sensing ward. The staff would know if someone used magic, yet they weren't supervising the room. Emily couldn't help finding that ominous. If Frieda was in real trouble, surely the staff would be keeping a closer eye on her.

But they'd have to be careful, she thought. Keeping an eye on the students is one thing, but spying on them in their bedrooms and bathrooms was quite another.

It wasn't a pleasant thought. Whitehall *didn't* have camera-like wards in every room, but it *could*. And *that* would drive students away faster than a murderous necromancer with bad intentions. *Emily* wouldn't have stayed if it had meant living in a goldfish bowl. She had no doubt that magical students needed to be monitored, but there were limits. It was perversely reassuring that *Gordian* seemed to be honoring them.

She sat on the carpeted floor and closed her eyes, reaching out with her mind. Frieda's wards—and her roommates'—were clearly visible to her magic, but there was nothing else apart from a handful of protective charms on the bookshelves. The room was almost completely clean. Emily tested the protective charms anyway, just in case one of the books was spelled to corrupt its reader, but found nothing particularly dangerous. A student who damaged one of the library's books would be frozen solid until one of the librarians arrived, not turned evil.

"Nothing," she said, opening her eyes. "Let's go."

She checked the wards outside, then led the way into the corridor. There was no sign of anyone, much to her relief, but the sound of younger students playing further into the dorms was growing louder. She wondered, absently, if Frieda was among them. Playing a game—even something as simple as freeze tag—would put her in a better mood.

"We should go to the library," Caleb said. He gave her a sidelong look. "Or would you prefer to go up the hill?"

Emily was tempted, more tempted than she cared to admit. It wasn't *that* late in the day. She could go for a walk, breathe the fresh air, gather her thoughts...

... And yet, going with Caleb made her feel uneasy. Not because she thought he'd do something stupid, but because she feared *she* would. Relaxing into his arms would be easy...

"I think I need to find Sergeant Miles," she said. One of the sergeants had taken a group of students on a forced march. She couldn't recall which one. Sergeant Harkin had told his class that it built character, back in first year. "And then..."

The wards *screamed* in her ear. She spun around, her body moving instinctively. Something was wrong at the far end of the corridor... badly wrong. She heard a scream, followed by another... the wards pressed against her mind, forcing her down the corridor. Her legs wobbled, as if they were no longer under her control. It was all she could do to keep herself from falling over.

She rounded the corner and froze. Frieda was standing there, angry magic crackling around her. She spun around, her plaits flying through the air. Her eyes went wide—with shock, with anger, with something Emily didn't care to recognize—when she saw Emily and Caleb. The wards were still sounding the alert, a noise thrumming in her ear that was threatening to drive Emily out of her mind. She honestly wasn't sure if it *was* in her mind or in her ears. The sound was so loud it was making it hard to focus on anything.

Caleb gasped. "What have you done?"

And then Emily saw Marian. "Frieda," she said. It was suddenly very hard to speak. "What have you done now?"

Chapter Twenty-Seven

"I SHUT HER UP," FRIEDA SAID. THERE WAS AN ODD TONE TO HER VOICE, A MIXTURE OF ANGER and self-righteousness that made her sound like a different person. "She wouldn't shut up until I made her..."

"Be quiet," Emily snapped.

She forced her shaken legs to carry her forward. Marian was sitting against the far wall, blood trickling from her nose. Her face was marred with twisted flesh—a pair of particularly unpleasant prank hexes, Emily realized—and her arm was warped into a misshapen lump that made Emily want to throw up. Marian was sobbing quietly, as if she was utterly unaware of her surroundings. She'd been hexed so badly, she'd need a healer to recover.

"I'm going to put you in stasis," Caleb said. He gave his sister a quick hug, then cast the spell. Blue light flared over Marian's body. The sound of sobbing cut off abruptly. "I..."

He rose, suddenly. Magic flared over his hands. "What were you thinking?"

Frieda gazed back at him, defiantly. "I taught her not to say stupid things in public," she snapped. "*You* should have taught her that..."

"You..." Caleb started forward, then stopped himself. "I'll..."

Emily cleared her throat, loudly. She wasn't sure *what* would happen if Caleb and Frieda started throwing hexes at each other—Caleb had more magical knowledge, but Frieda had the killer instinct he lacked—but there wasn't *time*. In stasis or not, Marian needed a healer as soon as possible. Emily wasn't sure *just* how many hexes Frieda had used on her, but it was clear that they'd started to bleed together. She doubted she could remove the hexes without risking Marian's life.

And Frieda will be in real trouble when Gordian finds out, she thought, numbly. The wards had stopped howling, but she had no doubt that Gordian and the other senior tutors had already been alerted. God knew *she'd* been in enough trouble when she'd almost killed Alassa. *She might get expelled.*

"Go to my office and wait," she ordered Frieda. She put as much force into her voice as she could. Perhaps, just perhaps, Gordian would let her deal with it. "I'll deal with you as soon as possible..."

Frieda glared at him. "You side with *him* against me?"

Emily felt her temper snap. "Go to the office or go to hell," she snapped. She didn't recognize Frieda any longer. "Wait there for me."

She watched Frieda turn and stalk off, every inch of her body language conveying the impression that she was being unfairly punished. Emily stared after Frieda, fighting down the mad urge to slap her... or to hug her and tell her that it was going to be all right. But it *wasn't* going to be all right. Frieda had assaulted a student three years younger than she was, a student who'd been recovering from a traumatic experience. Gordian would have all the ground he needed to expel Frieda...

... And the hell of it was that he would be right.

"I'll get her up to the infirmary." Caleb sounded tired, tired and frustrated. "Emily, you need to do something about her."

"I know." Emily felt a surge of bitter tiredness, mingled with the grim awareness that she'd failed. "I just don't know what to do."

Caleb stood, turning to meet her eyes. "Her behavior has been going downhill since before... since before Justice. You know it. She's been obnoxious and rude and thoroughly unpleasant, and sooner or later she's going to pull that shit on someone who isn't going to tolerate it."

He looked down at his sister's frozen body. "If she hasn't crossed the line today, Emily, she'll cross it soon. And you're pretty much the only person she actually *respects*. You're probably the only one who can knock some sense into her head before it's too late."

If it isn't already too late, Emily thought. She was sure Frieda respected Alassa—and Lady Barb—but both of them were hundreds of miles away. And yet... neither of *them* would have let Frieda get so far out of hand. *Perhaps I could send Frieda to Zangaria, if she gets expelled. Jade and Alassa would look after her...*

She sighed. "I don't know what to do!"

Caleb glared at her. "Put her over your knee or bend her over your desk and thrash her to within an inch of her life," he snapped. "Give her essays to write. Make her clean toilets for detentions. Force her to write lines or pick poisonous fruits or something else unpleasant enough to make it clear that she's being *punished*! Because if *you* don't stop her, what happens next?"

Emily swallowed. "She'll be expelled."

"Or Mother will seek revenge." Caleb levitated his sister's body into the air and directed it down the corridor. "She'll expect you to do something, Emily. So will I."

He walked off, floating Marian ahead of him. Emily clenched her fists as he walked away, fighting down a tidal wave of anger that threatened to overwhelm her. She wasn't even sure who she was angry at. Frieda, for assaulting Marian? Caleb, for putting the problem in such brutal terms? Or herself, for doing nothing until it was too late. And yet, she *couldn't* have kept Frieda with her, could she? There was no way Frieda could have gone straight into Third Year when she arrived at Whitehall.

She took a deep breath, then forced herself to turn and walk towards her office. Frieda would have gone there, wouldn't she? She had to know the consequences would be far worse if she had been caught by someone else. Unless... the possibilities ran 'round and 'round in Emily's mind, dragging at her feet as she hurried up the stairs. She didn't *want* to reach her office, or walk inside, or confront Frieda...

You walked into Heart's Eye, knowing there was a necromancer waiting for you, she told herself. *Why is it so hard to confront a friend?*

She sighed, inwardly. She'd thought she'd understood why inter-year friendships were discouraged at Whitehall, but she hadn't. Not until now. She was Head Girl, yet there was no way she could be dispassionate when dealing with *Frieda's* problems. Anyone else, she could offer advice from her lofty perch; with Frieda, all of her objectivity went right out the window. Frieda was more than a new bug, more than an irritating younger student to be ignored...

If someone else had assaulted a younger student like that, her conscience pointed out, you'd have demanded their expulsion.

She reached the door to her office and stopped. The wards confirmed that *someone* was inside, waiting for her. Frieda? Emily braced herself, fighting down an urge to run, to find someone else who could handle the situation, then pushed the door open. Frieda stood by the desk, one hand playing with the bracelet on her wrist. Emily allowed herself a tiny moment of relief—at least Frieda had gone to the office, instead of running—and then closed the door, slamming the most powerful privacy wards she could muster into place. No one, not even Gordian, would be able to eavesdrop.

But I'll have to tell him something, she thought. *That assault won't go unnoticed.*

She clasped her hands behind her back as she studied Frieda. The younger girl gazed back at her defiantly, her face somehow *different*. She'd changed, Emily reflected; she'd become a little harder, a little more determined to blaze her own path through the world. Her pigtails no longer looked girlish, somehow; her arms were strongly muscled, stronger perhaps than Emily herself. And her magic was ever-present, buzzing just below her wards.

"Frieda," Emily said. Her mouth was suddenly dry. It was all she could do to keep her anger out of her voice. "What happened?"

Frieda's face didn't change. "We were playing tag. She started to talk about you and me and... and stuff. I don't want to talk about it."

"You don't have a choice," Emily said, tartly. "What *sort* of stuff?"

"She was saying that you and I were having a relationship," Frieda said. "And that you broke up with Caleb because of me and... she just went on and on until I silenced her."

"Until you nearly killed her," Emily said. Marian had been bleeding. There could be internal injuries... or it could have been a force punch. Or a physical blow. Magicians rarely settled their disputes through brute force. A punch in the face would have surprised Marian more than a whole series of hexes. "She's a *kid!*"

Frieda snorted. "She's old enough to marry, old enough to bear children, old enough..."

"She's a firstie," Emily said. She felt her temper rise. "What were you *thinking?* Or were you thinking at all?"

"I was thinking that I could silence her," Frieda snapped. "I'm not stupid!"

"You could be expelled for this," Emily said. It was hard to keep her voice level. "You attacked a *firstie*. What sort of excuse do you have?"

"What sort of petty excuse did *Jade* have for knocking you on your ass when *you* were a firstie?" Frieda countered. "He did, did he not?"

Emily blinked. Jade—or Alassa—must have told Frieda that, back in Zangaria. "We were in Martial Magic," she said. Jade had been a good sparring partner, even though she was ruefully aware she'd never come close to matching him. "What's *your* excuse?"

"She deserved it." Frieda crossed her arms under her breasts. "I'm not sorry."

"You should be," Emily said. She forced herself to unclasp her hands. "Frieda, you could have *killed* her!"

"I didn't," Frieda said.

Emily felt her temper snap. "You assaulted a student who didn't have a hope of standing up to you," she snarled. That would have been true even if Marian *hadn't* been recovering from trauma. *Emily* had studied hard, but she'd never been able to match Jade or Cat in Martial Magic. "What the hell do you think excuses *that*?"

"She was lying about us, about *you*," Frieda snapped back. "She had to be silenced!"

And so you set out to silence her, Emily thought.

She groaned. She'd never liked the honor culture of the Nameless World, although she had to admit that she might have avoided Master Grey's trap if she'd been more aware of the pitfalls. A person who shot his mouth off *could* be challenged, he *could* be silenced by force... freedom of speech wasn't even a *concept* on the Nameless World. And a man who *didn't* challenge his detractors to put up or shut up would be seen as a weakling.

And that goes for magicians too, Emily thought. It was bitterly ironic. Mundane women were expected to ignore slurs against their persons—and mundane men were expected to ignore them—but female magicians were expected to defend their own honor. The one community on the Nameless World where sexual equality was actually a *thing* and it still managed to bite her on the behind. *Frieda thought she was doing the right thing.*

"You shouldn't let this happen," Frieda said. "Why don't you find whoever is spreading these rumors and *silence* him?"

"Because I don't know who to blame," Emily said. *Someone* was bringing the rumors into Whitehall. Perhaps she could find him and... *convince*... him to lead her to the true mastermind. But she had no idea how she could catch the rumormonger. "And even if I did, it would be wrong to silence him."

"These rumors are hacking away at your reputation," Frieda said. "What will people do if they think you can't respond?"

Emily sighed. She could face a necromancer, or a dark wizard, or an aristocrat with more good breeding than common sense. The threat was clear and present, easy to understand if hard to counter. But rumors? Rumors with no discernible source? She had no way to fight back, no way even to know who was behind it... all she could do was carry on and hope that nothing else happened before the exams.

And do you really think, her thoughts mocked her, *that you'll be that lucky?*

"That isn't the problem right now," she said. She walked forward and sat behind her desk, resting her elbows on the wood. Frieda turned to face her, slowly. "What should I do with you?"

Frieda's face twisted. "I was defending *your* honor!"

"I didn't ask you to defend it," Emily said.

She thrust herself forward before Frieda could respond. "You've changed. Your behavior has been going downhill for the last three months. And now you've stepped over the line."

"And now you're washing your hands of me?" Frieda asked. There was something in her tone that made Emily's heart want to break. "You're telling me that you don't want to be with me any longer?"

"I'm telling you that I can't ignore it any longer," Emily said. She thought back to Frieda's permanent record and shivered. "And nor can anyone else."

Frieda's face went expressionless. "What now?"

Emily looked her in the eye. "You are being an idiot. I know this year is hard—it was hard for me too! I had a tutor who was trying to kill me! And yet you're so wrapped up in yourself that you're on the verge of getting expelled."

"Celadon is being a prick..."

"Yes, he is," Emily agreed. "But you're not being much better."

She held up a hand before Frieda could say a word. "He's made a considerable improvement to the project proposal. Yes, he *should* have talked it over with you first. The damned project is about learning to work together, as well as trying to push the limits of the possible. But he has made it. *You* have to understand what he's done and then work to build on it..."

"So you're siding with him," Frieda said, flatly.

"I'm trying to help *both* of you," Emily said. What would Aloha do? Leave both parties to sink or swim? Or try to find a way to get them to find common ground? Or... would she even be involved? *Emily* wouldn't be involved if *Frieda* hadn't been involved. "You won't lose marks because he came up with the concept, Frieda. You'll lose them because you don't understand what he's done."

"I can't understand it," Frieda snapped.

Emily nodded, understanding Frieda's frustration. Celadon was so far ahead of her that it wouldn't be easy to bridge the gulf, even if he hadn't been smugly convinced of his own intellectual superiority and Frieda resenting the hell out of it. Hell, Emily wasn't sure *she* could explain the basics of magical theory to a firstie, not now. Years ago, Void had declined to school her in magic personally, pointing out that she needed to learn the basics first. She thought she understood his point now.

"You will," she said. "But that isn't the main problem. You've turned into a..."

"A bitch?" Frieda asked. Her voice was suddenly hard. "Was *that* what you were going to say?"

"A nightmare," Emily said. "You're snapping at everyone, you're aggressive... and now you've assaulted a firstie!"

"Who deserved it," Frieda insisted.

Emily met her eyes. "What do you deserve now?"

Frieda ignored her. "You're betraying me for her, for him, for everyone." Her voice rose, alarmingly. "Why are you still with *him*? He betrayed you for her and..."

"Caleb is not the issue here," Emily said. "We're friends..."

"And so you betray me for him," Frieda shouted. "That little bitch was right!"

Emily rose. "*Listen* to me," she snapped. "What will happen if Gordian decides you should be expelled? Where will you go?"

"I can survive," Frieda said. "I don't need anyone! I can go and..."

"... We'll all be sorry when you're dead?" Emily said. She felt her own voice rise and forced it down. "Stop feeling sorry for yourself and *look* at yourself!"

She sat back, wondering why everything had gone so badly wrong. Perhaps she should have kept a closer eye on Frieda. Perhaps... she shook her head. It didn't matter, not now. The situation had to be handled firmly enough to keep Gordian from doing anything else.

"You will report to the Warden." She hated herself for saying it, but there was no choice. "You will tell him that I am thoroughly displeased with your conduct and he is to take appropriate measures."

Frieda's eyes flashed fire. "Too weedy to beat me yourself?"

Emily was too tired to care about the challenge. "After you have been disciplined, you will write me a long essay on *precisely* why what you did was wrong. And *then* you will sit down and work your way through Celadon's proposal. I want you to understand the theory by the end of half-term."

"Or what?" Frieda challenged. "You'll have me beaten again?"

"I will tell the Grandmaster that you are probably going to have to repeat Third Year," Emily said, flatly. It was unlikely Frieda would be allowed to retake *just* Fourth Year. "You need to master the theory before you can move ahead."

She met Frieda's eyes. "I don't know what's wrong with you," she said. "But you are crossing the line. If you don't shape up, you might just be expelled. Go."

Frieda turned and marched out of the room. Emily watched her go, then covered her eyes as the door banged closed. There had been no choice. She told herself that, again and again, as the guilt threatened to overwhelm her. There had been no choice. And yet, she knew she would always regret it.

And I still don't know what's wrong with her, she thought. She hesitated, then rose. If Sergeant Miles was in the school, he'd be in the armory. *Perhaps he can offer some advice.*

Chapter Twenty-Eight

E MILY FEARED THAT FRIEDA MIGHT HAVE DONE *REAL* HARM TO MARIAN, THE KIND OF HARM that couldn't be repaired by magic, but Madame Kyla had no trouble repairing the damage. And yet, it was clear—the one time Emily looked in on her—that the incident had been traumatizing. Marian might be physically healed, but the mental damage was still extensive. Caleb told her, privately, that Marian had suffered a relapse. It wasn't clear if she'd be able to return to classes at the end of half-term.

"I hope you punished her," Caleb said, afterwards. "Because I can't keep this from Mother indefinitely."

"Yes," Emily said. "I told her off and I sent her to the Warden. She *was* punished."

She kept her thoughts to herself as the final days of half-term ticked away. She expected Gordian to say *something* about the incident, but he neither summoned her to his office nor ordered Frieda's immediate expulsion. Emily puzzled over it, remembering the story of the dog that didn't bark. Gordian knew—he *had* to know—about the whole affair. It wasn't like him to just let it pass. If nothing else, he had to make sure that Frieda was warned *never* to do anything like it again.

She'd hoped that Sergeant Miles—or someone else she trusted to offer good advice—would have remained at Whitehall, but he'd taken his students out on a character-building forced march. She wrote him a note anyway, then a longer letter to Lady Barb, but there was no response. Lady Barb was out of touch, she was told. Emily wished, grimly, that she'd convinced the older woman to stay at Whitehall. She might have been sharp and sarcastic if the Head Girl came to her for advice, but she would have given Emily advice regardless.

Emily *did* keep an eye on Frieda as half-term came to an end. The younger girl had been caned—of course—and then wrote an essay managing to combine an odd understanding of what she'd done wrong with a strange—and defiant—insistence that she'd somehow done the right thing. Emily read it and shook her head, unable to escape the sense that she was watching helplessly as a runaway train raced down the track towards disaster. If Frieda had been influenced by an outside power, it would have been understandable. Instead...

Instead, she was left wondering if she'd missed something. Or if she'd somehow failed Frieda.

It was almost a relief when classes restarted, even though most of her classes spent the first day reviewing material they'd covered in the previous term. Emily didn't blame Professor Lombardi and Professor Armstrong for wanting to make sure that everyone was on the same page, but she couldn't help thinking of it as yet another waste of her limited time before the exams. She hadn't gone home for the holidays. *None* of the older students had left the school for more than a quick walk up the mountains or a trip to Dragon's Den. And yet they had to review material before moving on. The only teacher who didn't seem inclined to hold a review was Gordian and she wasn't inclined to relax in *his* class. She *still* had no idea what he knew...

"Emily, remain behind," Gordian said, once his class finally came to an end. "Everyone else, dismissed."

Emily groaned inwardly, keeping her face impassive as the classroom hastily emptied. She had the feeling she would have enjoyed Ethics of Magic and Politics if Gordian hadn't been teaching it—the class did raise a number of interesting questions—but as it was she just wanted to sit at the back and not make waves. Gordian didn't let her, of course. He asked her questions more than anyone else, even the students who didn't seem to be paying attention. It was hard to escape the feeling that he had something up his sleeve...

Maybe he just wants to embarrass me in front of the others, she thought. It would be petty, if that were the case, but Gordian would hardly be the first sorcerer to indulge in a little pettiness. *Or maybe he thinks the Head Girl should be taking the lead.*

She sighed as Gordian sat down, facing her. She'd waited for five days, expecting the hammer to fall at any moment. And yet... it hadn't. She couldn't decide if Gordian was trying to outlast her or if he'd simply decided that she'd handled the matter in a suitable manner. Maybe he didn't know she'd been down to the catacombs. She knew they hadn't been caught.

"Lady Emily," Gordian said. "Do you know why I asked you to remain behind?"

Emily could make a number of guesses. But half of them would be revealing.

"No, sir," she said.

"A disturbing report reached my ears," Gordian said. "Your young friend assaulted a far younger student."

Reached your ears, Emily thought, sardonically. Gordian was connected to the wards. It would be hard for him to travel far from Whitehall without disconnecting himself and passing the wards to someone else. Doing that would be difficult, from what Gordian's predecessor had said. *You would have been alerted the moment the alarms went off.*

She kept her mouth shut. Gordian presumably had something to say. The sooner she let him say it, the sooner she could deal with it. Or just leave.

"The healer reported that the damage was quite significant," Gordian said, after a long moment. "Perhaps you could explain to me, young lady, why your friend should not be expelled?"

"She was punished," Emily said, flatly.

"Perhaps the punishment was not sufficient," Gordian said. "Perhaps it merits a far worse punishment."

Emily took a breath. Thankfully, she'd anticipated that question.

"Five years ago, one student accidentally injured another student," she said. "The wounded student had to spend several days in the infirmary. The student who cast the jumbled spells was caned, then forced to write an essay on the subject. I believe that is a suitable precedent for Frieda's case."

"You may be right." Gordian cocked his head. "Do you think that everyone will agree?"

"The precedent has been set," Emily said. It wasn't perfect, of course. Frieda was three years older than Marian, rather than being the same age. "And I believed I should follow it."

"I see," Gordian said. "I could, of course, overturn your decision."

"Not without calling my position into question," Emily said. She *had* made sure to read the rules, after she'd been told she'd be Head Girl. "It was my duty to handle the situation and I handled it."

"You were also quite soft on her," Gordian said, his voice surprisingly quiet. "Remind me, Emily. Which year is Frieda in?"

"Fourth," Emily said. "And Marian is a firstie. That does not change the fact that it was my task to handle the affair."

"No, but it does call your judgement into question," Gordian pointed out. "What would you have done if it had been someone else?"

"I think I would have done the same thing," Emily lied. Gordian had a very good point, damn him. Frieda was a *friend*. She wouldn't have been anything like so gentle with another student. "It *was* my call to make."

"It was, yes." Gordian met her eyes, evenly. "I don't think I have to warn you that this situation is already too far out of control. If Frieda does *not* shape up in a hurry, you may bear the brunt of the blame for her antics. And *she* will be expelled."

Because I didn't convince her to stop, Emily thought, sourly. *He has me whichever way I turn.*

"I understand," she said, tonelessly.

"She should also be removed from the dueling club," Gordian added. "Or should she stay, because she's one of the best duelists?"

Emily resisted the urge to roll her eyes. Frieda probably *should* be banned from the club, at least until her disposition improved. It wasn't something Emily had thought about, but... it was a good point. And yet, Gordian didn't *want* her to go. The irony cut at Emily like a knife. Frieda was being offered the chance to get away with something bad because she was good at sports.

And she'd hate to lose it, Emily told herself. *She is a good duelist.*

She looked back at the Grandmaster. "If she behaves, she should stay," she said. The club would give Frieda something to work for, if nothing else. "And if she misbehaves, she should go."

Gordian quirked his eyebrows. "Is that your decision, as Head Girl?"

Emily sighed. "Yes."

"Very good," Gordian said. "I believe the next contest is in a couple of weeks, right? Maybe she will do well enough to go into the final round."

"Yes, sir," Emily said. That would be good for Frieda, wouldn't it? Winning a contest on even terms, proving that she truly did have a place at Whitehall... it would be good. But after all the rumors spreading through the school, it might turn to ashes in Frieda's mouth. "I'm sure she will do well."

"She'll have to work hard to overcome some of the older students," Gordian said. "They won't underestimate her any longer."

He leaned back in his chair. "I trust you will also try to keep your boyfriend from making matters worse. We *don't* need angry parents descending on the school."

"No, sir." Emily rubbed her forehead, feeling a headache starting to pound under the skin. She'd have to have a talk with Caleb, soon. But she didn't want to take her attention off Frieda. "I'm sure that Marian will recover."

"Very good," Gordian said. "You may go."

Emily bit down on a number of sharp—and unhelpful—replies as she rose and hurried out of the room. It had been a long day and she was too tired for word games. And she didn't know what Gordian actually had in mind. She walked down the stairs, trying to parse out the problem. What was he doing? Trying to deal with too many conflicting issues...

... Or trying to push her into making a mistake?

She reached the bottom of the stairs and walked into the armory. Sergeant Miles was drilling a bunch of students in the correct use of the sword, alternatively encouraging or berating the younger boys as they took jabs at stuffed dummies. They wouldn't be allowed to use *real* swords in training, Emily remembered from her own days. The practice blades were wood, charmed to deliver a nasty whack without causing real damage. She'd staggered back to her room covered in bruises more than once, back in the early days.

Not that I'll ever be a swordsmistress, she thought, reluctantly. She knew how to handle a sword, but she was no match for Jade or Cat, let alone Sergeant Miles. *Many of these young men will surpass me.*

Sergeant Miles blew his whistle, scolded a young man who hadn't put his blade down fast enough and then dismissed the class. Emily stepped to one side as a mass of sweaty students pushed past her, all male. It didn't look as if there were any female students in this class, not entirely to her surprise. Men had always outnumbered women in Martial Magic.

"Emily," Sergeant Miles said, walking over to her. The training room was hot, but he didn't seem to be sweaty. "What can I do for you?"

"I need to talk," Emily said.

Sergeant Miles nodded. "I'll be in my office in five minutes," he said. The sound of punching and kicking echoed down the corridor, coming from the changing room. "Go there and wait for me."

Emily nodded, feeling a flicker of sympathy for the younger students. Sergeant Miles could deliver a devastating reprimand without ever raising his voice. Roughhousing had its time and place, she'd been told, but not in the armory. She turned and hurried to his office, feeling the wards part as she reached the door. It was unchanged, save for a large map of Farrakhan stuck to the wall. Someone had sketched an outline of the first and second battles for the city, then covered it with notes.

They're learning more about using guns in combat, she thought. The Orcs had received a terrible surprise, the first time they'd encountered muskets. They'd have been slaughtered within seconds if they'd faced machine guns. *Who knows what will happen next time?*

Sergeant Miles entered, looking grim. "Emily." He walked over to the sideboard and poured a glass of juice. "Drink?"

"Yes, please," Emily said. "I... I have a problem."

"You have many problems," Sergeant Miles said. "Which one are we talking about here?"

"Frieda," Emily said. "You do *know* you're listed as one of her guardians?"

"Barb convinced me to add my name to the list," Sergeant Miles said. "However, she is required to request my assistance if she needs it."

Emily sighed. "She needs help." She went through the whole story, starting with Frieda's increasing moodiness and ending with her assault on Marian. "I don't know what to do."

Sergeant Miles considered it for a long moment. "She *has* taken on rather a lot. I believe she even had a nasty fight with her teammates, a month or so ago."

"I know," Emily said. "Why did you let it happen?"

"Sometimes, you *have* to let things happen," Sergeant Miles said, curtly. "I didn't approve of the rest of her squad giving her a beating, even though I knew there would be no permanent harm. But, by the same token, I had to make sure that everyone *knew* there would be punishment if someone stepped too far out of line."

Emily swallowed. "That could have happened to me..."

"Only if you weren't trying. Or if you were making a fool of yourself. Or if you were costing the team its chance at victory." Sergeant Miles took a sip of his juice. "Believe me, there have been worse incidents. When I was a young man, newly assigned to a regiment on the border, we had a thief in the barracks. When he was caught, he was forced to run the gauntlet."

"And died," Emily finished.

"He went on to be one of the bravest soldiers in the field," Sergeant Miles said, quietly. "I believe he died in combat, ten years ago."

Emily felt sick. She'd seen a man run the gauntlet, back in the army camp. His beaters had not been gentle. He'd been covered in blood before reaching the end of the line. A healer could have fixed him up, if he'd been able to pay, but the lingering effects would have taken years to fade. How could a man who'd suffered like that go on to be a brave soldier?

"Trust has to be rebuilt," Sergeant Miles said softly, answering her unspoken question. "Sometimes, that means taking your lumps like a man."

I'm not a man, Emily thought. She remembered Lady Barb talking about respect, years ago. *If you want respect, particularly from men, you have to earn it. And that means acting like a man.*

She pushed the thought aside. "What do you suggest I do?"

Sergeant Miles looked back at her. "You cannot carry Frieda on your shoulders indefinitely," he said, flatly. "You have to let her work her way through this herself."

"She can't," Emily said.

"Then perhaps she shouldn't be here." He tapped his lips before Emily could say a word. "Frieda could learn a great deal from failure, Emily. And right now, she's setting herself up for failure."

"She might have to retake the year," Emily said. "Or even go back two years."

"Hopefully with the memory of her failure to sharpen her mind," Sergeant Miles said. "Her project isn't just about coming up with a great idea, Emily. It's about learning to work together, learning how to use one partner's skills to aid the other. Frieda will do better next time."

Emily sagged. "Are you suggesting that I just... give up?"

"I'm suggesting that you let her learn from her own failures," Sergeant Miles said. He held up a hand, calmly. "She has a problem. She has a whole set of problems, most of which she brought on herself. And she needs to learn how to deal with them, not... not try to get you to solve them."

"I can't," Emily said.

"That's the problem," Sergeant Miles agreed. "You can't save her from herself."

"I don't know what to do," Emily said.

"You've done all you can do," Sergeant Miles told her. "All you can really do—now—is hope for the best."

Emily sighed. "What advice would you give her, if she came to you?"

"I'd tell her to get her head out of her ass," Sergeant Miles said, bluntly. "She can put some of her classes aside, for the moment. She can get tutoring from older students. She can limit her other commitments until after she passes her exams, if she even gets that far. At worst, she can go to the grandmaster and ask permission to retake the year. She has options, Emily, and she knows it. Right now, she's too prideful to back down."

"I thought you said that backing down was a sign of weakness," Emily said.

"It depends on where you are," Sergeant Miles said. "Showing weakness to the wrong person can be disastrous. But overestimating yourself can be equally bad."

He looked up as someone rapped on the door. "She has promise. But she's not taking the time to develop it properly."

"They said that of me," Emily reminded him.

"Yes," Sergeant Miles said. "And didn't you have problems too?"

Emily made a face as she headed for the door. The sergeant could be right. She *knew* he could be right. But she didn't want to believe it.

And yet, she didn't know what to do.

Chapter Twenty-Nine

"YOU LOOK LIKE SOMEONE IN NEED OF A FAVOR," CIRROC SAID, AS EMILY APPROACHED HIS chair. He was sitting in the common room, reading a book. "What can I do for you?"

Emily frowned, inwardly. Did she *look* like she needed a favor? Imaiqah had always insisted that she had no bargaining face. It was why Imaiqah regularly managed to convince storekeepers to lower their price, while Emily was forced to either pay the original price or walk away. But then, she hadn't grown up in a country where bargaining was expected, let alone necessary. She doubted a Wal-Mart salesman would be impressed if she tried to haggle over the price of a box of chocolates.

And he probably wouldn't have the authority to offer a reduction anyway, she thought. *The person manning a fish stall, on the other hand...*

She pushed the thought aside as she surveyed the common room. Jacqui and Cerise were seated at a table, working their way through a large pile of books; Mathis and Pandora were sitting on a love-seat, looking unbearably lovey-dovey. Emily was tempted to tell them to get a room, but the common room was really for everyone. And there were too many listening ears for her peace of mind.

"I do need a favor," she said. Cirroc would want to bargain, of course. "Perhaps we could talk about it in your room."

Cirroc gave her a long look, then rose and led the way out of the common room. His bedroom was nearby, the door crawling with hexes that would take another student several hours to dismantle safely. Emily wondered, as Cirroc opened the door, precisely what Madame Rosalinda and her male counterpart made of it. They'd need to call on a wardcrafter if they wanted to open the door in less than twenty minutes. But then, Gordian could probably tear the wards down in a moment if he wished. The school's wards reigned supreme.

She found herself looking around with interest as they walked into the room. It was slightly smaller than hers, dominated by a large bed and a bookshelf groaning with textbooks. It wasn't what she'd expected from a young man who was far too close to being a jock, but being good at sports wasn't enough to get a student through Whitehall. Even the *jocks* had to study. A small basket of dirty laundry sat in the corner, waiting for someone to deliver it to the maids. The remainder of the room was surprisingly neat. She couldn't help feeling a flicker of amusement. Every time she'd imagined a boy's bedroom, she'd envisaged something that could have passed for a bomb site.

"Please, be seated." Cirroc sat on the bed, leaning back on his hands. "What can I do for you?"

Emily sat on the chair, resting her hands in her lap. She was surprised at her own daring, even though cold logic told her she was being silly. Five years ago, she wouldn't have willingly walked into a boy's bedroom... even if she knew and trusted him completely. And there *hadn't* been anyone she knew and trusted completely. She hadn't even spent much time in *Caleb's* room after they'd started dating. *Her* room had seemed much safer.

And you walked into a necromancer's den, she reminded herself. *What terrors does a bedroom hold in comparison to that?*

She leaned forward. "I read your permanent record. You spent part of last year tutoring younger students."

"I did," Cirroc said. He grinned at her, mischievously. His white teeth flashed against his dark face. "I was suitably rewarded, of course."

"Of course," Emily agreed. She'd been surprised when she found out, although she did have to admit that Aloha had helped her out a lot in her first year. Cirroc wasn't the type of boy she expected to host a tutoring session. "The tutors were quite impressed."

Cirroc shrugged. "I wanted some pocket money. And tutoring seemed an expedient way to make it."

"I know," Emily said. She'd never considered trying to sell tutoring services. In hindsight, it was something she'd overlooked. But then, she'd never had to make money after her first few months. "I was wondering if I could hire your services."

"I'm not allowed to tutor students in my year," Cirroc said. "And you..."

He stopped. "It's not for you, is it? It's for Frieda."

Emily nodded. There was no point in trying to hide it for a few seconds more. Cirroc had probably heard the rumors too. Emily had hoped that Frieda's attack on Marian would remain a secret, but parts of the story had leaked out. Thankfully, the full truth hadn't escaped or all hell would probably have broken loose.

"She needs a tutor," she said. "Someone she'll actually *listen* to."

Cirroc raised an eyebrow. "And you think she'll listen to *me*?"

"I think it's her best chance," Emily said. She'd read Cirroc's record very carefully. "You got high marks in both alchemy and charms, plus you have experience in breaking down complex subjects for novice students. And you're old enough for her to take you as a respected authority, rather than a fellow student. She might listen to you when she won't listen to me."

"I think you've never tried to tutor anyone," Cirroc said, dryly.

Emily shrugged. She'd found it easier to tutor her mentees than Frieda. They'd seen her as a senior student, rather than a friend. Frieda, on the other hand, had too much experience talking to Emily as an equal. Emily couldn't help wondering if Frieda had the same feelings towards *Emily* as she had towards Celadon. He was an equal and yet he was presuming to lecture her from a position of superiority.

"I can't tutor her," she said, shortly. "But you can."

Cirroc made a show of considering it. "I suppose I could," he said, finally. "What's it worth?"

Emily looked back at him. "What do you want?"

She held up a hand before he could say a word. "I don't have the time or patience to dance around the subject, with you hinting and me playing guessing games," she added. "A simple statement of what you want will be sufficient."

Cirroc grinned. "A date next weekend, in Dragon's Den?"

Emily felt a hot flash of rage, then realized he was joking. "Pick something else."

"We shall see." Cirroc shot her a challenging look. "The second round of the dueling contest will be held next week, won't it?"

"As you know perfectly well," Emily said, dryly. She doubted anything short of an earthquake would convince Gordian to cancel it. "We *have* been discussing plans for the last couple of days."

"Quite," Cirroc said. "I want you to hand the dueling club to me."

Emily fought down a smile. If Cirroc *wanted* to throw her in the briar patch, who was *she* to object? And yet, she would have to convince *Gordian* to let Cirroc take over. *That* wouldn't be easy. Perhaps she could make him see that she really *didn't* have the time to handle the dueling club as well as everything else, not if she was focused on the contest. Or maybe just make the transfer and then dare Gordian to do anything about it.

If he tries to override me, he'll call my authority as Head Girl into question, she thought, wryly. *And if he sacks me for gross insubordination, I won't be Head Girl any longer.*

She tried to sound reluctant, although she had the feeling she wasn't fooling him. "Why do you want it?"

Cirroc stretched. His muscles bulged against his shirt. Emily tried not to stare.

"To you, the club is nothing more than fun," he said. "To me, it's a chance to make myself look *very* good to the dueling masters."

"Fun," Emily repeated. She wouldn't have called the club *fun*. There were too many members who seemed to think that playing around with dangerous hexes was a perfectly reasonable way to spend the evening. "Are you sure that's what you want?"

"Yeah." Cirroc shot her a challenging look. "What *else* can you give me?"

Emily could think of a number of answers to that question, but most of them were either obscene or useless. Cirroc had a point. Practical experience running a dueling club *would* look very good on his record, as he'd said before. She could pour out enough money to smooth his path, but no one had enough money to guarantee he'd be taken as an apprentice. Real experience, on the other hand...

And it's not like I want to keep the job, she thought. *I had to let Cirroc run the show last week, just because I was too busy to be there.*

"I can let you take the club, as long as the Grandmaster doesn't object," she said. It would be easy to just leave Cirroc in charge, but that would cause problems further down the line. He might not be credited with running the club if he didn't have the formal position. "I trust that will be satisfactory?"

Cirroc gave her a look that reminded her of a cat eating cream. "It will be more than satisfactory. We can organize the transfer after the second round."

"You can run the contest too," Emily said. She had the feeling he'd want that more than the club itself. He'd be showing off in front of the third and final set of representatives from the dueling club. "I'm sure you'll enjoy it."

"Thank you." Cirroc leaned forward, smiling. "And when do I start tutoring?"

"As soon as possible," Emily said. She'd told Frieda to wait in the library, but she was reluctantly aware that Frieda might not have listened to her. Frieda had taken to vanishing at odd moments, spending as much time as she could out of the castle. For someone who was more sociable than Emily, Frieda seemed to be spending a great deal of time alone. "Now, if possible."

Cirroc rose. "Well, I don't have anything to do for the rest of the day," he said. Emily fought down a flash of envy, mingled with the droll awareness that Cirroc would consider keeping his side of the bargain more important than his formal schooling. "Unless you *want* to go to Dragon's Den."

Emily shook her head. She'd found herself *noticing* men more over the past year, after she'd started dating for the first time, but she didn't have the time to date. She honestly didn't know how Imaiqah had managed it. And besides, Cirroc was handsome, but he had the kind of hard *edge* that worried her. She was fairly sure she was a more powerful magician than he was, yet she still found his obvious strength a little intimidating...

And Caleb was hardly a weakling, she told herself as they walked into the corridor. For someone who would probably have been considered a nerd back on Earth, Caleb was amazingly muscular. But then, he *had* spent two years at Stronghold. *Do you think he couldn't have crushed your neck if he tried?*

She pushed the thought out of her mind, walking in companionable silence up to the library. It felt *odd* to spend time with a boy—a young man—who wasn't Caleb or Jade... she told herself, tartly, that she was being silly. Cirroc wasn't someone she knew very well, she had to admit, but he was hardly an *enemy*. And besides, he had something she wanted. The fact he wanted something she couldn't *wait* to give away was merely icing on the cake.

The library was thrumming with activity when she pushed open the door, a long line of students waiting by the desk to have their books stamped before they could be removed from the library. Several more were arguing with the librarians, insisting that they needed a particular book *instantly*; others were searching the stacks with the single-minded dedication of students who knew they needed to catch up on their studies before exam season rolled around again. Emily wondered, sourly, just how many books had been hidden behind the stacks or deliberately filed out of place. Too many students seemed to think that concealing books they needed was a completely new and original plan.

Frieda sat at a desk, looking tense. Frieda had a distracted look, as though she was talking to someone even though she was alone. Emily frowned as she led Cirroc over to the desk. Frieda looked up, her eyes going wide when she saw Cirroc. Emily hoped she'd look up to him, even if he was only two years older than she was. She'd definitely taken orders from him in the dueling club.

"Good luck," she said, as Cirroc led Frieda into a study room. "And thank you."

"I'll see you tonight, at the club," Cirroc said. "Take care."

Emily sighed, then looked around the library. A pair of students were making rude gestures at each other, mindful of the library's zero tolerance policy towards noise. She kept a wary eye on them for a moment, just in case they started shooting hexes at each other, then walked into the next study room. Cabiria and the Gorgon were seated at a table, working their way through a set of complex notes.

"Your friend nearly picked a fight with a senior librarian," the Gorgon said, by way of greeting. "Did she *really* hex someone into next week?"

Cabiria snickered. "I thought you didn't pay attention to rumors."

The Gorgon's snakes hissed, something Emily had come to recognize as embarrassment. "I try to ignore them," the Gorgon said. "But sometimes you just *hear* things."

"And sometimes you just listen." Cabiria grinned, sweetly. "It isn't as if any of *us* are going to blame you for listening. Anyone who wants privacy should cast a privacy ward."

Emily sat down. "She didn't hex someone into next week," she said, flatly. "She just... hurt someone."

The Gorgon blinked. "And you think that's acceptable behavior?"

"No," Emily said.

"Then do something about it," the Gorgon said.

Cabiria nodded. "Right now, there's a rumor going around that you let her get away with murder. You have to do something about it."

"I don't know what," Emily said. "Do you even know who's *spreading* the rumors?"

"You know how it is," Cabiria said. "Rumors grow and change in the telling."

Emily nodded, sourly. A rumor could be warped out of all recognition after passing through a dozen mouths. People would mishear, or add details, or even simply mingle details from two separate rumors into one. By the time she heard it, the original rumor might have been buried under a mountain of utter nonsense.

And the only good thing about it is that most people won't believe a word of them, she thought, ruefully. *But something might stick if it's repeated often enough.*

"I don't know who started the latest set of rumors," the Gorgon said. "But you have to find a way to stop it."

"You have to find a way to stop *her,*" Cabiria said. "I've got sisters. I know when someone is acting up to get attention."

"And you never did that," the Gorgon said, dryly.

"I got too *much* attention." Cabiria's face twisted into a bitter grimace. "I never *had* to act up."

The Gorgon shrugged. "Maybe Frieda is just being bitchy. You can tell *she* didn't have a good upbringing."

"She grew up in the mountains," Emily said. "She didn't have an easy life."

"That doesn't excuse bad behavior," the Gorgon said. "And while *you* might feel sorry for her, others will not."

"People always felt sorry for me," Cabiria put in. "I *hated* it."

"I bet," the Gorgon said.

"You're missing the point," Cabiria said. "I could get away with anything because... because I was a freak. People felt too sorry for me to do anything about my behavior. I was a little brat."

The Gorgon smirked. "And now you're a *big* brat?"

Cabiria shot her a two-fingered gesture. "You're missing the point. Everyone did it, even my sisters. You know, the ones who might be expected to resent any special treatment offered to the family cripple. And I hated it, because they weren't being nice to me because it was *me*. They were being nice because they felt *sorry* for me."

She looked at Emily. "Frieda doesn't need care and compassion. She needs someone who can give her a kick up the ass, someone who doesn't give a shit about her temper tantrums. Above all"—she pointed a finger at Emily—"she needs someone who can keep an emotional distance from her. You're too close to her, Emily, and she's too close to you."

Emily nodded, slowly. Cirroc could do that, she thought. But he was being paid to tutor Frieda... not, she supposed, that it mattered. He'd do what he'd agreed to do, unless it proved impossible. If Frieda acted badly, he'd just walk away.

And then we'd have to argue over who gets the club, she thought. *Joy.*

"It could be worse," she said.

"I suppose it could," the Gorgon said. "Now, are you going to study?"

Emily took the hint and rose. "I'll see you both at dinner," she said. She would have liked to stay, but she had her duties to attend to. "And thank you."

She walked back into the main library, taking the opportunity to glance into the next study room. Frieda and Cirroc were sitting at a table, their heads bent over a book. Emily hoped—prayed—that some extra tutoring would help. Frieda was far from stupid. A tutoring session might clear up the problem. If not... she couldn't think of anything else.

And I need to check on Celadon, she thought. *I don't know if his concept actually worked!*

Chapter Thirty

"So," Samra said, as Emily and Melissa stepped into the classroom. "I trust you have been practicing looking at yourself?"

"Yes," Emily said. She wasn't in the best of states for soul magic, but she had a nasty suspicion Samra didn't care. "I've been doing it whenever I have time."

"Very good." Samra waved a hand at a table. A pair of scrolls sat there, surrounded by a protective charm. "Emily, I need to have a word with Melissa. While we're gone, read those scrolls and consider them carefully. I'll call you into the next room when we're ready."

Emily nodded, shortly. The idea of sitting down sounded good, all things considered. It had been a long and thoroughly unpleasant day. Professor Armstrong had insisted she had to rework her personal wards, Professor Lombardi had questioned her judgement after a tiny error had threatened to snowball into a major disaster and Professor Thande had made the entire class repeatedly brew an alchemical concoction of no obvious value. If she hadn't been summoned to attend an impromptu class on soul magic, she would have gone straight back to her bedroom and taken a nap.

She sat down and opened the first scroll. It was nothing more than an attempt by an unknown writer to translate the terms of soul magic into something common magicians could understand. Emily found herself struggling to parse it out, understanding—not for the first time—why most magicians shied away from soul magic. Altering a single variable in a charm could prove disastrous, but the effects could be anticipated and countered, while in soul magic alterations and effects seemed to be completely unpredictable. The writer concluded by stating it should be possible to weave soul magic into a standard ward, but Emily couldn't swear to it. His argument relied upon so many buzzwords—half of which seemed to have been invented specifically for the scroll—that it was impossible to follow his words.

No wonder Frieda is having problems, she thought, feeling a flicker of sympathy. The writer seemed to be an older version of Celadon. *I can't make heads or tails of this scroll either.*

She put it aside and opened the other one. It felt old against her bare fingers. Whoever had written it had used Old Script rather than the common tongue, forcing her to translate it as best as she could. Her head was pounding by the time she managed to decipher the first passages, leaving her wondering why no one had bothered to do an official translation. But an account of the first person to experiment with soul magic—or at least the first person to survive the experience—wasn't something that anyone would *want* translated. It sounded as though the writer hadn't enjoyed himself.

The door opened. "Emily," Samra called. "Replace the protective charm and join us, if you please?"

Emily nodded, rolling up the scrolls before carefully resetting the charm. The parchment probably had some magic woven into the material, just to keep it intact. It awed her to think that it might have been passed down from master to master...

she wondered, suddenly, if it predated Lord Whitehall and his commune. She hadn't heard anything about soul magic during her trip to the past, but the commune *had* been fairly isolated. Magicians didn't start sharing secrets openly until after Whitehall School was established.

She rose and walked into the next room. Melissa was sitting in an armchair, so stiffly that Emily wondered if she'd been frozen in place. Only the rise and fall of her breasts—and her blinking eyes—suggested otherwise. Her face was so tightly controlled that Emily *knew* she was unhappy. She glanced at Samra, wondering just what the old woman had done. It would have to be something bad after everything *else* Melissa had done in the last few months.

"Close the door," Samra ordered. "Melissa, say something."

Melissa opened her mouth and brayed like a mule. Emily jumped. There was no shortage of spells that made people talk like animals—there was no shortage of spells to turn people *into* animals—but she wouldn't have expected one of them to work on Melissa. She was a sixth-year student, for crying out loud. Melissa should have had no trouble shrugging off a spell that even firsties could counter after a few weeks of training. And yet...

"Melissa has been cursed," Samra said. "Say something else, my dear?"

Melissa tried to say something, but clucked like a chicken instead. Emily reached out with her senses, but felt nothing. Melissa seemed to have removed all of her personal wards, leaving her effectively naked. And yet, there was no hostile magic surrounding her. A simple jinx should be easy to detect and remove, but...

"The curse in question is a very nasty piece of work indeed," Samra said, conversationally. Emily felt a flash of hatred that surprised her. Melissa didn't have to be humiliated, not like this. "I believe the person who invented it must have known *something* about soul magic, as the curse is quite hard to remove without *using* soul magic. And yet, it can be cast by any reasonably competent magician."

Emily made a face. She had been warned, time and time again, not to cast a spell if she didn't know what it did. On one hand, not knowing what the spell *did* would make it harder to cast; on the other hand, it would also make it harder to counter or remove the spell if it turned into something dangerous. Professor Lombardi had made them read hundreds of horror stories about magicians who didn't parse out spells before casting them. The lucky ones were often scarred for life.

Not that an angry magician would bother to read the warnings first, she thought. She'd read a couple of books on dark magic. *They don't care about the side effects.*

"Indeed, the vast majority of unbreakable curses owe something to soul magic," Samra added, seemingly unaware of Emily's growing anger. "They are simply too firmly embedded in a person's soul to be easily removed, at least without causing real harm in the process. The patients in the Halfway House, alas, cannot be cured without killing them."

"You cast the spell on her," Emily growled.

"Quite," Samra agreed. "Melissa knows she has been cursed, of course. And yet she can no more remove it than she can perform major surgery on her body. Variations on this spell make it impossible for her to speak of it, if she even realizes that she has been cursed."

"To speak of it," Emily repeated. Melissa brayed, loudly. "Why...?"

"She could write a note," Samra said, sarcastically.

She paced around Melissa and stopped, behind her. "Your task is to remove the curse. You have twenty minutes. I suggest you get it right the first time."

Emily glared at her. "If this could cause her permanent harm..."

"Name me a class in Whitehall that *doesn't* risk permanent harm," Samra challenged. She met Emily's eyes, silently daring her to object further. "And Melissa *did* volunteer for this..."

She'd be happier volunteering to take off her clothes in a junior healing class, Emily thought, grimly. Lady Barb had hired volunteers from Dragon's Den for anatomical studies. Emily suspected it had been a very good idea. Looking a fellow student in the eye—after that student had stripped naked in front of the entire class—would have been difficult. *This could be really dangerous.*

"You have twenty minutes." Samra pointed at Melissa's head. "Go."

Emily stared at her for a long moment, promising herself that she'd make Samra pay if Melissa was permanently damaged. Emily had enough experience with curses—and she'd read far too many books—to take *any* long-lasting curse lightly. The effects might seem humorous, but the long-term consequences could be disastrous for the victim. Emily had read about an obedience curse that had rendered the victim permanently servile, even after the spell had been removed. The victim had possessed almost no willpower of his own.

She leaned forward and touched Melissa's forehead, closing her eyes. An image of Spock mind-melding with Kirk flashed through her mind, an image she ruthlessly suppressed as she sent her thoughts flowing towards Melissa. There was no point in confusing someone who'd never heard of television, let alone *Star Trek.* Melissa had never spoken to her about any of the images she might have picked up from Emily's mind—Emily wasn't sure if Melissa could open such a conversation or not—but she was sure Emily's memories of Earth would be confusing. *Alassa* had found them confusing.

And we weren't anything like so close when I touched Alassa's mind, she thought. Blood magic allowed a mental link, but *soul* magic was far more intrusive. Or perhaps *inclusive* was the better word. *She will have seen too much of me.*

She slid into Melissa's mind, feeling a dull throbbing resentment pulsing through her thoughts. It was a strong feeling, one that threatened to overwhelm Emily and drive her back into her own mind. Of *course* Melissa was unhappy. The curse was dangerous, even if Samra was *sure* she could extract it without harm. Emily felt another flash of respect, realizing—suddenly—that she could no longer dislike Melissa. The girl had grown into a young woman who'd earned respect.

Thank you, she thought.

She started, surprise flickering through her mind—*both* minds. That hadn't been *her* thought... had it? Melissa was picking up on *her* thoughts! Emily felt her mind recoil in shock before she forced herself to remain calm. Melissa couldn't share whatever she saw in Emily's mind with anyone, without permission. And yet, it felt as though she was being violated on a very basic level. She hadn't volunteered for soul magic...

The thought faded away as she thrust deeper into Melissa's mind. Thoughts, emotions and images assailed her. Melissa owned a castle; no, a city; no, a spider-web that made up her innermost being. Everywhere Emily looked, there were memories and feelings and images that raged towards her, each one a distraction from her mission. And yet, Melissa wasn't even *trying* to fight her. Emily hated to think what it would be like if Melissa wanted to throw her out.

She saw herself casting a spell. It was odd... she'd been in first year, judging by her robes, but she hadn't been that pretty. Or had she? She'd never thought of herself as attractive, even after she'd started dating. And yet...how could she judge herself? She was seeing her body through Melissa's eyes and it looked different...

The memories grew stronger. Emily pushed them away as she worked her way down to the center of Melissa's mind. She could see Melissa's oaths—her marriage bond to Markus and the oath she'd sworn as a prospective healer—glowing in her mind, overshadowing her thoughts and feelings. A little of Markus's magic was mingled into the marriage bond—a link that would be unbreakable, save by death—but the healer oath stood alone. She'd sworn it herself, with total conviction. Emily couldn't help being awed. The oath wouldn't have taken if Melissa had harbored any doubts about her vocation.

She opened her thoughts... and saw the curse. It was black, reeking of evil... it looked like a poisonous spider, squatting on its victim. Emily recoiled, feeling herself tumbling backwards over and over until she remembered that she was in someone's *mind*. What she saw wasn't real. And, more importantly, she wasn't limited by her body. If she wanted to look like a bird—if she wanted to *be* a bird—there was nothing holding her back.

Bracing herself, she extended her mind towards the curse. It snapped and snarled at her, like a crab that didn't want to be picked up. Her thought gave it shape. Claws and teeth manifested from nowhere, snapping threateningly at her. Emily fought down the urge to run, telling herself that it wasn't real, that it couldn't harm her. And yet, she knew it *could* harm her if she let it. The curse changed shape again as she caught hold, becoming a sticky mess that threatened to leak into Melissa's mind. Emily tightened her grip, willing it to come free...

... It snapped free, then lunged at her. Emily recoiled as *something* landed on her face, tearing away at her bare flesh. For a terrified moment, she was *sure* the curse was trying to fight its way through every orifice and into her brain. She couldn't help thinking of a face hugger, trying to impregnate an unwilling victim. Her lips clamped shut, but *something* was trying to pry them open. Her thoughts had given it shape and form...

... She concentrated, then opened her mouth and breathed fire. The curse spun away from her, too late. She saw it wither and vanish, an instant before the fire vanished too. Emily hung in the center of Melissa's mind for a long moment, then pulled back hastily. The fire shouldn't have hurt Melissa—it shouldn't have been *real* to her—but there was no point in taking chances. She fled backwards...

... And then she was in her own body, jerking back from Melissa.

"Well done," Samra said. "You removed the curse."

"Thank you," Melissa said. She touched her throat, lightly. Her voice sounded odd, as if she'd been unwell. "That was... not pleasant."

"I'm sorry you had to go through that," Emily said, sincerely.

"We have all been through worse," Samra said, sounding like a fanatic. "Healers are often forced to put themselves in unfortunate positions. It is part of our calling."

"Yeah," Melissa said. "But does it have to be so unpleasant?"

Samra gave her a considering look. "There are few who would understand, outside the circle. They would not be sympathetic to our requests."

Her lips quirked. "Just be grateful you didn't have to have your arm broken, just so we could teach your fellow students how to mend it," she said. "*And* to teach you to be empathic for those who are in need of your skills."

Melissa stood up. "If you don't mind, I have work to do," she said. "Mistress?"

"You may go," Samra said. "Inform me at once if you notice any lingering after-effects of the curse."

Emily met Samra's eyes as the tutor looked back at her. "Are there *going* to be any long-term effects?"

"There shouldn't be," Samra told her. "The curse was not designed to survive, once it was yanked out of her mind. I don't believe that any remaining fragments would pose a danger to her. But in soul magic, it is impossible to be entirely sure."

"It tried to grab onto me," Emily said. "I saw it as... as a monster."

"Your perceptions were turned against you," Samra said. "It is vitally important to remember that you are fighting a battle of metaphor, rather than brute force. You could easily end up hurting yourself if you visualize the curse as a fly sitting on your nose, then punch yourself in the face in an attempt to get rid of it. Curses like that are practically *designed* to take advantage of your weaknesses."

Emily swallowed. "And once it grabbed on to me...?"

"Melissa would have a chance to practice removing curses too," Samra said. "You would not, I suspect, have been able to remove it yourself."

She paced the room for a long moment. "I'll keep an eye on Melissa, just to be sure," she added. "But I don't think there's any real danger."

Emily nodded, relieved. "No more. I mean..."

Samra turned. "No more?"

"No more reading her mind," Emily said. "No more poking myself into her thoughts. No more..."

"Do you want to learn or don't you?" Samra leaned forward. "This is *not* a skill you can learn from books, Emily. The only way to learn soul magic is by doing. You are extremely fortunate that you've been allowed to take lessons *without* committing yourself to the healing circle. Melissa has volunteered to allow you to practice on her..."

"I'll hurt her," Emily said. She remembered the images she'd seen of Melissa's childhood, back when she'd been under Fulvia's thumb. "Sooner or later, I'll do something wrong and..."

"She knows the risks," Samra said. "Melissa is a very brave girl."

She smiled. "And would you open your mind to her?"

Not willingly, Emily thought. The whole idea was horrific. *But if there was no choice...*

"I didn't volunteer to have my mind read," she said. She *knew* Melissa couldn't share anything she learned, not without permission. The thought was still unpleasant. "And I don't want to risk her any longer."

She looked down at the floor. "Why her?"

"She volunteered," Samra said, flatly. "*And* she has a marriage bond, which gives her some additional stability. Her classmates are rather less lucky."

Emily nodded, remembering the oaths in Melissa's mind. And her own, waiting.

"I was wondering if an oath could be removed," she said. "Is that possible?"

Samra made an odd sound. "There are people who would demand your immediate execution for daring to ask," she said. It took Emily a moment to realize she was trying not to laugh. "I don't think a sworn oath, one made of your own free will, could be removed. Even *trying* could be lethal. But an oath someone was forced to swear... maybe. It isn't something I would care to try."

She nodded to the door. "You'll be back, of course. Next time, perhaps I'll find you a more challenging opponent."

Emily swallowed, but said nothing.

Chapter Thirty-One

"IT'S A BRIGHT, SUNNY DAY," CIRROC SAID, AS THEY WALKED OUT ONTO THE GROUNDS. "JUST right for a dueling contest, don't you think?"

Emily bit down a whole series of nasty answers. The weather was perfect, absolutely perfect, for a long walk in the mountains. She could have gone, perhaps with Frieda, if she hadn't been expected to supervise the dueling contest. But instead... she groaned as she saw the vast number of people taking their seats in the arena. Gordian had insisted on holding the second round in the arena, where there were seats for the entire school to watch. And it looked like the entire school *had* turned out to watch.

And place bets, she thought sourly. *And try to use the contest as an excuse not to turn in their work on time.*

She sighed as she walked through the doors and into the waiting room. She'd only been there once before, when Alassa had tried to convince her to play *Ken*. Now, all thirty remaining duelists were sitting on benches or trying out moves until it was their turn to step onto the field. Even with four duels taking place at once, Emily thought, it was going to take some time before the first set of engagements were completed. Perhaps some of the audience would lose interest and wander off.

Frieda sat on a bench, seemingly alone. Emily gave her a sharp look, wondering what the younger girl was thinking. Her face was blank, her pigtails tied into a bun that made her look very different from her normal self. Emily wanted to walk over to Frieda and say something reassuring, but nothing came to mind. She was ruefully aware that being seen in public with Frieda would only add more meat to the rumors.

"She has been improving," Cirroc said, quietly. "But she needs to work more on her theory."

"Which is precisely the section she doesn't like," Emily answered, equally quietly. She wasn't sure how much Cirroc would tell her, although she *was* employing him. "Did Celadon's idea actually *work*?"

"Two times out of four," Cirroc said. "It's a very complex spell."

Emily kept her thoughts to herself as she walked to the front of the chamber. If Celadon's idea had failed outright, Frieda would probably have felt vindicated. It might have made her be more reasonable afterwards... along with Celadon himself, who wouldn't have been winning any prizes for extreme cleverness. A partial success wasn't bad—Frieda could help weed out the bugs *and* probably cast the spell herself, something she was good at—but Celadon had excellent reason to feel vindicated. It struck her as a recipe for disaster.

She cleared her throat, glancing from face to face. Adana and Tiega had made it through, along with two other Second Years, but everyone else was Third Year or older. Emily couldn't help wondering just how much of that had been sheer luck. Adana was good—Tiega was better—but neither of them would be any match for a fifth-year student. They might just have been lucky in who they faced, the first time around. The odds were a little steeper now.

And there's a greater chance of facing someone superior to them, Emily thought. They *would* have to start separate contests for each year, sooner or later. Cirroc could handle that, fortunately. Emily had every intention of handing the club over to him as soon as the second round was over. *He can make sure the odds are a little fairer next time.*

"Welcome to the second round," she said, flatly. It was hard to work any enthusiasm into her voice, but she tried for their sake. At the back, Jacqui and Cerise looked thoroughly unimpressed. "Eight of you will be on the field at any one time, so pay attention to your referee and ignore the others. Remember the rules and *don't* break them. The entire school is watching."

"That never stopped anyone cheating at *Ken*," someone muttered.

Emily sighed. The standard interpretation of the rules of *Ken*—as enthusiastically embraced by Alassa—was that it was only cheating if you got caught. Everything from *accidentally* hexing a part of the pitch to turning one's opponents into toads was perfectly legal, as long as the referee didn't notice. And she had long-suspected that the referees were all blind. The watching audience booed cheaters, even if the referee didn't see the cheating.

"This isn't *Ken*," she said, firmly. "The rules are not to be broken."

She nodded at Jacqui and Cerise, then led the way out onto the pitch. The audience roared in approval, their bellows shaking the stands. Emily told herself, firmly, to forget that there were hundreds—if not thousands—of watching eyes. And yet, she *couldn't* forget. The dueling league representatives weren't the only outsiders visiting Whitehall. Far too many parents had also come to watch the first dueling contest in years.

I wonder if Void is here, she thought, as she passed out the tokens. The selection was still random, although—with the numbers reduced so sharply—the odds of an unbalanced selection had been reduced too. *He could be anyone.*

The noise grew louder as the first set of duelists took their places in the circles. Emily forced herself to relax as she studied *her* duelists: a pair of Fourth Years, one of whom she vaguely recognized. The other was a complete stranger. She heard Cirroc blow his whistle behind her, then blew her own. The two duelists eyed each other warily for a long moment, then started trading hexes. They'd learnt a great deal since the first round.

They don't want to take risks, Emily thought, as the duelists circled the ring. She couldn't help feeling a flicker of annoyance. Losing in the first circle would be embarrassing and awkward, but not disastrous. *And they're reluctant to commit themselves.*

She cast a noise-cancelling charm, silently wishing that someone had thought to put one on the entire arena. Alassa liked being cheered, but *Emily* didn't. The noise was a distraction, if nothing else. She could hear the crowd going wild behind her, but she didn't dare look to see what had happened. Jacqui's duelists had probably already won and lost. She wondered, absently, which was which.

Her duelists paused, then leapt at each other. Emily braced herself, unsure if she should intervene as hexes crashed into wards and sparks of magic flew in all directions. It was suddenly hard to keep track of their movements, no matter how carefully she watched; the slightest movement could signal a spell being launched or... or nothing at all. The flares and flashes grew stronger, then one of the duelists managed to land a significant blow. His opponent was stunned, just for a second. It was long enough for him to land a second blow and end the match.

Emily nodded, curtly. "Well done," she said. The crowd grew louder, so much louder that she could hear the racket despite the spell. "Take your opponent back to the changing room and wait."

She checked the wards, then looked around. Adana had won her contest, it seemed; Frieda had won too, knocking down her opponent with brutal force. Cerise's contestants seemed to have managed to turn each other into animals, much to the crowd's amusement. Their boos and jeers grew louder as a rat and a tiny mouse struggled to break the spells before it was too late. The crowd even joined in the last few seconds of the countdown.

Cirroc wandered over to join her. "Should we class that as a mutual kill?"

"Probably," Emily said. It would unbalance the scoreboard and probably cause problems later on, but she found it hard to care. Besides, in a real duel, a mutual kill would leave both contestants dead. This way, they'd have a chance to win their next two duels. "Turn them back, then let them go wait for the next round."

She caught sight of Gordian, sitting in the tutor's box and watching the game. The Grandmaster looked almost childishly pleased, talking excitedly to a pair of younger men sitting next to him. Emily wondered, suddenly, just how old Gordian actually *was*. His predecessor had been in his second century, but he hadn't looked over fifty. Gordian was clearly quite a bit younger.

Probably in his fifties, at least, Emily thought. *He'd have had to build up a reputation before trying to become Grandmaster.*

The crowd laughed as the two unhappy contestants marched off the dueling field. Emily felt a flicker of sympathy, combined with a certain wry understanding that accidents happened. It was impossible to be sure, but she *thought* the two must have dropped their guard in a desperate bid to win. Perhaps they'd both been trying to hit their opponent with a prank spell...

It did work, she told herself. *The problem is that it worked for both of them.*

She took her flask from her belt and took a sip of water as the next set of contestants marched onto the field. They looked slightly more serious, now they'd realized the crowd was watching. Emily allowed herself a flicker of amusement at the way one of the young men was playing to the crowd, swaggering around as if he thought he was God's gift to women. The crowd cheered loudly, then settled down. Emily could see the telltale signs of bets being placed, heads huddling together as amateur bookies discussed the odds. She wondered if Gordian knew what he'd unleashed. Betting rings could easily turn into real problems if poorer students got involved.

He'll have to deal with it, she thought. *I won't be here next year.*

She blew her whistle. There was a brilliant flash of light a second later, so bright that it made her eyes hurt. One of the contestants had cast a light spell, scaling it up as much as possible; his opponent rubbed at his eyes frantically, hurling desperate hexes in all directions. The crowd laughed and cheered as the first contestant carefully placed a single spell, winning the match in less than a minute. Emily wasn't entirely sure if that counted as cheating or not, but she had to admit it had been ingenious.

Although it's an obvious trick, she thought, as the winner bowed to her. *Most sorcerers used a simple ward to keep themselves from being blinded. He'd have looked like a bloody idiot if it hadn't worked.*

The roar of the crowd grew louder as the loser stumbled off the pitch. Emily caught him and checked his eyes, making sure there was no permanent damage. It didn't look that way, but she told him to go see the healer anyway. She wasn't a trained healer. It was possible she might have missed something that would do real damage, if left untreated.

"Don't come back until they clear you," she ordered, flatly. "Please."

She shook her head, then turned to watch the other contestants. Most of them had *definitely* improved, although a couple seemed to be pushing the edges of the permissible. The spells they used weren't *lethal*, but they were right on the edge... used badly, they could kill. She ground her teeth in frustration, silently glad she wasn't in the ring. Holding back when she'd been dueling with Casper had been harder than she cared to admit.

And no wonder the referees didn't realize I gave him an opening deliberately, she thought, as another duel came to an end. *An opening that only existed for a second wouldn't be anything like long enough for them to think I did it on purpose.*

The other two pairs of contestants were clearly made of sterner stuff. Two Fifth Years stood, far too close together for her comfort, and battered away at each other with a constant string of nasty hexes. Emily shook her head in disbelief as the duel intensified, wondering just what they were thinking. The one who lost their wards wouldn't have a chance to dodge before they were stunned or frozen or...

"And that's a win," Jacqui declared, as one contestant was thrown backwards and slammed into the wards. His opponent hit him with a stunner before he had a chance to recover from the impact. "Well done, Marti!"

"She must like him," Cirroc muttered. "That wasn't well done at all."

Emily elbowed him. Marti was a fifth-year student. It would be unusual for Jacqui to know him, let alone show any *interest* in him. She could date someone a year below her if she wished, but it would turn her into a laughing stock. A girl shouldn't be looking at a guy a year younger than her...

Which isn't entirely fair, Emily thought. *Caleb is a year older than me.*

The crowd didn't seem any more inclined to leave as the first set of duels came to an end, leaving fourteen winners and sixteen losers. Emily checked to make sure the losers wanted to continue—no one wanted to leave, although the duelist who'd been blinded hadn't returned from the healers—and then reshuffled the tokens as the duelists ate a quick snack. It was good thinking on their part, Emily noted. A duelist who ran out of magic in the first round would be utterly curb-stomped in the second.

"They want us back out there," Cirroc said. He patted Emily's shoulder. "You're doing fine, so far."

Emily shot him a nasty look—she wished she was somewhere else, anywhere else—and then led the contestants back onto the field. The crowd was still placing bets, now the odds were a little clearer. Emily wondered, sourly, just who was the favorite to win, then decided it was a stupid question. It would almost certainly be one of the Fifth Years.

"Those who win two rounds will go on to the *final* contest," she said, her amplified voice booming over the crowd. It didn't seem to do much for the racket. She honestly didn't know how sports announcers did it. Merely saying two lines—and not very clever lines—left her feeling drained and exposed. "Those who *lose* two rounds will not continue!"

She gritted her teeth as the roar grew louder, then carefully recast the spell. It didn't seem to have worked properly, much to her irritation. The wards covering the arena were wearing it down, piece by piece. She made a mental note to suggest it be changed before the final contest, then turned to watch the first contestants enter the rings. Her eyes narrowed as she realized Adana was going to face Frieda.

Crap, she thought. Someone was going to say she'd helped Frieda. She was sure of it, even though Frieda *was* two years older than Adana and a Martial Magic student besides. *This is not going to end well.*

She turned, half-hoping to swap rings with Cirroc, but his contestants had already started hurling curses at each other. Jacqui and Cerise were deliberately not looking at her, as if they *wanted* to see what would happen. Emily bit down on a nasty curse, then signaled the contestants to get ready. Maybe it wouldn't look as bad as she feared. Frieda shouldn't have any trouble stomping Adana into the ground.

Don't make it too rough, please, Emily pleaded, silently. She tried to meet Frieda's eyes, but the younger girl was keeping her eyes firmly fixed on Adana. It was what *Emily* would have done, she knew. It didn't make it any easier. *Please...*

She blew her whistle. Frieda opened the match with a powerful hex that was borderline illegal, trying to smash Adana's wards into fragments before she could muster a response. Adana jumped to one side, avoiding the hex; she threw back a series of her own, some of which seemed to sink harmlessly into the ground. Frieda's eyes narrowed with cold fury, an instant before she launched a second hex. Adana seemed torn, just for a second, between trying to block it and dodging, again. And then she leapt out of the way.

Good move, Emily noted, coolly. Adana wasn't stupid enough to try to engage Frieda directly. Keeping her distance was her only hope of prolonging the fight. *She clearly learnt from the others too.*

The duel grew more intense as the two duelists closed. Frieda blocked everything Adana hurled in her direction, rather than trying to dodge. Her face was growing darker and darker with frustration, even though Adana hadn't come close to scoring a hit. Emily felt a flicker of sympathy, combined with a nagging worry that something wasn't quite right. The magic field was shifting...

The ground suddenly bulged with green creepers, reaching up towards Frieda. Emily gaped—the roar of the crowd suddenly cut off—as the creepers lunged forward, grabbing hold of Frieda's legs and her left arm, yanking her down to the ground. Adana had modified a quick-grow spell, then turned it into an unconventional weapon. Emily was torn between being impressed and horrified. Frieda wasn't going to like that at all. It wasn't technically cheating, but it was certainly bending the rules. *And* humiliating as hell.

Frieda's magic flared, burning through the creepers. Burning ashes flew in all directions as raw power tore the roots from the ground and incinerated them. Adana struck Frieda with a hex a second later, leaving her stumbling backwards against the wards. Frieda's face contorted with fury; magic crackled around her, burning bright with rage. She gestured...

... And Emily realized, a fraction of a second too late, what was about to happen. "No," she shouted.

It was too late. A wave of force picked Adana up and slammed her hard against the wards...

... And her body fell to the ground and lay still.

Chapter Thirty-Two

FOR A HORRIFYING MOMENT, THE WORLD SEEMED TO FREEZE.

"Stay still," Emily shouted. The fury on Frieda's face was terrifying. She honestly wasn't sure if the younger girl would obey. The arena wards weren't *designed* to stop someone in their tracks, even if it was necessary. "Stay still!"

She ran forward, heading straight for Adana. The younger girl's body lay on the grass, unmoving. Emily heard others running towards her as she skidded to a halt and knelt down next to the broken body. Adana was alive, but barely. Her breath came in ragged gasps, the sound tearing at Emily's heart. There was no visible damage, save for a trickle of blood leaking from her mouth, but there was clearly severe internal damage. Emily had seen a force punch crack or shatter ribs. Frieda had hit Adana far harder.

Stasis, she thought. She was so shaken it took her two tries to cast the spell. *Get her to the healers, let them work on her...*

She turned to look at Frieda as two of the healers arrived, levitating Adana's body into the air and steering her towards the school. Frieda looked... odd, her face curiously blank. Her hands were clenched, as if she expected to fight, yet there was no anger on her face. One of her plaits had come loose, slowly coming apart. Her trousers had been torn, revealing bare legs. Emily could see nasty bruises on her upper thigh.

Gordian appeared, looking grim. "What happened?"

Emily tried to think of an answer, but couldn't. Frieda had panicked and lashed out and Adana... had been seriously wounded. Perhaps even *mortally* wounded. Everyone had known there was a risk of serious injury, of course, but... she shook her head. There was going to be trouble. Frieda should never have been allowed to remain in the contest, not after she'd hurt Marian. Anyone who wanted to make political hay out of the whole incident wouldn't hesitate to point that out as often as possible.

"Sergeant Miles, take Frieda back to my office and hold her there," Gordian ordered, when Emily said nothing. "Remain with her until I arrive."

"Yes, sir," Sergeant Miles said. Emily hadn't even seen him *arrive*. He must have been in the audience, heroically refraining from commenting on the show-offs taking the field. "I'll see to it."

Frieda's face didn't change as Sergeant Miles caught hold of her arm, leading her firmly out of the arena. The crowd booed loudly, despite angry shouts from supervising tutors. Emily felt a wave of disgust, mingled with grim amusement. The dueling league's tournaments often ended with one party seriously injured—or dead. Dueling was a blood sport and only a fool would claim differently. The only advantage it held over hunting was that the two duelists were usually fairly evenly matched.

And the ones who appear weaker can come up with new tactics, Emily thought. She looked at the ashes on the field. Adana's creepers had been an unpleasant surprise, one that had come far too close to working. Emily would never have dared waste magic on something like that in the middle of a *real* fight, but she had to admit it had proved effective. It just hadn't been good enough to win the fight before Frieda broke free. *She panicked and...*

Gordian cleared his throat. "The contest is ended, for the moment," he said. His voice sounded strong, but she could hear an undertone of... *something*. He'd certainly played a role in the whole disaster, even if it hadn't been his fault. His enemies would not hesitate to capitalize on the blunder. "Go to the infirmary until... until the healers have finished, then report to my office. Cirroc can clean up the mess."

Poor bastard, Emily thought.

But she knew she should be grateful. The last thing she wanted was to work on the field when Adana was fighting for her life. God alone knew what would happen to Frieda. Gordian would need a scapegoat if the politics turned savage and Frieda was the obvious candidate. A young common-born girl from the mountains had few friends in the seats of power. King Randor was hardly likely to use some of his political capital to save Frieda's life.

Unless he got something from me in exchange, Emily thought. *But what would he want?*

She nodded curtly to Gordian, then walked over to Cirroc and told him he was in charge. The dark-skinned boy didn't seem too affected, much to Emily's annoyance. But then, he *had* been planning to become a professional duelist. He'd been taking part in contests ever since he came into his magic. Someone being injured—even killed—was hardly *new* for him.

"I'll take care of it," he promised. "You go see to your little friend."

Emily swallowed several nasty rejoinders, then turned and walked back into the castle. The corridors were deserted, thankfully. Most of the students had gone to the arena and those who hadn't were taking advantage of the peace and quiet to study. She centered her mind as best as she could, trying to gather her thoughts. Frieda had panicked...

... And Adana had been badly injured, perhaps killed.

Adana has powerful relatives, Emily thought, numbly. She hesitated in front of the infirmary, unsure if she wanted to go in. *What will they say if she ends up dead—or crippled?*

The thought mocked her. Adana probably *wouldn't* be crippled, not physically. Frieda hadn't hit her with anything that might have lingering effects. But... what if she'd cracked her head against the wards? Or... anything physical could be mended by magic, given time and money. Mental damage was almost always beyond repair. The shock of being so badly wounded would be disastrous.

She pushed her hand against the door, stepping into the infirmary. It was empty, save for Melissa. The redhead sat on a bench, her face pale and wan. Adana was her cousin, Emily remembered bitterly. Melissa might have been disowned, but she still loved her blood relatives. And her tutors wouldn't let her operate on anyone related to her.

"She's in there," Melissa said, quietly. Emily wondered, grimly, if Melissa knew what had happened. She sounded too tired to be angry. "We have to wait."

Emily sat down next to her, feeling cold. Adana was injured, perhaps dying... how much of it was *her* fault? Perhaps she should have kicked Frieda out of the dueling club. Or perhaps she should have rigged the selection so Frieda faced someone a little closer to her in terms of power and training. Or perhaps... hindsight mocked her, as always. It was easy to see how a crisis could have been avoided, in retrospect. It wasn't so easy to avoid it beforehand.

Melissa said nothing as they waited, leaving Emily alone with her thoughts. It was creepy, in many ways, just how well she *knew* the other girl. Emily had lost most of the memories she'd pulled from Melissa's mind, but enough remained for her to understand Melissa better than anyone else. She loved Markus, yet she missed her siblings and cousins. Emily had never really understood what it meant to have brothers and sisters until she'd peered through Melissa's eyes. The mixture of love and annoyance, of understanding and irritation... she felt a hot stab of bitter envy. *She* would have liked siblings too.

No, you wouldn't, she corrected herself. *You wouldn't want them to grow up with your stepfather.*

It was nearly an hour before Madame Kyla stepped out of the operating theatre. She didn't look to have changed in the years since Emily had known her—she was still a middle-aged woman with prematurely grey hair—but there was a grim expression on her face that Emily didn't like. Madame Kyla eyed her for a long moment, then shrugged. Emily hoped—prayed—that was a good sign. She didn't think she'd be allowed to stay if Adana was dying—or dead. Her family would be summoned as quickly as possible.

And they'd probably kick Melissa out too, she thought, sourly. *Legally, she's no longer part of the family.*

"Adana has been badly injured, but will recover," Madame Kyla said. "She's out of immediate danger now."

Emily sagged in relief. The last thing she needed—the last thing *anyone* needed—was House Ashworth declaring a blood feud. Frieda was in no state to fight. The magical community would find it amusing—Adana had known the dangers, when she'd stepped onto the field—but that would be no consolation. Frieda would have had no choice but to run.

Melissa sighed in relief. "How bad is it?"

"Her ribs were shattered by a powerful blow," Madame Kyla said. "It was sheer luck that one or more of the splinters didn't penetrate her heart. One of her lungs was punctured and started to fill with fluid. Thankfully, she was put into stasis before the damage grew out of control."

Thank God, Emily thought.

"We're going to put her back in stasis until we can fix the remaining damage, then slowly bring her out of it," Madame Kyla added. She looked at Melissa. "Do you want to see her now?"

"Yes, please," Melissa said.

"Inform the Grandmaster that Adana is out of danger," Madame Kyla said to Emily. "And she should be returning to classes in a couple of weeks."

Emily nodded, unable to hide her relief. Adana would recover! Frieda hadn't killed her, accidentally or otherwise. She rose and headed for the door. She'd take a moment to collect herself, then go straight to the Grandmaster's office. And then...

She sighed as she stepped through the door. Gordian wouldn't be pleased, even though *someone* getting injured was predictable. Emily herself had *killed* in a duel. She wasn't sure if Frieda had broken the rules or not—the spell she'd cast wasn't designed to be lethal—but she *had* done considerable damage to her opponent. It wasn't going to reflect well on anyone.

Jacqui was waiting outside, looking smug. "Emily," she said. "Perhaps we could walk for a little bit."

Emily eyed her, sourly. "Why aren't you at the arena?"

"Cirroc is throwing his weight around and I got tired of it." Jacqui gave Emily a sidelong smile as they started to walk, then cast a privacy ward. "You really should choose your friends better."

Emily's eyes narrowed. "What do you mean?"

Jacqui smirked. "A princess, a commoner, a... *creature*... a freak... and another commoner who happens to be an itty bitty child."

"Frieda is not a child," Emily said. She was too tired for word games. "What do you want?"

"Frieda has already managed to get you in trouble... how many times?" Jacqui made a show of brushing the hair back from her face. "You really shouldn't hang out with her any longer."

Emily felt a flash of hot anger. "And why shouldn't I?"

"Because she can't do anything for you," Jacqui said, in tones that suggested she was explaining things to a child. "Frieda's friendship is not *advantageous* to you."

Her smirk grew wider. "Unless you *enjoy* having someone around to feel superior to."

Emily resisted—barely—the urge to say she felt superior to *Jacqui*. She'd never thought much of the other girl, but then... she hadn't paid too much attention to her either. Jacqui had always seemed a hanger-on, a crony rather than a person in her own right. And yet, Jacqui was no longer Melissa's satellite. She had a mind and a will of her own.

"It isn't about advantage," she said, finally. "Frieda is a friend..."

"Who just managed to land you in hot water, again," Jacqui pointed out. "I don't think I'd stay friends with someone who did that to me, repeatedly."

"*Melissa* managed to get you in trouble from time to time," Emily snapped. She was *definitely* in no mood for verbal fencing. "How many times did you get caned because of her? Or wound up spending hours as a toad?"

"Melissa could do great things for me, once upon a time," Jacqui said. "What can *Frieda* do for you?"

"It isn't about what she can do for me," Emily said.

"It *is*," Jacqui insisted. "You choose your friends because of what they can do for you. I can help my friends, just as they would help me. Being *here*, Emily, is all about making contacts, about meeting the people who can help you get along. But *you* seem to have missed the boat."

Emily raised her eyebrows. "You don't think the Crown Princess of Zangaria can help me get along?"

"Not for those who matter." Jacqui clicked her fingers. Emily braced herself, half expecting to be hexed. "If we who wield power wanted to take her kingdom, we *could* take her kingdom. We *choose* not to control the mundane world, Emily. We are not *incapable* of controlling it."

"Alassa and Jade would give you one hell of a fight," Emily said, stiffly. "Or do you think *he's* overrated?"

"He could certainly have married better," Jacqui said. "A year and a half and still no sign of children."

Emily felt her temper begin to fray. "Is there a point to this?"

Jacqui stopped and turned to face her. "It's time you learnt to choose your friends better," she said. "Join us."

"What?"

"Join us," Jacqui repeated. "You need help from people who *can* help you, not a little brat who acts like a complete idiot. How old is she? Six? Seven?"

"Nineteen," Emily said, flatly.

"That's not an improvement," Jacqui said. "She's old enough to take responsibility for herself, isn't she?"

She looked down the long corridor. "Frieda is going down. And when she finally hits rock bottom, she'll take you with her. There is *nothing* she can do for you, while *we* have power and influence you cannot even begin to comprehend. Your father has not taught you even the *basics* of building up a patronage network. Let *us* teach you."

Emily took a long breath. "And if I choose to say no?"

"That will be your choice," Jacqui said. "Like I said, you should choose your friends better."

"I don't think my friends would have dumped me if I'd been disowned," Emily said, sardonically. "Alassa didn't stop writing to me because her father banned me from his kingdom."

"Politics." Jacqui shrugged. "Sometimes, you have to cut someone out of your circle for the circle to flourish."

Something *clicked* in Emily's mind. "For the *quarrel* to flourish."

Jacqui didn't seem surprised that Emily knew the term. But then, it probably *wasn't* a surprise. She knew Emily had been to Mountaintop, where the quarrels were far more prominent. Someone might even have told her that Emily had been offered membership in several *different* quarrels. She'd declined, at the time.

"Quite," Jacqui said. "You'll be leaving Whitehall at the end of the year, if Frieda doesn't get you kicked out first. What then? You will need help and support as you enter the community and it's pretty clear that your father isn't going to provide it.

Even if he did, how could he *understand* your needs? It's been decades since he was your age. You need people who are loyal to you."

"And how loyal were you to Melissa?" Emily asked. "You didn't stick with her when she was disowned."

"That was necessary," Jacqui said, stiffly. "Her family had already disowned her. We were pressured into abandoning her."

"How... *loyal*," Emily said.

Jacqui eyed her for a long moment. "And you expect Frieda to remain loyal to *you?*"

Emily hesitated. A year ago, she would have said *yes*. Now... Frieda had changed. Emily didn't understand why her friend was changing, but she couldn't deny it. Frieda was growing dangerously unpredictable. It was hard to escape the feeling that Frieda was careening towards disaster.

"I choose to remain loyal to her," she said, finally. "Does that answer your question?"

Jacqui shook her head, disdainfully. "You are willing to throw away your own future for her?"

"There's no guarantee I will lose my future," Emily said. "And I can't just abandon someone because they're going through a bad patch."

"That's a foolish attitude," Jacqui said. "You could lose everything."

"But at least it's mine to lose," Emily said. She met Jacqui's eyes, silently challenging her. "What do you want?"

"A more... *even*... relationship," Jacqui said. "You scratch my back and I'll scratch yours."

"Really," Emily said. She forced herself to think. Jacqui had stayed at Whitehall over the half-term, hadn't she? She *could* have carried the pamphlets into school, if she wished... hell, she could have spread the rumors too. But she had no proof, nothing she could take to the Grandmaster. "I think I prefer Frieda to you."

"You're making a mistake," Jacqui said.

"Maybe I am," Emily said.

Emily shrugged. "Seeing you have nothing to do tonight, you can supervise detentions in Room 101," she ordered. It was petty, but she wanted to shut Jacqui up. "I'm sure the younger students will be grateful."

Jacqui curtseyed. "Enjoy that badge while you have it," she said. "I'm sure Frieda will ensure you lose it soon."

She turned and walked down the corridor. Emily stared after her, gloomily sure she'd missed something important. But what? If Jacqui *was* spreading the rumors, what did she have to gain? Or was she jumping to the wrong conclusion, again? She'd have to be careful if she wanted proof. Making the accusation—even a correct accusation—without any real proof would be disastrous.

Something will turn up, she told herself firmly. *And when it does, I'll be ready.*

Chapter Thirty-Three

"TAKE A SEAT AND WAIT," MADAME GRISELDA ORDERED, WHEN EMILY STEPPED INTO THE antechamber. "The Grandmaster is currently busy."

Probably telling Frieda off, Emily thought, as she sat on the hard bench. *There's no point in playing power games now.*

She tried to force herself to relax, despite the disturbing conversation with Jacqui, but it wasn't easy. The bench seemed *designed* to make her uncomfortable. Gordian could have easily put a more comfortable sofa—or a set of armchairs—into the antechamber, if he'd wished. She couldn't help wondering if he subjected outside visitors to the bench or if he had a second office for non-students. Perhaps the latter. She'd met people who would take mortal offense if a single one of their titles was left out when they were announced. The ugly bench made it clear that anyone who visited wasn't welcome.

It's probably grounds to start a feud, she reflected. The thought wasn't really funny, but she was desperate for relief. *A death-match fought over a particularly uncomfortable piece of wood.*

Madame Griselda sniffed loudly, then returned to her work. Emily kept a wary eye on her—she'd often wondered if Gordian's aide was more than she seemed—but the secretary just kept working her way through the files. *Someone* had to keep the bureaucracy moving, even in Whitehall. Secretary or not, Madame Griselda was in a position of considerable influence and power. Stalin had been a secretary too, if Emily recalled correctly. Being able to alter the minutes and set the agenda had probably made his takeover considerably easier.

The inner door opened. Frieda emerged, looking weepy. She glanced at Emily, then hurried through the outer door before Emily could say a word. Emily stared after her, wondering just what Gordian had said. Had he expelled her? Or beaten her himself? It *was* within his authority, just unusual. Emily rose, unsure if she should go after Frieda or not. If nothing else, Frieda needed to know that Alana would recover...

"Emily." Gordian stood in the inner door, arms crossed over his chest. "Come."

Emily sighed and followed him into his office. It looked as cold and unwelcoming as ever, she noted as the door closed behind her. A dozen wards hung in the air, pressing against her magic. Half of them seemed designed to monitor flares of power within the room; the other half had no purpose at all, as far as she could tell. But that might just mean they weren't active, yet. She resisted the urge to poke and prod at them as Gordian took his seat behind the desk. *That* would have been very rude.

So what? her thoughts asked. *Not bothering to give you a chair, let alone a chance to sit down, is rude too.*

She pushed the thought aside as she clasped her hands behind her back. Sergeant Miles would have been proud of her, the irreverent part of her mind noted. Standing at parade rest, ready to accept praise or blame or whatever she was offered without complaint... it was something she thought he would have understood. She wondered, absently, where Sergeant Miles actually *was*. There had been no sign of him on the way to the office...

"Emily," Gordian said. "I trust Adana will recover?"

"She's out of danger, sir," Emily said. "I was told she'll be back to classes in two weeks."

"Good," Gordian said. For an instant, she saw naked relief on his face. She didn't really blame him. Frieda wouldn't have made a suitable scapegoat if Alana had died and her family had demanded vengeance. Gordian's own head would be on the chopping block, perhaps literally. "Being in Second Year, losing so much time will not make that much of a difference."

"No, sir," Emily said. She'd lost more time than that, thanks to Nanette. "I believe she will not have trouble catching up."

"Good, good." Gordian shifted, uncomfortably. "I had a very unpleasant conversation with your friend."

Emily nodded, slowly. "Can I ask what happened?"

"If you wish," Gordian said.

He paused. Emily frowned, wondering if he wanted to make her ask. It would have been a petty power game, not something anyone would do when the stakes were so high. Unless... it dawned on her that Gordian didn't *want* to talk about it. But he didn't really have a choice.

She took a breath. "What did you say to her?"

"Frieda was completely unable to account for her behavior," Gordian said, flatly. "She insists that the creepers panicked her, making her lash out. I did not find the explanation satisfactory."

"Grown adults have been known to panic too," Emily said evenly, choosing not to mention the fact that most societies *would* consider Frieda a grown adult. "The creepers were not a conventional attack."

"But one that could be handled by a lowly firstie." He tapped the table, firmly. "Worse, this is merely the latest in a string of incidents involving your friend. It is clear that standard punishments have failed to curb her behavior. There comes a time when more... stringent methods are necessary."

Emily felt cold. There was no pretense that the principal was your pal, not at Whitehall. The Grandmaster and his staff were in charge. No one was allowed to doubt it. Their authority was enforced by everything from unpleasant detentions to corporal punishment. And if those methods failed... what then?

"I have suspended Frieda for two weeks," Gordian said. "During that time, she will not attend classes, nor will she be permitted to take part in any organized out-of-class activities such as the dueling club. She will take her meals with the servants; she will be permitted to make use of the library, but otherwise she will be expected to remain in her bedroom."

Emily stared at him for a long moment. "That... that will force her to retake the year."

"Perhaps," Gordian said. "She *will* have access to the library and study notes, even if she doesn't attend classes. An able student will be able to lay the groundwork for catching up with the rest of the class, when she is permitted to return."

"She will also need to work on her joint project," Emily said. "She'll need access to a spellchamber and a workroom."

Gordian quirked an eyebrow. "And you believe she should be *allowed* to work on her project?"

"Yes," Emily said. "I understand that Frieda needs to be punished. But if the joint project fails, Celadon will fail too. That would hardly be fair."

"The world is not fair," Gordian said.

"That doesn't mean you have to make it even *less* fair," Emily pointed out. She pushed the issue as hard as she dared. "Celadon did not take part in the dueling contest. There is no logical reason to punish him for Frieda's mistakes. And it will look very bad if someone decides to challenge his marks on the grounds that *someone* refused to allow his partner to work."

Gordian gave her a sharp look. "Do you think that's a valid argument?"

"I think you don't need the hassle, *sir*," Emily said. She felt her head starting to pound. "He is dependent on Frieda's contribution. If he doesn't get it, the best he can hope for is a bare pass. And that will look *very* bad to his family."

"Whoever taught you to argue should be thrashed," Gordian muttered. He glared down at the table for a long, chilling moment. "Do you think his parents would have a case?"

Emily took a breath. The Nameless World didn't believe in helicopter parents. A student who got bad marks could expect to face the wrath of his parents, rather than watch the parents descending on the school like angry gods. No one would complain if Celadon was marked down for not doing the work. But they *would* complain, she thought, if Celadon had been deliberately deprived of his partner. *That* would make him suffer for Frieda's faults.

"I don't think that matters," she said. "What matters, sir, is if *they* think they have a case."

"True." Gordian looked up at her. "Very well. She may work with her partner, under supervision. *Your* supervision. And *you* will be held accountable for anything that goes wrong."

And perhaps give him grounds to try to expel me, Emily thought. She felt the wards at the back of her mind. She *still* had no idea what Gordian had been trying to do to them, but she was fairly sure it involved trying to remove her influence. *Or push me into a place where I have to surrender the wards.*

"Very well," she said.

"Good," Gordian said. "I believe we will have to hold the second round again..."

"I will be handing the dueling club and contest over to Cirroc," Emily said, flatly. She never wanted to see a dueling ring again. "He can take control of both, now they are up and running. I believe he will be far better at handling them."

Gordian's eyebrows rose. "As Head Girl, it is *your* responsibility to make them work."

"I *did* make them work," Emily said. She'd done her best to anticipate everything Gordian would say and come up with counterarguments. "The dueling club now meets regularly, two days a week, and we are well on our way to finding a yearly champion who might even go on to the league! I don't think the club needs me any longer. Putting someone else in charge, someone who has the talent and determination to make it work—and the time to dedicate himself to the club—would be far more efficient."

She paused. She was fairly sure Gordian would respond better to an argument that benefited him in some manner, but she was uneasily aware that he was at least thirty years older than she was. If he spotted her trying to manipulate him, and she knew she wasn't very good at subtle manipulation, he might react badly. And the only way to counter *that* was to put the argument in a way that laid all the advantages out before him.

"Cirroc has ambitions to join the league and become a dueling master," she reminded him, carefully. "A strong tie between the club and a dueling master will benefit us in the future, will it not?"

"True." Gordian gave her a sharp look. "And you think he has a chance of succeeding?"

"I don't intend to join the league myself," Emily said. She certainly had no intention of becoming a dueling master. "And nor do Jacqui and Cerise. Cirroc is the only one of us with such ambitions. He's the only one who *might* succeed."

Gordian nodded, curtly. "Very well. You can pass the club to him."

Emily allowed herself a moment of relief. She'd been fairly sure it lay within her authority, but Gordian might have tried to overrule her. Coming to think of it, he might even have tried to pass the club to Jacqui or Cerise. *That* would have been embarrassing. But Cirroc offered the greatest long-term advantage, as far as Emily could tell. Gordian evidently agreed.

"You can inform Frieda that she will be permitted to work on her joint project." Gordian met her eyes, warningly. "And if I were you, I would be reconsidering my friendship with Frieda. Her behavior has become thoroughly unacceptable."

He pointed a finger at the door. "Go."

Emily turned and walked through the door, keeping her back ramrod straight. She didn't allow herself to show any emotion as she passed through the antechamber, only sagging when the outer door was firmly closed behind her. Frieda was suspended... she groaned as the full implications struck her. If Frieda failed her exams, she might not be allowed to repeat the year. Her behavior had been appalling, after all. And even if she passed, she might not get good enough grades to pass into Fifth Year. There wouldn't be much hope of an apprenticeship if she left Whitehall with low marks.

Fuck, she thought, numbly.

She cursed Gordian under her breath. Expelling Frieda would have been kinder. God knew hardly anyone—apart from Emily—would challenge the verdict. And yet, she did have influence over Whitehall's wards. Gordian might have been trying to find a compromise between punishing Frieda and *not* alienating Emily herself...

Too late, she thought.

"Emily," a voice said. Emily turned to see Melissa, looking tired. "A word, please?"

Emily raised her eyebrows. "Did Jacqui send you?"

Melissa gave her an odd look. "Why...?"

"Never mind." Emily leaned against the walls, feeling power thrumming through the stone. "What can I do for you?"

"My cousin was badly injured by your friend." Melissa's face twisted. "That is *not* going to look good."

"I know," Emily said. She wondered if Melissa was going to challenge her, or merely throw a hex without bothering with a formal challenge. Adana had been Melissa's baby cousin, once upon a time. Melissa had every right to be upset. "I'm sorry."

"The family isn't going to be pleased." Melissa walked up to Emily and stood next to her. "I know she'll recover, physically. Mentally...?"

Emily nodded. She'd taken weeks—months, really—to recover from Shadye's attack on Whitehall. Or the Mimic. Or Mother Holly. Or the moment when she'd killed Master Grey or watched, helplessly, as Casper died. The Nameless World could heal anything that wasn't instantly lethal, if the victim was taken to a healer. But mental damage was beyond repair.

And no one wants to try to find spells to help deal with it, she thought, morbidly. *They're too scared about accidentally creating a whole new breed of powerful necromancers.*

"I've been through worse," Emily said, quietly. "Adana will recover."

"I hope so," Melissa said. "But if she doesn't..."

Emily sighed. "What will your family do?"

"I don't know." Melissa sighed. "It's not as if they invite me to conclaves now." She snorted, bitterly. "They didn't invite me before, of course. Fulvia just told us what to do and everyone went along with it. She decided who I'd marry and... they just agreed."

Emily pulled herself upright. "Why did they even *listen* to her?"

"She was old and powerful and knew where most of the bodies were buried," Melissa said, sardonically. "And very few people dared to challenge her."

"Oh." Emily started to walk down the corridor, Melissa falling into step beside her. "What happened between you and Jacqui?"

Melissa frowned. "Jacqui and Cerise both come from families that are connected to mine," she said, slowly. "We were the same age, so we were put together when the families met and... and expected to get along. We did, of course. It was *expected* of us."

She sighed. "And then I was disowned and they dumped me," she added. The bitterness in her voice was palpable. "Jacqui even turned around and practically *ran* up the corridor, just to make it clear she wasn't spending any time with me. So much for everything I did for *her*! *Gaius's* friends showed more loyalty."

"Jacqui invited me to befriend her," Emily said. "Why?"

Melissa stopped, dead.

"Because she thinks she can use you, I suspect." She snorted, rudely. "I wasn't taught to have *friends*, Emily. The people we were taught to court were the ones who could help us."

"Jacqui said much the same," Emily commented.

"Well, of *course*," Melissa said. The hurt in her voice grew stronger. "We had the same lessons."

She ran her hand through her hair. "You know—you *should* know—that people are expected to help their friends. But there's also..."

Melissa sighed. "Jacqui sees advantage in courting you. I suppose there's something *honest* about it. She's not some man pretending to be interested in whatever boring subject you're talking about because he wants to lift your dress the minute you're alone together. She will be honest about trading favors for favors, about owing obligations, about speaking for you as you will speak for her."

Emily lifted an eyebrow. "How many men spoke to you like that?"

"I was the Heir," Melissa said, in a faintly pitying tone. "Men would have buzzed around me like flies, even if I was a hunchback with a wooden leg. I could have jumped in a cesspit—" she snickered, humorlessly "—and they would have been complimenting me on my perfume."

She looked sad, just for a moment. "And then I was disowned and suddenly... no one was interested in me."

"You're married," Emily pointed out. "And Markus is a great guy."

"Relationships aren't just about sex, Emily," Melissa said. "I was taught to build up a web of people who owed me favors, who would repay them when I called. Now... I have to start again, from scratch."

"Or refuse to play at all," Emily said.

"Which feels unnatural," Melissa said. "Markus is doing the same, of course. He'll be head of the banking guild when it is formally announced. His contacts with the other bankers make it a certainty."

She shrugged. "If you want to befriend Jacqui, then befriend her," she said. The pain in her voice was clear. "But watch for the web of obligations. You might find yourself committed to something you don't want."

"Thank you," Emily said.

Melissa snorted and walked away. Emily stood there for a long moment, centering herself as much as possible, then reached out to touch the wards. She'd never liked using them to locate someone, even a tutor, but she didn't have a choice. She certainly didn't have the time to search the school from top to bottom.

She sighed. Frieda was in her bedroom. And that meant...

Time to go talk to her, Emily thought. *And then... what?*

Chapter Thirty-Four

"THE FOUR OF YOU SHOULD KNOW BETTER THAN TO HURL DANGEROUS HEXES AROUND," Madame Beauregard thundered, as Emily stepped into the dorms. For an awful moment, she thought it was Frieda getting told off *again*. "You're certainly not supposed to set the common room on fire!"

Emily peeped into Madame Beauregard's office. Four students, all boys, were cringing under the weight of her rebuke. She wondered, absently, what had happened to the housefather, then dismissed the thought as she made her way to Frieda's room. The housemother would be more than equal to the problem. She'd never seen anyone defy *any* of the housemothers twice.

She stopped outside Frieda's door and braced herself. Frieda hadn't *looked* happy when she'd left Gordian's office, which meant... Emily wished, suddenly, that she'd been there. She would have *known* what Gordian had said, even though her presence would probably have made Frieda feel worse. Shaking her head, she raised her hand and rapped on the door, firmly. The door swung open a moment later.

The tension hung in the air like a physical presence. Frieda sat cross-legged on her bed, while her two roommates eyed her nervously. Emily could sense dozens of wards floating in the air, brushing against each other to the point where she suspected it was actually counterproductive. She couldn't help wondering why Madame Beauregard hadn't intervened. There were so many spells in the room that they might be interfering with the school's wards.

"Emily," Frieda said, dully.

Emily looked at Frieda's roommates. "Go to the library for an hour." She felt a twinge of guilt at ordering them out of their room, but she wanted—she needed—to talk to Frieda in informal surroundings. "You can come back afterwards."

The roommates didn't hesitate. That, more than anything else, worried Emily. Something had gone badly wrong, so badly wrong they'd wanted an excuse to leave. And yet, retreating from their bedroom would have been a sign of weakness. Emily's arrival—and her orders—had cut through that particular dilemma.

"I'm going to sit on your bed," Emily said, once they were alone. "Drop the wards."

Frieda looked up at her, then waved her hand in a limp gesture. The wards faded into nothingness, allowing Emily to step up to the bed and sit down. Frieda shifted, bringing up her legs and wrapping her arms around them. Her plaits fell down, making her look ten years younger. It struck Emily, suddenly, that Frieda looked thin again. Had she even been *eating*?

On impulse, Emily reached out and pulled Frieda into a hug. The younger girl didn't move, even when Emily held her tightly. Her body felt limp against Emily's arms, as if she didn't have the strength to move. Emily held her for a long moment, remembering the days she'd told Frieda stories before they went to bed. Had she done the right thing, after all, by bringing Frieda out of Mountaintop? Or should she have tried to do something else?

She would have died, if you hadn't been there, Emily reminded herself. *And if she had lived, things might not have been better.*

Emily pushed the thought aside. "I'm sorry," she said, quietly. "I wish..."

She tried, desperately, to think of the right words. Lady Barb would have told Frieda off, she was sure. She would have lectured Frieda in her quiet manner that was somehow far worse than shouting, pointed out all of her mistakes in a way that would have left her feeling about a millimeter high. But *Emily* couldn't do that. Frieda was her friend and her little sister—in all but blood—wrapped into one. She could no more scream and shout at Frieda than she could beat her bloody.

And yet, she had to say something.

She wanted to demand answers, to know *precisely* what Frieda had been thinking. And yet, she knew demanding answers wouldn't help. *Gordian* had probably demanded answers, hammering away at Frieda until she was a nervous wreck. Frieda had probably been forced to relive the whole incident over and over, every detail etched on her mind... *Emily* knew *she* couldn't do that, not to her friend.

"It isn't good," she said, holding Frieda gently. The younger girl felt so small and slight in her arms. Frieda had always been small, even though she'd been putting on weight. "I don't know if you'll be able to pass the exams."

"He wants to be rid of me." Frieda sounded as if she wanted to cry, but didn't dare show weakness. Emily understood, more than she cared to admit. She'd never wanted to show weakness either. "I... I don't know what happened."

Emily frowned. "Do you want to talk about it?"

Frieda shook her head, but started to talk anyway. "I got angry. She was buzzing around me, tossing hexes at me... I got angry. I was... I don't understand it. And then the creepers caught hold of me and... I saw Dayan."

"Dayan?" The name meant nothing to her. It was masculine, she thought, but it was hard to be entirely sure. Gender-neutral names were unusual on the Nameless World. "Who was he? She?"

"He was in my class, back at Mountaintop... before I met you," Frieda said. "They gave me a basic class in reading and writing before they assigned me to you. Dayan... thought it would be funny to tie me up and dump me in a cupboard. I was there for hours before someone found and untied me."

Emily winced. "I'm sorry."

"I *saw* him," Frieda said. "And I panicked."

"And your magic blasted the threat," Emily said. "You nearly killed her."

"I thought I *had* killed her," Frieda said. "The Grandmaster didn't say."

Leaving Frieda with the guilt of thinking she'd killed someone, Emily thought. *And a fellow student, no less.*

She loosened her grip. "I should have barred you from the contest. I'm sorry."

"Not your fault." Frieda slowly uncurled, brushing her plaits out of her face. "I'm going to fail, aren't I?"

There was a wash of bitter resentment in her voice, mingled with naked shame and self-loathing. Emily felt a stab of pity and reached out to take Frieda's hand, holding it gently. A dozen possible answers washed across her mind, most entirely useless. There was no point in lying to her. Frieda could do the maths as well as *she* could. Being even a single week behind the rest of the class might make it impossible to catch up.

"That remains to be seen," Emily said. She sucked in her breath as Frieda looked at her, dark eyes shining with sudden hope. "You will have to catch up with some of your classes."

She made a face. Perhaps Cirroc would help tutor Frieda in other subjects. He'd probably want some other form of payment, but he could do it. Unless Gordian decided to be a pain and forbid Frieda from receiving any kind of tutoring. Emily made a mental note to do everything in her power to make sure he never found out, then pushed the thought aside. She had too many other problems at the moment.

"All right," she said. "What do you want to *be* when you leave Whitehall?"

"A combat sorceress," Frieda said. "You know, like Lady Barb."

"Yeah," Emily said. She took a second to compose her thoughts. "You will need Alchemy, Charms, Healing and Martial Magic, at the very least. You'll need advanced classes in all four subjects if you want to go straight into an apprenticeship after leaving school. That means you have to take them all in Fifth and Sixth Years."

"As well as others," Frieda said.

Emily nodded. "You can drop the other classes now," she said. She understood Frieda's reluctance to give up, but she'd really bitten off far more than she could chew. Aloha was the only student Emily recalled with a similar workload and Aloha had learned to read, write and study from a very early age. "I know you want to keep them, but you don't have time."

"I can't drop the joint project," Frieda pointed out.

"No, you can't," Emily agreed. She gritted her teeth. Celadon and Frieda would just have to put up with each other for a few more months. Then they could submit their project and settle their differences on the dueling field, if they wished. "You need to drop all of the other classes now."

"I'll lose marks," Frieda protested.

"You'll lose everything if your combined marks aren't enough to push you into the next year," Emily pointed out, a little more sharply than she'd intended. Frieda cringed, as if Emily had slapped her. "You can't handle so many classes, not now. Drop them and concentrate on what you need."

Which might not be enough. Emily thought. *Her behavior will not make the tutors eager to see her next year.*

She forced herself to think. It wasn't unheard of for a student to go into an apprenticeship after Fourth Year, but it was very rare. Frieda certainly wouldn't be offered the chance to apprentice with a combat sorcerer, unless... Emily considered a handful of possible options, one by one. Sergeant Miles would flatly refuse to take Frieda, she suspected, along with most of his peers. But Jade might... he was a master, authorized to take students if he wished. And he owed Emily a favor.

Alassa might be glad to have another combat sorcerer—even a half-trained one—nearby, Emily told herself. And Jade certainly doesn't have time to raise a conventional apprentice.

"You need to pass those four subjects," she said. "Everything else, you can study during the holidays and take the exams before classes resume."

"Like you," Frieda said. "What happens if I fail?"

Emily shrugged. There *were* options. Frieda wouldn't have any qualifications, but there were places so desperate for magical help that they probably wouldn't care. Or she could find a private tutor if she got kicked out of Whitehall. Or...

"Concentrate on not failing," she said, firmly. She untangled herself from Frieda. "How many hexes have you placed around your desk?"

"They kept trying to break in." Frieda waved a hand towards the desk. "I wanted to keep them out."

Emily sighed. It sounded as though Frieda needed new roommates too. She wasn't sure what she could do about that. Students weren't supposed to change rooms without a very good reason. Perhaps she could talk the housemother into authorizing a change, if Frieda found someone willing to swap with her. But the way she'd been behaving recently, Emily doubted she would have any takers.

She used to get on with her classmates, she thought. Frieda had always been more sociable than Emily. *She was the one who invented freeze tag! What happened?*

There was a small notebook on the desk, sitting next to Frieda's class schedule. Emily saw it and winced. Frieda had hardly any time outside classes at all. *That* wasn't going to be a problem for the next few weeks, she reflected as she listed the classes Frieda would have to drop. She understood wanting to learn as much as possible, but there were limits. Frieda had clearly met hers quite some time ago.

"Write a formal note to the year head, informing him that you intend to drop all but those four classes," she said. She picked up the notepad and held it out to Frieda. "And then I'll take it down to his office."

"You shouldn't do that for me," Frieda said.

Emily shrugged. Gordian was on the warpath. There was no point in giving him an excuse, no matter how thin, to turn Frieda's suspension into an expulsion. Frieda would be better off staying in her room anyway, at least until dinnertime. Adana's friends were likely to hex Frieda in the back if they saw her. They might be two years younger than Frieda, but if they were angry enough they were unlikely to care.

"I'll take it," Emily said. Frieda didn't need to get into trouble for hexing younger students *again*. "*You* can start working on your study plan."

Frieda blanched. "Study plan?"

"Yes." Emily reached for the bookshelf, then stopped herself. "Remove the wards?"

Frieda scowled, but did as she was told.

"There's a course outline in your year handbook," Emily said. She'd studied hers religiously, once upon a time. "You can see what the tutors are teaching over the next three to four weeks. *Your* task is to work out what you need to study to catch up with the minimum of trouble."

"I won't be able to do any practical work," Frieda objected.

"That might not be a problem," Emily said. Gordian *had* agreed that Frieda could use a spellchamber. He'd meant for the joint project, but Emily figured she could stretch his rules a little. Besides, she could alter the wards to keep him from peeking. "For the moment, though, you need to concentrate on theoretical work."

She passed Frieda the handbook, then sat on the bed. "You won't get another chance," she warned. "You *cannot* afford to let this one slip by."

Frieda looked down at the floor. "I'm sorry. I just... I just don't know what happened."

Emily frowned. She'd checked Frieda's room—and Frieda herself—for outside influence, finding nothing. Frieda hadn't been enspelled, nor was she being drugged or manipulated by magic. And that meant... what? That Frieda was acting of her own free will? Or that someone had managed to manipulate her without magic? Emily honestly wasn't sure which possibility was more disturbing.

She really did take on too much, she thought. Even *Aloha* had become cranky, as exam season approached. She'd once turned Emily and Imaiqah into tiny statues, just for talking too loudly when Aloha had been trying to study. *And Frieda might be cracking under the strain.*

"It doesn't matter," she lied. It wouldn't be long before Adana's parents heard what had happened. And then... what? There was no way to predict their reaction. Thankfully, Gordian would have trouble issuing more punishment—or handing Frieda over to Adana's parents—without an additional excuse. "What matters now is coming to grips with the problem."

She leaned against Frieda, wrapping her arm around the younger girl's shoulders. "You can cope with this," she said, as reassuringly as she could. She tapped the notebook, meaningfully. "Start writing the note now."

"All right," Frieda said. "I..."

She looked up. "I'm sorry, Emily," she said. Her eyes were bright, but there was something odd in her voice. "You've been a really good friend."

"So have you," Emily said. Frieda had saved her life, back in Beneficence. "You *will* be fine."

She watched as Frieda carefully wrote out the note, word by word. Her handwriting had improved immeasurably since they'd first met—Emily's hadn't been much better, given she'd never used a quill pen before coming to Whitehall—but she still labored over the paper. Master Tor was the sort of person who'd reprimand her for not crossing every 't' or dotting every 'i,' although—after everything that had happened over the last two months—his reprimand would probably be meaningless.

"Very good," she said, when Frieda had finished. "I'll take it now."

Frieda looked alarmed. "And you'll come back?"

"I need to have a word with Cirroc," Emily said. By her offhand calculations, Cirroc should have finished clearing up the mess by now. If not... well, she could find him anyway. "I'll come back after dinner."

"I have to eat with the servants," Frieda said, looking downcast. "Everyone will laugh at me."

Emily winced. Frieda was probably right. Eating with the servants wasn't something *she* would have considered a punishment, but it meant everything to status-conscious students at a boarding school. The servants were at the bottom of the social hierarchy, after all. Forcing Frieda to eat with the firsties would have been less of a humiliation.

"Just be glad you're eating," Emily said. She briefly considered inviting Frieda to eat in her suite, before deciding it would be a step too far. Gordian would be keeping an eye on Frieda now, if he hadn't been already. "The food will be edible."

She smiled. Lady Barb had told her that the cooks always kept back enough food to feed the staff, save perhaps for certain rare delicacies. Frieda might not *enjoy* eating with the servants—there'd be no chance to banter with them, or to discuss classes—but at least she'd have something to *eat*. The servants wouldn't know what to make of her, Emily supposed... she shrugged. Frieda would be able to eat, and that was all that mattered.

And no one will see her eating with the servants, she reminded herself. *Unless someone decides to go cadge a late-night snack...*

She groaned. Someone would. *Of course* someone would.

"I'll be back soon," she promised. There was probably no way to keep the rest of the school from noticing that Frieda was eating with the servants. Frieda would just have to put up with the taunts. "And I want you to have the study plan ready by the time I come back."

Frieda smiled, but there was an unsteady edge to it. "And if I don't?"

Emily frowned. "I'll put a *geas* on you to *make* you do it," she said, only half-joking. She wasn't sure *what* she'd do if Frieda refused to take advantage of her last chance. "And then I will leave you to the tender mercies of your tutors."

She rose, trying to ignore the flicker of pain in Frieda's eyes. "This is your last chance," she said, flatly. "Please. Don't waste it."

Chapter Thirty-Five

"THAT YOUNG MAN NEEDS A SLAP ACROSS THE FACE," CIRROC SAID, QUIETLY. THEY SAT AT one edge of the workroom, watching Frieda and Celadon try to work together. "Or probably a thrashing with a belt."

Emily nodded, sourly. The last two weeks had been better than she'd feared—Frieda had improved, after dropping a number of classes—but the joint project was the *real* problem. And it was almost completely insurmountable. Frieda was starting to master the material, but Celadon—suddenly aware that his grade depended on her contribution—was trying to push her forward too fast. Emily was morbidly certain that the only thing keeping them working together was the looming presence of two seniors in the background.

And if they don't hang together, they'll hang separately, she thought. Celadon's family would not be happy if the joint project failed—or his GPA fell past the point where he could automatically transition into Fifth Year. Having to retake a single year—let alone two—would not reflect well on him. *At least he understands what's at stake.*

She sighed. Celadon wasn't *bad, per se,* but he wasn't the ideal partner for Frieda. He was too impressed with his own brilliance to tolerate someone slower, too concerned about making a splash to worry about the groundwork. Celadon might have been better off sticking with the original plan, then working on his own concept over the summer holidays. It would have ensured that he got full credit for anything workable.

"You have to cast the spell *precisely,*" Celadon said. He sounded more like a condescending older brother than a student talking to a peer. Emily didn't need to see Frieda's face to know the younger girl wasn't happy about his patronising tone. Too many people had talked down to her in her life. "If you don't get all the moving parts going in the right direction, the spell will fail."

Frieda's temper flared. "And you never heard of the KISS Principle?"

"This isn't something that can be kept simple," Celadon said. "Mixing a potion, let alone an alchemical brew, is complex. The magic must be inserted in precisely the right form or it will fail."

Emily shared a long look with Cirroc. Sergeant Miles was *very* fond of the KISS Principle—he'd often explained that complex plans had a habit of going badly wrong from the start—but Celadon had a point. Alchemy was far more than merely throwing ingredients into a pot, inserting a little magic and hoping for the best. Anyone stupid enough to try would be lucky if they merely blew off their own hands. Brewing required a delicate touch and careful handling. Emily had never liked it. The slightest variation could have unpredictable—and spectacular—results.

"And how many alchemists are going to take the time to charge the fingers?" Frieda demanded, harshly. She picked one of them up and held it in front of her eyes. "Anyone who might *want* one will have the fine control necessary to brew the potion without it!"

"The idea is to market them to people who want to make potions *without* spending years mastering the skill," Celadon reminded her. There was a hard edge to his voice, but Emily could hear desperation under it. "Or even to people who don't have *magic!*"

Frieda glared at him, then cast the spell again. Emily watched grimly, knowing it was unlikely she'd be able to make the spell work while she was in a bad mood. Anger could power some spells, but none of them were particularly stable. Celadon's spellwork was far too unforgiving, too complex to allow raw magic to overpower any flaws in the spell itself...

She blinked. *It worked?*

"It worked?" Celadon stared at Frieda. "It worked?"

"It worked," Frieda said. The finger glowed in front of them, ready to use. "I cast the spell."

Cirroc nudged Emily. "I have to go down to the dueling field," he said. "Will you be okay here?"

"Probably," Emily said. Gordian hadn't commented on Cirroc tutoring Frieda, but Emily would have bet good money that Gordian would object if Cirroc missed dueling. The second round of the contest had to be repeated, after all. "I'll see you later."

She watched him go, feeling a flicker of odd affection. Cirroc was the sort of guy she would have found frightening, back on Earth. Strong enough to take what he wanted, *used* to taking what he wanted... Emily had never understood why some women found that enticing, even attractive. A man strong enough to pick her up was also strong enough to force her down and *take* her. And yet, Cirroc was far from just dumb muscle. Stupid magicians simply didn't last very long.

"The finger isn't quite stable," Celadon said. Emily dragged her attention back to him. "We need to make them with more care."

"You made this one," Frieda jibed. She pointed a finger at a mark. "That's your sigil there, isn't it?"

Celadon scowled. "I was expecting you to ruin it," he said, nastily. "I didn't bother to make them perfectly..."

Frieda's face darkened. Emily felt her magic surge.

"Behave," she said, sharply. She glared at Celadon. "You should be pleased that someone else has actually managed to master your spell."

Celadon looked back at her, then nodded curtly. Emily sighed, inwardly. Cirroc had told her that Celadon found her more intimidating than *him*—something Emily still found a little unbelievable—but he was also more inclined to challenge her. Most magicians didn't seem to *like* the thought of dealing with someone far more powerful than themselves, even if it was a fact of life. Perhaps *that* was the real reason students were separated by age and ability, Emily reflected. The younger students would be spending far too much time, otherwise, trying to knock the older students off their pedestals.

"Cast it again," he ordered, shortly. "We cannot afford to fail when they inspect our work."

Frieda's face darkened, but she cast the spell again and again. Emily nodded in approval. A good spellcaster—and Frieda *was* good—would find it easier and easier to cast the spell as they practiced. Celadon looked irked, then relieved. Emily watched as he organized the fingers, before starting to cast the spell himself. He was right, unfortunately. Failing to cast the spell—even once—during the presentation would probably get them marked down.

"I'll set up the caldron," Celadon said. "You get ready to insert the finger."

Perhaps another name would be better, Emily thought. Professor Thande would probably insist on it. A student who put a *real* finger in a steaming caldron would instantly regret it, if he survived. *But that isn't a problem right now.*

She tossed possible alternatives around and around in her mind as Celadon set up the caldron and started to brew with practiced skill. The more complex healing potions were never easy to brew, not even for a skilled alchemist. Emily couldn't help wondering if there would come a time, soon, when people would bless Celadon's name. Healing potions were expensive simply because they were very hard to brew. Anything that made them easier would be warmly welcomed.

Except for the alchemists who feel they've lost status, she reminded herself. *And everyone else who had something to gain from keeping the potions expensive.*

It wasn't a pleasant thought. The Accountants Guild had collapsed when the New Learning had exposed just how badly it had exploited its position, but its absence had played a major role in Vesperian's Folly. And *that* had nearly destroyed a city. She wondered, idly, just what consequences might follow if the alchemists lost some of their influence, then dismissed the thought. The consequences were probably unpredictable. Besides, the fingers couldn't be used to produce *tailored* potions. That required a skilled alchemist with plenty of spare time.

"The brew is ready," Celadon said, softly. "Insert the finger... now."

Emily leaned forward, watching with interest as Frieda gently lowered the finger into the yellow liquid. She wasn't sure if Celadon should be counted as a genius or not, but she had to admit that very few people would willingly try to use a wand—or anything charged with magic—to make potions. Professor Thande had warned them, time and time again, to be very careful that their tools were cleansed of magic, pointing out that an unexpected surge of magic could be very dangerous. Celadon had looked past the dangers and seen opportunity.

The liquid started to bubble, then turned a sickly green.

"That's not meant to happen," Celadon said, surprised. He sniffed the air over the caldron, then sat back hastily. Emily muttered a charm to dispel the stench before it spread any further. "What did you do?"

"I didn't do anything," Frieda said. "The spell was perfect."

"The brewing was perfect too, until you inserted the finger." Celadon picked up one of the other charged fingers and examined it. "You must have messed up the spell, somehow."

"Or you messed up the brew." Frieda's fists clenched as she stepped back from the worktable. "The slightest mistake could have caused an unexpected reaction."

"I didn't *make* a mistake," Celadon snapped. "This potion is so simple a *child* could do it!"

"Then why didn't you?" Frieda slammed her hand onto the table. "The spell was perfect!"

"You probably didn't anchor it properly," Celadon said. His voice lowered, becoming more annoyed than angry. It grated on Emily's ears as Celadon picked up three of the unused fingers and waved them at Frieda. "Practice again, on these three and..."

Frieda snarled. Her magic flared around her. "Do *not* talk to me like that!"

Emily cleared her throat, loudly. "Calm down, both of you," she snapped. "Did you expect success on the very first try?"

"It worked for me." Celadon didn't even *look* at Emily. "Why wouldn't it work for *Frieda?*"

"Because you messed up the brewing," Frieda snapped. Her fingers were playing with her bracelet. "You said yourself that the spell was perfect!"

"It only takes a tiny error to mess up the potion," Celadon countered. "And if you can't master the spell, what hope do you have of passing? You're going to fail because you're too stupid to count to eleven without taking off your shoes!"

Emily saw disaster looming and started forward, but it was already too late. Frieda lunged forward, grabbed the caldron and tossed the boiling contents at Celadon. Emily reached out with her magic, but she couldn't cast a shield in time. The liquid struck his chest, making him scream in pain.

Frieda screamed too, a sound of pain and rage and bitter hopelessness. There was something *in* the sound, something weird and alien and utterly *wrong*. But there was no time to analyze it. Frieda's magic flared out of her, slamming into Emily with staggering power. The force picked her up and threw her against the wall, hard. She heard alarms ringing in her head as she fell down and crashed to the ground, landing badly. The screaming was so loud she could barely think... the world went dark, just for a second. When she opened her eyes, there was no sign of Frieda.

Fuck, she thought, numbly. Her entire body felt battered and bruised. *What happened?*

The door slammed open. Gordian charged into the room, followed by Sergeant Miles and Master Tor. Emily barely registered his presence before he was casting spells over Celadon, trying to save his life. The shock of being drenched in boiling liquid alone might kill him, Emily thought numbly. She had no idea how hot the potion had been, but most brews had a boiling temperature well above water. And he'd taken the potion to the chest...

A strong arm grabbed hers, hauling her upright. She found herself looking at Gordian.

"What happened?" Gordian asked. Behind him, she could see Sergeant Miles levitating Celadon out of the room. "What happened?"

"I'm not sure," Emily temporized. Frieda had drenched Celadon in boiling liquid, then attacked Emily herself... and yet, there had been that weird sensation in her magic. "I..."

"Look around you," Gordian snarled. He didn't let go of her. *"What happened?"*

Emily forced herself to focus. The workroom was a broken mess, the walls cracked and broken, the floor covered with sawdust. She couldn't see the table... it took her several seconds, in her dazed state, to realize the table had been reduced to dust. Her wards were damaged too... she'd known Frieda was powerful, but not *that* powerful. If she'd blasted Emily with the sort of power it took to damage the walls, Emily would have died.

"Damn you," Gordian snarled. He slapped her face, hard enough to get her attention. "What happened?"

"Let go of me," Emily said. He was too close to her, his anger all too clear. She shrugged off his arm, leaning back against the wall. Her legs still felt unsteady. "Frieda... Frieda went mad."

"Mad," Gordian repeated. "What happened?"

Emily glared at him. She knew Gordian had used the wards to keep an eye on Frieda. Even if he hadn't, the workroom was monitored. Had Frieda somehow disabled or destroyed the spells? She tried to reach out with her mind to touch the wards, but her thoughts were too unfocused to make contact. Frieda might have hit her harder than she'd thought.

"Celadon and Frieda had a fight," she said. She forced herself to go through the entire story, despite the pain and bitter guilt. She'd failed both of them. Frieda would be expelled and there was nothing Emily could do about it. "Frieda... where is she?"

"I don't know," Gordian said. "She isn't within the school."

Emily eyed him suspiciously. How long had it *been* since Frieda had blasted her? Had she blacked out for hours? No, that was clearly impossible. Celadon might not have *survived* if it had been longer than a few minutes. The wards would have sounded the alert the moment Frieda lost control.

She could have gone down to the tunnels, Emily thought. *The wards don't reach down there.*

She dismissed the thought a second later. *Frieda* didn't know the wards didn't extend into the catacombs. And she knew she was being watched. Emily and Cirroc had drilled that into her head, time and time again. Frieda was no fool. She'd have known the only hope of escape was to get out of the school before it was too late.

And she can run faster than anyone else, Emily reminded herself. *Straight down the stairs and out onto the grounds, then directly into the forest.*

Gordian leaned forward, looming over her. "Where would she go?"

"I don't know," Emily said. Where *would* Frieda go? Dragon's Den was the only settlement for miles. But Frieda could live off the land for quite some time, if she wished. She certainly didn't have any of Emily's qualms about catching rabbits and other small animals for food, or remaining unwashed for days or weeks. "She could go anywhere."

She stepped away from the wards, thinking hard. Frieda couldn't teleport, as far as Emily knew. She'd certainly burned up much of her power destroying the room. But merely getting a few miles away would make pursuit impossible. Frieda had been *good* at Martial Magic. She knew how to cover her tracks and throw pursuers off the scent. And if she reached a large city—or even crossed a border—she would be impossible to find.

"I should have expelled her," Gordian said. His voice was angry, filled with bitter self-reproach. "When she hurt Adana... I should have expelled her."

"Something is wrong with her," Emily said, quietly. "I..."

Gordian's face darkened. "Yes, there is. You should have given her a slap and told her to behave, or else. Her behavior was unacceptable. You should have drilled this home to her until she got the message or quit! Instead, you tried to help her."

Emily tapped the badge he'd given her. "Isn't that my job?"

"There are limits," Gordian said.

He sighed, turning away from her. "I'm going to have to alert the authorities," he said, softly. "She's a rogue now, one who has to be hunted down..."

"You can't," Emily said. "They'll *kill* her!"

"Don't let your feelings get in the way of what has to be done," Gordian said, harshly. "A student lies at death's door, thanks to your little friend. How many more excuses are you going to make for her?"

"There's something wrong with her," Emily insisted. "You have to listen..."

"It's too late," Gordian said. "People will demand answers, Emily. Answers I will be unable to give them, because I didn't expel Frieda when I had cause. Celadon's family will *not* let this pass."

"And you're prepared to sacrifice Frieda to keep your post," Emily said.

Gordian's magic flared, just for a second. Emily stood her ground.

"If you weren't one of my students, I would challenge you for that," Gordian said. His voice was almost a hiss. "And as a probationary student, you can be expelled at any moment."

"Fine time to remember that," Emily snapped.

"Go see the Warden," Gordian said. "And then go back to your room and *wait*. I daresay the inquest will consume all of your time for the foreseeable future. You might want to start working on your defense."

He paused. "Oh, and if you happen to think of a place where your friend might be hiding, you should tell me. It will be taken into account during the inquest."

Emily scowled as she headed for the door. Frieda could be anywhere by now. She didn't have the slightest idea where to look...

She stopped. There *was* one place Frieda might go. And no one would think to look for her there.

Except me, Emily thought. She was certain she was right. *Because I'm the only one who knows she can get into my house.*

Chapter Thirty-Six

GORDIAN WOULD NOT BE PLEASED, EMILY KNEW, IF SHE WALKED STRAIGHT OUT OF Whitehall without bothering to ask for permission. Not, she suspected, that he'd give her permission if she bothered to ask. Celadon's family *would* demand answers and there would be more than enough blame to go around. Frieda would be expelled and convicted of mutilation and attempted murder, but that wouldn't be enough. Gordian might lose his job over the whole affair, if his political opponents tried to drag him down.

They'll say he should have expelled Frieda after Adana was injured, Emily thought. *And hindsight will suggest they were right.*

She walked down the stairs and headed for the door, reaching out with her mind to commune with the school's wards. Gordian would be monitoring her, of course. He'd want to be sure she'd gone to the Warden before going back to her suite and... and then what? Emily touched the badge on her breast, feeling unwilling to simply give it up. She'd never wanted to be Head Girl, but she thought she hadn't been doing a bad job...

And one failure is enough to erase a hundred successes, she reminded herself as she altered the wards. Gordian would think she was still in the school until she was well away from the building. He wouldn't be happy about that either, although it was a minor matter compared to everything else. Her lips twitched in bitter amusement. *He's going to have some problems deciding what to put on the expulsion paperwork.*

Outside, the sun beat down on the grounds. The students lying on the grass or kicking a ball around the field didn't seem to know that *anything* was wrong. Emily could hear cheers drifting from the arena, where the duelists were still competing to go into the third round. Gordian must not have alerted anyone apart from the tutors that there had been yet another incident. She felt a stab of bitter resignation as she walked down the path towards the edge of the wards. Some of the students must have seen Frieda as she ran past, but hadn't thought anything of it. Frieda would hardly be the first student to make a run for the outside world after leaving class.

She looked back at Whitehall's towers, then resolutely turned her back. Gordian would definitely try to have her expelled for this, which would set off a power struggle she might lose. She didn't know what he'd been trying to do to the wards, let alone how they'd react if she tried to push him out of the school. Or if he tried to evict her. Perhaps he *would* have expelled her by now, if he hadn't known she could influence the wards. He'd certainly done his best to discourage her from returning last year.

And Frieda... Emily sighed, bitterly. She was still no closer to understanding what was wrong with her friend. She'd done everything in her power—perhaps too much—to help Frieda overcome her problems. What else *could* she have done? Threatened Celadon to force him to go back to the original concept? Bullied him into treating Frieda with a little more respect? Or maybe even just banged their heads together, hard. It would hardly have hurt as much as a cauldron of scalding liquid. But that hadn't been her responsibility. They'd been meant to carry out the project on their own.

She wondered, suddenly, if she should send a note to Caleb. Or to the Gorgon. Or someone—anyone—else who might be trustworthy. Caleb would guess where she'd gone, wouldn't he?

No time, she thought. *I have to get there before her.*

She pushed the thought to the back of her mind as she stepped through the outer edge of the wards. She'd half expected them to try to deny her passage, but they didn't even flicker as they brushed against her magic. Gordian hadn't realized she'd left then, not yet. She took a long breath, then carefully tested her magic. She *should* have enough to teleport, but she wasn't sure...

There's no time to find a horse or a coach, she told herself. She'd never liked riding, even though Alassa had seen to it that she'd learnt to ride. Horses took one look at her and started plotting to act up. *And besides, she might get there first.*

Concentrating, she closed her eyes and cast the spell. The world lurched around her, the teleport striking her with all the force of a punch in the belly. She staggered, landing on the tiny patch of grass outside the house. Her legs buckled a second later and she fell to her knees, half stunned. She'd pushed too much magic into the teleport for safety.

She forced herself to reach out with her mind, testing the household wards. They were depressingly simple—and stupid—compared to Whitehall's, but at least they were easy to operate. Her eyes went wide as she realized that someone—Frieda—was already inside the house. It was impossible. If Frieda had stolen the fastest horse in the stables, and ridden him without regard for her or anyone else's safety, there was still no way she should have reached the house ahead of time. Had she teleported? She had the raw power—after what Frieda had done to the workroom, Emily had no doubt Frieda had the power—but not the skill.

Maybe she was desperate enough to make it work, Emily mused. She'd heard *stories* of magicians who somehow managed to teleport by accident, although most of those stories had ended badly. *Or... did she bribe an older student into helping?*

She tested the wards, carefully. Frieda had access rights, but *Emily* had admin rights. There wasn't anyone else in the house, certainly no one who registered on the wards. Maybe Frieda had talked someone into teleporting her to Dragon's Den... it was the only explanation that made sense. There was certainly no way she could have set up a portal. She lacked the skill to even *begin* such a task.

Emily walked towards the door, then stopped. She'd been right—she'd guessed where Frieda would go—but the knowledge brought her no pleasure. She didn't want to walk into her house and confront Frieda... again. Celadon was hurt, Frieda a wanted fugitive... what could they say to each other? Emily was torn between a desperate desire to help her friend and a grim understanding that Frieda might have put herself beyond help. And yet...

I have to know what happened, Emily thought. Frieda might have snapped under the workload. Or she might have been influenced by someone else. Or... she might have just decided she no longer cared to work. *I have to know before it's too late.*

Ignoring the little voice at the back of her mind that insisted it was already too late, she pressed her fingertips against the wooden door and touched the wards. Normally, they would alert anyone inside the house when someone opened the outer door; this time, she took several moments to ensure that the wards wouldn't react to her presence. She didn't want to sneak up on Frieda, but she wanted—she needed—to know what Frieda was doing in her house.

The door opened, slowly. Emily slipped inside, raising one hand in a defensive pose. The wards hummed around her, fading rapidly as she made her way into the living room. Frieda was in the library, it seemed. Emily tensed—there were some books there she'd rather never saw the light of day again—as she heard the sound of someone flipping pages at a fearsome rate. Frieda? Or had someone managed to subvert her wards? Grandmaster Hasdrubal had built them—and Void had checked them, when Emily had inherited the house—but they lacked the power and sophistication of Whitehall's wards. A skilled wardcrafter, already inside the house, might be able to weaken or destroy them with ease.

She felt her heartbeat start to race as she reached the library door and peered inside. Frieda was sitting at a desk, her back to the door, reading a book with terrifying speed. Emily's eyes narrowed... was that even *Frieda?* Shapechanging spells and illusion magic was commonplace, although replacing someone for more than a few minutes was extremely difficult. Emily peered forward, trying to determine if 'Frieda' was surrounded by a haze of magic, but there was nothing. The wards certainly hadn't hesitated to let Frieda into the house.

Emily cleared her throat, gently. Frieda spun around, her hand snapping up to cast a freeze spell. Emily blocked it, careful not to step too far away from the door. If that wasn't Frieda, or if she'd gone completely off the tracks, she might need a line of retreat. Trying to teleport out of the house would be extremely dangerous, if she'd had the energy. She hated having to consider her friend a potential enemy, but she had no choice. Frieda had badly wounded at least three people, as far as Emily knew.

"Frieda," she said. She found herself utterly unsure what to say. "What are you doing?"

There was an odd flash of... *something...* in Frieda's eyes. "Studying." She rose slowly, moving to hide the book. "I thought you wanted me to study."

Emily met her eyes. "Back in Mountaintop, I did something to you, to show you what might happen if you went too far. What did I do?"

Frieda's eyes went wide. "You smacked my bottom, then stuck me to the ceiling," she said, after a moment. "I remember."

"Yes," Emily said. She didn't think anyone *else* knew what had happened. Unless someone had dragged the memory out of Frieda's mind... she shook her head. The girl in front of her *was* Frieda. There was no point in trying to hope otherwise any longer. "You have gone too far, now."

Frieda looked sullen. Her fingers played with her bracelet. "What do *you* care?"

"I care because you're my friend," Emily snapped. She felt her patience start to snap. "I have defied the Grandmaster and ignored his orders to come after you. There is a very good chance they won't let me back in the school! So tell me... what were you thinking?"

"I wanted him to shut up." Frieda looked down. "He just wouldn't shut up."

"Look at me," Emily snapped. "You shut him up, all right. You poured enough boiling liquid on him to do *real* harm. He could be dying now!"

Frieda shrugged. "Serves him right."

Emily felt a hot flash of anger. She controlled it ruthlessly.

"And what do you think people will say when you get hung?" she demanded. "They'll say it served *you* right!"

She glared at Frieda, daring the younger girl to look away. "I ignored orders to go to the Warden and came straight here," she added. "That's something else Gordian can beat me with"—*perhaps literally*, her thoughts added—"when I get home. I came because of you!"

"You came to see me instead of getting caned." Frieda laughed, a humorless sound that sent chills down Emily's spine. "I feel *so* flattered."

"I might just have thrown away my schooling," Emily snapped. "Do you think the Grandmaster is going to let me back in?"

"You're the most important student in a generation." Frieda's voice wobbled for a long moment. "Of *course* he'll let you back in. Not like me..."

"Stop the pity-party," Emily ordered, icily. Running away from the Warden was bad, but injuring three students—one of them a firstie—was far worse. Frieda was in deep shit. "Perhaps you should feel sorry for the students you hurt."

Frieda's hand played with her bracelet. "Perhaps *they* should have shut up when they had the chance!"

"You turned into a bully," Emily said. "How are you any different from the students who tormented you at Mountaintop?"

Frieda recoiled, as if Emily had slapped her. "I'm *nothing* like them!"

"You do *not* hurt students three years younger than you without being called a bully," Emily said, flatly. "I don't care what she called you. I don't care what she said about me. I just don't want you to lose everything!"

"It isn't as if I'm going to finish the year," Frieda muttered.

Emily silently counted to ten before speaking. "I organized help for you," she said. It was hard to keep her voice under control. Cirroc had demanded a favor in exchange for extra tutoring, a favor to be called in later. And she'd be honor-bound to agree to whatever he asked. "I helped you cut down your classes to a manageable level. I even spent several days over the last couple of weeks helping you with your studies."

She felt her voice begin to rise. "You had every chance of getting through your exams until you decided to throw it all away!"

Frieda flinched. Emily took a long breath.

"But now, you're wanted for attempted murder! Does it really fucking matter if you finish your exams?"

"He didn't die," Frieda pointed out.

"He *could* have died," Emily said. *She* could have died, too. It wasn't something she cared to think about, not now. "A few more droplets on his face and he'd be dead. Or the shock of being scalded so badly could have killed him too. Or..."

"You came very close to killing him. And it will get you killed."

She walked forward. Frieda inched backwards, pushing against the table.

"You've thrown your life away," she snarled. "Why?"

Frieda held up a hand, as if she was about to cast a spell. "I... I... don't know."

"You turned into a monster," Emily said. She hadn't wanted to say it - she hadn't wanted to admit it - but it was true. She felt hot tears prickling at the corner of her eyes and blinked them away. "You bullied younger students, you fought with older ones... and you threw away your life. What do you think is going to happen now?"

She felt a surge of anger as Frieda lowered her hand. What had happened to Frieda? What had she become? And what would it take to put everything back to normal?

"I don't know," Frieda said. Her voice was almost a scream. "I don't know...!"

Emily looked past her, frowning as she saw the book on the table. "*Malice?*" She'd taken the book from Mother Holly, three years ago. It had been so crammed with dark magic that her skin had crawled every time she looked at the creepy leather-bound cover. She had no idea what animal had been used to make the cover, but the *pages* were made of tanned human skin. "What are you doing with *that?*"

"Studying," Frieda said, sullenly.

"Idiot," Emily said, sharply. Frieda knew better, didn't she? "Those magics are *dangerous.*"

She sucked in her breath. Lady Barb had urged her to destroy the book. Emily hadn't been able to bring herself to do *that*—burning books was akin to blasphemy, as far as she was concerned—but she *had* stored it in a hidden safe. Frieda should never have been able to get her hands on it.

"How did you find it?"

Frieda shrugged. "I want them to respect me." Her voice was defiant. "Dark magics will..."

"No, they won't," Emily said, sharply. She understood the impulse far too well—it was better to be the victimiser rather than the victim, if those were the only choices on the table—but she knew it was dangerous. Frieda couldn't force people to respect her through dark magic. "It'll drive you mad."

"So what?" Frieda's hand played with her bracelet. "What do *you* care?"

Emily closed the book, trying to ignore the crawling sensation. Whoever had written the book—there weren't many copies, according to Lady Barb—had been a monster. And he'd created many *more* monsters. The spells in *Malice* more than lived up to the book's name.

"I am your friend," she said. It was hard, so hard, to put her feelings into words. "I taught you how to do magic—proper magic—at Mountaintop. I took you to Whitehall and arranged for you to have decent classes with decent teachers. I took you into my life... I even brought you into my *home*! And you ask why I care?"

"You abandoned me for *him*." Frieda's hand was still touching the bracelet, her fingers tracing the runes carved into the metal. "He was unworthy of you and..."

Emily's eyes narrowed. The bracelet...

Frieda had made it herself, hadn't she? It couldn't be dangerous, not when Whitehall's wards would have sounded the alarm. God knew there were a handful of students who brought prohibited items every year. But... it was new and Frieda's behavior had changed after she got it and... was it a coincidence? Or was it something to do with the bracelet...?

"Frieda," she said, slowly. "Take off the bracelet and give it to me."

Frieda seemed to hesitate. "Why...?"

"Now," Emily ordered. She was suddenly certain she was right. The bracelet was dangerous. If it had somehow been slipped through the wards, it could have been influencing Frieda for months. "Take it off and put it on the table."

"I..." Frieda stumbled forward. "Emily..."

Emily put out a hand. "I'm here for you," she said, as reassuringly as she could. She rested her hand on Frieda's shoulder. "But you have to take off the bracelet..."

Frieda leaned forward and kissed Emily on the lips, hard. The touch was so unexpected that Emily froze, just for a second...

... there was a flash of excruciating pain.

And then there was nothing, but darkness.

Chapter Thirty-Seven

EMILY HURT.

Her entire *body* hurt. It felt as if someone had beaten her bloody, then healed her only to beat her bloody again. Her limbs were stiff, flashes of pain coming from her wrists and ankles; there was a foul taste in her mouth, a taste so vile she wanted to throw up. But her body ached too much for her to even try. And the world was dark.

A finger poked her chest. "Open your eyes," a voice said. A *male* voice. "I know you're awake."

Emily forced her eyes to open, despite a puffy feeling suggesting at least one of her eyes had swollen. She was lying on her side in a darkened room... one of the rooms she'd never used for anything, she thought. Her hands were tied firmly behind her back. The only source of illumination was a light-globe hanging over the speaker's head, bathing the entire room in a faint radiance. She reached for her magic desperately, only to feel it recede from her grasp. The taste in her mouth confirmed that she'd been dosed with potion.

Durian-based potion, she thought. It would make it impossible to use her magic, as long as it stayed within her body. There were ways around it, but she doubted he'd sit down and let her work on them. *Shit.*

She twisted her head to look up at her captor. He was a tall man, wearing a long dark robe and a hat that cast an odd shadow over his face. And yet... she saw enough of his harsh, angular face to feel as if she'd seen him or someone like him, not so long ago. There was something oddly familiar in the slant of his chin and shadowed eyes. She stared at him, trying to place him, but failed. She'd met too many people over the last five years to remember them all.

Besides, it could be nothing more than an illusion, she thought. *For all I know, he could be a woman.*

"An impressive piece of work." He pointed to her chest. "I assume you carved it yourself?"

Emily looked down. He'd cut her shirt open, revealing the rune between her breasts. Oddly, he'd left the breasts themselves covered. She wasn't sure if it was a courtesy or an unspoken reminder that he could rip the clothes from her body at any moment. A skilled magician would have more on his mind than rape and molestation... she hoped. Whoever her new opponent was, he'd already put himself beyond the pale.

She cleared her throat, wincing at the taste. "Who are you?"

"Call me Daze." He knelt down next to her. "I've actually been looking forward to meeting you."

Emily frowned. The sense of familiarity was growing stronger. And yet... she still couldn't place him. She wished she had enough magic left to get a sense of *his* magic, but he'd forced enough potion into her to make it impossible. The only magic she seemed to have left was the familiar bond.

And if he tries to take my bracelet, he's going to be in for a nasty shock, Emily thought, grimly. She tamped down the bond as much as possible. A Death Viper made one hell of a secret weapon, but she didn't dare unleash the creature without a plan. Daze could easily kill the snake if he wasn't killed in the first few seconds. *If we're on the lower floor, I wonder if...*

She put the thought aside, for the moment. "What did you do to Frieda?"

Daze shrugged. "What do you *think* I did to Frieda?"

"You... influenced her in some way," Emily guessed.

"True enough." Daze shrugged. "Frieda spent two months working... away from you, away from anyone who might notice too soon. It wasn't too hard to start slipping commands into her mind, slowly turning her thoughts to violence. I'm actually quite impressed she lasted as long as she did before going completely bonkers. No one else has remained sane quite so long."

"She's not insane," Emily said.

"It's an interesting little trick," Daze said. "You *push* someone in a certain direction. If they get angry, you make them angrier. Something that annoys them will make them angry instead, making them less inclined to listen to sweet reason. All the little niggles and resentments of life become impossible to tolerate for a second longer. Anchor a little magic into something the victim keeps close to them and... well, it's hard for them to realize they're slowly going mad."

"Frieda made the bracelet," Emily said, slowly. She saw it now. "But she did it under your direction, right?"

"Of course," Daze agreed. "It was *her* magic, complete with her signature. I was fairly sure that Whitehall's wards wouldn't notice."

Emily felt her chest clench. Of *course* the wards wouldn't notice. They couldn't respond to magic students cast on themselves or the alarms would be going off all the time. Even firsties used protective spells and wards, once they realized the alternative was ducking spells all the time. The bracelet would have set off alarms if someone else had made it...

"She really does admire you." Daze glanced behind him. "She calmed down quite a bit, every time you spoke to her. I fancy the effect might have worn off completely without the bracelet."

Emily followed his gaze. Frieda was standing by the door, as stiff as a board. He'd cast a freeze spell on her, Emily realized. Now she was aware of his manipulations, it would be harder for him to control her. She wondered, idly, why *she* hadn't been frozen too. Maybe he just wanted to gloat. Or perhaps he had something worse in mind. He'd clearly already taken the time to study her rune.

"You bastard," she said. "Why?"

Daze smiled. "Why not?"

... She stands in line, beside a terrifying woman. She is a young girl, barely entering her teens. She feels utterly out of place as the young men approach the matriarch and bow, pledging their services. Daze is one of them, shooting a sidelong smile at his future

mistress even as he abases himself before his current matriarch. The smile is so creepy that it takes all of her training to keep her from stepping backwards...

... Daze is useful, says the matriarch coldly. She smiles at the little girl, but there is no warmth in it. Some people exist to get their hands dirty so others don't have to. They are there to be used, praised and then discarded. The little girl is scared, but she knows better than to show it. Embarrassing the matriarch in public would cost her...

Emily recoiled. A memory... not *her* memory. *Melissa's* memory. She'd been the one who'd seen Daze, years ago. The memory was jumbled—Emily wasn't sure just how old Melissa had actually been—but most of it was intact. And the matriarch had been...

"Fulvia," she said. "You're working for Fulvia."

Daze's eyes opened wide. "How do you know that?"

Emily ignored him. "Fulvia wanted you to drive Frieda mad," she said. Fulvia had lost her power base because of Emily. She had every reason to want a little revenge. "She assumed, no doubt, that her behavior would reflect badly on me. Right?"

"Something like that," Daze said. He cocked his head. "How *did* you know that?"

"You wouldn't be doing this on your own," Emily lied. "*Someone* had to be backing you. I thought she was the most likely suspect."

She gritted her teeth. Was Fulvia working with Gordian? Had Emily been appointed Head Girl so the position could be turned against her? To make sure she fell and fell hard? Or had her appointment come as a surprise? Gordian certainly hadn't been pleased. She didn't think he was that good an actor. Or... there were too many variables. Perhaps someone as smart as Fulvia had merely started the ball rolling and then sat back to watch and see what happened.

Maybe Fulvia had her plans and Gordian had his, she thought. *And the two plans collided.*

"Very clever." Daze smiled. "I must say you are as brave as you are beautiful, Lady Emily. I wasn't expecting you to come charging after Frieda."

"Oh," Emily said. She wondered if she could sweet-talk him into untying her, then dismissed the thought. That only worked in bad novels. "What did you expect to happen?"

Daze shrugged. "But now I have you." He smirked, unpleasantly. Emily felt a wave of unease that came from Melissa's memories. "And I think that opens up a whole new set of options."

"They know where I am," Emily lied. "They'll be coming here."

"Frieda reset your wards for me," Daze told her. "No one will be able to get into the house."

Emily shivered. Professor Armstrong and a team of wardcrafters could probably break through the wards, but Daze would have plenty of warning. He could send Frieda to cause a brief diversion while sneaking Emily out the back door... if, of course, anyone actually showed up. Gordian knew she had the house, of course, but she had no idea how long it would take for him to realize she'd gone there. Hell, the

thought of giving someone without a blood tie access to a private house would probably be beyond his comprehension.

She met Daze's eyes. "Whatever she's offering you, I'll double it."

"You can't offer me what I want," Daze said, pleasantly. "And besides, even if you
could, I don't think you'd want to."

He sat back on his haunches. "Fulvia wants you. She wants you broken. And I will
break you. I'm sure you will prove an interesting challenge, Lady Emily, but *everyone*
breaks eventually."

"Damn you," Emily managed.

Daze stood up. "I go now to make preparations. I'll be back soon."

He strode out of the room, extinguishing the light-globe with a snap of his fingers. The room plunged into darkness. Emily listened for a long moment, but heard
nothing. Grandmaster Hasdrubal had wanted his house to be quiet, hadn't he? He'd
worked silencing materials into the walls, as well as charms to keep out the slightest
sound from outside. Daze could be standing on the other side of the door and she'd
never know about it. Frieda was frozen, unable even to move an eyeball. She would
be quiet until the spell was released...

And perhaps unable to do anything to help, even if the spell was broken, Emily
thought, as she tested the bonds. Sergeant Miles had taught her that there was no
such thing as a knot that was impossible to undo, but she suspected freeing her hands
would take more time than she had. She hadn't even noticed her ankles were also
bound until she tried to move her legs. *How many commands did he put into Frieda's
head?*

She gritted her teeth. It was a painful thought. Frieda might never recover completely, even if she got the very best treatment. She might never—through no fault
of her own—be trustworthy again. Emily cursed Daze, and Fulvia, as savagely as she
knew how. Frieda had been turned into a monster, her reputation utterly destroyed,
as collateral damage. Emily had been the *real* target...

Spread rumors about me, then drive one of my closest friends insane, Emily thought,
angrily. *Was that the whole plan, or was there more on the way? Did she want to discredit
me? Or make it impossible for anyone else to trust me?*

Closing her eyes, she reached down to the familiar bond. It felt odd against her
mind—she was drawing on the bond itself, rather than her magic—but at least it was
intact. The spell holding the snake in place melted into the bond, allowing the snake
to return to normal. Emily grunted as Aurelius's thoughts slammed into her mind, at
once calmer and wilder than usual. She no longer had the magic to cushion the blow...

She peered through the snake's eyes. Aurelius saw the world differently: she was
a reddish mass, while Frieda's still form was flickering with magic. The rest of the
room was cold. Emily breathed a silent prayer that Daze hadn't put any wards of his
own around the storage chamber, then directed the snake towards the nearest vent.
Her wards wouldn't stop the snake. She'd allowed Aurelius to explore the ducts,
when she'd been alone in the house. He knew how to find his way from room to
room.

And I might have needed to use them myself, she thought. She'd done that before, at Whitehall. *It would let me move from room to room without being seen.*

Her head swam as the snake slithered up the wall and into the vent. Aurelius had no problems with heights, but *she* did... when the storage room suddenly looked bigger than Whitehall. The snake's sense of proportion was different to hers, too different. She gritted her teeth and forced herself to concentrate, steering the snake through the vent and up to the next level. It wasn't easy—the snake's senses were constantly assailed by potential prey—but somehow she kept her mind together long enough to get the snake into the upper chamber and look around. Her emergency kit was where she remembered.

God bless you, Professor Thande, she thought. As eccentric as he was, Professor Thande had drilled the importance of keeping a safety kit within immediate reach into her head. She'd made sure to keep hers well-stocked, even when she'd done as little alchemy as possible over the holidays. *You might just have saved my life.*

Aurelius climbed up the table leg and looked at the small collection of bottles and scented cloths. Emily had to force him to focus enough to pick out a purgative from the rest, even though the snake's nose was sharper than hers. Aurelius simply didn't care about flavors, let alone understand the urgency of what she was trying to make him do. The snake wasn't intelligent, not in any sense a human would recognize. Her more complex orders either caused confusion or were simply ignored.

And all of those talking familiars from storybooks were so smart, she recalled, feeling a flicker of envy. The Nameless World had never developed stories about talking animals, something that had surprised her until she realized that talking creatures were often very dangerous. No one in their right mind wanted to tangle with an angry adult dragon. *And no one who wrote those stories realized what a familiar bond might be like.*

She pointed Aurelius at the nearest purgative and commanded the snake to swallow. Aurelius resisted, just for a second. She caught a wave of what she would have unhesitatingly called grumbling in a human, a moment before the snake swallowed the bottle whole. It didn't sit well in Aurelius's stomach, but she ignored his increasingly annoyed protests. Instead, she directed the snake to hurry back to the storage room. She had no idea how long Daze would wait before getting to work.

He thinks he has time to do it properly, Emily thought. She had a *lot* of defenses against mental tampering, thanks to Lady Barb and Sergeant Miles forcing her to practice, but she knew that no defense was invulnerable. Daze was clearly practiced in mind and blood magics. She had a nasty feeling he might know something about soul magic too. *And he might be right.*

The thought chilled her to the bone. *Shadye* had influenced her, once upon a time. But Shadye hadn't been interested in doing more than using her as a tool. He'd never even seen her as a person, she thought. Daze, on the other hand, would break her mind and then hand her over to Fulvia. Or, perhaps, keep her for himself. If he realized just how many secrets were locked away in Emily's mind, if he realized just how many advantages she could give him, he'd never let her go. Fulvia could offer him all the wealth in the world and he'd refuse, because Emily could give him more...

She pushed her fear aside and kept a tight hold on the snake's mind. Aurelius growled—she'd never thought a snake could *growl*—as he crawled back into the vent. The sensation of sharp discontent grew stronger and stronger, tearing at her mind. She silently prayed that the snake's stomach acid wouldn't destroy the bottle before it was too late. The potion probably wouldn't do any harm to the snake, but she doubted she could make Aurelius go back up for a second bottle.

I might not have a choice, she thought, sourly. She racked her brains, but she couldn't think of any other way to escape in time. Daze clearly wasn't stupid. He wouldn't untie her until she was firmly under his control. Even *pretending* to be under his control would be very dangerous. *If this fails, I will have to try again.*

She allowed herself a moment of relief as Aurelius practically fell into the storage room, then forced herself to focus on the bottle. Aurelius stopped in front of her—her perspective shifted and shifted again, reminding her that she should be glad the room was dark—and slowly regurgitated the bottle. The sensations were so strong that Emily retched in sympathy, even as she turned her head to take the bottle in her mouth. Thankfully, the lid had been designed so that someone could flick it off with their tongue. Holding the bottle's neck between her teeth, she tilted her head to allow the potions to flow into her mouth. The taste was awful, but infinitely superior to the durian...

The first convulsion hit her a moment later.

Chapter Thirty-Eight

E MILY SHUDDERED, RETCHING HELPLESSLY.
It had been years since she'd swallowed a purgative. It wasn't an experience anyone wanted to repeat, even with a relatively mild potion. One experience had been
enough to make it clear that she had to be careful what she put into her mouth. The
purgative was designed to rid her body of potion as quickly as possible. Everything
from dignity onwards came second.

She convulsed as her stomach heaved, then threw up violently. Sweat ran down
her arms and back, a second before she retched again. She felt very ill, her legs suddenly weak... if she hadn't already been lying down, she knew she would have collapsed. Her stomach rumbled again. She twisted her body, desperately. The room
was sound-proofed, but if Daze was lurking outside he might hear the noise. And
then...

There were alchemists who tried to make themselves allergic to certain potions,
she thought, as her chest started to hurt. The taste of stomach acid flooded her
mouth. But none of them could ensure a mild reaction to the potion.

It wasn't a pleasant thought, but she clung to it as her stomach heaved again. She'd
eaten lunch—had it really only been a few hours ago?—and now she was throwing it up, expelling all that remained from her stomach. She should be grateful, she
knew, that her body hadn't had time to metabolize more of the potion. If nothing
else, it proved that she hadn't been unconscious for very long. She forced herself to
concentrate on alchemical formulas as she expelled the last of the potion from her
body, wishing she was back in school. Professor Thande would have helped her, if
she'd taken the potion in class. He'd have cleaned up the mess before it was too late.

Frieda must be terrified, Emily thought. The younger girl might be frozen, para-
lyzed by magic, but she could still *hear. She'll think I'm dying.*

She pushed the thought aside as she took a long shuddering breath, trying to
breathe through her mouth. Moving wasn't easy with her arms and legs bound, but
she managed to roll away from the vomit before slumping back to the ground. The
durian potion fumes might just impede her magic, if she wasn't careful. She concentrated, trying to call on her power. A tiny spark answered her.

Shit, she thought, as she fanned the spark into fire. *This could take a while.*

Panic yammered at the back of her mind. Daze wouldn't underestimate her a second time. He'd knock her out, then transport her to his lair... or straight to Fulvia, if
he decided against trying to break her. Emily had no illusions about what the elderly
woman would do to her, if she had Emily at her mercy. A woman who had no qualms
about using magic to torture her granddaughter wouldn't hesitate to rip Emily to
shreds, atom by atom. She forced the panic back, concentrating on her power. The
magic was rebuilding itself, slowly.

She focused, then cast a very basic untying spell. It struck her, a second too late,
that Daze could have charmed the ropes, but the knots came untied without resis-
tance. Emily pulled her hands free and sat up, casting a night-vision spell as she

moved. Frieda was still unmoving—and Aurelius was curled up by the vent, waiting for her—but the remainder of the room was empty. Emily mentally kicked herself for not concealing emergency supplies everywhere she could. But then, she'd never anticipated being taken prisoner in her own house.

Her head started to ache as she reached out to touch the wards. They felt odd, as if someone had been trying to fiddle with them. Emily recoiled, cursing under her breath. She'd worked her own blood into the spells, but given time a skilled ward-crafter could probably subvert them. Particularly if he had a sample of her blood... she looked down, but she couldn't see the remains of a cut in the semi-darkness. The thought chilled her to the bone. Daze could easily have taken a sample of her blood while she'd been unconscious, then healed the wound to ensure she never knew. She'd always *wonder* if a sample of her blood was out there, somewhere...

Later, she told herself, firmly. Daze wouldn't have left the house. *We'll have time to search for it later.*

Emily struggled to stand, despite her legs threatening to buckle. She hadn't felt so ill since she'd eaten something she really shouldn't, back when she'd been twelve. She'd thrown up repeatedly, then dry-retched when she'd finally emptied her stomach. Her stepfather, damn the man, had made sarcastic remarks for weeks afterwards. His lurking presence had forced her to go to school the day afterwards, even though she hadn't been well. The school canteen's barely-edible food hadn't helped either.

She tugged at her damp clothes, pulling them back into place as she tried to think. Getting out of the room wouldn't be a problem, but what then? Sneak back to Whitehall? Or confront Daze? She dismissed the last thought a moment later. She wasn't in any state for a confrontation. *And* she had no idea how Frieda would react. Daze had done a number on her brain. She might let Emily get her back to Whitehall. But she might also turn on Emily.

Crap, Emily thought. She didn't have the power to teleport, even if she did manage to make it out of the house. Even levitating Frieda to the nearest coachhouse would be a problem. *How much control does he have over her?*

She forced herself to think. Frieda couldn't have made it to Dragon's Den without teleporting—and *that* meant she'd met Daze outside Whitehall. And she'd let him into the house, something she *knew* Emily wouldn't like... Daze might not have *complete* control over Frieda, but he was certainly capable of manipulating her. Frieda might be able to resist, now she knew what was happening, yet... what if she couldn't? Emily knew just how dangerous mind magics could be. Frieda might well believe she was doing the right thing, even as she betrayed Emily to her enemies.

Frieda needs help, Emily thought. She called the snake to her. *And the only place to get her that help is Whitehall.*

It was a risk, she acknowledged. Gordian had presumably started the expulsion paperwork by now. Even if he hadn't, hunting parties were probably already being formed. They'd be convinced they were looking for a rogue magician. It was quite possible, Emily had to admit, that they might be looking for *her* too. She didn't dare assume Gordian hadn't realized she'd left school. If nothing else, there would be an alert when she failed to visit the Warden.

Aurelius crawled up her arm and settled into place, just inside her sleeve. The snake didn't *like* the smell—Emily recoiled at the sudden wave of sensations from Aurelius's twitching nose—but put up with it anyway. Emily braced herself, leaning against the wall for a long moment, then made her way towards Frieda. Perhaps she could levitate Frieda out of the house before ordering the wards to attack all intruders. She didn't *think* Daze could have subverted her wards to keep her from doing *that*.

She touched Frieda's arm, wincing at the unnaturally stiff sensation. "We'll get out of this somehow," she muttered, although she knew it wasn't true. Even if Frieda got the help she needed, even if her name was cleared, she was going to carry the mental scars for the rest of her life. "I'll get you home."

There was no response, of course. Emily gritted her teeth, silently promising herself that she'd make Fulvia pay. There was nowhere in the Allied Lands she could hide. Melissa might have been disowned, but she still had a blood-tie to Fulvia... and if she didn't, she wasn't the only Ashworth who owed Emily a favor. She'd track Fulvia down and use the nuke-spell on her hidey-hole, turning it into radioactive ash. They'd say the land was cursed for a hundred years.

Emily gathered herself, then cast the levitation spell. The effort tired her, even though it was a simple spell she'd mastered five years ago. Frieda floated into the air, wobbling unsteadily as Emily turned and guided her towards the door. It was unlocked, surprisingly. Or perhaps it wasn't *that* surprising. Stripped of her magic, Emily knew there was no way she could have untied herself in time. She felt the wards grow stronger as she levitated Frieda into the corridor, but they refused to help her locate Daze. It was impossible to tell if she just didn't have the energy to make contact—or if Daze had subverted them already—but it didn't matter.

I need a nexus point, she thought. *And there's one at Heart's Eye.*

The thought kept her going as she slowly slipped down the corridor, Frieda floating behind her. Heart's Eye was safe, secure... and *hers*. She could take Frieda there, then turn the former school into an impregnable fortress. Fulvia couldn't get to either of them there. And she could continue with her plans... invite Caleb to open the university, invite Melissa and all the others... build a community of her own, away from the Allied Lands. Who knew? It might grow into something great.

And then she heard someone clapping.

She froze. Daze was standing by the door, looking impressed. His smile—his creepy smile—was almost welcoming. And yet... another string of Melissa's memories rose up from the back of her mind, screaming a warning even as they threatened to overwhelm her. Emily forced them back, concentrating her mind. She was in no state for a confrontation, but she had no choice. Daze wouldn't make the same mistake twice.

"I am impressed, Lady Emily," Daze said. "There are fully-trained magicians who wouldn't have escaped."

Emily felt the snake, hidden in her sleeve. Perhaps Daze would come close enough for her to shove Aurelius into his smug creepy face. Or... she gritted her teeth, realizing how badly Melissa's memories had affected her. Melissa hadn't just disliked Daze, she'd found him thoroughly unpleasant and sinister. She forced herself to keep an eye on the older magician as she lowered Frieda to the ground. She'd need all of her power to fight.

"This is my place of power," she said, as defiantly as she could. "You can't fight me here."

Daze smiled, rather thinly. "I've taken the opportunity to examine your wards," he said, holding up a hand. Dried blood was clearly visible, forming a rune. "They are very well crafted indeed, but incapable of differentiating between Frieda and me. And you don't have time to reprogram before it's too late."

Emily cursed under her breath. He was right. She'd used the same trick herself.

"I don't know how you managed to recover your magic and escape," Daze said. "But if you could kill me, you'd have done it by now. Why don't you walk back to the cell and wait?"

"Because you'd kill me," Emily snapped. She tried, desperately, to think of a plan. She'd lose a straight fight and he was too far away to be *certain* of getting him with the snake. And if she *failed* to get him, he'd curse her into next week. "Or warp my mind for your mistress."

"I can always let your little friend go," Daze offered. "You are a far more valuable prize."

More than you know, Emily thought. She considered, briefly, offering to share what she knew, but she doubted he'd trust her. He'd want to control her, just to be sure. And that would be the end. *What the hell do I do?*

She stalled. "How do I know you'd let her go?"

"I could offer you an oath," Daze offered. "Her freedom for your surrender."

Emily winced, inwardly. It wasn't much of an offer. Frieda would *still* be mentally damaged, *still* be hunted by the authorities... she'd certainly never get the healing she needed to prove her innocence. Emily didn't think Daze could do anything about that, even if he wanted to. Frieda would walk out of the house, straight to her doom, while Emily remained to face hers.

She gritted her teeth. If she could get to a battery... it wasn't much of a plan, but it was the only thing she could think of that *might* give her a chance. She'd have to focus the magic manually too, channeling it through her mind rather than using a valve. Too many things could go spectacularly wrong. It might even drive her mad. And yet... she couldn't think of anything else.

"No." She gathered herself. "Walk out of here and I'll let you go."

Daze made a gesture with his finger. Emily barely had a second to react before an invisible force slammed into her, knocking her past Frieda and up the corridor. She gathered herself, then dispelled the magic a heartbeat before it would have thrown her into the wall. Daze walked past Frieda and advanced towards Emily, his magic crackling at the ready. She saw an unholy anticipation on his face and cursed, again. Melissa had been right. Daze was creepy as hell.

"You haven't recovered *all* of your magic," Daze said. Emily threw a hex at him, but he deflected it with a wave of his arm. "I imagine that whatever you did to purify yourself wasn't perfect."

He cocked his head. "How *did* you do it, by the way?"

"None of your business," Emily snarled. She tried to cast a series of wards to protect herself, but she could barely muster the magic to secure them in place. "That's *my* secret."

Daze seemed unconcerned. "I'll take it from your mind, once I've broken you," he said, calmly. His magic beat on the air, pressing lightly against Emily's makeshift wards. "I look forward to understanding how it was done."

"You'll never be able to do it," Emily managed. "It's my secret."

She tightened the wards, but she was grimly aware that they wouldn't hold for long. Daze was pushing his magic forward, seeking out and exploiting gaps in her spellwork. It would have been a mistake if she'd been at full strength. As it was, he'd done precisely the right thing. He'd break down her wards without causing significant injury.

"We will see." Daze sounded as calm as if he were ordering dinner, not slowly breaking down her protections. "I've often found it amusing how many exclusive spells can be reworked for others to use."

"Fulvia will use you and then discard you," Emily said. The pressure was growing stronger as her wards started to crack. "Do you think she'll reward you?"

"I think she'll pay through the nose to get her hands on you," Daze said. "Do you not?"

Yes, Emily thought. *Fulvia would shell out her entire fortune just to get her hands on me.*

Her wards shattered. Daze reached forward, magic crackling around his hands. Emily braced herself, then thrust the snake at him. Aurelius hissed, loudly; Daze froze for a split second, then jumped back in shock. A moment later, a wave of force slapped through the air, knocking the snake into the wall. Emily screamed as her bones shattered... no, *Aurelius's* bones. The familiar bond worked in both directions.

"A Death Viper," Daze breathed. "*Your* Death Viper?"

Emily gasped for breath. It was hard to keep her thoughts in order. He'd hit her... no, he *hadn't* hit her. He'd hit Aurelius. And yet, her ribs felt as if they were about to crack... no, they *had* cracked. She felt the bond waver as Aurelius fell into unconsciousness. It was luck—sheer luck—that Daze hadn't killed the snake. Emily wasn't sure what would have happened then, but she was fairly certain it would have thrown her into unconsciousness for a while too...

Daze reached out and caught her by the neck. Emily fought to muster her magic, but only a tiny flicker answered her call. It was hard to gather more, let alone shape a tiny spell in her mind. His power was crawling over her skin, checking for defenses...

she tried to push him away, but she couldn't even move her arms. A spell flickered on the edge of her mind...

... And she had an idea...

"There's no point in trying to cancel my spell," Daze said, as she cast the spell. His eyes bored into hers. "Even if you did succeed, I could just cast another one."

Emily spat, aiming for his face. Daze's face darkened with anger. She braced herself, expecting him to hit her. Fulvia would hardly complain if Emily was black and blue when she was handed over. But at least it would keep Daze focused on her. She hadn't aimed the spell at him...

"You are remarkable," Daze told her. Perversely, he sounded admiring. "But the game is over."

His magic pushed forward. Emily braced herself for the final struggle... then jerked backwards as Frieda slammed a deadly spell into Daze's back. Emily allowed herself a moment of relief as white lightning flashed over Daze's body, silently thanking all the gods of the Nameless World that Frieda was on her side. Daze hadn't realized that Emily had aimed to free Frieda, not cancel *his* spell. It had been a deadly gamble, but there had been no choice.

Daze fell to the floor, his body smoking. Emily fought the urge to cover her nose—she'd never grown used to the smell of burning flesh—as she looked at Frieda. Her friend was staring around wildly, her eyes flickering from side to side as if she was on the verge of bolting. An incoherent keening escaped from her mouth, drool dripping down to the floor...

... And then Frieda's hands shot to her own throat and started to squeeze.

Chapter Thirty-Nine

EMILY STARED IN NUMB HORROR, THEN PUSHED HERSELF FORWARD AS FRIEDA'S GRIP TIGHT-
ened. She pulled at Frieda's hands, trying to get them away from her neck. Daze must have programmed a suicide trigger into Frieda's mind, she realized as she struggled to save her friend's life. He'd wanted to be sure that no evidence remained behind, if something happened to him. And if Frieda killed herself, no one would know the truth.

"Let go," Emily said. She'd known Frieda was physically strong—good food and healthy exercise had worked wonders—but she hadn't realized just how strong. Her arms felt immoveable. "Frieda, listen..."

Frieda lashed out, throwing a punch into empty air. The second blow caught Emily in the shoulder, sending both of them falling to the ground. Frieda hit out time and time again, throwing punches in random directions... as if she thought, deep in her mind, that she was fighting a whole mob of people. Emily struggled to raise the magic to freeze her, or to stun her, or to do something, even as she tried to avoid punches that would do real harm if they hit home. Frieda was on the verge of tearing herself apart.

Damn him, Emily thought, as Frieda shoved Emily over and climbed on top of her. Frieda drew back her fist, as if she was about to start beating Emily into a pulp, then threw the punch into the air. *What did he do to her?*

Emily tried to think of a plan as Frieda waved her fists around frantically, her eyes flashing from side to side. She didn't have the strength to subdue Frieda—either magically or physically—and it was only a matter of time before one of Frieda's blows struck Emily hard enough to stun her. Whatever was going through Frieda's mind, she'd clearly lost all touch with reality. Emily wasn't sure there was *anything* she could do...

He cursed her mind, she thought, numbly. *And that means...*

A thought struck her. It would get her in real trouble, if someone chose to take a dim view of it, but it was the only thing that came to mind. She owed it to Frieda to take one last gamble before letting her friend kill herself. Besides, Gordian was probably planning to expel her already. She'd made so many blunders over the past few weeks. What was one more?

She reached up and caught Frieda's arms, yanking her down. Frieda struggled, fighting with terrifying force as Emily pulled her close, then pressed her bare hands against Frieda's cheeks. The last scraps of her magic rose up within her, allowing her to form a link between her mind and Frieda's. Samra would not have approved, Emily thought as she pushed her mind forward, but she couldn't think of an alternative. She *had* to remove the curse before it was too late.

Frieda's body jerked, violently. Emily wrapped her legs around Frieda, silently thanking Melissa for staying still while Emily probed her mind. Breaking contact *might* snap her back into her own body, according to Samra, or it might leave her consciousness trapped in Frieda forever. Magicians hadn't really wanted to experiment, Emily had been told. She didn't blame them for being wary of the dangers.

The maelstrom rose up and tore at her as she pushed her way into Frieda's mind. Emily braced herself as she was assailed by a dizzying array of memories and emotions, some close enough to hers to be confusing, then held herself steady. Frieda wouldn't welcome the intrusion, even from Emily. Her mind would fight to defend itself against what it would see as rape. Emily hesitated, repulsed by the thought, then pushed on. If Frieda decided to hate her afterwards... well, at least it would be her decision.

Melissa's mind had been a nightmare, but Frieda's was far worse. Emily peered through the hailstorm of thoughts and memories and saw... a dark lattice, woven through Frieda's subconscious mind. Merely *looking* at it made Emily's skin crawl. Daze had planted a seed in her mind, one that had steadily grown into a monster. Frieda hadn't known her thoughts and feelings weren't hers... in a sense, they *had* been hers. Daze had used her own magic against her. Emily swallowed as she realized just how hard it was likely to be to *prove* that it had been outside interference. The bracelet might not be enough proof to satisfy Gordian.

Because she made it, Emily thought. She gathered herself, then pushed onwards. *Daze might have told her how to make it, but it was Frieda who carved the runes.*

A voice boomed through Frieda's mind. "*GET OUT! GET OUT! GET OUT!*"

Emily cringed as the voice tore into her very being, burning through her thoughts. It was powerful, yet... she could hear a hint of desperation underneath it. She thrust herself onwards, remembering—again—that mental combat was all in the mind. Frieda could drive her out, she thought, but she couldn't do any real harm as long as Emily kept a tight grip on herself.

Samra should be here, Emily thought, numbly. *Or someone who knows what they're doing.*

She reached out, mentally, for the first part of the lattice. It was glued to Frieda's thoughts... no, it *was* part of Frieda's thoughts. Emily couldn't help thinking of it as malware, exploiting gaps in Frieda's defenses until it seemed *part* of her defenses. And yet, she reminded herself, again, to concentrate on visualizing the lattice as something that *could* be removed. If she believed it couldn't be removed, she wouldn't have a hope of removing it.

Frieda's thoughts raged around her, a razor-blade storm that threatened to dig into Emily's soul. She saw... *creatures*... running towards her, strange entities that flickered from shape to shape as they tried to lock onto her thoughts. They would be formless, she reminded herself, as long as her mind didn't give them form. She couldn't close her eyes, not in Frieda's mind, but she could ignore them. And telling herself—*convincing* herself—that they were harmless would make them harmless.

She touched the lattice...

... The father is angry, storming around the room. The girl recoils from his shouts. She tries to speak, to try to promise that she won't do it again if only he'll tell her what she did wrong, but the words refuse to form. He grabs her by the arm, throws her over the chair

and lashes her until her back is bruised and bleeding. She tries to ask, again, what she did wrong, but there is no answer. It isn't until much later that it dawns on her that she didn't do anything wrong...

... And recoiled in shock. A memory, overwhelmingly strong. Emily gritted her teeth as phantom pain burned her back and legs, telling herself—firmly—that the pain wasn't real. And yet, it had been real. Frieda had grown up with that man, her father...

Emily didn't want to press on, but she had no choice. She took hold of the lattice and pulled, hard. It resisted, shifting from form to form as it tried to find something that would give it a chance to remain embedded in Frieda's mind, but Emily refused to let go. She heard someone—or something—howl in pain as she tightened her grip, imagining that her hands were superhumanly strong. The lattice shimmered...

... The little girl stands in the square with her family and watches as the taxmen inspect the village. They go into every house, searching for hidden crops and livestock, then check the barns and other potential hiding places. The little girl feels the sullen anger and bitter helplessness pervading the villagers and wonders why her father does nothing, even when his oldest daughter is insulted, but she knows the soldiers will kill anyone who resists. And, afterwards, her father takes his rage out on her...

... The young girl is running, hiding. She can hear giggling behind her, a mockery of a hunting horn... she runs faster, only to trip and fall. Her pursuers are on her before she can rise, beating her with their fists and tearing at her clothes. She tries to kick out as they roll her over and over until she is covered in mud, but she cannot resist...

... The winter is cold. The little girl watches as Granny is marched out of the house by her son. She wants to cry, to scream, but she knows her father will merely beat her again. Granny is old and frail. She must die so the rest of the family can live. And when her brother tells her she will be the next one out the door, she believes it...

... The girl has just started to bleed, a day before the Harvest Festival. A sign of luck, perhaps...

Emily staggered under the wave of emotion, of self-disgust and bitter sickness and naked hatred. The memory seemed to laugh at her, taunting her... the lattice had found something that almost made her let go. She tried to concentrate, but the emotions pressed onwards, tearing into her mind. Frieda had been through hell. And now, if Emily wanted to free her, she had to face her friend's memories.

She braced herself, feeling a sudden flash of relief. She'd thought she'd had it bad, years ago. She had no doubt that neither her mother nor her stepfather were suited to bringing up a child. But her stepfather had never beaten her for fun, or to relieve his feelings... he'd certainly never put a grandma out into the cold to die. And if he had, he would have been arrested for murder, instead of being feted as someone who'd made the right decision. Frieda would have *killed* to have Emily's problems. She would have traded places in a heartbeat.

The lattice snapped and snarled, growing teeth and claws. Emily smiled, challengingly, and reached for it...

... The hunt is serious, this time. The boy is a few years older than her, on the verge of getting married. His father is a headsman; his mother the dame of the village. The girl knows better than to let him get too close, but he is too fast and strong and catches her away from the village. And then his hands are everywhere, pulling up her skirt and...

Emily felt sick, but she forced her way through the memory. The impressions grew stronger and stronger—a young man molesting her, a father who didn't care, a mother who couldn't defend her daughter—capped with a memory of the first time Frieda had shown magic. Even Mountaintop had seemed an improvement, at first. She certainly didn't want to go home again.

The lattice grew stronger, clawing at Emily's mind. Emily concentrated, then took hold and pulled as hard as she could. Frieda screamed—Emily couldn't tell if it was a real scream or just something in her mind—but Emily refused to be distracted. The lattice snapped and snarled at her, throwing memory after memory into Emily's mind, yet it was losing. And she knew it was losing. The knowledge gave her power, even as the last memory struck out at her...

... There is a girl. No, a young woman. Beautiful and clever and brave and... and a savior... HER savior. She wants to be with her. She hates it when she is with others. She wants her all to herself...

Emily blinked in shock. Frieda had a crush on her. She'd known Frieda had a crush on her, after Mountaintop, but she hadn't realized how *intense* it had been... It still was. She'd thought Frieda had got over it, yet Frieda had been jealous of Caleb and...

And how many of her feelings are real? Emily asked herself. *And how many are due to Daze playing games with her mind?*

She pushed the thought aside, sharply. It was something they would have to deal with, afterwards. She'd never thought of Frieda as anything other than a little sister... she'd never been interested in *girls*, not in that way. And even if she had been, Frieda was in no state to do anything. It was quite possible that the lattice had boosted her crush too.

Gritting her teeth, she took a tighter hold on the lattice and pulled as hard as she could. It struggled for a long moment, then came free... pulling a whole string of thoughts and feelings in its wake. Emily cursed as they assaulted her mind, trying to weaken her defenses so the lattice could worm its way into her thoughts. But they had started to fade the moment they came free. She concentrated on her defenses, watching coolly as the lattice and its companions started to vanish. Deprived of their connection to Frieda, unable to snag hold of Emily's mind, it was only a matter of time.

Emily wanted to pull back, as soon as the last one faded away, but she knew she had to be sure the curse was gone. She moved forward, feeling Frieda's thoughts pulsing around her. Wave after wave of sensation brushed against her thoughts—shame, guilt, fear, surrender—but they all seemed to be Frieda's. She knew someone more experienced would have to inspect Frieda's mind, just to be sure, yet...

She isn't trying to kill herself any longer, she told herself. *That is an improvement, isn't it?*

She snapped back into her body, instantly aware of a weight on her chest and liquid dripping onto her face. Frieda was crying silently, tears falling from her eyes and splashing on Emily's cheeks. She'd never cried loudly, Emily recalled. It had always earned her a beating, when she'd been a child. Now... now she could no longer cry normally. She rarely cried at all.

"It's all right," Emily said, softly. Frieda was shaking, her body shivering helplessly. "I've got you."

She gently pushed Frieda off, then rose and looked around. Daze was definitely dead, but she put his body in stasis anyway. The effort tired her more than she'd expected, yet she doubted she had a choice. Daze could have charmed his body to reanimate after his death—or worse. She couldn't sense any magic on the corpse, but that meant nothing. Her brain was too tired to work properly.

Frieda sat upright. "I'm sorry..."

There was something mournful in her voice, something that tore at Emily's heart. A bitter guilt, mingled with shame. Frieda hadn't been compelled to do anything, not at first. She'd been pushed and prodded, her tiny resentments and dislikes boosted until they'd overwhelmed her... it would be hard for an outsider to tell how much of her behavior had been hers and how much had been the result of manipulation.

The bracelet lay on the floor, glinting under the light. Emily picked it up and studied it, thoughtfully. The tiny charm was a masterwork, she had to admit. Frieda didn't have the skill to realize that it didn't *just* provide a degree of protection. And no one else would have noticed unless they looked very closely. She felt a stab of guilt. She *should* have looked closely.

"It wasn't your fault," Emily said. She looked down at herself. Her shirt was torn and damp, stained with the remains of the durian potion. "And we'll talk about it later."

She helped Frieda to her feet. "We'll have to get a wash and a change," she added. She didn't want to think about Frieda having a crush on her, not now. Somehow, the idea of a girl having a crush on her had never crossed her mind. It had taken her long enough to realize that Caleb liked her. "And then we'll have to go back to school."

Frieda jabbed a finger at Daze's body. "What about him?"

"We'll take him with us," Emily said. If they were lucky, Daze's body would be enough to keep Gordian from trying to arrest them both on sight. Melissa could presumably identify him, if nothing else. Adana too, perhaps. "And then we'll have to decide what to do next."

She picked up the snake and returned him to his bracelet form, then led the way up the stairs, silently grateful that she'd listened to Void's advice about stockpiling food and drink. They'd be able to get something to eat before they returned to Whitehall, as well as cleaning up the mess before it *really* started to stink. She'd never liked the idea of keeping servants, particularly when the house was supposed to be closed down while she was at school, but she could see the downside now. Someone else *wasn't* going to be doing the cleaning up for her.

"Get undressed," she ordered, as they entered the bathroom. She didn't think she wanted to be naked in front of anyone right now, but she didn't want to leave Frieda alone. The younger girl was still a suicide risk. "We'll take a quick shower and then have a bite to eat."

"As you wish," Frieda said. She sounded tired and depressed. Emily wondered if she should put Frieda in stasis too. "And then... what?"

Emily sighed. They'd have to face the music, of course. Legally, Frieda couldn't be blamed for anything she'd been *compelled* to do, but proving that she'd actually been *compelled* might be difficult. Daze's subliminal prompts were already fading into nothingness.

"I don't know," she said.

Chapter Forty

WHITEHALL FELT DIFFERENT, EMILY NOTICED, AS THEY MADE THEIR WAY UP THE DRIVE towards the gatehouse. Daze's body floated after them, bobbing in the wind. It was late afternoon on a weekend, yet there were no students or tutors in sight, something she knew was almost always a bad sign. The small collection of horses in the gatehouse was worse. Their caparisons suggested that they belonged to mediators or combat sorcerers.

At least they're not hunting for us, Emily thought, although she wasn't sure that was a good thing. The hunters would be annoyed if they discovered they'd wasted their time, but at least they'd be out of the way. A single spell-happy idiot who started casting spells before she could explain would be enough to cause a tragedy. *But where are they?*

Sergeant Miles stepped out of the gatehouse, his arms folded across his chest. "Emily. Frieda."

Emily swallowed. Beside her, Frieda shivered, brushing against Emily's arm. Emily shot her a reassuring glance, even though she didn't feel it. She'd prepared herself to face Gordian, not Sergeant Miles. But in some ways it was a relief. Sergeant Miles would *listen* to her, at least. She reached out with her senses, but felt nothing within the gatehouse. That didn't prove he was alone, she reminded herself sharply. Anyone could be hiding inside and she wouldn't know unless she drew on the wards.

"It wasn't her fault," Emily said. It struck her, suddenly, that Sergeant Miles might have deliberately *chosen* to greet her. He'd be as aware of the potential for disaster as Emily herself. "She was manipulated."

"I see," Sergeant Miles said. His face was unreadable, betraying nothing of his inner thoughts. It was impossible to tell if he believed her or not. "How?"

"Mind magics," Emily said. It wasn't a discussion she wanted to have in the open air, not when God alone knew who might be listening. "She needs medical attention."

There was a long, chilling pause. "I will escort her to the infirmary," Sergeant Miles said, finally. "And *you* will go straight to the Grandmaster's office. No *detours* along the way."

Emily hesitated, unsure. She didn't want to let Frieda out of her sight, even escorted by a man she trusted. Sergeant Miles wouldn't hurt Frieda, she was sure, but Gordian—or someone—could simply order him to hand her over at once. And then... she wished she knew just *what* Gordian had told the hunters. They'd be more inclined to attack first and ask questions later if they believed Frieda was an irredeemably insane rogue.

"I won't let anyone hurt her," Sergeant Miles added, quietly. "But you do have to speak to the Grandmaster before something else happens."

"I'll be fine." Frieda let go of Emily's arm. "You go see the Grandmaster."

"I'll take the body, too," Sergeant Miles said. "You won't want anything distracting you while you're talking to the Grandmaster."

Emily nodded, wordlessly.

She felt the castle's wards grow stronger as she stepped into the building. Gordian had been busy, she thought grimly. The wards weren't entirely friendly any longer. He knew she'd left the building, then. She wondered, sourly, if Gordian was working hand in glove with Fulvia. But then, he wouldn't want to put himself *too* far out for her. A Grandmaster was supposed to be above the political fray.

Emily watched them head down to the infirmary, then climbed the steps slowly to Gordian's office. The corridors were deserted, the wards humming a warning note to anyone stupid enough to be out of their dorms. Normally, someone sneaking through the school in the middle of the night would be tolerated, as long as they weren't caught, but not today. Now, everyone was in their dorms...

And it isn't even sunset yet, she thought, wryly. The last time everyone had been confined to their dorms, a Mimic had been prowling the school. *They'll be wondering just what the hell is going on.*

Her footsteps echoed in the empty air as she walked down the corridor and into the antechamber. There was no sign of Madame Griselda, not at her desk nor poking through her filing cabinets. Instead, the door to the inner office gaped open, invitingly. Emily gathered herself, trying to think of everything Gordian might say, then stepped into the office. The wards brushed against her magic, testing her identity, as she closed the door behind her and looked around. Gordian stood behind his desk, wearing battle robes. One hand was hidden inside his pocket.

"Emily," Gordian said, shortly. A wave of emotions crossed his face, ending in weary resignation. "I believe I gave you some very specific orders."

"Frieda was manipulated," Emily said, flatly. She thought, fast. Gordian was resigned... but resigned about what? Surely, he didn't think she was going to dictate to him. "She isn't responsible for her actions."

Gordian's eyebrows rose. "I see," he said, in precisely the same tone Sergeant Miles had used. "Perhaps you should start at the beginning."

Emily clasped her hands behind her back, then started to explain how she'd deduced where Frieda was going and gone after her. Gordian listened, yet he only showed real interest when Emily told him about Daze and the bracelet. He sucked in his breath when she mentioned Fulvia, but he didn't ask any questions. Thankfully, he didn't ask any questions about how she'd escaped her bonds either. She didn't want to tell him she had a lethal snake for a familiar.

"And you used soul magic on Frieda," Gordian said, when she finished. "You *do* realize that using soul magic without permission is technically illegal?"

"I could have left her to die, instead," Emily said, sharply. She would have thought that *legality* would have been the least of his concerns. "And she would die with everyone thinking she'd gone rogue."

"True," Gordian said. "Do you still *have* the bracelet?"

Emily fished it out of her pocket. She'd cast a pair of protective charms over it, just in case it was still dangerous, but otherwise she'd left it untouched. Gordian took the bracelet and examined it carefully, turning it over and over in his hands.

Emily watched, nervously, as he pressed his fingers against the runes, then placed the bracelet on the desk. It didn't seem inclined to try to bite him.

"Powerless," Gordian said, finally. "And she made it herself."

Emily's eyes narrowed. "What do you mean?"

"I mean it proves nothing," Gordian said. There was another hint of bitter resignation on his face, briefly visible before it vanished. "Frieda would hardly be the first student to try to devise something to encourage her to study. Or to make a fatal mistake when she put it on."

"Daze taught her how to make it," Emily said. In hindsight, the trick should have been obvious. But she'd never thought about it. "And he was working for Fulvia."

Gordian met her eyes. "Can you prove it?"

"I can swear an oath," Emily said, sharply. Was *Gordian* working for Fulvia? Or was he merely concerned at the prospect of another political catfight? There would have been some frank exchanges of views after the near-disaster last year. "And Frieda's mind..."

"You can only swear to what you *believe* to be true," Gordian said. His voice grew darker as he looked down at the bracelet. "And while I understand precisely why you choose to enter Frieda's mind, you will have almost certainly made it impossible for a trained healer to evaluate the damage. It will be tricky to prove that Frieda was under someone's control and"—he held up a hand before she could speak— "impossible to prove that Fulvia was behind it."

Emily started. "Daze told me..."

"Yes," Gordian said. "But how do you know he wasn't lying?"

He picked up the bracelet and played with it for a long moment. "Celadon's family has demanded a formal inquest. They have dispatched a prosecutor to file charges against Frieda. The... incident involving Adana may be discussed too. It is possible that Marian's family will *also* insist on having a say. If Frieda is found guilty, or judged to be too unstable to handle magic, she will be executed."

"It wasn't her fault!"

"Prove it," Gordian said, calmly.

Emily stared at him. "Surely you can attest to her change in behavior..."

"She would hardly be the first student to go through behavioral changes as she grapples with preparing for her exams," Gordian said. His voice was hollow. It dawned on Emily that Gordian might have been hoping that she and Frieda vanished without a trace. "Any competent prosecutor would have no trouble knocking holes in *that* argument. Celadon's family wants someone to pay. Frieda is the unlucky one who *will* pay."

"Unless I can prove she was manipulated," Emily said, stiffly.

"Correct." Gordian looked up at her. "I didn't expel her, not yet. Frieda will get a fair trial, as laid down in the rules. I am *obligated* to make sure she gets a fair trial. And you will have a chance to prove that your claims—and your charges—are true. But if she is found guilty, she will be handed over for ultimate judgement."

"Fuck," Emily said.

Gordian sighed. "On a different note, your behavior has been very poor," he added. "You were appointed Head Girl, yet you failed to handle an obviously difficult student. You were too emotionally involved for your own good. Frieda... should have been brought up short, a long time ago. There is a *reason* we try to keep a social gap between the older and younger students. Their concerns should not have any significance to *you*."

And so you want me to turn in my badge, Emily thought, sardonically. *You never wanted me to have it in the first place.*

"Some students might be allowed a chance to correct their mistakes," Gordian added. "I could pardon *some* of your errors, if they weren't repeated. But I cannot look past blatant insubordination, disobedience and naked favoritism."

He held out his hand. "Give me the badge."

Emily reached into her pocket, feeling... she wasn't sure *how* she felt. She'd hadn't wanted the badge, let alone the responsibilities that came with it. She'd wracked her brain to find a way to get *out* of being Head Girl. She hadn't enjoyed disciplining younger students, patrolling the corridors or running the wretched dueling club. And yet, being stripped of her position and authority *hurt*. It was a punishment every bit as humiliating as being slapped across the face.

She was tempted to throw it at him. Instead, she merely dropped it into his hand.

"Another Head Pupil will be selected within the next day or so," Gordian told her. He looked down at the badge for a long moment, his face unreadable. "You will clear out your rooms and office, of course. Pass student files to your successor, move your own possessions into one of the empty chambers. I expect you to do everything in your power to ensure the transition of power is reasonably smooth."

"Yes, sir," Emily said. She thought she should feel something. But, apart from a dull ache gnawing at her, there was nothing. Too much had happened in too short a space of time for her to feel much. Besides, losing her position *was* something of a relief. "I'll see to it tomorrow."

"Very well." Gordian stood up. "I'll ensure that Frieda receives the very best of care, Emily. Hopefully, Madame Samra or Madame Kyla will find evidence to back up your claims. The inquest will not hold Frieda accountable for anything done under any form of mind control."

As long as it can be proven, Emily thought, numbly. She tried to remember what little she knew of the procedure, but there wasn't much. She'd never thought she'd need to look up the rules for a formal inquest. Normally, there was a clear and unchallengeable reason for any expulsion. *But at least we have hope.*

Gordian looked up, sharply. "The Prosecutor has arrived," he said. "She's making her way here now."

Emily nodded, slowly. "I should go."

"Stay and tell them what happened," Gordian urged. "She may as well hear the story from your lips."

"Yes, sir," Emily said.

She reached out with her mind, trying to sense the prosecutor's approach, but there was nothing. The wards weren't being cooperative. Gordian might not have managed to sever her connection to the school's wards—her connection outranked his—but he *had* managed to limit her ability to manipulate them. Somehow, she doubted he'd let her get back down to the catacombs to erase his modifications.

I suppose I should be grateful that he didn't simply try to kill me, she thought, morbidly. *But he would have no way of knowing how the wards would react.*

The door opened. She turned as the prosecutor entered the office...

"Fulvia?"

End of Book Thirteen

The Story Will Continue In

Graduation Day

Afterword

Well, here we are again.

Last year, when I wrote *Infinite Regress*, I noted that I disliked long-running book series where each book was nothing more than an oversized chapter. I felt—and still do—that the writers pad out their volumes to keep the series going as long as possible, even though it tends to be a little self-defeating. Quite a few people have told me that I would enjoy *Game of Thrones*, for example, but I have no intention of picking up a volume until the series is concluded.

My intention, regarding *Schooled in Magic*, was to work hard to ensure that each book would be relatively stand-alone. Obviously, later books would draw on earlier books—this book draws on ideas seeded as far back as *The School of Hard Knocks*—but they would not force the readers to wait impatiently for the next book. My first failure, insofar as that was concerned, was *Infinite Regress/Past Tense*. I found that there were two separate plots—the collapsing school and Emily's journey back in time—and while I could divide them to some extent, I couldn't tie the first one up without completing the second. *Past Tense*, therefore, followed on from the cliff hanger at the end of *Infinite Regress*.

I promised my readers, back then, that I would finish the first draft of *Past Tense* within two months. And I kept my promise.

The Gordian Knot had the same problem as *Infinite Regress*. There were elements that needed to be put in place before the original plot could actually begin, but those elements would either consume too much of the book or fail to receive the development they needed. Accordingly, I split the plot into two and ended *this* volume with a cliff hanger. By way of recompense, I intend to write *Graduation Day* within two months (September 2017) and—hopefully—have it out by the end of the year.

Thank you for reading!

Christopher G. Nuttall
Edinburgh, 2017.

About the author

Christopher G. Nuttall was born in Edinburgh, studied in Manchester, married in Malaysia and currently living in Scotland, United Kingdom with his wife and baby son. He is the author of twenty-six novels from various publishers and fifty self-published novels.

Current and forthcoming titles published by Twilight Times Books

Schooled in Magic YA fantasy series
Schooled in Magic — book 1
Lessons in Etiquette — book 2
A Study in Slaughter — book 3
Work Experience — book 4
The School of Hard Knocks — book 5
Love's Labor's Won — book 6
Trial By Fire — book 7
Wedding Hells — book 8
Infinite Regress — book 9
Past Tense — book 10
The Sergeant's Apprentice — book 11
Fists of Justice – book 12
The Gordian Knot – book 13

The Decline and Fall of the Galactic Empire military SF series
Barbarians at the Gates — book 1
The Shadow of Cincinnatus — book 2
The Barbarian Bride — book 3

Chris has also produced *The Empire's Corps* series, the *Outside Context Problem* series and many others. He is also responsible for two fan-made Posleen novels, both set in John Ringo's famous Posleen universe. They can both be downloaded from his site.

Website: http://www.chrishanger.net
Blog: http://chrishanger.wordpress.com
Facebook: http://www.facebook.com/ChristopherGNuttall

If you enjoyed this book, please post a review
at your favorite online bookstore.

Twilight Times Books
P O Box 3340
Kingsport, TN 37664
Phone/Fax: 423-323-0183
www.twilighttimesbooks.com/

CPSIA information can be obtained
at www.ICGtesting.com
Printed in the USA
BVHW032207180621
609956BV00011B/48

9 781606 193280